OF BREATH & BLOOD

AF604971

An Irish-Australian, Dorothy Simmons is an English/Drama teacher whose first published work was a performance: the stage play *Night Exercise*. Since then, publications have ranged from Young Adult novels to the historical fiction *Living like a Kelly,* from short stories to microfiction. Her work has appeared in *Best Australian Stories*, *Etchings*, *4W* (Fiction Prize, 2018), *Hecate*, *Newcastle SS Anthology*, Spineless Wonders' *On the Hour* (Best Writing, 2019) and *Time*. She holds a doctorate in Creative Writing (Melbourne University), comprising the critical *Myth and Meaning* and the creative work which became *Living like a Kelly.*

For samples of her work, please visit her website: www.dorothysimmons.org

OF BREATH & BLOOD

DOROTHY SIMMONS

ARCADIA

© 2020 Dorothy Simmons

First published 2020 by ARCADIA
the general books' imprint of
Australian Scholarly Publishing Pty Ltd

7 Lt Lothian St Nth, North Melbourne, Vic 3051
Tel: 03 9329 6963
enquiry@scholarly.info / www.scholarly.info

ISBN 978-1-922454-10-2

ALL RIGHTS RESERVED

Cover design: Sarah Anderson

CHAPTER ONE

In the Wash

'Look, look! One of them parrots, see? There, on top of the wall!' The girl tugged at the big woman's arm and pointed to the flash of colour. High above, perched on the sandstone wall, the bird flicked its bright blue head: danger? Danger? No: not from the women inside the wall, spinning or carding wool in the Factory's workrooms, not from the women down there by the river, scrubbing linen or twisting knitted stockings dry. The bird strutted a few steps.

Below the wall, a dirt track dropped steeply to the river. Week in, week out, it was tramped flatter by the boots of the laundry women who trudged the Factory linen down the track dirty, up the track clean. Past silver-skinned eucalypts, past feathery tufts of ti-tree they trudged, past peeling strips of bark and tall grasses which shivered unexpectedly; past the bald patch swarming with ants and the cluster of ferns, across the footbridge into the clearing and on to the flat rocks beside the river where they could drop their loads before picking them up again.

The river was racing now, reckless after rain, swirling and spitting at an indifferent blue sky. Scattered across the clearing, women scoured and rinsed, squeezed and shook, pegged and unpegged. Lines of drying clothes fluttered in a sudden breeze: the flaccidity of a private's long johns, the billow of a supervisor's nightshirt, the coy flutter of a petticoat.

The bird flexed emerald wings and was gone. The big woman raised a brawny forearm to shield her eyes from the sun and squinted after it. The girl heaved a sigh.

'Gone! Did you see, Molly?'

'Just the rainbow flash of him.'

'Rainbow, that's it! So bright, so fast ... what wouldn't you give to have wings?'

The big woman raised her eyebrows. 'Oh for the wings, for the wings of a dove, eh? Not the wings of a parrot, Em, you wouldn't want the wings of a parrot. A swallow, now, that would do, a glossy blue-black swallow with a forked tail; like a divining rod, you know, a magic wand that could fly you straight home, fly you across the whole wide world and never lose its way.' She grinned. 'I'll say that for this place. The birds are beautiful. They'd want to be, mind you, they sure as hell can't sing. Those bloody cockatoos ...'

'They can, but, some of them can! Those black and white ones that go oidel oidel ...'

'... and they call magpies even though they're nothing like. Big ignorant brutes of things they are. I'll give you that, though; they can sing. Pity they don't sing before they swoop. Come on, we're nearly done.' She tugged a sheet from an almost empty basket. No answer: the girl was still staring at the sky. 'Come on, Em, get a move on!' Em tossed her head; her ginger plaits glinted. 'Ah, to blue bloody blazes with it! Come on, Molly, come with me! Quick! Quick!' She darted towards the rocks.

Across the clearing, women were stacking washboards and wooden bats, lining up the baskets now filled with clean laundry. Soon, they would be lugging baskets and tubs and boards back up the track, soon the gate in the wall would be unlocked for them to troop back inside; soon, almost unconsciously now, their throats would tighten at the scrape of the key in the lock behind them. Soon the clean laundry would be put away, the empty baskets stored; soon they would be on their way to whatever workroom they'd been assigned to next. No rest for the wicked.

Save your energy, Molly opened her mouth to say, but Em was already skipping around the open space, already bouncing and beckoning at her: come on, come on! Molly looked toward the supervisor's bench, but Peg Sloane was not there. Where on earth could she be? Matron Raine would not be amused ... and where were the troopers on duty? 'Molly! Come on!'

Molly folded the sheet long-ways, wound it round and round her arm and hurried after the girl, rehearsing in her head: 'Sheets still damp, Ma'am, needed a last airing ...' Em met her halfway and pulled out the sheet's bottom corners. She skipped backwards till the sheet hung like a hammock between them. Women looking up from tub or board or basket grinned and wiped their hands on their hips. Stretching and rolling their necks, scratching armpits, digging fists into the smalls of backs, one by one they stopped whatever they were doing, folded their arms under their bosoms and watched.

'So, Ginger Em! Who's for the heave-ho today?'

The ginger plaits flipped side to side. 'Matron,' called Em, 'Matron Raine, who else? It's our last chance, innit? This time next week she'll be gone. And good riddance to bad rubbish!'

Planted opposite, mobcap pulled low and fists clenched around the sheet, Molly looked like some gnarled, ancient tree. She took a last look around: still no sign of Peg Sloane. Nor the troopers. She turned back to Em, took a deep breath and nodded. 'Ready, steady, go!'

Two pairs of arms pumped. The sheet bellied up full sail, slumped down hollow, windless, empty as a pocket. Full, empty, full, empty: each time Em gave a little skip, each time her ginger plaits glinted. Molly's voice rang across the clearing, clear as a bell.

Heave her up and away she'll go;
Heave her down, way down below;
Heave her in where the river flows ...
Sink or swim, God only knows!

'Or cares!' chimed in Em, pumping the sheet in time. 'Or cares!'

Heave ho, Raine, Raine, go away,
Don't come back some other day!
Leave us be this sunny weather,
Birds of a feather flocked together!

'You should've told me the words, Molly, so I could sing too!'

'How could I? I only just made them up!'

The women laughed and clapped and shook their heads. Molly flashed a grin and backed towards them, tugging Em after her by the sheet. With a sudden rush, the girl was up against her, shoving her sheet corners into the big woman's fists, laughing and darting straight back on to the rocks. Arms stretched high above her head, she pushed herself up on tiptoe. Slowly, deeply she inhaled. Not a woman moved, waiting ... for the run, for the spring. Em's thin, bony legs were suddenly graceful as she cartwheeled ...

She bowed left, she bowed right. The women clapped and cheered; someone whistled. On tiptoe again, Em cartwheeled twice, thrice, four times, each spring as effortless as the first. More clapping and whistling: Em beckoned to Molly, who was laying the neatly folded sheet into its basket. The big woman hoisted the basket into the air and perched it on her head: 'Look, no hands!'

One step, two steps, three, before the basket shifted, slid ... and was caught.

Molly set it down beside the others. 'Done! All diddle daddle done!'

Em ran over and grabbed her hands. 'No, no, we're not done yet! Give us another song!'

'Nah ... don't push your luck, Em. Where the hell are they? Peg and those two troopers: has anybody seen them?'

A snigger: Molly glanced at two women leaning against a tree. One of them jerked her head toward the bushes at the edge of the clearing. The other waggled her eyebrows and made kissing noises. Em squealed and clapped her hands. 'True? Jesus wept, who'd a thought it? Peg-face: How about that!'

The second woman nodded. 'Yup. Don't miss a chance, our Peg. When we were all bums up scrubbing.'

'Tell you what, she's game! Rainey might have handed in her notice, but still ...'

Molly shrugged. 'Cat's away ... or on her way at least ...'

More chuckles and nudgings. Older women looked for a fallen tree or upturned tub to sit on, the younger fidgeted uncertainly. 'Any word about the new Matron?' asked one.

'Nah,' shrugged another.

'Who's going to give us word?'

'Well then, not our worry, is it? Or not yet.' Em clapped her hands again. 'Come on, Moll, not often we get a chance like this! Sing something. You can't be miserable all the time!' Alone on the rocks, she raised her arms and cartwheeled again.

'For goodness' sake, girl, that's enough!' snapped a woman with wispy white hair. She clicked her tongue. 'Enough, d'you hear me? They'll have you up for whatchamacallit: soliciting. Flashing your legs like that, God knows who might be watching ...'

Em pulled a face. 'God knows, God cares! Give us something we can dance to, Molly! Shift your arses, come on!' She darted forward and grabbed two of the younger women's hands; they stumbled after her, half laughing, half resisting.

'You'll cop it, you lot!'

'Who cares, who cares? How often do we get a chance like this? Once in a blue moon ... Peg's hardly going to squeal on us, is she, and as for old Rainey, she'll be too busy packing her bibles and beads. Hell, the laundry's done, innit? Or just about: come on!'

Molly looked toward the bushes, frowning. Finally, she tossed her head, grinned, and strode out on to the rocks. She stamped her foot and clapped her hands.

An old man came courting me, hey ding a doorum day;
An old man came courting me, me being young;
An old man came courting me, all for his wife to be,

Maids when you're young, never wed and an old man ...
For he's got no faloorum, faliddle – ayoorum,
He's got no faloorum, faliddleay-ey!
Maids when you're young, never wed an old man ...

Em stopped mid dance, flipped up her skirt and waggled her behind. Catcalls, whistles, laughter.

When this old man comes to bed, hey ding a doorum day!
When this old man come to bed, me being young ...
When this old man comes to bed, lays like a lump of lead ...
Maids, when you're young, never wed an old man!
So I threw my leg over him, hey ding a doorum day ...

'Stop! Stop! You women, stop this instant!'

A man's bellow. For a second, the dancers on the rocks froze in a single shocked tableau. Then they bolted. Tripping over each other in their panic, twitching aprons and tugging at jackets, tucking hair under and swiping faces, they stood to attention alongside washboards and baskets. At the footbridge, a tall man and an almost equally tall woman stood arm in arm beneath a parasol, still as a pair of porcelain figurines ... but radiating outrage.

No one moved, no one spoke. At last, the female figurine nodded to the male and they bore down upon the clearing. Back at her table, Peg straightened her skirt and bobbed a curtsey. Two flush-faced troopers snapped to attention. Out on the rocks, only Molly was left, stranded like some landlocked albatross. Hands locked above her head, left foot mid tap, she pressed her eyes tighter shut.

'Molly Malone. I might have known.' A woman's bray.

Molly lowered her arms and opened her eyes. She looked for Em. At the end of the row of women, the girl grimaced and turned up helpless palms. Molly drew herself to her full six feet and braced for the double glare: Matron Raine and her new lord and master.

'It didn't take you long, did it? Goodness me, it didn't take you any time at all!' Tapping a gloved finger against her throat, Elizabeth Raine uncoupled her arm from her husband's and stepped portentously forward. She paused, hand at her throat. With a world-weary sigh, she glanced over her shoulder. 'This is what I mean, my dear. Give them an inch and they take a mile. I thought a couple of weeks in Third Class would teach her a lesson, but evidently not. Evidently not.' She shook her head.

Leaning heavily on the curved brass handle of his walking stick, Edwin Raine nodded and tut-tutted loudly. 'Evidently not. Evidently not. As you say, my dear. How many times have I told you, you must not allow these reprobates, these quite irredeemable reprobates, to impose upon your good nature? Under, they must be kept under!' The walking stick thudded emphatically.

Molly raised her head, looking over the river and up through glinting eucalypt tips to the sandstone wall. *Done it again, girl, done it again. More fool you. When are you ever going to learn to keep your mouth shut?*

Thirds: it would be another stint in Thirds. It would be another summons to the office, where Matron would have reported back to Marsden and the good Reverend would have felt compelled to put in an appearance himself, if only to say that he'd told her so. Just like he had already told everybody else so. If only to pull off her cap and point at her shaved head. The man was a heathen pure and simple, for all he wore a collar. How long would they put her down for this time? Third class, poor lass: picking oakum, splitting stones. Did they pick oakum in Hell? It would be just the thing, you'd think ... pointless, painful, and never-ending.

Molly knotted her hands behind her back. Lifting her chin, she stared past Matron and Master to the river, following its course to where it wound out of sight, losing herself, willing herself to be swept away in the flood of it, to be one single solitary droplet hurtling unstoppably toward some all-immersive ocean. For a few seconds, one river became another, a headstrong, rain sequined race ... on the other side of the world.

CHAPTER TWO

Change the Subject

Matron Elizabeth Raine paused and looked down at Ann Gordon. 'Our little tour is very nearly complete.' She held up her hand, counting off each item on her fingers. 'I've shown you the living quarters for the different classes, Firsts, Seconds and Thirds. We've been to the kitchens, the lying-in rooms, the workrooms, the yards ... last but not least is the laundry.' She nodded. 'A vital occupation, of course. First and Second Class women only, for obvious reasons. It is much sought after, laundry work. If you'll just follow me, Mrs ... Matron Gordon, I should say!'

Ann Gordon hurried after the statuesque figure, conscious of her own lack of stature. *Height's not everything.*

At a gate in the sandstone wall, her guide selected a key from the metal ring clipped to her waist, unlocked the gate and held it open. Ann stepped onto a narrow track leading down to a bridge, a clearing and a river flowing past an expanse of flat rocks. Beyond the clearing, open bushland stretched away towards a featureless horizon. 'That is where the laundry is done; we are fortunate to have the river so close. Most convenient. Shirts, skirts, bedding, the convicts' slops, they all get washed here.'

Water sparkled; the uplifted limbs of the trees gleamed white against a cloudless blue sky. Ann smiled. 'What a pleasant spot! I can see why laundry work would be popular.'

No response.

'I suppose you post extra guards? In case some are tempted to abscond?'

Elizabeth Raine started, then waved a dismissive hand. 'My dear, where are they going to abscond to? Of course, the Thirds are desperate enough for anything, but we don't give them the chance. Quite apart from the fact that we want the clothes clean, you know! Some of the Seconds can be salvaged ... despite their recent lapse.'

Ann raised enquiring eyebrows. So many lapses: one for every part of the Factory she'd been shown. Hardly surprising, really, so many outcast women. Built for 300, but housing many more. 'Just last week, Mrs G. Just last week.' Matron Raine shuddered ostentatiously.

Mrs G? Who said she could ... never mind. Say nothing.

'Just when I thought I was done, you know: ship manifests, assignment contracts, in-comings, out-goings, all the books shipshape and ready for you to take over ... well! Just as I was taking a rest, a stroll with my dear lord and master ... outrageous! The patience of a saint, Mrs G, as the dear Reverend says, they would try the patience of a saint.' Matron Raine patted the enamelled cross at her throat, a gesture, Ann noted, that every 'lapse' seemed to trigger.

'Dear me. What ever happened?'

'Well ... perhaps I should say no more. Though, there again: you have taken on the position and they do say forewarned is forearmed, do they not? It is no small task you have been given, believe you me!' She heaved a sigh. 'Shameful, Mrs G, I did not know where to look. The embarrassment for my dear Mr Raine! In broad daylight, cavorting like performers at a circus, hair loose, laces untied, skirts flying ... legs, Mrs G, legs! Not to mention the extreme crudeness of the song ... I came down hard. I make no bones about it, I came down hard. The Reverend Marsden and I hit them where it hurts, in their stomachs. Remember that. The way to keep these women in order is through their stomachs. We rationed their bread and sugar. It's all they understand, just ask Reverend Marsden. Major Lockyer is a tower of strength as well, of course, but for day to day matters, believe me, the Reverend is the man. He knows what they're like. And yet he is a true Christian, a true man of the cloth, always reminding me that these women know no better. Licentiousness and loose living have been their lot from the cradle, the cradle, Mrs G! But of course they blame you for everything, everything they have brought upon themselves.' Elizabeth Raine shook her head wearily. 'If they only knew, Mrs G, how tirelessly that man has advocated for them! Why, he has taken on Governor Macquarie himself, actually gone and told him to his face that leaving these women in the kind of draughty barn which had been their accommodation before the construction of the Factory was as good as condoning prostitution! The Reverend Marsden does not mince words, Mrs G, he calls a spade a spade. But for his good offices, these women would still be in that barn, open to all comers! No better than a brothel, as he pointed out. Yet they turn their backs. They turn their backs, Mrs G. Irredeemable, as Mr Raine puts it. That is his name for them, the Irredeemables. Hitting the nail on the head exactly. Now, if you'll just step back inside ...'

Ann stepped, scanning the largely empty yard as her guide locked the gate. *Change the subject.* 'I see you grow your own vegetables, Matron.'

Her guide glanced at the old man digging in a kitchen garden. 'Yes, yes. The gardener you see there is Jake Barnes: ticket of leave man. Getting on now, not as stout and hearty as he was. Needs an assistant. He had his son, but the boy has run off, goodness knows where. Could be dead for all we know. Typical, I'm afraid: no loyalty, no sense of Christian duty.' She sighed deeply, then leant closer and nudged Ann. 'One of the tasks on your list now, Matron!' She smiled expectantly. Ann could only smile back.

'Not to worry, not to worry, Mrs G! The garden is not urgent. You will have plenty of other matters to keep you busy, that I can guarantee! We'll make our way back to the Matron's residence now ... as of tomorrow, yours!' She clasped her hands under her bosom. 'I do hope my little tour has been helpful!'

'Oh, indeed, indeed! I am most grateful to you for sparing me the time, I know how busy you must be. Having just moved myself, I know only too well what a job it is ... the furniture, the linen, the crockery, packing, deliveries ...'

'Deliveries! Don't talk to me about deliveries!' Elizabeth Raine shuddered again.

'Tradesmen and deliveries: my nightmare! Trying to find anybody that one might rely upon, such a nightmare! But say no more, say no more. My residence is just through here, please step this way ... I'm sure you are ready for a cup of tea. I know I am.'

'I hope I haven't put you to too much trouble ...'

'Not at all, not at all, fortunately I have one of the better maids, she knows what to do. Unfortunately, you won't meet my *caro sposo*: Edwin had church business to attend to, unfortunately. He is an elder, you know. We met through the church. Reverend Marsden often asks him to read the lesson. Never mind: we shall see you in the pews next Sunday, I'm sure.' Elizabeth Raine patted her cross and smiled.

Change the subject ...

***

Beyond the cosied teapot and the rose-patterned china lay the keyring, its keys splayed like finger bones. Ann's gaze kept sliding back to it: so many doors to open. She would have to learn what each was, memorise them ...

'You will have sugar, won't you?'

'Yes, please.'

'Tea's not tea without sugar, is it? Normally, I'd be using my best china in your honour, Mrs G, but I'm afraid it's all packed away. That box by the door. I packed it myself; Royal Doulton, hand painted. Can't be too careful. I've only ever had one plate chipped, and where do you think that was? At sea? Rough weather? At the docks, in the dray? Not a bit of it! All that way and it was chipped here in the kitchen. Of course, I got rid of the girl ... no idea, some of them, just no idea. Here you are ...'

'Thank you. A Royal Doulton tea set, all the way from England: that must have taken some packing!'

'Well, I just made up my mind, Mrs G, that life far from Home did not have to be life far from civilization. I would bring my civilization with me. My dear departed husband thought I had taken leave of my senses. Elizabeth, said he, Elizabeth, you cannot be serious! John, said I, John, why else would I be sitting in the middle of these boxes tearing up old sheets? And not a chip, not one single chip, all the way here. I should have known better, of course, than to leave the unpacking to the maid, but I wasn't quite myself at the time. As you may have heard, I lost my dear John on the journey here.'

'Yes indeed, Matron Raine, I have been advised of your sad circumstances. You were Matron Fulloon, I believe. Please accept my most sincere condolences. To lose your husband on the very brink of a new life: tragic. Quite tragic.'

'Yes, indeed, quite tragic. That journey, Mrs G, that journey! Can we ever forget it? The tropical sun, that endless tropical sun, mile after endless mile of ocean! Of course, the heat, you know, the heat meant there could be no delay: no notices, no church, no proper funeral. The Captain read out the service and consigned my dear John's remains to the deep. I collapsed, I confess, simply collapsed on the deck. What does the Bard say? Full fathom five ...' Elizabeth Raine patted her enamelled cross. 'We know not the hour. We know not the hour.'

Ann's eyes flicked between teacup and key ring: what to say? But her hostess had already moved on.

'And so I arrived in Sydney, a lone, lorn widow woman. I confess, Mrs G, for two pins I would have boarded the next ship Home. But then the Governor made me so welcome, you know, and the gentlemen of the Management Committee were so very accommodating ... not to mention the good Reverend. Quite apart from which, our house in London had been sold, our affairs wound up. And here was Parramatta's newly built Female Factory, in urgent need of a Matron. Here was Governor Darling, here was the Reverend Marsden and the gentlemen of the committee, pleading, positively begging me to stay. It was clearly my duty, my Christian duty, Mrs G. The Lord moves in mysterious ways. For here too, all unbeknownst to me, was my dear Mr Raine.

We have been married almost a year now.' The Matron paused, sipping her tea. 'I have been blessed, Mrs G, truly blessed. But now you must tell me something about yourself. Your husband was with the 48th regiment, I believe? In Ireland?'

'Robert? Yes; and I must apologise again. I don't know what can be delaying him ...'

Elizabeth Raine raised her eyes to the ceiling. 'Life, Mrs G, life! Another day, another delay, that is our lot; until that last delay of all ...' She patted her cross. 'More tea?'

'No, thank you. I was actually hoping ...' *to discuss moving furniture ...*

'I've always been so glad that I brought my Royal Doulton. Everybody admires it. A reminder of manners and morality, that's what it is. As my dear Mr Raine says, manners and morality.'

She told me the boxes would be gone this morning at the latest. How I am supposed to get organised ... never mind. Change the subject ...

'I believe you plan to open a school for young ladies, Matron, now that you are leaving the Factory ladies behind?'

'Factory ladies! Very droll, Mrs G! Yes, that is correct. An establishment for the instruction and moral guidance of young gentlewomen. The future wives and mothers of this infant society. A sacred trust, as Reverend Marsden puts it.'

Ann sipped her tea, eyes on the key ring. Elizabeth Raine set her cup down, picked it up and flicked through the keys. 'Kitchen, workrooms, sleeping quarters, offices: all as I've shown you. And this house, of course. All here.' She held up the heavy metal ring; the keys hung in thin clusters. *Like the long skinny leaves on the trees here. Spindly, untidy.* Ann bit her lip. As of tomorrow, hers.

'It is a relief, I have to confess, to hand them over at last.' Her hostess' lips twitched. 'My nerves, you know. One is constantly in demand. Three and a half years, Mrs G. I was beginning to think that this day would never come. So: well, why not? I have no further need of them. Edwin ... my dear Mr Raine, would be applauding. Quite the knight in shining armour he is, just longing to take me away from all this! So.' Smiling, she shook the ring so the keys chinked. 'Here you are, Matron! Congratulations: the

Factory is all yours! No, don't worry, there is a spare set. Just in case I might forget anything.' Ann smiled and took the key ring, turning it in her hand. *Matron. Matron Ann Gordon. In charge of these outcast women. As of now.* She pressed the keys to her breast.

Elizabeth Raine patted her cross. 'All yours, Mrs G, all yours! As Mr Raine says, I too have served my time! I have redeemed you, my dear, he said. This very morning, over breakfast. My duty here is done, Mrs G. They are all yours.'

Am I supposed to thank her?

'Are you familiar with Mrs Fry's work, Mrs Raine? Her success with the women of Newgate must surely give us hope.'

'Ah, the estimable Mrs Fry. Yes, Reverend Marsden has been in correspondence with her. And yes, of course we must rejoice over every single lamb saved out of the hundred who are not. Unfortunately, that still leaves us with the other ninety and nine, who, as the Reverend and I have often jested, Mrs G, all seem to have been sent out here! Mrs Fry means well, of course, terribly well, there is no doubt of that. She is to be congratulated on her good work at Home. But what can she possibly know of life in the colonies, Mrs G? And a penal colony at that? As the Reverend says, meaning well is one thing; doing well is quite another.'

Bite your tongue. She means ... well.

'Their immortal souls, Mrs G, the salvation of their immortal souls: we must never forget, that is our mission. If they will not seek the light, must they not be shown it? If they will not be led, must they not be driven? Born into a life of vice; taking vice in, as it were, with their mother's milk ... is it any wonder we seek to remove the children from their mothers' influence? I have even taken it upon myself, Mrs G, in the name of the Lord ... taken it upon myself to care for one such little one.'

'Indeed? That is true dedication. A girl or a boy?'

'A girl, naturally. Mary. In the name of the Lord.'

'She is a fortunate child. I am sure you will be rewarded in heaven as on earth.' Ann stood. 'But I am conscious of taking up your time ...'

'Not at all, do sit down!' Reluctantly, Ann sat. 'Now, Mrs G, just remember: anything you need advice on, feel free to call on me. A cup of tea and a chat, I have found, are most restorative.' Elizabeth Raine nodded wisely.

'The First Class women, of course, are rarely a problem. They will be assigned, get married, and get their tickets of leave. Marriage is to be encouraged, Mrs G. The state of holy matrimony is their golden opportunity to put their lives of sin behind them, to re-set their moral compass, as the Reverend so eloquently puts it. Manners and morality; they are what our mission revolves around. Second Class are more mixed, though they too may marry and some do see the light, so to speak, see the error of their ways. They are the ones to whom we can make most difference, Mrs G. They may have been hauled before us for drunkenness, disobedience, or simply idleness; but they can still repent and start again. Even, occasionally, you may find some woman among the Thirds who earns a move to Seconds. On probation, as it were. And of course, the lying-in rooms are in the Second Class area. Alas, I'm afraid the babes born there are born out of wedlock far more often they are in. They can't seem to help themselves, you know; simply beget and forget. Ah! My dear Mr Raine! Did you ever? Beget and forget!'

'Forget their own children? Surely such women are rare exceptions!'

'You would think so, but ... well. Be prepared, Mrs G. That is all I will say. Be prepared. Take a firm hand, right from the start. Even the better women, you know, the monitresses, portresses and the like: never let them become too familiar. Even the most sober, the most docile and industrious, Mrs G, will lapse, believe me. They will lapse.' Elizabeth Raine heaved a deep sigh and patted her cross.

Ann turned her keyring.

'Third Class, of course, is the Penitentiary Class. To be supervised at all times. They are strictly segregated: yards, workrooms and dormitories. Divide and conquer, you know. That is our Factory motto. It only takes one rotten apple to contaminate the entire crate, and we have more than one rotten apple, believe you me.' Elizabeth Raine patted her cross yet again.

'What else? Ah, yes: there will be times requiring more vigilance than others. When a new cargo of women arrives, or some particularly hardened case is returned. I showed you the cells; some are, as my dear husband says, simply Irredeemable. And public holidays, they can be difficult. Any excuse, you know ...'

The knock at the door was not loud, but Elizabeth Raine started. 'Who can that be? I was not expecting anyone.'

The door edged open. Ann leapt to her feet. 'Robert! Where on earth have you been? Here he is at last ... Mrs Raine ...'

In one fluid movement, Robert Gordon embraced his wife, moved across to Elizabeth Raine and raised her hand to his lips; she pursed her lips coyly.

Attaboy, turn on the charm. Where have you been?

'Sincere apologies: my horse had to choose today to cast a shoe ...' Robert waved his hand at the key ring in his wife's hands. 'Though I'm sure you two ladies have had plenty to discuss without me. Had a good look around, have you dear?'

'Yes indeed, Mrs Raine has been most generous with her time ...'

'Mr Gordon; will you have some tea?'

Not Mr G?

'Thank you, Ma'am, no; I took some refreshment while waiting for the blacksmith.' Robert glanced at his wife, who raised an eyebrow but said nothing. He turned in a circle and waved his arms expansively. 'What a fine room! Our new home, Ann!'

'You must forgive the state it is in, Mr Gordon; indeed, the state I am in! Between tradesmen and deliveries and disturbances, I believe I could sleep for a week! But I have given your wife the keys, I have handed over. She tells me you have lodgings in town. I shall be gone, yes, I shall actually be out of here at last, when you return tomorrow morning.'

'Think nothing of it, we know only too well the trials of moving, don't we, Ann? I hope you have not as much distance to cover as we had: Newcastle to Sydney.'

'Good Heavens, no. Sydney is quite far enough for me! Mr Gordon, may I at least offer you a biscuit? Do sit down!'

'Thank you, I will. I must say, we were not expecting quite such roomy accommodation, were we, Ann? And so private, for all we're within factory grounds. I do like sandstone as a building material, don't you? It certainly compares well with the grey stone of Portsmouth or Limerick, doesn't it, dear?'

'Indeed it does ...'

A loud crash made them all jump. Elizabeth Raine stepped backward, grasping the back of a chair. Ann and Robert rushed to the window. They could see nothing, only hear: raised voices, shouts, whistles, thuds.

Two young men in uniform burst into the room. 'Matron Raine! Major Lockyer says you are to come with us to the Barracks. They're looking for you!'

Elizabeth Raine clutched her cross with trembling hands. 'Who? Who are?'

'The factory women. They're running amok, rampaging about the yards this very minute. They're shouting your name!'

Robert went back to the window. Ann put her arm around the quivering Elizabeth Raine and steered her gently toward the troopers. *Nerves: is this why she was nervous? Why are they shouting her name?*

'I knew they were up to something, I just knew it. Muttering in corners, hushing up as soon as they saw me coming, hissing they were, hissing ...'

Ann handed Elizabeth Raine over to the troopers, who took her by the arms. 'Don't worry, Ma'am, we've got you. It's all right, the Major has everything under control. You come along with us, we'll look after you, don't worry.'

The dark-haired trooper patted the woman's arm, nodded to his sandy-haired fellow and steered the anxious woman toward the door. He glanced over his shoulder at Ann and Robert. 'Sir ... Madam ... you'd best come as well ...'

CHAPTER THREE

Bread or Blood

'Dear oh dear oh dear'. Elizabeth Raine's voice faded.

The Gordons looked at each other. Robert held out his hand.

'Give me the keys. I'll lock the door. They'll never know we're here.'

Vehemently, Ann shook her head. 'No! They won't know we're here, but they'll think she is, and it's her they want. Probably on their way right now. They're angry, Rob; can't you hear it? They're looking for somebody to blame ... and I don't want it to be me. No, we should not be found here.'

'But they don't know! Let them hammer at the door. No answer, they'll go away.'

'You think so? A mob of convict women? What about the windows? Have you forgotten the mob in Newcastle that barged into our offices? That was about rations as well. They're hungry, they're angry, probably every bit as angry as the Newcastle mob. They're certainly not in any state to meet their new Matron.' She peered out the window again. 'Those troopers said Major Lockyer had it all under control. I hope they're right. But he doesn't need anything more to worry about, does he? We lock up and head straight back to our lodgings.'

'I suppose ...'

'Come on, then. Quick ... don't you want to find out what's going on out there?'

They hurried out the door; Ann locked up. In spite of everything, she flashed a smile and chinked her keyring. But Robert was already out in the yard, beckoning. As she hurried after, Ann glimpsed the two troopers almost carrying Elizabeth Raine around the corner, heading towards the Barracks. She caught Robert by the arm: 'Listen!'

Voices: shouting, squalling from the far side of the archway.

'Christ, woman, I thought you said you didn't want to be seen here?'

Robert tugged at her arm. She brushed him off. Rolling her shawl into a long scarf, she threaded it through the key ring and knotted it firmly around her waist. She pulled the wool over the key ring and looked up at her husband.

'Just a peep. They won't notice.' She made for the archway.

'Ann, don't be so damn silly! Come back here!' He lunged after, cannoning into her when she stopped short. He had to grab her waist to stop her falling.

'Dammit, watch where you're going,' she snapped. She pointed at the expanse of grass across which, only a couple of hours ago, Elizabeth Raine had escorted her: the Bleaching Green.

In the fading light, the Green had become a blur of brown, a swarm of buzzing bodies. Women's bodies: full-breasted, flat-chested, sharp-elbowed, broad-beamed, pinch-lipped, gap-toothed, fierce-fisted, splay-fingered, aprons tied like cloaks or untied and brandished like banners. Unlaced jackets flapped, ragged skirts were hoicked up over ragged petticoats, rolled sleeves bared sinewy forearms: so many! Ann gasped. Who'd have thought there would be so many? Withered crones with white hair bristling under mob caps, freckle-faced girls with long plaits swinging, slatterns in torn stockings and clumsy shoes, hoydens with loose hair and torn skirts ... all swarming straight toward her and Robert ...

'You idiot, Ann, they've seen us! Christ, look at them! They'll tear us apart, come on! Come on, let's get out of here!'

'Don't be silly. Where are you going to get out to?'

Robert spun around, scanning the walled spaces: he shook his head, threw his arms in the air and slapped them against his thighs. He threw back his head and laughed. 'Hooray and up she rises!'

Ann flashed him a smile and braced herself, hands clasped firmly around the shawled keyring. Lips compressed, jaw set, she waited. Seconds later, the swarm was upon them, buzzing and smelly and loud. Robert drew himself up tall, crossed his arms over his chest, raised his chin.

Ann waited for the voices to die down, for the whispers, for the lull. She lifted her right hand, took a step forward and looked around. 'Ladies! Ladies, what is the meaning of this? Whatever do you think you are doing? It is Friday evening. It is the end of the working week. Your tasks are done, it is time to rest. You should be retired for the night, not charging about in this unseemly fashion! What do you think you're doing?' She paused and looked around again. Eyes: nothing but frowning eyes, all trained on her.

'Can nobody tell me? Whatever can be the matter at this late hour? I do not know; but what I do know is that creating a public disturbance will not solve whatever it is. I have no doubt that the forces of law and order are already on their way. They will arrive at any minute and they will not be amused. They will not be amused at all. My advice is that you do not wait for them. Disband, go to your quarters now. Calm yourselves; calm yourselves and retire for the night. You have beds to go to: I advise you to go. Quickly, before the troopers find you a less comfortable place to sleep.'

A giant of a woman shouldered her way to the front of the crowd. She towered above Ann: *six foot at least.* No mobcap: no hair either. Bald. *No, not bald, her head's been shaved, that's it. See the scabs on her scalp, the nicks from the razor, the places where the stubble is growing back uneven? Bruising, too; she must have put up a fight. Pity: she might have been handsome, once upon a time: good eyes, regular features.*

The woman folded her arms across her ribs and inhaled; large breasts bulged. 'Ladies, is it? Ladies? And who the divil might you be?'

Irish. Might have known.

'I am Mrs Gordon. This is Mr Gordon. We are recently arrived from Newcastle. We have a Female Factory there too; some of you might know of it. We have simply been for a walk, exploring the town. We saw the factory buildings and came to take a closer look. We were interested to see how the Factory here compares with the one in Newcastle. Idle curiosity, if you like.'

'Curiosity killed the cat. So: been taking a look, have you? And have you been taking a look at the good Matron never Raines but it bloody pours? Has she told you God's in his Heaven and all's right with the world?' The woman lifted her arm to quieten the chorus of catcalls and boos.

Ann knotted her hands tighter around the keyring and waited, again, for the voices to die down. 'Matron Raine has said nothing to us. For the very good reason that we did not find her at home. We have knocked several times at her door: no answer. We were on our way back into town.'

A stocky, dark haired woman at the bald woman's elbow plucked at her neighbour's sleeve. 'She's been tipped off, bet you what you like. Bolted. Likely sniveling to bloody old Marsden this very minute. Or saying her prayers. As well she bloody might. Or bolted for the Barracks; that'll be it, Molly, that'll be it. She'll be holed up in the Barracks.'

No doubt about where you're from, is there, hen? Glasgow, bet you what you like ...

Molly nodded, her eyes flicking from Ann to Robert to Ann. 'Well, Mrs Gordon, you may tell our good mates in Newcastle that we wish them well. Because whichever one of Her Majesty's boats any one of us came out in, we're all in the same one now. And it gets to the stage, don't you see, that you have to swim or you'll sink. And we're not for sinking. As for you and your man there, we've no quarrel with you, so just you keep right on going. Back to Newcastle.'

She turned to face the other women, holding her arms up for attention. The voices stopped; they listened. 'Ladies, now ... ladies! When was the last time any one of you was called lady? Never mind treated like one! So I think we will just let this lady and gent keep going about their business and we'll keep going about ours, all right?'

Cheers, claps, the occasional apron waving.

'It seems the old Rainey is not at home. Not receiving visitors. You'd nearly say she's done a runner. Never mind. That's all right, we've time enough. It's not like we're going anywhere, is it, not like we've too many other pressing social engagements? We'll give her a second chance, won't we, even if that's more than she's ever given us? What we'll do now is we'll take a wander on over to the Barracks and have a look around. A good look, mind, so she can take a look at us as well: so she can remember that we're here waiting. And we'll be here waiting come breakfast tomorrow morning; waiting to remind her that it's wonderful what a body will do for a decent cup of tea. Poor old pigeon, she'll be crossing herself, can you not see her?' Molly rolled her eyes as she crossed herself and patted her throat. 'She can cross herself as much as she likes, it's about time she damn well listened to our prayers for once! Enough is enough ... or more to the point, not enough. Nowhere like enough ... is it any wonder we're sour? I don't see too many plump pigeons here, do I? More like a mob of bloody scarecrows! There's a few of us here mind the Famine, don't we? The Great Hunger? There's a few of us here could tell you about gentry that ate white bread while bairns were starving in front of them! And what we said then is what we say now: bread or blood! Bread or blood!'

Ann braced herself, tightening her grip on the hard curve of the keyring as if it could steady her against the surge of voices. 'Bread or blood! Bread or blood!'

The big woman swung around and strode back across the green, her bald skull gleaming above the patchwork of dark heads and fair, of mob caps and high-flying aprons. They disappeared through the archway again.

In their wake, the aftershock of silence. Ann let herself lean against her husband and close her eyes. He squeezed her shoulders. She felt rather than saw his grin. 'No doubt about you, girl, no doubt about you! God Almighty, did you ever see the like? A pack of hounds in full cry, that's what they put me in mind of, for all the world like a pack of hounds: tantivy, tantivy, tantivy! A-hunting we will go!'

His wife smiled and slipped out of his arms. She clasped her hands behind her head and stretched her neck to one side then the other. Robert put out a hand to pull her back, but she shook her head. Instead, she gave her skirts a little shake, her keys a little chink, and set off briskly for the archway through which the women had disappeared. For a moment, smiling and watching her go, Robert didn't move. Then, with a few long strides, he caught up. On the far side of the yard, the women were gathered under a big tree. The bald woman was talking, her palms upturned as if explaining something that surely must be obvious. Robert rested a hand on his wife's shoulder.

'Well, Matron Gordon? How do you like your new charges?'

CHAPTER FOUR

To Sleep, Perchance ...

It had been her turn for the big bed, her turn to stretch out full length instead of wrapping her arms round her knees and waking in the pre-dawn dimness with stiff joints and numb fingertips. So why couldn't she sleep? It wasn't as if she was not tired, you couldn't be anything else in this place: tired of this work, tired of that work, tired of asking leave to do this, tired of being refused leave to do that, tired of the dirt in your very pores, tired of the stink of your own sweat ... Molly scowled into the dark. Go to sleep, go to sleep! What's wrong with you, girl? She laid her hands over her eyes: *shut up, brain, for chrissake! You'll be no use at all in the morning ...*

The morning. What have I started? All very well, out there in the yard with Joan and all the others clapping and cheering, all very well sailing along on a high tide of words; not so well here in the dark on her own. Like they said, no rest for the wicked. Wicked. With a capital letter, you could hear it, the stamp, the sizzling brand of it in the judge's voice. 'Wanton Wickedness.' What was it about 'w'? Wanton, willful, wayward, wrecked ... wicked, witch ... wishful, witchful thinking ...

What's the capital W worst they can do to us if we go ahead and do it? If we actually break out? They'll round us up again, of course they will. Might just about last the day, but that'll be it. But what then? More rations? Lock us up? So how are they going to get their spinning and carding done?

Who's going to pick their oakum?

Anyway, that's not the point. What is the point? To show them what happens when people see that they've got nothing to lose ... when they stand together ...

So they round us up again. Going to need somebody to blame, aren't they? That'd be me. Of course. The big bald bitch, who else? They can't shave me again, though: nothing to shave. They can, probably will put me down to Thirds. Back in the yard with Bridget, splitting stones. But I'm too big for the bullies, and too sharp for the bitches. And Bridget will be there, we'll be swinging sledges together like last time. Unless they've seen that we're mates; might put me on to oakum instead, make me pick my fingers raw stripping rope. How long for, that's the question. What if they make it permanent?

Killing time. How long before time kills me?

Or there's solitary. Most reckon that's the worst, that they do it so you go demented and then they can forget about you. Out of sight, out of mind in every possible way. Not me though. Last time wasn't so bad. It's a matter of practice: re-membering, re-calling ... I mean, I've been doing solitary ever since I landed, really. Until Em ...

Molly turned to face the curved back on the far side of the bed. The girl was deeply asleep, her breathing slow and rhythmic, her knees tucked in tidily and her hands in prayer position, cushioning her cheek. Like her own Maeve as a little girl, way back then, way back when ...

Only as a little girl, though. The grown Maeve could never have shared a mattress, too like her mother, too big. Junoesque, that was the word Frank used when he came courting. Molly smiled to herself; she used to tease him about it. Junoesque? Say what you mean, man: good childbearing hips! Maeve would squeal with irritation: oh, for God's sake leave us in peace, Ma!

Molly reached across and touched Em's tousled hair. Junoesque: not a word the girl would even have heard of. Gently, she twisted a thick ginger curl around her finger. A long time, such a very long time, since anyone had run up and flung their arms round her like Em had after they let her out of solitary. Ginger Em. Good name: she'd certainly gingered things up in the yard since they'd sent her back from assignment. Skipping instead of trudging, pulling faces, cheeky as they come: she made them smile. She made the days go quicker. Nobody could do anything about the nights.

The darkness hummed tunelessly on, breathing in, breathing out, scratching, sighing, squeaking, monotonous rhythms punctuated by phlegmy snorts or grunts from elbowed snorers. It was a female darkness, dense with the secretions of women's bodies: the oniony smell of armpits, the rising fumes of a fart, the sour tang of menstrual blood; a darkness full of urgent fumblings, dream whimpers, inaudible mutterings and random shouts: Hot Cross Buns, Hot Cross Buns! No Pope Here! Jack's The Lad! So many Jacks, thought Molly, so many Jills: so many hills to fall down. It was a darkness full of memories.

October 26th. Maeve's birthday. Tomorrow. 1827. 29: she'll be 29.

Christ! That was middle-aged. Her little girl! And what did it make her? 44. Christ: 44. Five years now, five years of her life she'd been here. No, five years since her life; five years since life turned into a life sentence. Funny, calling it a 'life' sentence when what it was, really, was a postscript: an afterlife.

She'd asked her father once if he believed in an afterlife. He said he did, but not the kind they preached in church. She never did find out what he meant by that; never would, now. But never ever would it have been this kind of afterlife, never this kind of slow-motioning ...

It was the pointlessness that was hardest, that and the boredom; like hanging around after your own funeral, when anybody who'd ever loved you had long since said goodbye, long since tucked you away in some neat little 'sacred to the memory of' corner of their minds. Which was as it should be, of course, exactly as it should be. Why should they be miserable? They had their own lives to get on with. Maybe it would have been better, after all, if they had seen her hanged. Billy Orr, remember Billy Orr? The man's neck broken, his trousers wet with piss, his poor skinny corpse turning in slow circles before they cut him down ... no. No: you wouldn't wish that on anybody. Not after '98, not with all that slaughter still raw in people's minds. Which was why they hadn't had the nerve to do it, to put a public full stop to a woman whose father's name was a byword for decency, and the price he'd paid for that decency known to all ...

Stop it. What's done is done. Think about what was still to be done; what she could still do to give half a chance to Em, her daughter come lately ... though never instead of her Maeve, never that. As well as ...

Happy Birthday, Maeve. Every one of the last five years I've sung happy birthday to you; I wish you could know that. Even though I'll never see you again, I wish you could know that. How has your life been, sweetheart? You with your Frank and his school and your little Molly and whatever bairns have come since ...

And Sam, my good brother, my good, good brother: what are you now, 46? Yes, 46: none of us getting any younger. Hammering away there at your anvil, you'll not be able to keep that up for too much longer. I hope you and Abby have enough put by, that it didn't all go on lawyers to speak for your headcase of a sister. Dawn to dusk, in there with the big fire blazing behind you, hammering away, sending the sparks flying up the forge chimney, up and out into the high air over the Six Mile Valley ...

Little Molly will be 12. Just budding. What's in a name? Nothing. Pray to God, nothing. For the child's sake.

Em shifted in her sleep: the curl slipped through Molly's fingers. She crossed her hands on her chest and stared at the ceiling; it was just starting to get light. Morning: morning soon. So stop havering on and think, Molly, think! It's not like this is just a spur of the moment thing. No, we've talked about it, we've seen it coming. This is the moment, now, when there are chinks in the armour, when they're between Matrons. So the next one knows what she's getting into and that there's a limit to what we'll put up with. Seize the day, that's what they have to do. Carpe Diem: she could hear her father's voice saying it. Ever since she'd swung her sledge hammer in Thirds and looked round at the other stone splitters, at the corded veins in their necks and the dust creasing their faces; ever since she'd looked at the guards yawning at their posts and the Matron bustling across the yard with a handkerchief held to her nose, ever since she'd looked at Bridget and Bridget had grinned and farted on purpose ... she'd known that there would be a day to seize. This was it.

Bridget was going to smash the gate. She said it'd be like old times, breaking machines. She said it was a lot easier than breaking stones.

Bloody old Marsden in church the other day. Let us pray. Glad to see you on your knees, Molly. Let us pray. Let us pray for your immoral soul, Molly. Immoral soul: the snigger of him. His own private little joke. Bloody heathen.

Pray: now, how do you spell that, Reverend Marsden, please? E Y, isn't it? P R E Y. What? A Y is it? Well, you learn something every day, she could have sworn it was P R E Y. What did she mean? Nothing at all, Reverend Marsden sir, what could I mean?

Thinking, that's her way of praying. Never a day she doesn't think about them, Maeve and Molly and Frank and Sam and Abby and little Sam and little Sal. Her fingers might be stiff and sore from picking oakum, but her head could still be flying across the world, watching them go about their lives, wondering what they might be doing, where they might be going, who they might be seeing. *The kettle's spitting on the range, I can smell wheaten farls on the griddle, hear the children singing in the schoolhouse, or answering one after the other as Frank calls out their names; their faces are soft in the firelight, sitting round of an evening, talking about who's died and who's wed, whose pigs got out, whose horse would win at Lisnalinchy and how were they ever going to get the hay in with all this rain?* In her head, she spoke all their parts; sometimes, on her own, she did the actions as well: Abby rubbing the back of Sam's neck for him, Maeve tossing her head, Frank pushing his spectacles back up his nose. All those weeks in the hold of the ship, that was what had kept her sane. From the first stagger on to solid land, to the outhouse where they'd lodged her on her first assignment, to lying here in the dark, remembering was what kept her sane. Remembering what was real.

Though it started long before that, the remembering. Charlie, it was her Charlie, way back in '98. It was how you kept them alive, your nearest and dearest, in your mind's eye. You just had to set your mind's eye to it. It was what her father did after he was blinded, set it all up in his mind's eye: what people looked like: the house and garden, the books on his shelf. He mapped them all out in his head.

Molly held up her fingers and wriggled them in the dark. Would she still be able to write? Bloody oakum ... not that writing was any use to her now. She would like to think she still could, though; that she could still make her fingers work if she had to. So many words in her head, so many songs, verses, snippets from the newsletter, and no way of keeping them in order, no way of checking she was remembering right. Some of the verses she used to read her father, for instance; she'd have every line memorised, every single line, all but the one word. And she could find a word that made sense, but she knew it wasn't the one, and it niggled and niggled, and the more it niggled the further she'd be from getting it. It drove her demented at first, until she realised that the only way to get it was to let it go, not think about it. Then it might ... just might ... rise to the top of her mind, like a trout in the Six Mile rising to the fly ...

And of course people got older, children grew up; that was all right. That was good, that kept her mind working. What would they look like now, where would the lines have fallen, the calligraphy of smile and frown? There would be a fair few changes over five years. Not like here, year after year, day in, day out, same old, same old ... don't tell Em. She'll find out soon enough.

They were getting on with their lives: Maeve, Frank, Sam, Abby and the children. The next generation. She had to believe that. Life went on, with or without you.

Remembering to sing happy birthday was the closest she could get to making it with. Even if they couldn't hear, she still sang the whole verse out loud; like carving your initials into a tree made of air. One time she'd sung it with a crowd of women on the Bleaching Green and a woman had started crying because it was her birthday too. Fifty she was, but so pleased, so delighted just to hear the song again. Molly had asked Em when her birthday was, but the girl had shrugged and said her mother had never been exactly sure on account of being drunk ...

All the stored songs: she sang them, she made herself sing them, even if it was just in her head. Because if you couldn't remember, what could you do?

She remembered God: sometimes. And her immoral soul. Now and then. What must I do to be saved? Me or any of us in here? No answer. Like the Majors and Magistrates, she supposed, God hadn't a lot of time for the wicked.

Stop it.

Would there be sugar in their tea in the morning, that was the question. A few grains of sweetness first thing? No. In her gut, she already knew that there wouldn't be. So it would be on. The tools were ready, stashed away behind looms, buried under coils of rope. Amazing what you could do when you put your mind to it; when you put three or four or five minds to it. And time: when you had time to kill. It had swirled her back to those whispered meetings in '98: *by the rising of the moon, by the rising of the moon; the pikes will be together by the rising of the moon ...* no pikes though. Nasty, brutal things, pikes. Shocking what they could do to a human body: no. Not a matter for pikes. Couple of crowbars, shovel or two, couple of sledgehammers, that was all they needed. To get them through the gate. To get them out on the town! Oh, that would wake them up all right! That would show old Rear End Marsden and the good Matron when enough was enough. And serve notice on the new one, whoever she might be.

If it doesn't work, though, what if it doesn't work? If the others don't turn up, if Bridget can't break the gate down, if they're surrounded before they get out? What if they're no better off, if they're sent back to work harder and longer, if their rations are cut even more? That'd be the worst; she could cope with solitary if she had something to show for it. But what if she hadn't, what if she only made matters worse?

It was like Bridget piling the stones they'd split into little cairns about the yard: you found things to do. Even if you had to undo them straight after. But you couldn't scatter the stones so quick if they were all in one big cairn. If they stuck together, that was the thing; then they couldn't single women out. Then they might get somewhere, might make it better for the young ones like Em or that Sarah, the new girl with the strawberry mark on her face. It was worth a try. Molly flexed her fingers. She might not be able to write copperplate anymore, but she could still use a stick of charcoal: she could still stir them up. Up the Pope ... with a poker! Graffitied in tar ... the bucket of the stuff left by the wall, the sudden irresistible urge: worth getting her head shaved for? Yes, dammit, yes. The Matron's face ... never mind Marsden's. Just about busted out of his collar. Besides. Got rid of the nits.

Em read the Pope graffiti all by herself. She said it was the best reason for learning her letters she'd heard yet. Sheer luck, coming across that tar: you could still see it, no matter how hard they'd scrubbed. Better than scoring the dirt with a stick and scuffing what you'd done out every time you saw somebody coming.

She was bright, Em; she caught on quickly. And if she could say she could read, once she was put up for assignment again she'd have a chance of being sent somewhere decent. Shouldn't be too much longer; Molly glanced at the sleeping girl. No more singing the alphabet, no more spelling in the dirt, no one to teach new words. How would she fill her days then?

It had made all the difference, these last few months. Something to look forward to in the spare minutes off work, snatched before and after: something to share besides bedbugs. Em just needed to keep that ginger head of hers down. If the breakout went ahead, she would find an excuse to keep her in the crowd, out of sight. Tuck her plaits away under her mobcap. Make her stay down. Girl didn't stop to think, girl just flung herself at the enemy. Same as she'd done herself, and look where that had got her.

There'd be hell to pay, of course there would. But there was hell to pay anyway, so what was the difference? A stint in Thirds. Price to pay. Split stones, make herself too tired to think. For a while. Third Class, crime class: she supposed she was lucky she hadn't been put in Thirds all along; she was, after all, guilty of criminal assault. She never did ... most likely never would ... find out what strings Sam had pulled. Her good brother: his earnest face looking at her across the courtroom and giving her the thumbs up ...

Molly yawned, stretched, scratched and slapped. Bedbugs. Needed to jump in the river again. From somewhere outside came the warbling of one of those fake magpies. The tunefulness of it made her smile, vicious brutes though they were, swoop you soon as look at you. She lifted her head, squinting at the windows. Like a bruise, the dark had almost faded. Morning was here ...

Beside her, Em rolled on to her back. 'Molly? Molly, you awake?'

'Yes. Ssh! It's not time yet.'

'I know. I bin awake for a bit. Had a dream.'

'What, London again? That Charlie of yours?'

'I wish. No, it were here. Down by the river, at the laundry. I were turning cartwheels, only once I started I couldn't stop. I done more and more and more, faster and faster, till I come right to the edge and I fell in. And there were no rocks, no nothing, it were cool, all lovely and cool; only when I tried to climb back out I couldn't on account of there weren't nothing to grab hold of ... then the river started rising, started swirling me round and round and round and down ...'

'Like a whirlpool, you mean? That could happen when it's in spate, you know. Like the other day. You want to be careful.'

Em wriggled closer. 'Molly, listen. Something to tell you, ain't had a chance. Like, not just with the two of us.'

'Not exactly just the two of us now.'

'I know. Whisper.'

'What?'

'At the river that day, when we got sprung dancing. When they were herding us back up the path. I were the last one, see. Looked back down at the rocks, and what do you think I seen?'

'What?'

'A black.'

'A savage, you mean? A native?'

'Yes. Only it were a girl. I mean, she'd hadn't hardly nothing on, you could see her titties and everything. She were standing in under the trees.'

'What did she do?'

'Nothing. Only stood there, watching us climb back up the path.

Then she run out on to the rocks, went up on her toes and stuck her arms in the air. Still as a statue, for about ten seconds ... shiny, like a carving or something ... then crouched down and reached out her hands.'

'Must have been watching. Maybe saw you cartwheeling.'

'You reckon?' Em made a pleased little noise. 'That's what I thought, I thought maybe she were going to try and do one, only she didn't.'

'Did you tell Matron? We're supposed to, if we see them near like that. In case they're planning something.'

'Like we are, you mean?'

Molly grinned and nodded.

'No. Why would I? They shoot them, don't they?'

Molly nodded again. 'Yep. If she's any sense she'll run back to wherever they are out there in the forest and stay there. Out of sight, out of mind. So what did she do then?'

'It were like a sort of dance, only like I said she ducked down like she were grabbing something and then there were a shout from the track and she bolted. It were all over quick as anything, but that clear, that ... exciting, you know? I've not said to nobody but you, on account of they wouldn't believe me, but it were true, true as this.' She pinched Molly's arm.

'I couldn't see what it were she grabbed, it were over so quick. That fast she was; fast as me. Or me like I used to be in London.'

Molly tousled Em's hair; it sparked ginger in the dawning light.

'I know what it was. That she reached for, I mean. The laces from your jacket: bet you that's what it was. Remember you pulled them out because they were loose? And dropped them? I meant to remind you, only what with all the Rainey carry on I forgot.'

'Yes; yes, that'll be it, right. Sheesh. That Rainey: don't take much, do it?'

'Well ... not everybody would think flashing your legs through the air wasn't much.'

'D'you think she seen that? I thought she just seen the singing and dancing. Just the having a good time.'

'Don't know.'

'Dammit. How am I ever going to get back in her good books? She's never going to pick me for assignment now ... and how am I ever going to find my Charlie when I'm stuck in here?'

'But she's going, remember? You're in luck. You'll just have to behave yourself with the new one. Which reminds me: I want you to lay low tomorrow ...'

* * *

Ann tugged at the heavy brown blanket; Robert always took it all. He lay inert, slack jawed, arms by his sides. Still a good-looking man, she thought, with or without the uniform. At least he doesn't snore, like Martha says George does. Though she supposed you would get used to it; probably end up counting snores the way people are supposed to count sheep. She had been hoping they might actually have been able to move that same evening, but even if Elizabeth Raine's boxes had been out of the way, Lockyer wouldn't have heard of it. He'd even been dubious about the next day. Still chancy, he said. You never could tell with these women; as far as they were concerned, 'Matron's Residence' still meant Matron Raine and, as Ann had seen for herself, she was the one they were after.

That was the problem with these women; Lockyer had said, shaking his head. You never knew what they were capable of. It didn't pay to underestimate them, they weren't stupid. On the contrary: a few of them could even read and write. You weren't just talking about shop lifters or smash and grabbers: smart as paint, some of them. Had to be, to survive on the street. Forgers, fences, blackmailers, housebreakers; the lot. And then you had your machine breakers and anarchists. Not that he wanted to alarm her. Just a little more time to make sure everything was in order, that was all he asked. Yes, he supposed they could move in tomorrow; the women would be safely back inside by then. To be frank, the sooner she was in there and set up as Matron, the happier he would be. But right now, no need to pay for another night's lodging, there were some vacant rooms in the Married Quarters at the Barracks, he'd made enquiries. Would they care to dine with him there? It would be an opportunity for her to meet some of the officers. Much better to stay there tonight and make a fresh start in the morning, didn't she think?

Yes, she did think. A fresh start was what she'd been saying she needed all along. Major Lockyer was most considerate. Edmund, he said, call him Edmund.

She tugged at the blanket again. So much unpacking still to do, so much to organise. The children would be here soon, along with the rest of their luggage. Stop fussing, woman, said Robert. You've done all you can, it will all work out. Oh will it, she'd hissed as they followed Lockyer into dinner. And how would you know?

He seemed to think he had the Storekeeper job in the bag. Which was a big relief; at least she wouldn't have to waste time worrying about what he was getting up to every day. It was a proper job, too, there'd be no more snide remarks about Mr Matron. Not that those had ever seemed to bother him, water off a duck's back. That was Robert: not an anxious bone in his body. No, things always worked out for Robert. Home and hosed. In the bag. Ann turned on her side and looked at the sleeping face. Things always worked out for that face, right down to her. Gone through the whole performance, hadn't he? Her hands in his, pulling her in close; would she do him the honour, would she say 'I do'? Of course she was going to say 'I do'. What else? How could she say no? Second hand goods: who else was going to make her an offer?

She grimaced. She'd found out later that he'd actually advised the army of his change in marital status the day before he'd proposed. Give him his due, though, he had never cast Letitia up at her; he'd dandled her on his knee like his own daughter. What's sauce for the gander is sauce for the goose was what he'd said at the time, and God knows, there was more than one woman in Portsmouth had been sauce for his gander. But that was all behind them now, thousands of miles behind them, faded into the mists of memory like the coast of Ireland.

Everybody moaned about the hardships and discomforts of the voyage: for her, it had been the honeymoon she'd never had. Robert had been at his most charmingly attentive; well, nothing else to do, had he? When they crossed the Equator, he'd played the part of Neptune, swathed in the folds of her old green cape and waving a pitchfork with the spike of a bayonet tied in between the forks to make it a trident; how they'd laughed! And she'd stroked her belly and thought she'd have said yes even if she had had any choice. They had seen flying fish that same day, and later he had called her up on deck to see a whale breaching, its sudden enormous bulk, the sparkling plume of spray. He'd reached his arms round her whale of a belly and laughed and said lucky old Jonah. When she carried baby Maria up from the cabin for the first time, he had played chasey with Caroline until the child fell asleep in his arms. Later, she had stood with his arm round her and he had pointed out the faint scribble on the horizon which was New South Wales ... so yes. Yes, even if there had been a choice.

The scribble took shape: sunlight sparked off harbour waves and long ribbons of sand edging steep cliffs; pale stemmed trees struck unlikely poses and dark, more stoutly limbed ones braced stubbornly under a cloudless blue sky. The colony itself she liked immediately; the people were friendly and down to earth. They didn't put on airs and they didn't ask too many questions. They knew what it was like, being a stranger in this strange land; they listened, they nodded, they showed her how to do things. The years slipped away: children, friends, housekeeping, charities, official functions: dinners to be given, a household to be run. Until the day that Robert walked in as she was writing a letter home and told her he had resigned his commission. For a few seconds she simply gaped; then she stood up slowly and hissed. 'You've what? Without even asking me? What in God's name were you thinking?'

He took both her hands and made her stand still. It was all right. The regiment wasn't being sent back to England. Or Ireland. They were being sent to India. India! Blacks everywhere there, not to mention cholera, and cows in the streets, and stinking heat the whole year round. What about the children? She sank back into her seat, silenced. She didn't want to go there any more than he did. But how were they to live? What was he going to do instead? Would he get a pension? How were they going to manage?

When she saw the position of Matron at the Parramatta Female Factory advertised, she didn't hesitate. The letter arrived the very day Robert heard that his bid for the property at Burragorang had fallen through. She read it out loud. Your application has been successful. For the first time in weeks he flung his arms around her and spun her around. Matron Gordon. From now on, she was Matron Gordon. She smiled in the dark: the governor himself had shaken her hand, Governor Darling. He had led her into dinner, ahead of all the others. He had introduced her to the other gentlemen on the committee; that was the first time she had met Lockyer. At the end of the dinner, Darling had stood up and waited until he had their attention, their undivided attention. He asked them to charge their glasses, raised his own and turned towards her: 'To Matron Gordon! Our chief Lady!'

Such a long way, such a very long way from the attic in Portsmouth, the garden, the main street, the Assembly Rooms; such a very long way from Limerick and militia balls and shooting parties. Ann took a deep breath in, arched her back and stretched her arms above her head. A world away: it was mainly times like now that she thought about it, times when she was lying in bed awake, twitchy, anxious, second guessing the day ahead. Here she was, Ann Gordon, King that was. Once upon a time. Here she was in New South Wales. As far away from Portsmouth and Limerick as you could possibly get: the Colonies, the Antipodes, the ends of the earth. For better or worse.

A whole wide world away from the Assembly Rooms and the soldier boys on leave, the gallant soldier boys with their red coats and their curly side whiskers, their red lips and tight breeches; from the low, caressing voice that suggested a turn around the gardens ... and around and around; from a fourteen year old girl sobbing to Martha and Martha blaming her mother for making her take her little sister to the Assembly in the first place, how was she supposed to keep an eye on her the whole time? From Mother with her fan and her fainting, from Father pacing up and down in front of the fireplace, hands behind his back, studying the carpet; such a very long way from that lonely first trip to Ireland with a big belly and no wedding ring.

Sometimes she wondered what had happened to him: was he dead?

Was he alive? No way of knowing: no way of ever knowing any more than a name, the memory of a few enchanted moments in a garden. Letitia would never know her father. Blood strangers His regiment had been shipped back to France the very next day, before it even occurred to Ann that she might be pregnant. Hardly even time to say goodbye, just a promise to call when they docked again. Days of hope, days of wonder: day after day of nauseous realization.

He never did dock again. He turned into a picture in a frame, a fading miniature of dark eyes and crooked smile, a blur of dancing, faster and faster in the warmth of the night, dizzy and dizzier ... like in that advertisement for mesmerism she'd seen in the newspaper. How could you, said Martha, how could you? What do you mean, you didn't know, how could you not know? Mesmerism was the only word that came anywhere close. When she told Robert, he just grinned and waggled his eyebrows. He was a good dancer too. She smiled to herself, thinking of Robert, Martha, George and her: those were the days, dancing together at Limerick militia balls ...

Bad luck, Martha called it. Just plain bad luck. Later, that was: once there was no ignoring her sister's burgeoning belly. There's many a girl that's made one mistake and got away with it, she said. But ... big sigh ... not you, pet. Not you. Put it behind you. Nobody in New South Wales need ever know.

Letitia. The entry in her father's big Latin dictionary read joy, happiness. So that was what she called her baby: little Letty. A grown woman now. Left behind in Ireland when she and Robert set sail, but all the better for that. The right decision, absolutely the right decision to leave her behind. They'd all agreed, Martha, her father, her mother ... George, Robert. Even though it had broken her heart; even though never a day passed that she didn't lift her hand to her locket and the curl of hair inside. It was for the best, she had to do the best she could for her little girl. It wasn't her fault, was it? In fact, now she came to think about it, even though she'd protested when Matron Raine had told her what the Factory's policy was regarding babies, it was really the right one. It was better to take the women's babies. It was better to give those children a chance to make something of themselves. And once you had made up your mind about that, the best thing was to do it early, before the children knew what was happening. Before the mothers had the time to get attached as she had. Because it wasn't like with decent families, it wasn't like these women were married or had a home for the children to go to, never mind be brought up knowing right from wrong. It wasn't like they were going to be writing letters or sending birthday presents. Sometimes you had to be cruel to be kind.

Stop it. She had Maria and Caroline and Henry and Sarah to think of now. Not to mention her new position, her fresh start, her chance to finally make something of her life. As Mrs Fry might say, to lift those who had fallen. Starting today. She looked toward the window; it was getting light. Time she was up and about. Lockyer had promised to take them straight to the Factory.

Her first day as Matron Gordon. There was her dress, dark blue with a lace collar, hanging starched and crisp in front of the wardrobe. There was the keyring, her keyring, on the bedside table. Time to put them on.

She threw back the blanket, swung her bare feet onto the floor and shivered. Robert grunted. Over by the wash basin, pouring water from the jug, she watched him turn over, grope the empty space by his side, open his eyes and peer in her direction.

'Time to get up. Mr Matron.'

He grinned and stretched. 'Mr Storekeeper, don't you mean? You just mind your Ps and Qs, my girl, or you could find yourself missing a few deliveries.'

She squeezed out the washcloth and pressed it to her face; it was icy cold. She soaked it again and threw it at him.

'Dammit, Ann ...' he sat up, grabbed the cloth and threw it back at her.

Three loud thumps on the door stopped them mid throw.

'Matron Gordon, Major Lockyer says he'll see you downstairs. Straightaway. There's trouble at the Factory again.'

Ann dived for her dress. Robert leapt out of bed.

CHAPTER FIVE

Thick as Bees

'A numerous party again assailed the gates, with pick axes, axes, iron crows ... the united force of which, wielded as they were by a determined and furious mob, soon left a clear stage and the inmates were quickly poured forth, thick as bees from a hive, over Parramatta and the adjoining neighbourhood. About one hundred came into town, exclusive of numbers that took different routes. Constables were seen running in all directions. A captain, a Lieutenant, two serjeants; and about 40 rank and file, were seen flying in all directions with fixed bayonets, for the double purpose of securing the fugitives, and staying the mutiny; and so violent were the Amazonian banditti that nothing less was expected but that the soldiers would be obliged to commence firing on them ... as they ... went along, carrying with them their aprons loaded with bread and meat ...'

– *Sydney Gazette*, October 1827

***

Molly sighed. Running a hand over her bare skull, she scanned the miles of wilderness, the dark graffiti of trees that individually, she knew, had bark as pale and scabby as her own skin. It seemed to her like some endless parchment unscrolling to the farthest horizon, the very edge of the world.

What was out there, she wondered. And who? That girl Em had described, how long had she been watching them? Had there been others? She'd heard there were tribes scattered all over this strange land: though of course it wouldn't be strange to them, would it? She felt the weal under her arm where the jacket had chafed the skin, but resisted scratching. She could understand why you would go without clothes in this climate. But how did they live? What did they eat? There were wild stories about savages with mutilated bodies and spears: not, she thought, that the blacks had any monopoly on savagery. When you thought about it, what was a bayonet but a fancier kind of spear? She looked at the women scattered round her and smiled.

This was her tribe.

They sat companionably back to back, propping each other up; or leaning against outcrops of rock eating bread begged, borrowed or stolen during the rampage through town. Some of the younger women lay full length on the ground, heads in one another's laps. Waves of voices rose and fell: Cockney, Yorkshire, Scots: she could pick them all. Plus Irish, of course: North and South. That should never have been divided ... where was Bridget? Bridget was born on a farm outside Londonderry. There you had it, the division, all in one name. But where was she? Ah: over there, sitting wide legged with her back to ... Betty? Yes, Betty Chambers. They were sharing a loaf of bread. Got to keep your strength up, as Bridget said. Often. Fair enough too. They would never have got through that gate without Bridget.

Not all were talking or eating. Some were dozing, making the most of the sunshine and not having anything to do but breathe. One or two, like herself, were staring towards the blue-grey shimmer that marked the edge of sight. The sheer distance, that was what you couldn't get over: greater than anything any of them could ever have imagined. What meadows and streams, what lanes and alleys could compare with this? Molly looked around the gossiping, grimacing, giggling faces, each with its own little world inside, a world now blown away like heads of seed from a dandelion. *Blow the wind southerly, southerly, southerly*: she hummed the tune in her head. Except the sea wasn't bonny blue and there was no true love waiting. Instead, a world where the seasons ran back to front and the stars reeled like they were pissed out of their minds.

What were those faces thinking right now? The same as she was, most likely. What happens next? What are they going to do to us? What can they do? And what do we do to stop them? With a sigh, Molly heaved herself to her feet. She stretched up on her toes, reaching skyward as if to call down some god to explain how they got here, to make some sense of it all. Clasping her hands above her head, she closed her eyes and rolled her neck in a slow circle: *breathe in, breathe out. In, out ...*

She opened her eyes on a sea of expectant faces. She shook her head and laughed out loud. 'Christ, take a look at yourselves, would you? What do you think this is, Sunday school?'

A few chuckles, scattered nods and grins. More shrugs, raised eyebrows and muttering. One or two shaded their eyes and looked across the plain at the other groups, the ones closer to town. Small knots of women were sitting wherever there was shade, passing bottles, sharing bread, waving aprons. Further away, on the outskirts of the town, scurrying figures ducked from door to door. Occasionally, a flicker of scarlet appeared, or a brisk scarlet caterpillar came marching left, right, left right. Somewhere a bugle sounded faintly, followed by a cheer – or was it a jeer? The cavalry appeared, trotting through the gates of the Barracks then cantering off in the direction of the Governor's house. Molly sucked in her breath, thrust her chest out and started to march on the spot. She swung her arms to a martial beat and sang.

The Grand old Duke of York ...
He had ten thousand men;
He marched them up to the top of the Hill ...
And he marched them down again!
And when they were up, they were up;
And when they were down, they were down;
And when they were only half way up ...
They were neither up nor down!

The laughter was more widespread this time. Molly glanced across at Bridget, who was clapping her hands in time. She opened her mouth and jerked her thumb towards Parramatta. Molly shook her head: time enough. No need to go back inside just yet. On the ground to her left, propped comfortably against a rock, Joan yawned and shook her dark hair.

'That's the way, Moll. No hurry.'

'None. None in the wide world.' Molly waved to the others. 'It's all right, we'll tell you when it's time to go.' She sat down, drew her knees in to her chest and rocked herself gently. Joan brushed crumbs from her apron. 'Not a cloud in the sky. In October. Tell you what, you wouldn't get weather like this in October in Glasgow!' She smiled and patted her stomach.

'I'm full. Can you believe it? Full.'

Molly grinned. 'With more than just bread. You're starting to show, Joanie.'

'I know, I know. No point going to Rainey, though, not now. I'll go straight to the new one. Never know, she might not be such a holy roller. They should have moved her in by the time we get back. So. I'll go see her, tell her I'm up the duff tomorrow. And while I'm at it, I'll tell her she needs another midwife. Somebody to give old Mary a hand: the poor old biddy's well past it. Tell you what, I wouldn't want to be counting on her to cut my cord! Got the shakes coming, you can see it. What they need is somebody hearty like me, somebody who's been there, done that. How'd you like me for your next lying in, girls?'

The sharp faced woman sitting next to her snorted. 'Well, you been there, done that, that's for sure. No lack of experience, eh? Who is he this time? Or don't you know?'

'No need for that, Agnes Rowley, sour bitch that you are. You know perfectly well who the father is. Jealousy, that's all's the matter with you. I know what I'm doing, don't you worry.'

'So you say, Joan Campbell, so you say. But there's many a slip ...'

Behind Joan and Agnes, the girl lying with her face buried in her arms rolled on to her back. In one lithe movement, she sprang into a squat, ginger plaits swinging, balancing easily on her haunches. 'But do we? Do we know what we're doing? I mean, are we really just going to walk back in there like nothing's happened? Molly, some of them soldiers had bayonets out, seen that, did you? Bayonets! Half a chance and who do you think would be spitted on the end of them? We'd be well and truly fucked then ... well, we would! I'm only saying what we're all thinking, Moll! Now we're out, what's next? That's what I want to know; what are we going to do now? They'll come after us, right? Round us up and chase us back inside, just exactly the way we were! I mean, what's the point if that's all that happens? Yessir, nossir, three bags full sir? We should make a run for it, some of us at least might get away.'

Molly held up her hand. 'Yes, Em, yes. I hear you. But run where? They'd catch us in the town and who's going to give any of us a lift to Sydney? And it's not like we're natives, is it?' She gestured towards the horizon. 'We'd never survive out there on our own. Anyhow, you're wrong. It won't be the same. It won't be like nothing's happened, it can't be, because something has. And it's something they never thought could. They won't forget this day in a hurry! We have joined together, you see, worked together like they never thought we could. We got out, didn't we? They never thought we could do that. Now they know we can, we can! They're not going to forget that in a hurry. Now they know there's only so far they can push us. They couldn't stop us and that's got them worried. Because if we've done it once, we can do it again. That's what they've been scared of all along. What do you think all the different yards, what do you think dividing us up into classes is about? To split us up, just exactly that, stop us getting together and turning on them like we just did. Divide and conquer, ever heard of divide and conquer? That's what they do. Only now we've divided and conquered them.'

'So you say, so you say ...'

'Yes, Em, so I say. It's splitting us up. Like when you split stones in Thirds till there's only dust and rubble: rubble, rabble, see? That's us. It's why they keep shifting us, one here and one there, one up, one down for no reason; it's why they play favourites, so we bitch at each other. Divide and conquer. Suppose we were all to run off like you say; how long do you think we'd last? How long before we had to come limping back? How long before they caught us? On our own, none of us have any chance, not even with shoulders the size of Bridget there. But if we can stick together, we might be able to do something. Not win, I'm not talking about winning. We've already lost. But that's it as well, we've nothing more to lose. Better make sure we keep what we've got instead of picking new fights.' She pointed to her bare skull. 'They can't shave all our heads.'

Em twirled her plaits and spat. 'Like to see them try!'

Molly shook her head. 'They'd do you like anybody else, Em, on your own. We stick together or we've no show. Like, even shaving. It takes three of them to shave any one of us ... one to shave, two to hold ... four if it's Bridget. No way could they shave the whole lot of us!'

'They don't have to, they pick on people, you know that. Like you say, divide and conquer. Any of us, could be any of us. To make an example of. Like they done with you, Molly; or like putting me in the cells that time.'

'Em, you were fighting! What did you expect? And they put Lizzie Adams in as well.'

'There's worse than the cells.' Bridget ran a hand through her hair and shrugged. 'In cells you just shut your eyes and go to sleep.'

'Sleep?' Em stared at her. 'By yourself? Locked up in a black box?'

'Yup. Few hours, that's all. Have a rest.'

'Feels like the rest of your life!'

'All right, all right!' Molly clapped her hands. 'Look, all I'm saying is it's easy to keep one of us under, not so easy to keep us all. There's more of us than there are of them; that's what we've got to remember. Sticking together is the only way we'll get them to listen. Because in the long run ...'

'But what about the short run? I'm not Bridget, Molly, and nobody's ever locking me in a cell again, I'd die first. No air, no room, no light, all on your own ... stand up, lie down, three steps left, three steps right ... the only blink of light way up above your head, and not so much as a toehold in the wall.' She shuddered and shoved her fist in her mouth.

'It won't happen, Em. We won't let it happen.'

'Easy said. I'll be back in the bad books after this. She'll tell the new one. Just when she'd got the letters the Harveys sent back with me, saying I'd given good service and they were returning everybody, not just me, on account of moving back to England. She stopped me in the yard, Moll; said she might see if there was another place. Rainey, I mean. Only then I seen that damn Lizzie and I lost it and now I'm back where I bloody started! God only knows where Charlie is by this.' Em bit down on her knuckles. Joan reached out and yanked her arm away. 'Chrissake, Em, stop that god-awful chewing. It's disgusting. You say you want to get assigned again; who's going to want a maid with hands like raw meat?'

'Oh, shut up Joan. What the fuck would you know?'

'A damn sight more than you, you silly little bitch!'

Molly grabbed Em by the shoulders as she lunged. 'Stop it, stop it, you two! Joan ...'

'What? Who the hell does she think she is?'

'I know more than you think!'

'Oh give over, you two! This is all we bloody need! Come on, Em, come on! Work yourself into a state and you're no use to anybody.' Molly gave one of Em's plaits a gentle tug. 'Yourself included. They can't lock us up, there's too many of us. Not enough cells.'

Em sniffed and lowered her hand. 'Rainey'll be dead set against me now, she'll start picking on me, same as she picked on you. I were right beside you at the gate, Molly, she were pointing at me, I seen her! Bald head and red head ...'

'I told you to keep your cap on!'

'Got pulled off, didn't it? Anyhow, don't matter. They already know who they're going to nick. Marsden'll have his list. That's what I'm saying, we're out, we're out! Why go back in? We'd manage somehow!'

Molly heaved a sigh and waved her hand at the interminable bush. 'Jesus Christ, girl, take a look! Mile after mile after mile after mile, acre after acre of sweet F. A! Like God was on some kind of bender ... how long do you think you'd last out there? This Charlie of yours, I've no idea where he is, but I'm damn sure he's not out there. We're going back, of course we're going back. We were always going back. We've done what we meant to do, we've taken a stand. A stand that'll make them think again next time they want to starve us. Make them realise there's limits to what they can get away with. Now they know what we can do when we put our minds to it. And so do we! Think about it. They've shipped us over here to serve our time. Free labour, that's what we are, for her Majesty's government. So, free labour it is. But we can't labour if we're not fed right. Stands to reason. If they're not feeding us, what have we got to lose? Might as well kick their rotten gates down! That's what you've got to remember, Em, they need us. Can you not see that? Who else is going to spin and scrub and comb and card for them? Who else is going to pick apart the sodding ropes that hold their sodding ships together?' She held up stiff, calloused fingers. 'These used to play the fiddle; I told you that, didn't I? See them? Used to hop about the strings quick as fleas. Jigs, marches, come all ye's, I could do them all ... but never mind that. Try to understand what I'm trying to get into that daft ginger head of yours ... and anybody else's with the same notion. Em, you'll get your ticket, but only if you have the wit to bite your tongue now and then! Never mind keeping your fists to yourself. If the new Matron's any way decent, you might even get it sooner than you think.'

'She might be worse.'

Molly shrugged. 'She might. But why would you suppose that? What's the point of supposing that? That's like saying you're beat before you even begin. We're not. As long as we stick together, we're not. When we go back in, we'll all be walking alongside each other.' She nodded towards the groups of women scattered across the open land between them and the edge of the town. 'We'll link arms, it'll be like a procession. Remind them how many we are. They might be able to keep one or two down, but they can't squash us all.'

'Hear hear!' Joan sat up very straight and clapped. 'Good idea, Moll, that linking arms. That's how they marched in Ireland, isn't it? Them hunger marches you told me about? The bread or blood ones?'

Molly nodded. 'That's right. Bread or blood.' She grinned. 'Know what? We should call ours bread for blood! Because that's what it is, really, isn't it? Give us this day our daily bread and we'll give you our blood, sweat and tears! That's how it is; exactly how it is.'

'Bread for blood, bread or blood, whatever. How about it, Bridget?' Joan jumped up and clapped again. Bridget thrust both fists in the air and beamed: 'Bread for Bridget! Bread for Bridget!'

Molly rolled her eyes, reached down and squeezed Joan's shoulder. 'We need to be back by dark. That gives us another hour or so. We join up on the way so by the time we get to Fleet Street we're all linked up. All right?'

'All right. Here you go, Bridget.' Joan held out what was left of her loaf. 'I'm stuffed.'

CHAPTER SIX

Meanwhile

From the Barracks door, Ann scanned the yard: there he was. The tall, commanding figure of Edmund Lockyer stood before a semi-circle of uniformed men. He was clearly giving orders; man after man saluted and strode off. *All his right hand men: what does that make me?* Robert nudged her. 'Come on. Let's see what's going on.'

Lockyer saw them coming and raised a hand in salute. 'Robert! Just the man. You wanted to have a look round the stables? Well, here's your chance.'

Matters were not quite settled at the Factory yet, but they were making progress. While he was reluctant to inflame the situation by calling it a riot, that was what it was. The women had stood up from their breakfast benches and walked out. God knows where or how, but they had got hold of a couple of sledgehammers, broken through the gate and bolted. Run amok, straight through the town and out into open country. Hard to credit, but there it was. A few strays were still staggering around the streets, but you would find most of them camped on the slopes outside the town. God only knew what had possessed them. Never mind: Lockyer nodded reassuringly to Ann. They wouldn't go far. They'd be back by evening; when they got cold and hungry.

As was already becoming a habit, Ann gripped the keyring at her waist: *not a good start.* She waited, turning the ring slowly in her hands. Lockyer sent the rest of his men off. He was right, of course. Like hens out of their henhouse, they'd scratch around for a bit, then come home to roost. Nothing to eat, no tea, with or without sugar; nowhere to go. As for what had possessed them, that was easy: anger. Those women she'd seen yesterday were unmistakably angry. Manners and morality, forsooth: what did manners and morality matter when you were hungry and outcast? When you were already the lowest of the low? They would come back because they had no other choice. They would come back like whipped dogs with their tails between their legs. Snappy. Snarling. Scarcely in the mood for a fresh start. When the last men had been sent off, she walked up behind Lockyer and tapped him on the shoulder. He spun to face her.

'Major Lockyer. What would you like me to do?'

'Mrs Gordon ... Matron, I mean Matron Gordon. This is not the kind of start you would have wished for.'

'Indeed not. But it is what it is: what can I do?'

'Never fear, Ma'am, I guarantee we will have them all back under lock and key by this evening. What can you do? Well now, this would be a good opportunity to start moving into your new residence; I think you said that Matron Raine had given you keys? Take advantage; there certainly won't be anybody there to bother you at the moment!'

'Major, I am sure there must be something more generally useful I can do. Give me a job.' Lockyer's rather bushy eyebrows drew together for a moment, then lifted. 'I'll tell you what you could do which would be useful. If convenient, of course ...'

'What have I just said? Name it.'

'You could take a message to the Reverend Marsden for me. He will be at his residence, writing his sermon. He plans to hold a special service for the women once we have them back in the Factory. His house is only a five-minute walk away, the large house on the corner. If you go down to the corner of the Barracks there, you will see it.' He pointed; Ann looked and nodded. 'Tell him that I've got men working on the factory gate. Ask him to check on them for me, say in an hour or so. If any of his own men are available, tell him to send them along. We need that gate fixed by this evening. And you could give him this ...' Reaching into his pocket, he pulled out a large sheaf of paper. 'This is a list of the women's names. We'll need a special roll call.' He smiled. 'That would be most useful, Matron. How you occupy your time otherwise, I must leave up to you. No doubt you will use the time profitably. I must run, I need to catch up with my men. I can count on you to do this for me?'

'Of course you can.' She held out her hand for the envelope. 'When do you expect to be back?'

'That depends. I shall be in and out, it depends ...' He shrugged. '... on the women, really. You understand. Besides, it will be a chance for you to meet Elizabeth.'

'Mrs Raine? But ...'

'No, no, another one. The Reverend's wife, Mrs Elizabeth Marsden. I'm sure she will be delighted to make your acquaintance; you might even wait at the Reverend's house until we have the women back inside.'

I might nothing of the sort. 'When do you expect that to be?'

'By tomorrow. Certainly. We will have them rounded up before dark, then it will simply be a matter of restoring order.'

'Very good. I shall be at my office in the Factory or at the Matron's residence. I know where it is, I have been given the tour, remember? I have the keys.' She patted her waist.

Lockyer bowed. 'I commend your presence of mind, Matron. Very good. Right then, I shall be off. I will see you when I get back. I shall make a point of informing you personally on whatever transpires.'

'Thank you, yes. Please do.'

Lockyer strode purposefully away. Ann watched him go, then turned to the papers in her hand: four pages of names. Name after name after name, starting with her own, Ann. The list was in alphabetical order: Austin, Brown, Cartwright, Dixon ... Grimes, Lord: then all the Macs: four handwritten pages: the names of what was it? 366 women, Lockyer had said last night. The place was bulging at the seams. Representations had been made to the government in England, but the ships just kept coming. The

Major had shaken his head. Too much pressure on the assignment system; it was increasingly difficult to accommodate such numbers. Shipload after shipload of women, all to be registered, accommodated and given something to do. Some women had been here for weeks; even some of the better sorts were still waiting to be assigned. Plus you had to make room for women sent back from their assignments as unsatisfactory, there were always a few of those. Then that meant bigger numbers in Third Class, and that in turn meant more guards, more regulations, tighter discipline. And then there were the freed women who had re-offended. Lockyer threw his hands up in mock despair; it was if it were in the air, as if crime was something they breathed in! And they hadn't even got to the women who were pregnant, or sick, or simply too old and done and decrepit to be any use to anyone.

She folded the pages and slipped them into her handbag. No point looking at them now. That would be one of her first jobs, though, to get a list of her own and work through it, put names to faces and faces to names. But for now, that reverend house on the corner ...

* * *

Imposing classical columns flanked a dark timber door. Nothing classical about the door knocker though: it was a brass fox head. She lifted the narrow muzzle and made the fox snap. Snap, snap. No response. She snapped louder. Footsteps, finally: the door swung inwards. A flush faced maid curtsied awkwardly

'Reverend Marsden's residence: can I help you, Ma'am?'

'Sally, Sally, come back! Dear, oh dear, who can that be, he can't be back already ...' The voice was a woman's, high pitched and panicky. Ann hesitated, then nodded at, she presumed, Sally.

'Good morning. Is the Reverend Marsden at home?'

'No, Ma'am, sorry Ma'am. The Reverend ain't home. He had to go and see a man about a sheep.'

In the hallway, a thin, high shouldered figure appeared, wringing her hands and muttering. 'Dreadful, just dreadful. What am I going to do?'

Clearly not a good time: should she excuse herself, come back later? But when? She had promised Lockyer ...

'I have a message for Reverend Marsden. Will he be gone long? Is there someone to whom I might speak?'

Sally stepped back to make way for the wringer of hands: evidently her mistress. Ann bowed. 'I do apologise, this is clearly not a good time to call.'

'Oh, don't apologise, it is I who should apologise; such a reception! It's just ... such a thing to happen! Reverend Marsden will be ... oh dear. Yes, I'm afraid it is, rather a bad time, yes ...'

The woman put a hand to the wall to support herself, lips twitching. Sally hurried to support her; below the maid's rolled up sleeves, her bare forearms showed angry red weals. Hastily, Ann stepped forward. 'Good God: has there been some accident? What can I do?'

Sally's mistress was leaning on the maid's arm; Ann reached out her own. 'Mrs Marsden, I presume? Mrs Elizabeth Marsden? You don't look at all well, Mrs Marsden, we must find you a seat ...'

'Yes, Elizabeth Marsden. There is nothing you can do, nothing anybody can do, I'm afraid. They are all dead!'

Ann stopped short. 'Dead? Did you say dead?'

'Whatever am I going to tell him? Such a thing to happen, the poor little babies ...'

God Almighty: babies? Dead babies? What?

Sally was waving her free hand and shaking her head. 'It's all right, Ma'am, it's all right,' she hissed. 'It's the rabbits, the baby rabbits!'

Elizabeth Marsden moaned and clutched at her maid. Ann grasped her other arm.

'This way, Ma'am,' said Sally. Between them, they helped the unsteady woman to an armchair in the sitting room. She leaned back with a sigh, eyes closed. Then she twitched and blinked at her visitor. 'I do beg your pardon, Mrs ... Mrs ... I didn't catch your name?'

'Gordon, Mrs Ann Gordon. I am the new matron at the Factory.'

'Ah yes, yes, so I have been told. My husband has spoken of you; he is most gratified that a replacement has finally been found. Did you say something about a message? I'm afraid he is not at home. I hope it is not urgent?'

'Not especially; but a matter that needs his attention. My apologies for intruding at such a time, I was told he would be at home.'

'He is. I mean, he was. He was called out unexpectedly, quite unexpectedly. The stockyards. A new ram has arrived: a purebred Merino. For sale. My husband is a breeder, you see. Of Merino sheep. The purest, finest wool, everybody says so.' *To see a man about a sheep ...*

'They are on his farm, of course: his run, as they call it here. One day he hopes to be able to reside there permanently, but at present his religious duties keep him in town. Not to mention his civic duties. Being a magistrate as well as a minister, you know, he is in constant demand. There is simply nobody else with his qualifications ... dear oh dear, he will be ...' Elizabeth Marsden bit her lip, her rather protuberant eyes bulging. 'He did not expect to be more than an hour and he has been gone at least that. It put him quite out, he had dedicated this morning to composing his sermon. I hope you can wait a little; I am sure he will be back very shortly'

Frowning, Ann perched in the armchair opposite her hostess. 'Yes, I can wait for a little. I do not like to leave you like this; you still do not look very well. Perhaps ... Sally, is it? Perhaps Sally might fetch you some water.'

'Yes. Yes, water, thank you. How thoughtful. It did give me quite a turn, you know, really it did. Yes, thank you, I will stay where I am for a little, catch my breath. Oh, but Sally ... Sally!'

'Yes, Ma'am.'

'You must get rid of them, you understand? The little bodies, you must get rid of them all ...'

Sally curtsied and left. Frowning, Ann folded her hands around the bag in her lap and studied the woman opposite her. She was staring at the carpet. *What on earth to say?* She cleared her throat. 'That's right, Mrs Marsden. You just sit there and catch your breath.'

Sally reappeared with the glass of water for her mistress. She looked enquiringly at Ann, who shook her head. 'Off you go. We shall be quite all right.' *Off you go: to get rid of little bodies?*

Elizabeth Marsden sipped slowly, put down her glass and fanned herself with long fingered, elegant hands. She opened her mouth, shut it again and nodded. Ann smiled, waving her own square, unremarkable hand. Her hostess picked up her glass and sipped again, her eyes on the mantelpiece clock.

This is ridiculous.

'Mrs Marsden. Please don't think me rude, but really ... what is going on?'

Elizabeth Marsden pulled out a handkerchief and dabbed at her lips. She cleared her throat and leaned forward. 'I'm so sorry, you must be wondering, indeed you must. You must think this all so very odd! You see: well, the thing is, my husband, the Reverend Marsden, keeps rabbits. White Angora rabbits. They are his hobby, really, his relaxation. He takes all our visitors out to the garden to show them off. They are often surprised, you know, to find that so prominent a person in the colony, one so frequently called to pass judgement on matters of life and death, has a softer side. My husband says it is important to show that softer side from time to time. The human touch, he calls it.'

Elizabeth Marsden closed her eyes and drew a deep breath. 'I don't know if you are familiar with Angora rabbits. They are very handsome. Quite aristocratic. Pure white, and large, very large. For rabbits, that is. Well. Normally he takes care of them by himself. You know, feeding, tidying cages, that kind of thing. His relaxation, he calls it, his light relief. It gets him out into the garden, into the fresh air. It takes his mind off the responsibilities of his position. He had them sent out from his cousin in England, who breeds them. Well. This morning while he was tending to them, a messenger came from one of his sheep breeding friends. He advised him to go down to the stockyards to see this ram, this purebred Merino. My husband had just put the rabbits out in their runs; they get a daily run, you see, and then he feeds them. He had intended to go straight from the garden to his study to write his sermon, so, as I said, he was quite put out. What was so urgent, he asked.'

Elizabeth paused again, nodding to herself. 'Well. The man said there were a number of breeders interested in this ram and it would be first come, first served. So my husband went immediately. He told me to finish feeding the rabbits and put them back in their cages. I have done it before, he has shown me what I must do many times. I was at my piano; I play, you see.' She flexed her fingers. 'Sacred music. For the church. It was a new piece, quite difficult, and I was right in the middle, so after he left, I let them run about a little longer before going out and popping them back into their cages. Well. I was in the shed getting their feed when I heard screams: the most shocking high-pitched screams! I was terrified, absolutely terrified! I rushed out and the mother was killing her babies! Shaking them from side to side, banging them against the side of the cage, and eating them! Tearing them apart and eating them! Only then I realised that it wasn't the mother, it was the father; the mother was screaming and pawing in the next cage ...'

She covered her face with her hands and sobbed.

'What I'd done, you see, what I'd done was, I'd put the father into the babies' hutch instead of the mother! They all look just the same, you know, just exactly the same, big and white with these red, red eyes ... so I shouted for Sally, and she got a sack and opened the cage and managed to get him out and back in his own cage, but by then it was too late of course.' She pulled out her handkerchief and blew her nose. 'Dear oh dear. Blood, all over the straw, and these chewed up little corpses ... little bunny corpses.'

It's not funny, don't you dare laugh. It's appalling ...

'How awful for you! How absolutely awful; no wonder you were upset!'

'And he'll be back any minute, though since you are here ...' Elizabeth sat up straighter. 'Well. I won't tell him just yet, because he had better see you first, hadn't he? Yes, business first, much better. And by then Sally will have finished clearing up, and there will be his sermon still to write, he will probably go straight up to his study. Yes. I won't distract him just yet.'

'I really did turn up at a bad time, didn't I? My goodness, I had no idea that rabbits could be so savage!'

'Oh, neither did I, I assure you. Neither did I!'

'Lucky you have such a capable maid.'

'Yes, she is good, I must say, Sally is very good. Quite superior, for a convict. I hope he didn't scratch her too badly. It must have been when she was getting him into the sack.'

'Yes. Brave girl, by the sounds of it.'

Abruptly, Elizabeth sat up very straight. A key could be heard turning in the front door. She clasped her hands together under her chin. 'It's him! He's home!'

'Elizabeth!' boomed a voice from the corridor.

I remember that voice ... the Governor's dinner ...

'In here, dear, in here!'

Marsden filled the doorway. Elizabeth cleared her throat and fluttered her fingers towards her guest. 'We have a visitor, dear; your new Matron ...'

Reverend Marsden swept off his hat and bowed. 'Matron Gordon! What a delightful surprise! To what do we owe this pleasure? Elizabeth, have you not offered our guest some refreshment? A cup of tea, some cakes ...'

'I have just this very minute told Sally ... I will go and see to it ... I shan't be a minute!' As Marsden stepped into the room, his wife fled out the door and down the corridor.

Tell him. Break the news. Poor thing, she's obviously scared stiff ...

Ann rose, holding out her hand. 'Reverend Marsden, how do you do?' His hand closed round hers and tightened. 'Good to see you again, Matron.'

'Likewise, Reverend Marsden.' She stretched her fingers. 'I must apologise for this unannounced visit; I come on an errand from Major Lockyer. First of all, however, I hope you won't think me impertinent if I draw your attention to your wife. She has had a rather nasty shock.'

'A shock? What's wrong with her?'

'There's been an accident. No, please don't be alarmed, nothing serious. Just one of those things, one of those unfortunate things. Some of your pet rabbits, apparently, were accidentally returned to the wrong hutches. The male rabbit attacked and killed his offspring. When your wife went to feed them, she was confronted with a hutch full of little corpses. It must have been quite horrible: I had no idea rabbits could be so bloodthirsty! By sheer coincidence, I came knocking on your door only minutes after this had happened. As you might imagine, everything was still all at sixes and sevens. Your poor wife had to turn round and entertain me, even though she was clearly still distressed. As much on your behalf as her own, I believe: she told me how fond you were of them ...' She looked up enquiringly. Narrowed eyes drilled into hers, narrowed lips curved downward.

He turned to the door; she darted forward and touched his arm. 'Wait, Reverend Marsden, wait! If I may ... I do suggest that you wait. There is nothing to see, your wife and maid have already cleaned everything up. Order is restored! Father and mother have been returned to their proper hutches. Do wait: your poor wife needs time to regain her composure!' She tapped his sleeve. 'I'm sure the litter will soon be replaced. Rabbits being rabbits.'

She smiled; he did not smile back. She took a deep breath and carried on. 'Your poor wife is really quite shaken. She should perhaps lie down for a while.'

He crossed to the fireplace and swung round to face her, legs planted wide, hands behind his back as Ann could imagine him in a courtroom. Judgement pending.

Pending; why can't things just be over and done with? That's it. All you can do. Change the subject.

'Now. If I may, Reverend, my message from Major Lockyer. He is, as you know, fully occupied dealing with the women who broke out of the Factory this morning. Two things: firstly, he asked if you would check progress on the repair of the Factory gate, and send any extra workers that you might have so that it might be repaired as quickly as possible.'

Marsden nodded and opened his mouth to speak; hastily, she continued. 'The second thing was to give you this.' She pulled the envelope out of her bag. He held out his hand, took it and glanced inside. With a nod, he set it on the mantelpiece.

'Roll call. Good. Thank you, Mrs Gordon, for your trouble. Not a promising start to your tenure, I'm afraid. Most unfortunate. Let us hope that you will not be deterred. We must battle on, Mrs Gordon. We must battle on.'

'Exactly, Reverend. We must battle on.' His features relaxed slightly;

with a nod, she added: 'Major Lockyer seems confident of restoring order by this evening.'

'I should think so! Disgraceful, absolutely disgraceful behaviour. Alas, Mrs Gordon, it is what we have come to expect from these wretched women. But I shall have a few words to say to them, never fear! I shall give them a sermon they will not quickly forget. They will see the error of their ways, don't worry. I can see that you are a sensible woman, Mrs Gordon. I can see that you will not stand for any nonsense. I flatter myself we have chosen well; let me assure you, here and now, that you have the full support of myself and the committee with whatever discipline you choose to impose. As did the worthy Mrs Raine before you. Not to mention the full weight of the Law, both the law of the Land and the law of the Lord. The law of the Land and the law of the Lord, Mrs Gordon, these are the twin forces which we bring to bear on these wretched women! They must be made to see not so much the error, but the sheer wickedness of their ways.' He shook his head. 'Just when one thinks they can fall no further, that is exactly what they do: fall further!'

Elizabeth Marsden hovered in the open doorway. 'My dear ... Mrs Gordon ...' She crossed to a low table, beckoning Sally to follow her with the tea tray. The maid set the tray down and stepped back; she had pulled her sleeves down, Ann noticed. Elizabeth was just lifting the teapot when her husband held up his hand. 'Let the maid pour, my dear. You do not look at all well; you had better go and lie down.'

'No need!' Ann rose from her seat. 'Allow me! Do sit down, Reverend.' She picked up the teapot and smiled at Sally. 'You may go.'

Sally curtsied and fled. Ann started to pour. Marsden stood over his wife and patted her head. 'Mrs Gordon has told me all about it, Elizabeth. You have had a nasty shock. I insist. You must go and lie down.' He turned to Ann. 'My wife has never been strong, unfortunately. Something to do with the artistic temperament perhaps. She is musical, you see.'

Elizabeth's glance flicked from husband to Ann to husband; she opened her mouth to speak, shut it again.

'Go now, go on!' Marsden gestured impatiently. 'You really must take better care of yourself, my dear. Go and lie down as I've told you.'

'Well ... thank you, dear. Now that you mention it, I do still feel a little faint. I shall do as you say. Thank you.' She rose and nodded to Ann. 'And thank you, Mrs Gordon, thank you too. So very nice to meet you, I do hope you will call again at some more opportune moment ...'

'Indeed, I hope so too.'

She left.

Ann held up the milk jug. 'Milk? Sugar?'

'Thank you. Two.' She reached him his cup, then the plate of jam drops. The Reverend helped himself. She put the plate down and picked up her own cup of tea.

'You won't have a biscuit, Mrs Gordon?'

'No, thank you. I won't.' *Little clots of blood ...*

'I gather Mrs Raine has shown you around the Factory.'

'Indeed she has, she has been extremely helpful.'

'I don't doubt it. A true Christian spirit, Mrs Raine: a shining example for these wretched women, had they the eyes to see. I will draw their attention to her example in my sermon. We shall continue the rationing she so judiciously imposed. Crime and punishment, Mrs Gordon, crime and punishment. As ye sow, so shall ye reap.'

Ann hesitated. Was this the time? *Yes, dammit. Start as you mean to go on.* 'In this case, though, Reverend ... I do wonder whether reducing what are already fairly basic rations is the most effective punishment. These women do work long hours, as you know, and for that they do require adequate sustenance. It is in nobody's interest for them to fail to complete their quotas in spinning or weaving due to weakness ...'

Marsden chewed his biscuit. 'Weakness, Mrs Gordon? Don't you believe it. Hard as nails, these women, hard as nails. The only way is to hit them where it hurts, and that, Ma'am, is in the belly. They must never, on any account, be allowed to think they have succeeded. This is most particularly important right now, as authority is passed from one matron to the next. The timing of this incident is no accident, I fear. Change presents challenge; it is a time when the rules must be applied with particular vigor.

Punishments must be enforced. Not to do so is to show weakness, which we, of course, must never allow. Take my advice and make every use of the authority we have vested in you. There must be no chink in our armour. Weakness?' he snorted. 'The only weakness these women show is a weakness for strong liquor. The weakness of sin, in short, that same weakness which brought them here in the first place. We must not only be, but must be seen to be, above all that.'

Ann sipped her tea and said nothing. No point. Yet.

CHAPTER SEVEN

Oranges and Lemons

With a wag of her finger, Joan leant towards Em. 'What would I know? I'll tell you what I know, my girl, and if you've any wit you'll mind me. It's not only skivvies, it's not only washerwomen and spinners and weavers that's needed to fetch and carry and clean up after them, there's men in this town that's lost for it. Lost for it, know what I mean? Now, if I was young and pretty as you are, pet, I'd be thinking that there's more than one Charlie in this here town that's been shipped out here on his ownsome. Sydney or Parramatta, place is full of them. And don't you screw up your face at me, Agnes Rowley, that's the nub of it and you know it as well as I do. Ticket of leave or ticket of love, that's what we're after. One or t'other, that's our ticket out. That's our chance to make some sort of a life for ourselves!'

'Some bloody chance!'

'Well, Agnes, I told you he was a wrong 'un, didn't I? Not my fault you didn't listen ... anyhow. More fool him. Win some, lose some; no use whingeing. What Em here needs to see, aye, and young Sarah there too, all you young lasses, is that a girl's got to look out for herself. Because, guess what, nobody else is going to. Don't just stand there looking at the ground, you've got to look up, you've got to step up. Finding the right one, that's the trick. The ones that are quick enough to throw back the blankets for you of a night can be just as quick to pull them off you of a morning and toss you out on your ear. That's not what you want. No, what you want is a man that knows there's two sides to a bed, and that two's warmer than one.'

Em held up her hands and sighed. 'Look, Joan. I shouldn't have swore, all right? I'm sorry, all right? I know you mean well, you've got my best interests at heart and all that, but give it a rest, will you? Just on account of I'm not as old as you, just on account of I never learnt to read before Molly showed me, don't mean I'm dumb. You go on like I ain't seen nothing, but I seen plenty, and so has my Charlie. I know what you think; you think he's no different from all the rest, only out for what he can get, but he is. Different, I mean. I've knowed Charlie Mason all my life. We was born in the same street, played in the same backyards, nicked apples off the same barrow, run up and down the same alleys. He were the brother I never had. Only then we grew up and I looked at him and he looked at me and there weren't nothing brotherly about it. That were it. From then on it were him and me: oranges and lemons, say the bells of St Clements. Oranges and lemons, swings and roundabouts, bread and butter: that were us. Couldn't have one without the other.' She paused, then shrugged.

'We got in with Smithy, see, learned how to work the streets. Shops, markets, fairs. The two of us: a team. Then he moved us on to the bigger stuff. Houses. Breaking and entering. Except it was more climbing and tiptoeing than breaking. And balancing: walls, planks, ropes. Amazing, the number of upstairs windows you'll find just that teensy bit open ... anyhow, we just got better and better till we were the best. Smithy used to bum about us to his mates. Should of seen us: flitting shadow to shadow, stopping by the wall of some big mansion; drainpipe, lamppost, whatever way it was we were going to get up to that window, we'd have studied it, we'd have worked it out. Charlie would give me a leg up, I'd tie the rope, he'd come spidering up behind and there we'd be, the pair of us tippy toeing along some balcony ... like this, see?' Em spread her arms out wide and tiptoed across the dirt like it was a narrow course of bricks. She crouched, measuring an imaginary distance with her eye, leapt, landed and flourished a bow. Jean and Molly grinned at each other and rolled their eyes; Bridget clapped loudly. Em flourished a bow.

'Oh, Charlie is my darlin', my darlin', my darlin' ...'

Em started and looked around. 'Who's that? Ain't heard that in years ...'

Molly turned and took a sandy haired girl by the hand. 'Sarah, come here ...'

'Molly, no, I didn't mean ... it just came out ...'

Molly pulled the reluctant girl forward. Em's eyes widened; her first thought was blood. But no: the purplish stain trickling down over the girl's forehead to the corner of her eye was permanent: a birthmark.

Molly smiled. 'Em, this here is Sarah. I've been meaning to get you together. She's your age, only just arrived. What, a week ago, is that right?'

Sarah scuffed the ground with her boot and nodded.

'Same place, too.' Molly looked from one to the other. 'London.'

Em shrugged. 'Sounded more of a Scotty to me.'

Sarah glanced up. 'Aye, well. That would be because I am. A Scot, that is. Born and raised in Edinburgh. My Da's head gardener in Holyrood. The palace.'

'Ooh! The palace!' Em rolled her eyes, then winced as Molly dug her in the ribs.

'That's it. I only come down to London last year.' Sarah tossed her head. 'Work for my Aunt and Uncle. Shop in the East End. Brick Lane ...'

Em's mouth fell open.

'Brick Lane? Beside that great big place that smells like a brewery?'

Sarah nodded. 'That's right. Bob's Baccy.'

'Sign of a pipe, right? With smoke curling up over a smiley face?' Em mimed puffing a pipe. 'Such a good picture! Charlie read me the name: good name too.'

'That's Uncle Bob. He married my Aunt Jean.'

Em laughed. 'Would you believe it? And there's this wall just past it ...'

Sarah was smiling now. 'Where the lane is.'

'We had to bolt up that lane, on account of we'd been sprung jumping out a window. These two narks were on our tail, but thank Christ there was a lamp post ...'

'Yes! Yes! I know the exact one!'

'... just the exact right distance from the wall, so we shinned up it, then up and over the wall ... the narks ran straight past.' Em put her hand on Sarah's shoulder.

'Come on, tell me where else you know ... see that rock? Race you!'

She took off. Sarah shrugged then hurried after. Molly turned to Joan: 'Told you. Someone her own age: calm her down a bit. Come on, let's put our feet up while we still can.'

Perched on the rock, Em waited for Sarah to come panting up, then skipped down beside her. 'Weird, innit? I mean, there we were, might even have walked past each other ... and here we are now. What'd they do you for? I mean, if you were with your family?'

Sarah shrugged. 'Not my proper family. I hadn't seen Aunt Jean for years, not since her and Uncle Bob moved south. None of us had. Christmas letter, that was about it. Bumming about how well they were doing. Anyhow, Da had this idea. They didn't have any children, see, and I'm the eldest of six. He wrote and asked if they needed help in the shop and if I could work there for a year. Learn about running a business, that sort of stuff. They pretty much jumped at it. So he packed me off on the train; that was the last time I saw him, waving out the train window ...'

Sarah's eyes filled; she sniffed. 'Sorry. He said they'd pay me, so I could pay my way home again. But when I got there Aunt Jean said she liked his nerve, she was doing the family a favour and I'd get me board and learn a thing or two and think myself lucky. She said he'd cheated because he'd never said a word about my face. What customers were going to want served by a face like mine? What if I put them off? But the first day their usuals came and they were just interested and said how good it was of her and Bob. And then she fell and sprained her ankle. So I had to serve, no choice. She taught me how to work the till and write up accounts and orders; it didn't take long to learn. I could do the books better than her. But she still didn't pay me. After me nursing her and all.'

'Did you not get a message to your Da?'

'He'd enough on his plate, what with Ma and the others. And he wasn't a well man.' Sarah bit her lip. 'Even then, the gardens were getting to be too much. It was only going to be a year, see. Then we were going to set up on our own, selling flowers and vegetables and that. Stupid, stupid, stupid!'

'So what did they do you for?'

'I was at the Markets, running messages. Never done running bloody messages. Never done, full stop. 'Giving' me my keep? I bloody well earned it! Up first thing to light the fire, stack shelves, sweep floors, then serve customers all day. We sold pipes, tobaccos, all sorts. Liquorice all sorts: what wouldn't I give for a liquorice all sorts!'

'Only sweets we ever got was what we lifted.'

'And sherbet. What wouldn't I give for a bag of sherbet! One of those ha'penny bags with a stick of liquorice in it; you could make them last for ages.'

'But you didn't get done for nicking sherbet, did you?'

'Nah. A shawl. I nicked a shawl. At the Markets. Prettiest thing ever. I can see it yet, this foresty green, with roses embroidered round the edges, and little sparks of gold thread all through it.'

'Lovely.'

'Yes.' Sarah drew her hand across her face.

'Ah: so it hid your mark?'

Sarah nodded. 'Yes. Stupid, stupid, stupid. It had rose borders, like Da's garden. Anyhow. Tried it on and just had to have it ... nobody about but me ... stuffed it into my bag. But the stall holder saw me and yelled and I bolted, only I bolted down a dead end street. So that was the end of that. I mind turning round just as Big Ben chimed; by the time it had done chiming that beautiful shawl was back in the stall holder's greasy mitt – he was an Iti – and I was squashed under this big policeman's smelly armpit.'

'What did your aunt and uncle do?'

'Nothing. Didn't want to know. Couldn't afford to, not with Uncle Bob running his books. Last time I seen Aunt Jean, she said I'd made my bed, to lie on it.' Sarah shook her head. 'Hope to Christ she posted my letter to Da like she promised. I don't know what he'll do ...' She paused.

'For all I know, he could be dead.'

'She'll have posted it, course she will, be the least she could do! Or your Da will have sent to find out ... They'll know what happened. It's not like you're dead.'

'Might as well be.'

'Don't say that. Don't let Molly hear you say that. She'll tell you to nil desperandum.'

'What does that mean when it's at home?'

'It's one of them languages nobody talks any more. For don't give up. Don't ever give up. She's clever, is Molly. Educated. She's teaching me to read. Can you read?'

'Of course I can. You have to if you work in a shop.'

'Sorr-ee! S'pose you went to school.'

'Not at first. Our neighbour, Mrs McKee, she taught me my letters first. Mrs McKee, she said to me, why don't you sing me your ABC.' Sarah smiled. 'We had to sing the letters back to her.'

'That's like Molly did, she got me to sing as well!'

'She made it fun. Except then she died.'

'Molly makes it fun too. Writes stuff for me to read. Funny stuff. That's how come she got her head shaved, writing stuff on the walls. Up the Pope with a poker. And No Pope here.' Em laughed. 'That'll be the day, when there's a Pope here! Seriously, but: you stick with Molly, she's been here for ages and she knows what's what. Joan's all right too, except she's never done going on about men and how you've got to look out for yourself.' Em tossed her head like Joan and fluttered her eyelashes. 'I'm telling you, girls, you just do whatever it takes. Screwing's one thing, keeping your heads screwed on is something else again ...'

Sarah laughed. 'True enough, though, isn't it? Keeping your head screwed on, I mean. Doing whatever it takes. You have to.'

Em frowned. 'Depends what the take is. Not saying she's wrong. But everybody's different. And she never shuts up. Like she thinks you haven't got the message.'

'That's what I didn't do. Keep my head screwed on. Fooling about with shawls ... that's just exactly what I was, a fool. Nearly there too. Nearly enough money for my fare home.'

'Thought you said they didn't pay you?'

'Out of the till. Because once they saw I didn't put customers off, they had me in there all day every day. I heard Jean saying to Bob they came on account of they felt sorry for me. More than they did, they just squeezed whatever they could out of me. Must have thought I was stupid as well as ugly. Half time they didn't know what customers were in, they too busy out the back running their book and making their fortune. Once I knew how to work the till, I just decided I'd pay myself. It was slow, a farthing or two here, threepenny bit there, nothing they'd notice. Till had to tally at the end of the day. But it was mounting up. I had my fare and more. Under my bed: loose board.'

'True? Still there?'

'No. Harry will have got it.'

'Harry?'

'Harry worked for Uncle Bob; used to run between him and the other bookies. I told him last time I saw him. To lift it and take it to my Da.'

Sarah leaned her head back and closed her eyes. Em studied her good side.

'That's a big ask.'

Sarah bit her lip and nodded.

'He your fella?'

Sarah nodded again. 'Auntie Jean couldn't believe it. Me neither. I thought he was just being kind, and so he likely was at first. He worked at the stables down the road. I used to go down to stroke the horses. Always liked horses; used to stroke them at the Holyrood stables as well. Then he'd come into the shop asking for Uncle Bob. He'd have tips from Newmarket, or some of the other bookies. Sometimes Uncle Bob would be out, so he'd have to wait and we'd get chatting. Just chatting. Till one day he reached out and touched me, right on it, you know ...' Sarah raised a hand to her forehead. 'Said it was no different from a blaze or a star. Like, on a horse.'

Em sucked in her breath. 'Did you not belt him one?'

'No, because what he meant was, it didn't make any difference. And because he was kissing me.'

Em whistled. 'Good for him. I mean, if it wasn't for that you'd be real pretty.'

Sarah pulled a face. 'Ha ha. I still made sure I slept with my good side up.'

Em waggled her eyebrows; Sarah tossed her head.

'That was why I wanted the shawl. We were going to go to the races, just the two of us. Only we never did.' She shook her head. 'He came to see me in prison. And then to say goodbye. That's when I told him about the money. He promised.' Sarah put her head in her hands.

Awkwardly, Em patted her shoulder. 'Not fair, is it? Not bloody well fair.'

Side by side, lost for much more than words, they sat staring at the distant horizon. Em broke the silence first. 'I've got a fella too. A proper fella, like you. He's here somewhere, I just got to find him. Charlie, his name is, Charlie Mason. The one I told you about before, the one that read your sign. He's smart, see. We worked together, the two of us. For Smithy. Dunno what you'd call Smithy, bur he'd lots working for him, all over the East End. He found the jobs, set his people up to do them Cat's whiskers, that's what he called Charlie and me: the cat's whiskers. Walls, gates, drainpipes, no object. Always carried a rope, never know when you might need a rope. With a loop ready tied, so we could toss it up round some railing and haul ourselves up or let ourselves down, whatever. I tell you, you don't want to play quoits nor any of them throwing games with Charlie or me, you've no chance! Swinging up on to a window ledge or spidering down a drainpipe, though; I had the edge on Charlie there. He got too big; you got to be skinny, you see, little like me; and you got to have a good head for heights so you can jump from roof to roof. Smithy used to say we should've been in a circus, only there weren't none in the East End. Walking the tightrope, that would have been our trick.'

Em sighed and paused for a moment.

'When we started, some of Smithy's crew used to laugh at us because we were so skinny: pipsqueaks, they called us. But they soon found out different. Thick as two short planks they were, where Charlie and me, we were always a couple of jumps ahead. Ducking and weaving, weaving and ducking, in one door and out the other, nobody any the wiser. Come up with the goods, every time. Smithy said we were the quickest on the uptake he'd ever had. Cat's Whiskers!' Em crooked her fingers like claws and meowed. Sarah laughed.

'So how come you got done then? If you were so good?'

'Breaking and entering. Upstairs, downstairs, in my lady's chamber: jew'lry and stockings and lace and shawls. What Smithy used to call easy lift, easy shift. The best bit was showing him what we'd got; he used to make us try it on, stick our noses in the air and parade up and down like toffs. We never got caught in the act, it was after we got lifted. We'd just made it back and all the stuff we'd nicked was still on us when they raided the house. Thanks to the bitch who ratted on us. Lizzie Adams.'

'There was a Lizzie Adams on the ship with me; what does she look like?'

'True? Buck teeth and big googly eyes? Black eyes. I give her one.'

'What, you fought her?'

'I were walking back from seeing Matron Raine, see, happy as can be. She'd got the Harveys' letter of recommendation, she was going to see what she could do. Talked about some family in Sydney town, the very place I know Charlie is! So I'm daydreaming away when who comes strolling across the yard but Lizzie Adams! Large as life, the same bloody bitch! Last time I seen her were in the court room; the time before that were when we got sprung ... narks thumping up the stairs, turning the place upside down, finding the jewel'ry, dragging us out on to the street. Bitch were standing smirking at the foot of the stairs, all cosied up to one of the narks. Only then she seen them drag Charlie down as well. That fair wiped the smirk off her face! They were only meant to nick me, see, she thought Charlie were off on another job and I were on my own and this were her chance. She'd always fancied him, see, but he'd never looked near her on account of me. So she had to get rid of me. But what happened, he never went to that job on account of Smithy got word of this better one that needed the pair of us. We'd only just got back when they raided, just spread the jools on the bed.

Caught red handed. They hauled Charlie down one road to the men's lock up and me down the other to the women's.'

Em stuck her fist in her mouth and closed her eyes for a second. When she opened them again, they were teary. 'Next time I seen my Charlie, it were in the Criminal Court, stood up in front of all them coats of arms and long robes and daggy old wigs and far better looking nor any of them. Anyhow, bang goes that judge's hammer and that's the end of that. Big bull of a nark heaving Charlie out the door, Charlie craning back over his shoulder and me waving and yelling 'I'll find you, I'll find you!' Em dropped her hands and tucked them under her arms. She looked at Sarah. 'And I will, if it's the last thing I ever do, I'll find him! And he knows, he seen me, heard me. Never looked at her, for all she was standing there wagging her stupid arm off. Him and me, that was all mattered. That's all's ever mattered.'

Em hit her fist against her mouth. 'Then it were my turn, and I got seven year too. And I were glad, on account of going to the same place. No sign of her in the court then; just as bloody well. I know how to spit. Anyhow, when I got here I was assigned to people called Harvey, on the Sydney road. Only then they decided to up sticks and go back to England, so I landed back in the Factory ... anyhow. That day. I seen her and she seen me exactly the same second. And she knew, by God she knew! She went to bolt, but I took a flying leap and tackled her to the ground ... she's screaming blue murder and the nails are out, and the teeth, and next thing I know half the Factory's there going 'Fight! Fight!' The guards come running, and Rainey, and that holy bloody roller Marsden. Solitary we got, her and me both. So at least she copped it too. Not seen her since, thank God. Molly says I've to turn and walk the other way when I do. Stop me kicking her head in.'

'That's right, you'll walk and keep walking, girl. Or you really can kiss that ticket goodbye.'

Em jumped at the flick of her plait. Molly smiled at them. 'And the same goes for you, Sarah. However mad you are, just you turn yourself around and keep walking. Scrag fights; all you can expect from the likes of us, aren't they? Up in the Barracks, they lay bets on them. Don't give them the satisfaction. Lay low: bide your time.' She flicked Em's plait again. 'They'll forget about it. Bridget says they've no room in Thirds as it is and there's more cargoes of women arriving all the time. They'll be wanting to shift us and if they think you're a fighter or a troublemaker, they'll send you as far as they can: back of bloody beyond.'

'That's right.' Bridget loomed up behind, arm in arm with Joan. 'And some of them backs of beyond, I'm tellin' you, cells are nothing to them. You want to try waking up in a barn with a snake curled up next to you.'

Em gasped. 'A snake? True? What did you do?'

'Big brown bugger. Asleep in the straw beside me. What did I do? Nothing. Nothing. Lay there playing dead. Trying not to breathe. Seemed like hours. Morning, barely light. I heard this scratching over by the door. So did the snake, its head reared up, I seen that forked tongue flicker. A chicken it was, one of them little fluffy yellow ones. For all of about two seconds ... then it were dead and I were hanging from the rafters screaming like a bloody banshee.' She shook her head. 'Never seen anything like it, the speed of that snake. Lightning: forked bloody lightning.'

Joan shuddered. 'Ugh! Don't know how you did that, just lay there looking and not moving ... I'd have been bit for sure.'

'Did they ever catch it?' asked Sarah.

Bridget shrugged. 'Dunno. Didn't matter, I weren't going to sleep out there again, not for nobody. They slung up a hammock under the trees outside. That was all right; more than all right, I used to just lie and look up at the stars. Only then it started getting cold, brass monkey weather. So when this hawker come through in a cart, I climbed in the back and pulled his big oilcloth over me. By the time he found out we were halfway to Parramatta. Chinese he was, and he'd been smoking, like they do, so I don't know what he thought he was seeing when he seen me. Anyhow, his wee slits of eyes were sliding all over the place and he reached out his scrawny yellow hand and I shook it. That was it. We done a deal; he let me stay in the back and I did the cooking till we got to Parramatta. Only then we stopped at an inn and I got into a fight and ended up nicked again.'

Bridget tipped her head toward Molly. 'She's right, you know. Fighting's no use.'

'Especially if you're like Bridget here and don't know your own strength. That's when they'll come down on you, if they think you're capable of doing damage to more than yourself. That's when they say you're incorrigible.' Molly slapped the other woman's burly shoulder. 'Reprehensible, recalcitrant ... They've any number of words for us, and they're none of them kind.'

'I know, I know.' Em chewed at her knuckles. 'Done it now, but. Old Rainey seen the fight. So I'm one of your re-whatsits.'

'Em, Rainey's gone, remember? The new one won't know you ... unless you give her reason.' The big woman shrugged. 'Like I say, just keep that red head of yours down. What the eye doesn't see, the head won't blame.' She paused and grinned. 'Wonder Rainey did see you, really, what with her eyes turned up to heaven the whole time. You take a look some time, Sarah. She never looks at you when she's talking, just rolls her eyes up and talks to the sky.' Molly laughed, rolling up her own. 'Em and Lizzie thrashing away there in the dirt and her saying her prayers!'

Em snorted 'Turn ye aside from anger, turn ye towards the light ... that's what she said. Then what? Shoves ye into a black box with only a slit of a window way over your head. Locks ye in all on your own, not another soul, just them walls closing in and the dark.' Em shuddered. 'Like being buried alive ...'

Molly set her hand on Em's shoulder. 'But you weren't, were you? And you won't be. They've got an awful lot more than you to worry about. Right now, they'll be busy working out how to get us all back inside. Old Rear End will be getting a sermon ready. One of his brimstone specials, warning us what's in store for us, hey Joan?'

Joan snorted. 'That'd be right. How sinful we all are, yielding to temptation instead of him. Some temptation he'd be: face like a skillet with two eggs sizzling. Look, Molly, look over there! They're waving their aprons.'

In scattered groups women were standing, shaking themselves out and stretching. Molly patted Em's shoulder. 'Out of sight, out of mind, that's the way, sweetheart. All right, everybody? Up you get. Stick together, remember? Link arms, make sure they see how many we are. Come on ...' All around, women were getting to their feet and shaking themselves out. Molly linked with Bridget and Joan. Em and Sarah tucked in behind.

Joan stood on tiptoe and waved her arms. 'All right, all right! Keep together, keep walking, and don't go off on your own. Arm in arm, right? Just keep telling yourselves, they can't do without us. They can't. The place would fall apart. Rainey's overstepped the mark and they know it! Like Molly says, they can't shave us all. And what about when the next ship comes in? What are they going to do with the women off it? We're crowded enough as it is, can't hardly scratch ourselves, never mind our best friend, hey Susie? Oh, for goodness' sake, only joking! Christ, what's wrong with you lot, don't any of youse know how to take a joke anymore? Numbers, that's all I'm saying. We got the numbers.'

Molly clapped. 'Joan's right. Be prepared. We can't be seen to have got away with it, they'll have to think of some sort of punishment: save face, if nothing else. But there's too many of us to come down hard on. And I tell you what, the new Matron, whoever she is, she'll think twice before she cuts rations again.' She glanced towards the other groups. 'That's Peg's apron. Come on!'

In twos and threes, the women set off, gathering up aprons now mostly empty, brushing down skirts, tying laces. Molly watched, arms folded across her chest. 'That's it, here we go! Put us together, that's a lot of women, isn't it? That's a street, that's a village. What are they going to do to us all? And the ships keep coming, keep sailing in through those Heads, keep bringing more of us. That's it, see? Every single one of you, whatever boat you sailed out of London in, you're sure as hell in the same one now. We're mates! Ship mates!'

Molly moved to the front of the crowd, Bridget and Joan following. She ran her hand slowly over her head, watching the lines of women converge, arm in arm, heading for Fleet Street and the Factory walls. Em grabbed Sarah's hand and they ran up alongside the big woman. Twisting two fingers of her free hand together, Em held them up. 'Mates. Like

Charlie and me. Oranges and Lemons.'

'Say the bells of St Clements,' chimed in Sarah. Molly cuffed Em lightly on the head. 'One track mind, that's all's wrong with you. Come on.'

Trickles then streams of brown and blue merged into a broad river flowing toward the town, where troopers on horseback rode up and down for no apparent reason. Shopkeepers, housewives, tradesmen with their carts stood in small clusters outside buildings or on street corners, talking or simply staring. Children jumped up and down and waved and shouted till their elders boxed their ears and sent them inside. The women kept coming, through the town gates, round the corners, along Fleet Street. There were the Factory walls, there was the big gate, solid as before, waiting to thud shut behind them There were the troopers stationed along the way.

Em tugged Molly's sleeve. 'A song: how about a song, Molly?'

Dear God, think, woman, think ... 'Right, then. Clap your hands; here we go ...

There was an old prophecy found in a bog
Lilliburlero, bullen a la!
This land shall be ruled by an ass and a dog ...
Lilliburlero, bullen a la!
Lero, lero, lilliburlero, lilliburle-ero bullen a la ...

CHAPTER EIGHT

Starting Over

October 1827
My dear Letitia,

You will be wondering at not having heard from me. Quite simply, I have been run off my feet. First, the big move from Newcastle to Sydney: packing, getting the children organised, not to mention transport for furniture etc. and our own travel. All still to unpack and reorganise! Then there have been various meetings and one official dinner. Governor Darling is very distinguished and considerate; he made me very welcome. I have signed the legal documents and met the gentlemen from the management committee to whom I will be reporting; the keys to the Factory are beside me as I write. Yesterday afternoon I was given a tour of the Factory buildings by my predecessor, Matron Raine. It was useful, of course, though I would have preferred to spend the time moving the rest of her boxes out of the Matron's residence and moving ours in. As it turned out, though, our move was delayed in any case because of a disturbance among the women. They claimed to have grievances because their rations had been cut: no sugar for their tea, and a smaller allowance of bread. Apparently this was a disciplinary measure ... a mistaken one, in my view. Today they have actually broken out of the Factory, actually out through the gate! As you might guess, chaos reigns. Clearly, it is an unfortunate beginning to my tenure as Matron, but do not let it alarm you. After all, I am sitting here comfortably writing a letter, am I not? Major Lockyer is confident that order will be restored and the women back in the factory tomorrow. As he very sensibly remarked, where else are they going to go?

They are currently still at large: 'on the town', I'm afraid, in the most literal sense. As I say, however, I am confident Major Lockyer has the matter in hand. The militia have been called out and the gate is being repaired as I write. All will be in order for their return. It is reassuring to know I have such support.

So: no cause for alarm, I am undeterred. I think I told you in an earlier letter about an article I read recently about Mrs Elizabeth Fry ... yet another Elizabeth: hard to believe the same name applies to three such different women! Anyway, I have been quite inspired by reading about Mrs Fry's progress with the women of Newgate prison. I cannot remember her exact words, but they were to the effect that the purpose of punishment should be reform rather than retribution and that such women should not simply be dismissed as lost causes. Indeed, they may actually have skills which can and should be used for the benefit of society.

I was taking tea with my predecessor, Elizabeth Raine (the second Elizabeth) after she had shown me round the Factory when we had our first warning of the unrest. Two young troopers were sent to the Matron's residence with orders to escort her to the Barracks; Major Lockyer was concerned for her safety. With some reason, to judge from the shouts we could hear outside! So they took her off and left Robert and me to our own devices. I will confess to a few anxious moments after leaving the house, when we came across a large group of Factory women. Fortunately, they did not know who I was and we were able to go on our way unmolested. Their leader was a large, fierce looking Irishwoman; I was reminded immediately of our time in Limerick. Despite her appearance, however, she was prepared to listen to reason. While they eventually returned to their quarters, Major Lockyer insisted that we spend the night at the Barracks. We dined with him, which was very pleasant. I am frustrated by the delay, however. I had hoped to have at least our cases unpacked by now: so much to do!

The breakout, of course made for more chaos, with whole gangs of women running amok through the streets of Parramatta! They are still out. Hence this letter: there is nothing I can do at the moment but wait until I hear from Major Lockyer. As I say, most frustrating.

The Factory itself is a handsome sandstone building. Fortunately for the colony, though not for him of course, one of the convicts sent out here is an architect by the name of Francis Greenway. He has designed a number of buildings, apparently. I believe he advertised his services on arrival and has been in demand ever since, obtaining his ticket of leave almost immediately. One more example of a person who has defied the odds and made a successful life for himself out here! The building is three storeys high and generously proportioned. There are workrooms for the various industries in which the women are employed, spinning, carding and the like. There are separate yards for First Class, Second Class and Third Class convicts, the latter being the Penitentiary class. The building backs on to the Parramatta River, which is very convenient for laundry work. The Matron's residence, our new home, stands within the grounds and is really very convenient and comfortable. I have an office in the main building, of course, and am writing this at my desk. My carriage clock, of which you have the partner, is before me, keeping time as faithfully on this side of the world as it did on the other. I am now officially Matron. It is a relief, as you can imagine, to be settled and secure again after Robert's resignation and the anxiety of wondering how we were to support ourselves. I expect the children to arrive early next week; I don't think I will feel truly 'at home' until they are here.

Ann paused and surveyed her office. The far end had been arranged like a sitting room, with a sofa and armchairs around a low table. Matron Raine had told her that the Reverend sat in the right hand armchair, the better to admire her china rabbit on the sideboard. 'Belique china, Mrs G!' No rabbit now: she must have taken it, along with the rest of her knickknacks. Just as well.

She looked down at her letter: 'at home'. Not much longer, hopefully, until the children were here and they were properly settled into the house. At least her escritoire had been delivered, without a scratch so far as she could see. Such a find, the little mahogany desk with its neat compartments and drawers; she had been determined not to leave it behind. She would set it up next to the drawing room window so that she could see people coming and going; when visitors came, she could simply close the lid. Most of her work would be from her office here, of course, but there would certainly be times when she would have to take work home. She had added the escritoire keys to those already on her keyring. She smiled to herself as she went back to her letter.

Our other good news, of course, is that Robert has been appointed Commissariat Storekeeper of the Factory: Hurrah! I am delighted. It is quite a responsible position, administering both civilian and military stores. I suspect it will occupy him rather more than he blithely supposes at present. And of course, with the four little ones, the extra income will not go astray.

So, my dear: despite this initial set back, I am in good spirits. I like Major Lockyer; he is a military man, but not at all pompous or arrogant. He has been most helpful. This morning I took a message from him to the Marsdens' residence, where I met the third Elizabeth, Mrs Marsden: a timid sort of woman; very musical apparently. She is clearly in awe of her husband, the Reverend and I can see why. I must say I did not take to him, though I gather I have him as well as Mr Greenway to thank for the Factory. Previous arrangements were, to put it mildly, primitive: little more than a shed. While the decision to build was Governor Macquarie's, apparently it was Reverend Marsden who convinced him of the need for such a place for the women. I have also been told that he corresponds with Mrs Fry, which is encouraging. I must not rush to judgement; but he is certainly quite fixed and rigid in his views, particularly regarding convict women. In one breath, he talks of their immortal souls, in the next of lost causes! He keeps rabbits ... but I will save that story for my next: this is already too long and I have to go and meet Robert.

I feel confident that, with a firm but fair hand, the Factory will soon be running smoothly again. I mean to establish a strict routine which will keep the women usefully and gainfully occupied. The rules will be made quite clear to them, and the penalties. I do not want there to be any excuse for bad behaviour. The divisions between the classes will be maintained; I agree wholeheartedly with Major Lockyer that every effort should be made to prevent the 'old dogs' from teaching the 'new dogs' disobedient tricks. I shall be firm; firm but fair, and make sure I am seen to be so. Women who do well will be recognised. In a nutshell, I mean to put the present unrest behind us as quickly as possible and restore peace and quiet.

I must finish. My dear child, it does my heart good to think of you so well established. It is hard to believe that so many years can have passed since I kissed a little 5-year-old girl goodbye! Is it not strange that you, like your mother before you, should have followed your husband to the ends of the earth? Yet there you are in New Zealand, with your own family! How I should love to see my little grandsons! Write soon! Your loving mother.

Ann signed and sealed the envelope. She stood and went over to the window. In the distance, she could see what looked like a slow brown river trickling towards the Factory gate.

* * *

'Look out, George, here they come!'

The broad shouldered, freckle-faced trooper pushed himself off the wall against which he and his companion had been lounging, stamped his feet and straightened his jacket. Beside him, George spat out his quid of tobacco and grinned, his eyes on the advancing women. 'Well, well. Ain't that nice: arm in arm. The animals went in two by two, Hurroo! Hurroo!'

'They just want us to keep watch, don't they, George? Just let them file in quietly? Not arrest them or anything?'

George yawned and ran a hand through his mop of curly dark hair.

'Arrest? Where would you even start, man? Nah, we're just here in case any of them decide to do a last-minute runner. Keep them moving straight along Fleet Street, straight through the Factory gates, straight back inside. Lockyer will get them all inside those walls before he starts worrying about arrests.'

'Do a runner? Down the town, you mean?'

'Down the backstreets, down the dives, is what I mean. Won't be the first time some of them have been out. On the street, in every sense. Some of them have got friends ... family, even. They didn't all come on the last ship, some of them have been in and out of the factory for years. On assignment, or tickets of leave: let them out one day, off they go and get pissed, lock 'em up again the next. Even if they do get some sort of job, it's usually just a matter of time before they're caught nicking something again. Can't help themselves. And then there's the brawlers and shit stirrers.'

'Really? That bad?'

'Trust me, mate. Just wait till you've been here a bit longer, you'll see. Look, it's that big bald bitch in front, and her mate beside her. Tell you what, it'd want to be hellish dark before you'd tackle either of them!'

'What about the shorter one beside them? She looks a better sort.'

'Too long in the tooth. You want to steer clear of the older ones, Andy my boy. They're the ones most likely to give you a nasty little present. The young ones, the ones just off the ships, they're a better bet.'

'Wasn't planning to bet on any of them. I'm engaged, remember?'

'So you are; bloody hell, so you are! What's her name again?'

'Emily Luttrell.'

'Luttrell: that'd be the surgeon's daughter? Well done you; she'd be worth a bob or two. Handy Andy, eh? How did you nab her?'

'It wasn't nabbing, George. It just worked out. Like it was meant to be, really. See, her father knew mine before he came out here, they studied medicine together in London. I think they might even have shared a surgery for a bit. When I got posted, my father wrote Luttrell a letter. He got one back just before I left, saying that he and his family would be delighted to see me. They asked me round the first week I got here.'

'What's that, a month ago now? Still makes you a pretty fast worker, boyo!'

'No.' Andy shook his head. 'We just hit it off, that's all. What speeded things up was they got a letter from her grandmother in London wanting to know what ship she'd be coming backon. They'd been planning on sending her over there for the season, you see. Make her debut.'

'Find a husband, you mean. And she didn't jump at the chance?'

'No! She can't stand the old bag. Besides, her father's not been too well lately. She's close to her father.'

'Never thought of it yourself? Medicine?'

'Never had the brains, George. There's a stack of exams you have to pass, books you have to read: anatomy, stuff like that. That's what Alexander did. He's my older brother: he's the one got all the brains. He was always the one going to take over from Father.'

'So you took off to seek your fortune!'

'Not much choice. Not much fortune. Twins after me. There was a bit of pressure.'

'Well, it's one way of seeing the world. Even, like they say, if it is the arse end of it. Oops ... no reflection on Emily, mate! God, no, I meant ... you know what I meant!' Andy grinned and nodded. George slapped his shoulder. 'So when's the big day?'

'Twentieth of November.'

'Bloody Hell, that's not far away, is it? You'll have to have a stag night, boy! We'll go to Harry's, he runs a clean house ... tell you what, I'll have a word with him this very night, book us in. We'll pass the word, get a few of the boys together ...'

'Hold on, hold on, I'm not sure ...'

'Course you're sure! Randy Andy, eh? And if you're not, it's about time you were! Want to be able to show her a thing or two, don't you? Leave it to me ... uh oh: here they come. Crossing the road now, we'll get the whiff of them soon ... the animals went in two by two ... horses, donkeys ... plenty of dogs ... whole mob of sheep, baa baa black ... dammit, look at that one! Somebody must have puked on her.'

'That's a strawberry mark. Father had a baby like that in the surgery once. They're born that way. Nothing you can do about it.'

'See the one she's linked with? See the redhead? That's her!'

'What do you mean, that's her? Which her?'

'Shut up. Wait till they're past.'

The two stood to attention, staring straight ahead as the women, arm in arm, filed past. Some stared fixedly straight ahead, more kept their eyes on the ground. Some talked, some whispered, a few staggered and stumbled, the worse for drink. A few shot furtive sideways glances, but for the most part the women barely glanced at the troopers lining the road. When they did look up, the Factory gate loomed, yawning like the jaws of

Jonah's whale, ready to swallow them whole. George nudged Andy. 'There she goes. See? The little red head linked to the strawberry?'

Andy narrowed his eyes and nodded. 'Yes. She is kind of pretty. Bit too skinny for me. What about her?'

'She's the one I saw down at the river that day. Remember, I told you? Doing the laundry.' George's lips curved. 'Turning cartwheels, she was. You could see right up her fanny.'

CHAPTER NINE

The Word of the Lord

Ann drummed her fingers on the table. It was a rather fine mahogany table, had anyone been able to notice it under the boxes of invoices and receipts, the ledger books, the manifests of ships and convicts, the inventories for looms, spinning wheels, carding combs, blankets and linen. Ann sighed and stilled her fingers. *You can do this; this is straightforward, this is the easy bit.*

She hadn't slept well, that was the trouble. She had woken up in the wee small hours with a lurch in her stomach that she hadn't felt in years: the lurch that went with the losing Letitia dream. She frowned: a panicky, illogical nightmarish thing. She'd almost forgotten it. Such annoying things, dreams. And no getting back to sleep, just when she needed to. She had slowed her breathing, made lists in her head, turned from one side to the other: still no sleep. Beside her, Robert had heaved over once and chuckled: nothing wrong with his dreams. He was probably greeting the children this very minute, cracking jokes, showing them their rooms, hoisting Caroline on to his shoulders. She should have been there with him, but there was too much to do. She must see about getting a domestic. Two: a cook and a maid. She drummed her fingers again and picked up a list of names. No shortage of women to choose from.

Women for assignment: women not for assignment. Names to be

added, names to be crossed off: pregnant women, babies, women for laundry, women for spinning, for carding, for stitching and patching and sewing a straight seam. Monitresses, portresses, cooks, gate keeper: she had to see them all. Lists and more lists: the management committee was strong on lists. Not so strong on doing anything about them. Though the gate had been fixed, thanks to Lockyer and Marsden.

Had she done the right thing? Standing there at that gate as the women came marching in, two by two? They would have had no idea who she was; with Marsden and Lockyer either side, most of them probably didn't even notice her. She had to be seen in her own right ... not easy when the men were so much taller Though there again, Elizabeth Raine was tall and she hung off Marsden's every word, Reverend this, Reverend that. No wonder he was full of himself. Maybe she should just have left the men to it ...

No. She had to be there. It was her responsibility to be there. Being in charge meant knowing exactly what was going on. She was Matron Gordon: she made the rules. She was the one they would go to for permission, she was the one whose signature they would need ... for pretty much everything.

Matron Gordon: firm, but fair.

She crossed to the window and, with some difficulty because the latch was stiff, pushed it open and looked down. The yard was heaving. Directly underneath, two women lurched drunkenly off the wall; she had to smile as the first squared up like a prize fighter to one of Lockyer's men. Not to be outdone, the second flung her arms around his offsider and would not be dislodged. Over by the wall, a dozen or so troopers feinted and lunged with their rifles, but every time they relaxed, one or another of their carefully lined up women ducked under an arm or a rifle, dodging through the crowd until they were dragged back squalling. Some of the troopers stayed tight lipped; others shouted and swore. A few of the younger ones were actually laughing; they whistled and egged each other on, grabbing random women, tripping them up, yanking them back to their feet. Only the men posted at the entry stood to stiffly expressionless attention, staring over the heads of the swarming women as if by ignoring their existence they could erase it.

Two troopers led a horse and cart into the middle of the yard, ignoring the protests of its evicted owner. Major Lockyer and the Reverend Marsden were studying what looked like the list of names; the Reverend was jabbing at it with his forefinger. There was a clear space around them, an unlikely still point amid the general confusion. The two troopers took up positions either side of the horse, waiting for instructions.

Aprons lay scattered about. Some, still knotted around food, looked like mouldy cannonballs; some lay trampled and torn, fallen women with outflung arms. Two women, brown of skin and skirt, wrestled fiercely over a brown bottle. It fell from their grasp and bounced across the dirt. They dived after it, were dived after themselves. Four troopers hauled them up and dragged them, mumbling and squirming, into line. Near the main gate, half a dozen First Class women stood in a rigid row, hands knotted at their waists, chins tucked under, eyes downcast. *Where have you seen women like that before? Lining up to disembark, that was it, that momentary limbo after you'd stepped on to the gangplank and stood above that dark strip of water, before you'd stepped off into this new world ...*

A heavily pregnant woman clutched at her stomach and staggered. The women nearest flung their arms around her and half dragged, half carried her towards the lying in rooms. What state was old Mary in, Ann wondered; she'd passed the rooms on the way to her office that morning, and yes, that was snoring she'd heard. She poked her head around the door to see Mary flat on her back on one of the pallets, jaw fallen open, eyes closed. She had thought to wake her, but something about the old face had changed her mind. The rooms were empty; let her lie.

A shot cracked through the air. Men and women alike sprang to attention, pivoting as one towards Lockyer and Marsden. The Major lowered his pistol and stepped forward, list in hand. He read out a list of names and his men, clearly briefed, made bee-lines for their owners. From her vantage point, she could see women ducking for cover, smaller behind taller. Some women, their arms still linked, stepped forward or backward as the listed ones ducked and dodged.

Ann frowned. Lockyer had said that they needed to make an example of one or two; she had agreed. But this wasn't one or two, this was four, five, six and counting ...

Last to be pinioned was the big bald Irishwoman. Ann leant forward to see better. The woman was head and shoulders above the uniforms clamped to her elbows, yet she made no attempt to resist, as most of the others had. She simply allowed herself to be led to the wall. *What are they going to do with them? This isn't what we agreed. Time I was down there ...*

Keep them under, keep them under. In her head, Elizabeth Raine's words drummed a rhythmic tattoo as she hurried down the stairs. Or were they Marsden's words? These outcast women ... must serve their time, must repay their debt to society, must pray for forgiveness. All well and good, but one or two was enough of an example, surely? Not nine or ten ... what were they going to do with them all? *Get yourself down there ...*

Ann rounded the corner into the yard and pulled up sharply. Instinctively, she grabbed at the two flying figures who had almost skittled her. She braced herself, hands clamped around their wrists. They jerked to a standstill and she drew herself up very straight. 'Stop this minute! You two: where do you think you are going? What do you think you are doing, bolting like this?' Shifting uncomfortably, the two she had pinioned kept their eyes on the ground. *Girls: they're only girls: not even Letitia's age.*

The girls fidgeted, shooting furtive glances at each other and this fierce little woman from nowhere whose hands manacled their wrists.

First impressions, remember, remember. Keep them under. Ann dropped their wrists and fixed her gaze on the red head, standing with her head down and one fist pressed against her lips.

'Well? I asked you a question: two, in fact. Who are you and just where do you think you are going?'

'Emily Kelly per Janus, Ma'am. Nowhere, Ma'am.'

'You are in a very big hurry to be going nowhere.'

The girl shrugged, keeping her eyes on the ground. Ann turned to the other one.

'And you?'

The girl looked up and Ann winced, registering the strawberry mark.

'Sarah Scott per Harmony, Ma'am.'

Dear God: who names these ships? Slow down, take your time; take your time.

'Well, Emily Kelly and Sarah Scott, what do you think you're doing? Why are you not in the yard like the other women? Has Major Lockyer dismissed you? Has the Reverend Marsden dismissed you?'

Sarah straightened her cap and glanced at her friend's bent head. She sniffed and bobbed a curtsey. 'Yes, Ma'am. I mean, no Ma'am. We didn't mean nothing, Ma'am. It's just ... everything's that confused, what with us all crammed in together and all the swearing and shouting and shoving and grabbing, and nobody knowing what's supposed to be happening. We didn't know either, all we knew was we didn't want to get into strife, so we thought we'd just duck out of the way for a bit, Ma'am. We never knew we were meant to stay and be dismissed, Ma'am.'

'Never knew much, did you?'

'No, Ma'am, that's right, I never did. And now I know even less. Only just got here a week ago, Ma'am; don't know nothing, that's about the height of it. Honestly.'

Harmony: that's right, the manifest's on my desk ... last week ...

'I see. Well, Sarah Scott, I would have thought that would be all the more reason to wait for orders and do what you're told in the meantime. What about you, Emily Kelly? How long have you been here?'

'Six months. Ma'am.'

'Is that so? And what do you know?'

'Nothing. Ma'am.'

'Nothing? Look at me when I'm talking to you. You must surely know more than your friend here.'

Green eyes flared: Em raised her chin. 'All I know, Ma'am, is the same as her. We never done nothing wrong. Or at least, we never meant to. Only you can't never tell in this place.'

The sound of a bugle. *Now what? I should be out there ...*

'Well, know this. I am your new Matron; you will address me as Matron Gordon. I have no time now, I will deal with you later. Follow me, this way. Quick smart, now, quick smart!' Ann stopped at the archway into the yard. 'Now, stand by the wall there. Just there, that's right. Wait there till I get back.'

Lockyer and his men had the women lined up to face the cart, which was to become a pulpit. Reverend Marsden climbed up, set his legs wide apart and punched the sky. *Pay attention, God!* Ann hurried off across the yard. 'Wait, mind!'

'Yes, Matron Gordon.' Two voices chimed obediently.

'Hear ye the word of the Lord!'

Ann stopped behind Lockyer, who was standing off to the side of the cart. Looking across the rows of bowed heads, Ann felt no need to bow her own. She stood on tiptoe and scanned the crowded yard. A hammer: that was what Marsden's voice reminded her of, a blacksmith's hammer. Except that it wasn't metal he was hammering.

'And the Lord God said on to the woman, what is this that thou hast done'? You women gathered here before me, this is your text for today. Listen well. 'And the Lord God said on to the woman, what is this that thou hast done?' Marsden's forefinger stabbed the air above the rows of bowed heads. He sucked in his breath.

'And I say on to you, on to each and every one of you gathered here in this factory this day, what is this that thou hast done? This very day? You must know ... each and every one of you must know ... that you have sinned, most grievously sinned. You have risen up against those set in authority over you. You have turned your hands against those appointed to do God's work, those who seek to lead you from the wilderness of wickedness on to the road of repentance! You have sinned against those appointed to save you from the wages of that very sinfulness, to save you from the fires of Hell and everlasting damnation!'

The accusing forefinger stabbed again. 'Once more I say onto you, what is this that thou hast done? Yesterday, today? You have squandered the chances given you! Not only squandered your immortal souls through your disobedient and licentious behaviour, through your depravity and your deceit, but spoiled them for your fellow sinners by dragging them down with you, down, down into that sulphurous pit! For the Lord God says: except ye repent, ye shall all be thrown into that everlasting pit! Except ye throw off your sins like the dirty rags they are, except ye don the shining white raiment of humility and obedience, ye shall perish! You must throw yourselves on God's mercy; for only He who is Our Maker, only He who is Lord of All, only He can redeem you and make you fit for salvation!'

The Reverend dropped his arms into prayer position. 'Yet God in his Mercy is great; as he saved the poor thief who repented, as he has saved miserable sinners the world over, so may he yet save wretched outcasts like you. But ... but! Only if you repent, only if you obey His Will, only if you do not yield to temptation! The good Lord has warned you, time and again He has warned you against the sins that mortal flesh is heir to! Time and again He has warned that there shall come a Day of Judgement when the wicked shall be cast into the Fiery Furnace, when there shall be weeping and wailing and gnashing of teeth! Pay heed, oh, pay heed! For if you do not, if you do not repent and mend your wicked ways, then, oh, then you must abide His Wrath. And I tell you, that Wrath will be most terrible.'

The yard was a silent sea of mobcaps, Marsden perched above them like a messianic crow.

'For His is the power and the glory! Vengeance is mine, saith the Lord; I will repay. So pray, pray for forgiveness! You know, each and every one of you must know how unworthy you are, how sinful: repent ye therefore! For should you go and sin again, should you persist in disobeying the Word of the Lord, know that you will not escape His Wrath, His most righteous Anger. And from that Last Judgement, hear me, from that Last Judgement ... there will be no ticket of leave!' Marsden sucked in his breath, steepled his hands and bent his head. 'Let us pray.'

Ann looked across at the row of women whose names had been read out. The big Irishwoman was last in line; she was looking up at something. What? There, strutting the length of the wall: one of those blue and green parrots ...

For the duration of the prayer, long after the bird had flown away, long after the cart had been returned to its grumbling owner and the other women had been dismissed, the bald-headed Irishwoman stood staring upwards.

CHAPTER TEN

Tattoos

Backs to the wall, the girls watched their new matron march briskly towards the cart. Em closed her eyes; with a low moan, she spun towards the wall and started punching it.

'What the hell d'you think you're doing?' Sarah grabbed her arms. 'Stop it! Stop it!'

Em tugged herself free, glared at Sarah and slumped against the wall. She shoved her hands under her armpits and rocked side to side, a lone tear trickling down her cheek. Sarah stood close; from the yard, the Reverend's voice boomed. Em held out her hands, grimacing as she tried to flex them.

'You want to run those under cold water.'

'Don't see too many pumps handy.' Em sniffed; little beads of blood were forming on her skin.

Sarah shook her head. 'What in hell was the point of that?'

'No point, no bleeding point.' Em shook her fingers. 'No bleeding point to anything. So much for getting in with the new matron!' She spat on her knuckles and sucked them. 'To hell with it: back where I started, ain't I? What's the point? What's the point even trying?'

'Yes, but what's the point of not? I mean, what else are you going to do? You've got to do something! And it's not like we were nicking stuff or on the grog: just out of line, that's all. She might be all right, that Matron

Gordon. You know, she looked me in the eyes when she talked to me.' Sarah tapped her forehead. 'And she could easy have handed us straight over to the troopers, there's enough of them about. But she said to wait here. So we'd better wait. Work out what we're going to say.'

Em leaned back against the wall and. sighed. 'All right. Just tell her it was a call of nature. Or tell her we were scared we'd piss in the middle of the Reverend's sermon. I mean, you can't piss away your sins, can you?'

Reluctantly, Sarah grinned. They looked across at the Reverend, who was taking a cautious step backwards ... the cart was not entirely stable. His arms went out and up ... and steadied.

'Thought he was gone for a minute there.'

Em shoved her hands under her armpits again. 'No such luck. But call of nature's as good as anything. What's it matter? She won't believe us anyhow. You got any better ideas?'

'We could just tell the truth.'

'What, that I was going to show you me tatt? That'd go down well. Then they'd want to see it.'

'Well: so what?'

'Just be another black mark ... black mark, ha ha!'

'Lots of people have tattoos. My Uncle Bob had a mermaid. Got it done when he worked on the docks. Must have taken ages, went right from his wrist to his elbow. Scaly tail, long hair, big round titties, nipples like bullseyes.'

'Must have hurt, getting it done.'

Sarah shrugged. 'S'pose. Prob'ly did it when he'd had a few. What he used to do for the customers when they asked, see, he used to hold his arm up and hump the muscle of his arm so it looked like she was humping too. It did, I swear. Disgusting, it was; but the punters loved it.'

'My one's only little, and that was sore enough.' Em shifted closer to Sarah, angled her left shoulder forward and pulled down her jacket. 'Have a look now. Pull down my jacket; you should be able to see the head.'

Sarah pulled and peered. 'A cat's head? Yes ... yes, I can see it. Hey ... whoever did this was really good!'

'I know; watched him do Charlie's. Every pin prick, just exactly right. Cat's whiskers, that was Smithy's name for us, that's why we got them done. His missus even made us black masks, last Christmas that was. You know, with holes cut out for eyes.' Em sighed. 'Only last Christmas.'

'I like the way it's jumping.'

'That's right: black moggy, jumping through the air like we did. Real artist, that gypsy. Tattoos all over himself.'

'Better than a ring. Can't lose a tattoo, can you?' Sarah stood off the wall and stretchedher arms above her head. 'Fair goes on, doesn't he? At least we don't have to stand out there in the sun.'

'Old Rear End? Yep.'

'Rear End?'

'Molly's name for him.'

Sarah grinned. 'Smart, isn't she? The way she can think of names and that. You'd wonder how somebody like her ever ended up here.'

'I know. I've asked her, but she never says much. Just that it were her bad temper that got her here and let that be a lesson to me. I said I'd never seen her lose her temper, so how did she know what it was like? And she lifted that eyebrow like she does and started talking about this red veil that kind of drops down on you, and makes everything throb and bleed into everything else and all you want is to make sure that whoever you're looking at is bleeding too ... well. I just looked at her in the eye and nodded. She'd got it exactly right, and how did she know? She just laughed.'

'Whoever you're looking at?'

'Whoever's making you mad. For me, Lizzie Adams. For Molly, I reckon it was a man. Sometimes she says stuff in her sleep, stuff about branding, and for the term of his damnable life ... *his,* see? I told you she's learning me my letters, didn't I?'

Sarah nodded. 'Really good of her. You never went to school?'

'Nope. Ma never bothered and I never really had a Da. There was a bunch of us lived in Stitch Street and we just ran about. Never any call to read. Not till they nicked me. I mind standing there waiting to go into the dock, and this clerk holding up this big book and pointing to a big black sign like a whip. He said it was a 7, and it meant 7 years. What I'd get. Charlie could read a bit, his Ma showed him. He always said he'd show me one day, but we never got round to it. No Mrs McKee where we lived.'

'Mrs McKee was only when I was little. She lived up the road, used to mind us when Ma and Da had to go away somewhere. But there was a kind of a school. Old Mr Beggs ran it; he used to be a minister, only he lost his religion. I always thought that was funny, like he just accidentally dropped it or something. Billy Beggs, paper legs ... we called him that because he was old and doddery. He taught my Da as well. I asked Da if he thought Mr Beggs was still looking for his religion, but he said no. So then I asked if we should help him look, but Da said the best way to do that was to learn my letters. Which didn't make much sense, but I did anyway.'

'You got on with your Da and Ma, didn't you?'

'I did. We all did. We were happy at home. Didn't have much, but enough to go round. That's why Uncle Bob's was such a shock. Couldn't wait to get back home again ... Harry was going to go with me, cause he was sick of running back and forward for Buggerlugs Bob. That's what he called my uncle.' She threw up her hands. 'And look at me now! All gone. All on account of a fancy shawl. Ain't it funny, the little things that change everything? If that man hadn't turned round and seen me ... or going to London, there's another one.'

'That's not a little thing. Besides, if you hadn't gone, you wouldn't have met Harry.'

'True. I thought of that on the way out, thought about it over and over. One minute I'd think I couldn't bear to have missed my time with Harry, I mean, with my face and all. But the next, I'd think of Da and all we'd planned. And how if I hadn't gone, I'd never have known what I was missing.' Sarah shrugged. 'And now? Dunno. Like I said, don't know nothing anymore. Don't care.'

'Who's a misery guts now? We're here, and that's it.'

'It's all very well for you, at least that Charlie of yours is here somewhere. You just got to keep trying.'

'That's like something Molly would say.'

'What would she say if she saw your hands? Is she teaching you to write as well?' Em held out her hands. The knuckles were red and angry looking. She shrugged. 'They'll mend.'

'They'll be worse before they're better. You really do want to soak them in cold water. Take some of the swelling out. Run to the horse trough, go on. Marsden's still going strong and she won't come back till he's done. It'll only take you two minutes.'

'Right. I'm off.'

'Quick! Don't want to be on my own when she comes back!'

'Two ticks, that's all!'

Em ran. Sarah slumped against the wall. She closed her eyes; the world seemed to pitch and roll, like being back at sea. She stiffened; what was that ... down her inner thigh ... yes! Yes, it must be, finally, it must be! Thank God, oh, thank God for that!

She raced after Em.

* * *

'... and deliver us from Evil ...'

Ann looked up at the man in the cart. *Bit of a late delivery for this congregation, Reverend ...*

'Let us pray.' Marsden bowed his head.

Ann sidled forward and tugged at Lockyer's sleeve. He looked down and smiled. 'Mrs Gordon ... Matron!' he whispered. 'You shouldn't sneak up on a man like that!'

'I came to see how things were going,' she hissed back.

'Well, well: going well. No need to worry, everything's under control. Soon as the Reverend's done, the women will report to their workrooms or yards. Except for those women lined up by the wall, they're from the Reverend's list. Ringleaders, remember? There have to be consequences, and seen to be. The wages of sin.'

'As I remember my Bible, the wages of sin are death. This is hardly a matter of life and death!'

Lockyer looked taken aback. 'Indeed, indeed! The Reverend can get rather carried away at times ... it never ceases to amaze me how much of the Bible he has committed to memory. Chapter and verse, he can quote you: a walking Authorised Version, that's what he is. Of course, you won't have been to one of his sermons yet. This is nothing, this is just off the cuff ... he does take his position very seriously.'

'So it would seem. But this is not what we agreed, Major. One or two ringleaders was what we agreed.'

'Moral gravitas, that's the phrase I believe. Not too much moral gravitas in New South Wales.'

'Rather too much here in the Factory, Major. Surely you are not trying to tell me every one of those ten women is a ringleader?'

Lockyer glanced at the line of women; they stood braced, hands behind their backs, staring at the ground. 'No, I suppose not. But, as the Reverend says, better safe than sorry. We can probably let a few go. Have to, in fact; not enough cells. I've detailed some men to keep them lined up there till the rest are back to work. Bit of suspense won't do them any harm. We can sort them out once we've had another roll call and made sure the majority are where they should be. Getting the Factory back to normal, and seen to be so, that's the first priority, as I think you said yourself.'

'That's right, I did. Back to normal, and the sooner the better. To that end, Major, our aim should surely be to make little of this unfortunate disturbance rather than a lot, which is precisely what drawing attention to so many will do. What concerns me most is that the bigger an exhibition we make of a few refractory women, the more importance, notoriety even, we are giving to their behaviour. Get them back to work, all of them. No time to think, no time to gossip, just straight back to work. Tire them out.'

Frowning, Lockyer stroked his chin. 'Yes. I see what you mean.' He looked across at the Reverend in his cart, his head still lowered and his hands still steepled in prayer, then at the rows of women. They stood with their heads bent, but there was constant shifting from foot to foot, nudging and twitching and sideways glances. How many was it again? He checked his men, strategically placed around the yard. He nodded.

'Yes. The first thing is restoring order, and putting them back to work is the best way to do so. I take your point, Matron. To subject too many to severe punishment may create as many problems as it solves. We will have to increase patrols as it is. I shall raise it at the meeting. For the moment, let's just get the main body back to work. First things first. Then we shall decide what to do about the list. I have already reminded Reverend Marsden that we are to meet in your office presently. That still suits you?'

'Certainly. As arranged.'

'Good. A firm line, that's the ticket. I will see to the rollcalls in each work shop and be with you directly.'

'Very good. I will be waiting.'

Lockyer bowed, and strode over to where Marsden was steadying himself on a trooper's shoulder as he descended from the cart. Watching him turn to the Major, Ann was struck by how much shorter the clergyman was than his voice suggested. He nodded to Lockyer, pulled out his list and jabbed at it again. *I need to get hold of those lists.* The two men stood with their heads together, talking and jabbing. Those two girls: Ann spun around.

Dammit, where are they? She hurried across the yard. At the wall by the archway she paused, looking left and right. No sign of them. Tight lipped, she made for the stairs. 'Matron Gordon! Matron Gordon!'

The girl with the birthmark: Sarah ... Scott. Yes, that was it. Scott. By name and by nation. Ann stopped and drew herself up severely. 'Sarah Scott. Where have you been? And where is Emily Kelly?' Sarah ducked her head, twisting her hands together. 'Well ... well, the truth is, Ma'am, it's that time of month. It just come on me, and I had to make a run for it, if you know what I mean. Fix myself up.' She looked up and bobbed a curtsey. 'But I have, I've done it. It's all right, Ma'am. It's all right!'

Ann eyed the flushed face sceptically. For some reason, the birthmark seemed darker. *She's looking very pleased for somebody who has no right to be ... or maybe she has. Yes, that smile is relief. I'm sure it is. You can't fake relief. And I suppose that's one less thing to worry about, for both of us ...*

'Very well. I will take your word for it. For now. But where is Emily

Kelly?'

'Emily? Emily ... well, that was a call of nature, too, Ma'am. Before me. Not like me, though. I mean, hers was just your ordinary call. Didn't want to cause embarrassment, see. On account of Reverend Marsden being in the middle of his sermon, Ma'am. She said to tell you a call of nature.'

'Did she indeed?' *Nonsense, and the girl knows it.* 'Where is she then? No, never mind. I have more urgent matters to deal with right now than two silly girls. But I will not forget. You are new, Sarah Scott, as you said. You should be trying to make a good impression. Or at least not making a bad one.'

Sarah curtsied. 'Yes, Ma'am.'

'You may go. For now. But you are both to report to me: tomorrow morning first thing. The first thing you should know is that you do what you are told. When I say wait, I mean wait. You at least have some excuse. For now, you will go straight to your workroom. Make sure you tell Emily Kelly. She has a lot to answer for. Consider yourself dismissed.'

Sarah stared at the Matron's retreating back for a moment; then she hugged herself and skipped toward the carding room.

CHAPTER ELEVEN

Wages of Sin

Ann sat at her desk with her head in her hands. Wearily, she glanced at her clock: ten minutes, she still had ten minutes.

Pity of that girl. Whatever she did, it's hard enough being shipped out here without a blemish like that. Not like that other little baggage: Sarah Scott wants to watch the company she keeps. Still: nothing more you can do about that now. Meeting with Marsden and Lockyer: start like you mean to go on.

She surveyed the room. Usher them straight through to the armchairs by the fireplace as Elizabeth Raine evidently had? No. This was work. Theirs as well as hers. Keep it that way. Those two straight backed chairs by the window, they would do.

She lifted them one by one and set them in front of her desk. She shifted the piles of ledgers and files to the right and left sides of her desk so that she had a clear view through the middle. She set her day book in front of her, open at today's date. Inkwell, pen, blotting paper, pencils, all there. Her carriage clock gave her five more minutes. She studied the two straight backed chairs, then went back down to the end of the room, picked up a cushion, and brought it back for her own chair. That would add a bit of height. She perched and looked across the desk. Yes: better.

She was at the window looking out over the now empty yard when she heard their footsteps on the stairs. Hurrying back to her desk, she stood waiting, hands clasped at her waist. A perfunctory knock, and the door swung open. Marsden was puffing a little; the stairs were steep. He made straight for the fireplace. Behind him, Lockyer bowed and stood behind the right hand chair. The Reverend paused, realizing. Ann beckoned.

'Reverend Marsden, Major Lockyer: welcome, gentlemen, welcome. Do sit down. I'm sure you will be glad of a seat; you have been on the go all morning.'

'Indeed, Mrs Gordon, indeed!' Marsden lowered himself on to the second chair with a grunt. 'Straight down to business, I see. That's the way, that's the way. No nonsense, eh, Major?'

Already seated, Lockyer simply nodded. Ann perched on her cushion. 'I take it all the women have been put back to work?'

'They have. Praise be. Disgraceful business. And on your first day as Matron! Most unfortunate. Yes, the miscreants are back where they belong. A few still unaccounted for, but not for long, don't you worry, not for long!'

'I am glad to hear it. But this is disturbing; how many are still unaccounted for?'

'How many, Lockyer?'

'Two or three. Nothing to worry about; they'll come in when they get hungry.'

'Your confidence is reassuring, Major.'

Lockyer smiled. 'In my experience there is no arguing with an empty stomach. Back inside and back to work. As you said yourself Matron, back to normal.'

Marsden clapped his hands. 'Back to work, indeed: best thing for them. The Devil finds mischief for idle hands, we all know that. The Major tells me that you came down to the yard for my little impromptu sermon, Matron; I am flattered. I must apologise for not greeting you. I would have done, of course, had I known. But I was in full flight, as it were.'

In a cart, as it were ...

'Please don't apologise, Reverend. You were doing your job. I had no intention of interrupting you, I merely wanted to see for myself what was going on.'

'A distressing spectacle, I'm afraid. I trust I will be able to treat you to a rather more elevated discourse next Sunday!'

Ann inclined her head. 'Major Lockyer tells me your knowledge of scripture is formidable.'

'The word of the Lord is formidable, Matron: I am merely His humble mouthpiece.'

Humble? Not a word that springs to mind ...

'You underestimate yourself, Reverend, I'm sure! But to the task in hand: these women. Getting this place up and running again. Major?'

Lockyer nodded. 'Workshops are back in production. Gate repair complete. Rolls checked, monitresses to report back on any signs of restlessness. Extra men posted.'

'Excellent.' Ann smiled and ticked off those items in her book. 'Now. That list of names you were checking in the yard, can you give me a copy please? I presume it includes the names of those you consider the worst troublemakers?'

Marsden wagged his forefinger. 'No considering about it, Matron, let me assure you. It's knowing. We have some very hard cases here, Ma'am, I must warn you. Lost causes, long lost causes. Worse than the men in many ways. More devious. This latest outrage must have been planned well in advance. And when there is trouble, we know where to look, do we not, Major?'

'Well, we certainly have a fair idea. You have the list, Marsden, have you not? Why don't we just go through it? I can have another copy made for you, Matron.'

Ann twiddled her pen. 'Thank you Major, I would appreciate that. In the meantime, I shall jot them down as we go. It will help me learn names. If I am to keep order, gentlemen, I must know the source of the disorder. I too must know where to look. These names will be a good place to start. Where are they now, by the way?'

'Still waiting under guard.' Lockyer coughed. 'Matron has suggested, Reverend, that we have been somewhat over enthusiastic in our cull. Ten ... it was ten in the end, I think? She has a point, you know, ten is a lot.

Hard to see how ten could have got together for any length of time without somebody noticing. Quite apart from the fact that we do not have ten cells, detaining so many suggests we are giving this disturbance an importance it does not merit. We do not want to give what is mainly folly and agitation the status of rebellion.

Marsden switched his gaze sharply to Lockyer. 'Major, I am astonished. Astonished! Folly and agitation? These women have wantonly destroyed property. They have disturbed the peace; they have disrupted an entire township with their riotous behaviour! The excesses of the French Revolution sprang from just such agitation! I presumed we were of one mind, Major, on the need to stamp down hard, to crush the smallest seeds of rebellion. Nip, as it were, insurrection in the bud.'

Lockyer raised a protesting hand. 'No, no, you mistake me, Reverend! Of course such behaviour cannot be tolerated, obviously not. As Matron Gordon will tell you, I have constantly emphasised the need for her to take a firm line. But we must also consider how our response will be viewed. The more women we incarcerate, the more examples we make, the more their peers are likely to think we feel threatened by them. They may even conclude that we take them and their "grievances" seriously. Do you see? Even if we do, we don't want them to think that we do.'

'Exactly!' Ann leant forward earnestly. 'They may, in fact, even find common cause and stir up more disturbances. We should bear in mind that each of those ten will have friends among the other women, sympathisers so to speak. Discontent may spread, rather than being contained.'

Marsden's eyebrows climbed; he looked at Ann as if her hair had come undone. 'But we must not be seen to be weak, Mrs Gordon. You, above all, must not be seen to be weak. Particularly now, if I may say so, before you have had a chance to set the stamp of your authority on them. These wretched women, if they think for one minute they can get away with such behaviour, then we shall have more of it. And the next time it may not be so easy to restore order.'

'I am well aware of that, Reverend. I fully intend, as I have said to Major Lockyer, to be firm. But I also intend to be fair. That is my plan:

to be absolutely firm, but absolutely fair.' She paused, looking from one man to the other. Lockyer nodded. 'Now. We make a point of separating the women into classes in order to keep the more hardened from those we can salvage, do we not? In the case of these ten, we seem to be making no distinction between them at all. It seems highly unlikely that all ten can be ringleaders. Are we not uniting rather than dividing them?' Ann glanced at Lockyer, now sitting back in his chair with his arms folded across his chest. He nodded again.

'Matron Gordon makes a good deal of sense, Reverend. The very timing of this disturbance, as you noted, casts it in a different light. It is an interregnum, as it were, a changing of the guard; and we know that these women do not cope well with change. Matron Gordon here should be given a chance to make a fresh start, to set up a new regime rather than simply carrying on the old. And we do not have ten cells. We cannot isolate them all. When I talked about lending importance to the riot, I meant in their eyes rather than ours.'

Marsden frowned. He pulled out a large white handkerchief and blew his nose. For a moment there was silence. Then he nodded at Lockyer. 'I see. Yes, I can see the point you are making, Major. The cells are a problem. To put such women in together would quite defeat our purpose. They are hardly likely to reflect on the error of their ways if their partners in crime are in there with them, are they? Very well then; let us cull.'

Yes! Yes!

The Reverend steepled his hands under his chin and closed his eyes as if in prayer. Lockyer waited for a moment, then coughed. 'Very well. Have you got the list there, Reverend? Would you like me to read it out?'

Marsden blinked and reached into his waistcoat. He passed Lockyer some rather creased pages. 'There you are, then. Let us begin.'

In her day book, Ann printed two headings, 'Leaders' and 'Followers'.

'Go ahead, Reverend.'

Marsden jabbed a finger at the list. 'Bridget Murphy. Well! No doubt about her nationality, is there? No work in Ireland, so she was sent over to Yorkshire. Convicted of arson: burnt a barn. One of that shocking bad batch, you remember, Lockyer, the Nelson, was it? I think it was the Nelson ... Machine breakers, Luddites. Nothing but trouble. Sent some of the worst offenders on to Moreton Bay; this Bridget was one of them. Unfortunately, we had to take her back because she and some other woman fought every time they saw each other. Apparently they were involved in the same crime; revenge, payback, God only knows. But they could not be in the same space without going for each other, tooth and nail. Had to be torn apart.'

Lockyer shook his head. 'You'll find that, Matron. In practical terms, sometimes the best remedy is simply to separate them. Since she's been back here, this Bridget hasn't really been a problem ... up till now. Third Class, of course. But more brawn than brain, if you know what I mean.'

'Yes, it's inbred, I'm afraid. The Irish. What's that joke?'

Ann eyed Marsden dubiously. 'Joke, Reverend?'

Marsden held up his forefinger. 'What is the difference between an Englishman, a Scotsman and an Irishman?'

Anne tipped her head to one side. 'I don't know. What is the difference between an Englishman, a Scotsman and an Irishman?'

'The Major there knows it, don't you Major? An Englishman, you see, will die fighting for his country. A Scotsman will die fighting for the savings under his bed. An Irishman? An Irishman will die fighting!'

He slapped his thigh. 'Bit of a classic, that one.'

Ann smiled politely.

The Reverend went back to his list. 'Yes, that's Bridget Murphy for you. Hasn't died fighting yet, but it's not for want of trying. She was the one took the sledgehammer to the gate: have you seen the size of her? Like a battering ram! They'd never have got out without her. For the cells. Definitely.'

Ann wrote 'Bridget Murphy' under 'Leaders'. She frowned and added a question mark. The Reverend jabbed his page again. 'Agnes Rowley. We could probably let Agnes Rowley go. Harmless enough, it's the company she keeps. Can't read or write: scullery maid. Did a good job polishing the church candlesticks a couple of weeks ago. So she should, mind you; she's had plenty of practice. That's why she's here, stealing silver: spoons, knives and forks. In broad daylight, her mistress said. How the stupid woman thought they wouldn't be missed ... well, she didn't, did she? Think. Think. Like most of them. Wouldn't know how.'

Ann wrote 'Agnes Rowley' under 'Followers'.

'Charlotte Barnes. Now there's a piece of work. Saving your presence, Mrs Gordon, better known as Charlotte the Harlot. Last time she was out on assignment, she was found flat on her back in a house of ill repute in Fleet Street.'

'What did she do yesterday?'

'Yesterday? Ducked off on the way back. Had to send a couple of troopers after her. Had to be dragged out of ... shall we say, licensed premises?'

'But hardly a leader of the disturbance? Major?' Lockyer shook his head.

'No. Hopeless case, but no leader. More trouble to herself than anybody else.'

Ann listed another follower. The Reverend contemplated the list and heaved a windy sigh. In short order, Sarah Jones, Matilda Grey and Lucy Saunders joined the followers. Shiftless, shameless, slovenly: typical of the type of woman they had to deal with. But not leaders.

'Joan Campbell,' read Marsden. 'Now there's one to keep an eye on. Bit more up top than most: knows how to add and subtract, can read a bit too. But you wouldn't turn your back on her, not for a second. In her case, though, it might be worth waiting. We might get rid of her yet. Not unattractive, you see. She has been out on assignment and seems to have given satisfaction. Only returned because of a death in the family. Here's the thing: her employer was one of the local publicans, actually keeps one of the better houses. The other day, he stopped me in the street to make enquiries about her. Seems it was the wife that died, and whatever relatives he's had in helping have gone home, so he's left with a business to run and two small boys to look after. The man is actually prepared to marry her, so I told him to come along next Market day.'

'Market day?'

'It's a service we offer here at the Factory, Mrs Gordon. Given the shortage of females in the colony. You've been told about it yet? There should be a log book there ... It's for men needing a cook, cleaner, housekeeper. We set a date for interested men to come along for a look and line the better women up so they can take their pick. If a man sees one he fancies, he comes and applies to us. They have to marry her, of course; no immorality, Mrs Gordon, not on my watch. We give the one he's picked the nod, and he asks her himself. She can say yay or nay, I might add, we do not force the women to agree. It is all quite above board: the women can say no, and the men have to marry them. We've had quite a few taken off our hands that way, haven't we, Major?'

Lockyer smiled and shrugged. 'As the good book says, Matron, man wasn't made to live alone. Even out here. Some of the marriages actually work out very well; the women mostly see it as a fair trade, you know: gets them out of the Factory, puts a roof over their heads. The Reverend here marries them.'

'I see.' *Not really, but no doubt I will.*

'Maggie Crowe. Hard looking ticket if ever there was one. Resisting arrest, Major, at the gate, right in front of everybody. She's for the cells. And that Betty Chambers. Drunk and disorderly, as per usual. Where they got the grog I do not know, but they were an abomination, the two of them. Disgusting.' The Reverend shook his head and watched Ann write down the two names before going back to his list. 'Well, well: who have we here? Molly Malone. God help us. Molly Malone.'

Ann laughed.

Marsden sat up straight. 'Something amuses you, Mrs Gordon? Let me tell you, this woman is no laughing matter.'

'No, no, Reverend, I'm sure she isn't. It was just the name, you know. Molly Malone, can there really be a Molly Malone? Like the song? You must know the song.' Marsden looked blank. Lockyer smiled and leaned forward.

'Molly Malone is a character in a well-known Irish folk song, Reverend, that's all. That's what Matron Gordon found amusing. That's it, Matron, is it not?'

Ann nodded. 'Yes. I used to hear it often when we were living in Limerick. I was just struck by the absurdity of it, that's all. I'm sorry, Reverend, I thought you would know the song.'

'Some kind of street ballad, I suppose.' Marsden sniffed and leaned back in his chair.

'Correct. *In Dublin's fair city,* don't you know,' said Lockyer. 'How does it go, Matron? *In Dublin's fair city, where the girls are so pretty ... I first set my eyes on sweet Molly Malone ...* think of the Molly we know, Reverend. I'm sure you can see the absurdity of it!'

Marsden raised his eyebrows and cleared his throat. 'Certainly no girl, and certainly not pretty.'

'And of course, she's not from Dublin either. She's from the North of the country, from Belfast's fair city. Transported for life: I must stress, this actually is a dangerous woman, Matron. Violent, reckless. You may have noticed her already; it is difficult not to, really, particularly since her head's been shaved. Tall, far too tall for a woman: broad-shouldered, too. Bit of an Amazon.'

'Yes.' Ann nodded slowly. 'Yes, I know the one you mean.'

Mention our encounter? No, not now ...

'As you say, it is hard not to notice her; she stands head and shoulders above the other women. And a lot of your men as well. But violent, you say?'

Lockyer sighed. 'I'm afraid so. Life sentence: grievous bodily harm. And extremely lucky they didn't string her up.'

'Intent to kill,' Marsden jabbed his forefinger at Ann. 'I do not doubt for one minute that there was intent to kill. You only have to look at her. Regrettably, given the public unrest in Ireland at the time and a clever lawyer pleading mitigating circumstances ... her family had a good name, I believe. Sadly, there is always a black sheep; they were probably glad to get rid of her. Ireland, you know. Ready to die fighting! Never learn, either: she was returned from her last assignment for assault.'

Ann frowned. 'Fortunate, then, that she didn't start something in the yard. I was watching. She let your men lead her away without any resistance at all, which is more than I can say for some of them. Nor any sign of drink on her that I could see; again, unlike the Betty Chambers of this world.'

Marsden frowned, leaned forward and tapped his forefinger on the table.

'Be warned, Mrs Gordon. Thick as two short planks, most of them, but not this one. Molly Malone is far from stupid; this is what makes her dangerous. She is perfectly literate; some misguided person has given her an education. You must keep your eye on her at all times. Blood will out, Mrs Gordon. This is what we have to contend with. Blood will out. Song or no song, Molly Malone is a dangerous piece of work. Her temper is violent, her nature vengeful. This is not the first time she has been in the cells, nor the first time I have had to come down hard on her. I have wrestled with her in prayer, Mrs Gordon, wrestled with her in prayer. Sadly, I fear she is guilty of the greatest sin of all. Pride. Of course, that is quite ridiculous, what could such a depraved female possibly have to be proud of? But proud she is. Proud and devious. As I said, transportation was the best she could have hoped for. But is she grateful? Does she give thanks to her Maker for preserving her? No. Quite the reverse: she is blatantly inattentive in church. I have watched her, staring out the window, yawning and fidgeting. Sets the worst kind of example; sows the seeds of discontent and disobedience, Mrs Gordon.

'Why has her head been shaved, you might ask? Graffiti, that's why. Profane language: wanton destruction to property. It has been removed, of course, though with some difficulty. Somehow she got hold of some tar. It was particularly offensive as it was clearly aimed at Matron Raine, who, as you have no doubt gathered, is a most pious lady. It is a rare Sunday that she is not sitting in my front pew.

'But back to Molly Malone: six men it took to shave her. And yet only a few weeks later, there she is, at it again, leading the others on. Down by the river singing lewd songs, the foul words ringing out clear as a bell! I have no doubt that she is the prime mover of this latest outrage. The cells. Absolutely the cells for her.'

Ann wrote Molly's name below the other three. 'You say that she has been in the cells before. They do not seem to have done her much good.'

'Sadly, no. She may need a longer spell than the others. We persevere, Mrs Gordon, we do our best to make these wretched women see the error of their ways. We have sent her down to Third Class twice now. But they gather round her, unfortunately, they do gather. She talks, you see, and they listen: the likes of Bridget Murphy, for example. Now there is a truly unholy combination; the main reason, in fact, that we have not sent her permanently down to Thirds. It will be a comfort to know that for your first days at least you will not have Molly Malone to contend with. Out of sight, out of mind.'

And yet she let us go on our way ... 'I see. Well. The sooner I get her and Bridget up in front of me the better.'

'In front of you?' Lockyer and Marsden looked at each other.

Ann drew herself up. 'Yes. I intend to hold as many as I can to account, starting with those in the cells. I shall be able judge for myself; and they need to know who their new Matron is. Major, kindly arrange for your men to bring them to see me. One by one, starting with Molly Malone.' Lockyer nodded; Ann turned immediately to Marsden. 'So important to know what one is dealing with, don't you agree, Reverend? I am told inspections by the Matron are regular procedures for women newly admitted. It seems an obvious way of establishing my authority.'

Marsden leant forward, clearing his throat. 'Authority: I am gratified to hear you use that word, Mrs Gordon, gratified that you understand the need to establish your authority. Inspections: that is what you mean. Indeed, it may well be a time for closer inspections. Draw up a schedule and we will arrange to be there. A tribunal: we could make it a tribunal. Yes. Good idea.'

'No! No, you mistake me, Reverend. Much as I appreciate your generous offer, which of course I do, I have determined to see these women on my own. For the exact reason that you mention: to establish my authority as Matron. To establish beyond any doubt that it is I to whom they must answer.'

'Indeed?' Marsden sat back. 'You are very decided, Mrs Gordon. You probably do not yet quite realise the full depravity with which you will have to deal: time enough. Time enough. However, I must advise you not to be hasty. The timing of this outbreak, on the very day that you take up your position, Mrs Gordon, makes it all the more outrageous. It is incumbent upon us to back you to the hilt, our authority being, of course, in some part vested in yours. These women must know that any disobedience, any refractory behaviour and we will come down on them like the proverbial ton of bricks.'

Not so proverbial ... 'I am aware of the authority vested in me, Reverend Marsden. I very much appreciate your concern. However, I believe I am capable of dealing with any refractory behaviour on my own; I believe that is the reason I have been employed. I do not expect you to concern yourself with what is my responsibility. And in any case, I will have one of Major Lockyer's officers just on the other side of that door, will I not, Major?'

'Of course. Let us give our new Matron her head, Marsden. The women do need to know who they must answer to; we do not want any more days like this. They need to understand quite clearly that it is to the Matron that they must apply for whatever needs, whatever permits, assignments, or allocations they might seek. Let her go ahead. We are always there if need be.'

'If need be. We can only hope that there will be no need be.' Marsden shook his head. 'Well. So be it. We have restored order; let us maintain it. I shall pray, Mrs Gordon, I shall pray for you. God is on our side. We must never forget that God is on our side.'

Pray for me, indeed ... no. Don't say a word. Bite your tongue. Ann tapped her pen. She looked from one man to the other and smiled. 'Well, then. That leaves us with Bridget Murphy, Maggie Crowe, Betty Chambers and Molly Malone for the cells. An improvement, I think!'

Marsden held out his hand for the list. 'Certainly. We have done well. But we shall see what we shall see. Remember, Matron, you must not hesitate to approach us at any time. The minute you think things look like getting out of hand ... just call on us, Mrs Gordon. Now. Moving on. Matron Raine's rationing of provisions will continue until such time as we consider the women have learnt their lesson and acceptable behaviour has resumed. The Major's men have already informed them of this; Ma'am, so that is one less thing for you to worry about.'

'Really? I was not aware you had made that decision. That was next on my list.'

'Self-evident: self-evidently in everyone's best interests, Mrs Gordon; no need to waste further time on the matter. Punishing the ringleaders is all very well; but their followers must be made to feel the consequences of their actions also.'

Bite your tongue, bite your tongue. The man's used to ... what? His will being done on earth, I suppose. Ann set down her pen, aware of Marsden's eyes on her. 'Well. What's done is done. We have not exactly had much time to inform each other of our decisions, have we? Although in my view, it will be better that the time set for rationing be short. After all, we want the women in a fit state to fulfill their quotas of work. And speaking of time, how long might the four be confined in the cells? Overnight, I presume, and then?'

Marsden frowned. 'For time in solitary confinement to work, Mrs Gordon, we must allow precisely that ... time. Time to reflect upon their sins. Nothing between them and their Maker, nowhere to go, nowhere to hide. I have known a spell in solitary to break down the hardest cases, to bring grown men to their knees. I recommend two days for Crowe and Chambers, four for Murphy and the full week for Malone.' He raised his hand as Ann opened her mouth. 'Believe me, Mrs Gordon, I know these women. You will see what I mean when you have Molly Malone back in the yards. As we said, a hardened criminal. But we shall see what a week on bread and water will do. Agreed, Major?'

Lockyer shrugged. 'It's not her first time. One can only hope.'

Marsden slapped his thighs and stood. 'Mrs Gordon, we will not keep you any longer. I can see that you are being most diligent.' He waved a hand at the crowded desk and turned to Lockyer. 'We must congratulate ourselves, Major, on having made such an excellent choice for our new Matron!' He thrust his hand across the desk, gripping Ann's outstretched one so tightly that she winced. 'Good to have you on board, Matron,' said

Lockyer; his handshake was mercifully light.

'Thank you, Major,' she smiled. 'And you, Reverend. I hope that one day both of you gentlemen, together with your good lady wives might like to join Robert and myself for afternoon tea ... perhaps next week? I trust Mrs Marsden is quite recovered?'

'What? Oh, Elizabeth. Yes, yes, that's all sorted out. The woman will have to be returned, of course, but in view of present circumstances, I'll keep her a few more days. You have enough on your plate, Mrs Gordon.'

The woman? Who, his wife? No, don't be silly ...

The Reverend shook his head regretfully. 'It's an absolute nuisance, of course, most inconvenient. But one thing I will not tolerate in these women, is a vengeful nature. Like the Malone woman we have just been discussing. As Elizabeth pointed out, Sally never has liked me. It now seems likely that she knew Fitzgerald and those other Irish hooligans that I had to deal with so severely ... oh, some time ago now. They don't forget, these vengeful natures, they do not forget. The rabbits were just her underhand way of getting back at me.'

Ann stared at him blankly. Lockyer looked from one to the other, totally at a loss. The Reverend explained. 'We are talking about my rabbits, Major. My Angoras. Everyone knows how fond I am of them. There has been an incident. A most unfortunate incident.'

'Incident? Don't you mean accident, Reverend?'

'I wish I did, Mrs Gordon. But sadly, one cannot turn one's back for a second ... I had to go down to the stockyards unexpectedly, Major. Good thing I did, managed to get in first. Just arrived, a purebred Merino ram, particularly fine specimen. He will make all the difference to my flock. But that is by the way ... I was in the middle of attending to my rabbits when I got the message, so I left Elizabeth to put them back in their hutches and feed them. She had gone into the kitchen to get something or other when she heard squeals from the garden. She ran out to find a most bloody scene. Our maid Sally had put the male and the female in the wrong hutches. Deliberately and of malice aforethought. Of course the male had gone berserk and killed the entire litter. Shocking. And particularly distressing for Elizabeth, who as you know is not strong. When Mrs Gordon here called, she found her in a state of shock. You remember, Major, your message about the gate.'

'I'm very sorry to hear that.' Lockyer frowned. 'Most disappointing. I had your Sally down as one of the better ones.'

'Yes, yes. No telling, unfortunately. Poor Elizabeth. Just goes to show, you can't trust any of them. Goodness, is that the time? I must go. Places to be, people to see!' Marsden headed for the door, which Lockyer was already holding open. Ann stood staring long after he'd closed it behind them.

CHAPTER TWELVE

Confinement

'Stop! Stand over there.'

Wearily, the women lined up in front of the cell doors. Molly looked up at the sky: fittingly enough, it was overcast. Beside her, Maggie hissed at Betty to stand still; Bridget nudged her arm. It made no difference, Betty kept on shifting from foot to foot. For once, the two guards didn't notice; they were intent on the Sergeant's progress as he unlocked the cell doors. The scrape and chink of keys was the only sound.

He shoved the last door open.

A sudden gush and splash of water. The sergeant swung around.

'What the ...?'

Then he saw. They all saw: the spreading puddle between Betty's feet. The acrid stench of urine pinched their nostrils.

Silence.

First to move were the guards, spluttering and covering their noses. The sergeant bared his teeth. A grubby tear trickled down Betty's face. 'Sorry, Sir, sorry, jus' couldn' hold it in no more ...'

'Just as bloody well we're holding you in, then, innit?' snapped the Sergeant. He lunged towards her, then pulled himself up sharply and beckoned his men. 'You! You and you, over here! Get this stinking pisspot the hell out of my sight!'

The troopers exchanged grimaces and stepped forward. Faces averted, they half carried, half dragged Betty's limp body to the nearest cell, shoved it inside and slammed the door. Hurrying back to their post, they snapped to attention as the Sergeant locked the door. The first guard sniggered and elbowed the second. He nodded at the damp patch of dirt. 'Like a fucking mare in season, mate!' The snigger became a snort, a raucous hoot. Until he looked up and saw Bridget towering above him, fist drawn back.

'My nose! My nose, she's broken my fucking nose!'

***

The bolt clanged behind her. Molly stood perfectly still, hands pressed to her head. *Bridget, you idiot, you bloody idiot!*

The key scraped in the lock. She lowered her hands around her neck. A collar. A spiked metal collar. How could you bear it? Just the weight, never mind anything else ... you couldn't breathe, let alone speak, let alone sing ... and stuck in that cell by yourself! For God knows how long. Nobody to hold it up off the bone for a single minute ... Drive you demented, drive you up the screaming walls. Shaving was nothing to it, once that's done you just ignore it, walk about, talk, sleep even. God help her. *And not a damn thing I can do ...*

She looked up to the narrow strip of window, the tiny glimpse of blue sky. That parrot would still be flying about up there; or maybe she's found some comfy perch, and *tucked her head under her wing, poor thing ...* Molly spread out her own arms like wings and stood on tiptoe. Then she touched her hands together, palm to palm, as high above her head as she could reach. Six foot of her still wasn't tall enough. It was a window never meant to be reached.

Dropping her arms with a sigh, she looked around. Same as last time, and the time before that. There was the pallet bed, there was the bucket underneath. There were the walls, the door with the food hatch and the spyhole. She ran her hand over the bed: scratchy, harsh, just like before. Her jacket would be her pillow. It would be chilly enough tonight, not midsummer like last time. She twisted left, she twisted right; three steps left, three steps right. Not enough room to swing a cat, as they said. Whoever 'they' were; whatever they wanted to swing a cat for.

A sledgehammer: that was what they made you swing. Plenty of room to swing a sledgehammer in Thirds, to raise any amount of dust. When she'd walked out into that high walled yard the first time they sent her down, Bridget was already out in the middle, swinging her sledge. Head and shoulders above the others, she put Molly in mind of her Father's stories about Finn McCool, the giant hurling rocks across the sea to Scotland. Bridget's sledge split the stones, sent the dust spinning high and low. Molly took to her instantly, the sturdy, wide legged stance of her, the brawny arms arcing up and down, up and down: like she was ringing bells, like she was scything grass, like she was a pendulum marking time. Which, of course, was exactly what she was doing; what they were both doing. Though Bridget could mark time better than her; Bridget swung herself into a trance, hour after hour, her blisters long since turned to callouses, her aching back numbed. Molly shook her head, recalling the blind staggering exhaustion of those first days. Some choice: that or picking oakum. She preferred the sledge. It stopped you thinking; no splitting hairs when you were splitting stones.

And Bridget made her laugh. Not because she was witty or smart, not because she had anything clever to say, or even much to say at all. Bridget was not clever. 'Nothing much to say, Moll. Nothing much up here, know what I mean?' She would tap her head and try to cross her eyes, which she couldn't do because one eye had a cast in it. When you talked to her, one eye was looking at you and the other way off into the distance, as if everything you said went in one eye and out the other, flying off into the distance like one of those bright parrots, or the one that used to sit on the wall and watch them, the scruffy bird with the bandit face and the blue flash on its wings. *Hahaha hohoho!* That was how Bridget laughed. She liked to laugh, it was her way of marking time, laughing and looking to laugh. You wouldn't think there would be much to laugh at in the third class yard, but whatever there was, Bridget found it: a split seam in a pair of breeches, a split lip on some hungover guard's face, a bee on Matron's bonnet, a fart ... farts were the best. You could always laugh at a fart. She'd screw up her nose and try to cross her eyes again ... you had to laugh.

They'd told Bridget she was built like a horse, same as they'd told Molly. They should make up their minds, Bridget said: first they called her a stupid cow, now a horse. Did they not know the difference? Anyhow, some of her best friends were cows and horses ... or used to be, on the farm in Ireland and then in Yorkshire. She used to plait the plough horses' manes for the show ... Molly sighed. Plough horses' collars were leather, soft thick leather, padded and oiled till it shone. Not metal, never mind metal spiked so you couldn't lie down, so there was no way you could rest your head. And nothing she could do, nothing but watch them clamp it round her neck, nothing but lock eyes with her friend before they were shoved into separate cells.

Molly looked up at the window again. She supposed she could pray; should pray, her father would say. Lord have mercy on me a sinner. On Bridget a sinner: on the whole godforsaken lot of us sinners. But that was it. God forsaken. What was the point of praying when God had abandoned ship somewhere between the old world and the new?

She sat on the bed and closed her eyes, breathing slowly in and out. In, out. Out, in. Out of sight, into mind ... here we go, here we go, here we go: up the long slow incline to Umgall cemetery with her Father on her arm. At the entry stile, turn and look back down across the Six Mile Valley; how many times had they walked up there, just the two of them? Her cue: tell him what she could see. Who was out in the fields? Whose cart was trundling along the road? Which trees were in leaf, was the Six Mile running high or low, was it sparkling as it wound in and out the meadows and past the white washed farm houses, was the patchwork of small fields with their scatter of cattle bright in the sunlight? Had there been rain? Of course: there had always been rain. The grass gleamed, lushly, greenly, field after field sloping lazily away towards the soft blue hills.

'Good girl,' he'd say, 'good girl. That's the way, that's the way I remember it. *In the springtime of the year* ... I can make it springtime any time I like now, you know. Never thought of that, did they? Spring: any time I like.' And he'd tap his forehead. 'All in here, Molly. It's all in here.

They couldn't take that away.' She gave him her elbow and they went through the cemetery gate, up the path by the dark stand of yew trees, left and then right along the pathways between the graves. Some of them were tumbledown, briars grown feral over faded names and long-ago dates; some were polished and freshly buttonholed with flowers, dated yesterday or the day before. After he died, she still went up there. *In the springtime of the year*, every year, she stood in front of the grave nearest the wall, the tall headstone peering out over the valley all on its own. Frank Malone: 1730–1818: To Liberty Prove True.

She opened her eyes and looked round her cell. *All in here. They couldn't take that away.* She wasn't so sure about that anymore, what they could or couldn't take. Even stone walls crumbled and tumbled at last. How long, she wondered. How long before the way it once was finally gave up on walling out the way it was now and the weeds took over? How long before the colours finally blurred and ran into each other and all that was left was existing from grey day to grey day?

She jumped to her feet and shook her head fiercely. What sort of a hole are you digging yourself into, Molly Malone, what are you thinking? Look up, look up for goodness sake, while there's still light to see!

The strip of blue was dimming; from the bed, the far end of the cell was dungeon dark already. Was that deliberate? Could you not at least put it off for a bit? Drag the bed down the other end, get the last of the light? So when you sat on it you could look up and out instead of down and in? She bent over the bed, reached her hands under the pallet, and braced. Could she shift it? Heavy: but yes. Yes, but could she get it past the door? Angle it? Yes. She heaved, leant, braced. Paused, caught her breath. Was it worth it? How much difference would it really make? What would they say, would they call it wanton damage to property? Willful destruction? Willful, that was her problem: willfulness.

How long was she in for? You could sit on the floor at the other end and just use the blanket. Cold stone floor. No. No, keep going. *Finish what you started.*

If she'd known how hard it would be, she wouldn't have bothered. But she did it. And once she'd done it, she sat on the bed and said 'good for you, Molly Malone' out loud. Then: *To Liberty Prove True.* Twice.

Funny word, prove. When you proved bread, you kneaded it, but in between you let it rest, you allowed the yeast to rise. But when they proved you guilty, they never stopped kneading, they kneaded and kneaded till every last tiny iota of rise was kneaded out of you. Kneadless: you became needless. Even words, even sentences: their word against your word; their sentence against your ... full stop.

Remember, re-member: that was another funny word. Member, as in a cock, a pizzle, a spouter ... what else? Love truncheon ... maybe that was where they got 'banged up' from. Then there was your Member of Parliament. Your Honorable Member. And member-ship of course, crew members, cargo members: day after day at sea, each big ship with its cargo of little member-ships. All the women in the Factory, each with her own personal hold, her own ballast and rigging. All the lives and limbs shipped out of sight, out of mind. Out of memory. Not important enough to be forgotten: just un-remembered. Dis-membered.

Nonsense. That's what her father would say. *Your head's a marley, Moll.* Look up.

So: to remember, whatever way you looked at it, was to put back together again. *There was an old man called Michael Finnigan, he grew fat and then grew thin again; then he died and had to begin again, poor old ...* Moll Malone again.' Her laugh chimed up and out the slit of window, the musicality of it briefly softening the featureless gloom. *I can still laugh; my laugh still sounds the same.* Remember that. All these years, year after year, that was how she'd survived: re-membering. Even picking oakum, all you were doing was taking it apart to be put back together again. How many ropes could you unpick in a life time? If you knotted them together, how far could you throw them?

Surprising how much you could remember when you put your mind to it. When you'd nothing else to do, when you had to keep your mind occupied, when there was nothing to do but have to begin again, turn yourself into Moll Malone again ...

Pay attention, child, do you want to help me or not? Here, do these addresses. Neatly, mind, neatly!

Yes, father. Remember, re-member. Sitting myself down at the big table next to the printing press, flicking back my plaits, picking up a pen and pulling the list of names towards me. Copying them out, letter by letter, the tip of my tongue curling over my lip ...

Calligraphy: the hours he'd made her practise. *You'll never be any good if you don't keep at it.* The art of ornamental penmanship. She could still do it, she was sure she would still be able to do it. That was what gave her away when she did the graffiti, the fancy letters. 'No Pope Here.' Well, there wasn't, was there? Just stating the facts, Matron Raine.

Facts. A middle-aged jailbird on the other side of the world, doing time.

Re-membering time. Even though you couldn't re-do it, you could re-mind yourself.

Trying to teach a street urchin to read. In the dormitory at night, or snatching odd moments at breakfast or dinner, in the yard ... printing letters in the dirt with her fingers. How bloody minded was that? Minded, it did feel minded: or at least it felt like something instead of nothing: like she still had skin instead of callouses. These last few months, it had become something to look forward to. She'd nearly forgotten what that was like, having something to look forward to. Ginger Em: her little Ginger Em.

They hadn't put Em in the cells. That was the main thing. Molly winced, remembering the shivering wreck she'd rocked through the night that time after they let her out: like some old drunk with the shakes, and her not much more than a child. City born and bred, that was the trouble. Her entire life spent on the streets, never been on her own before; closest she got was breaking into houses and then she'd had that Charlie of hers with her. Cat's whiskers. Molly smiled. That Smithy, whoever he was, was right; the girl should have been in a circus. Handstands, somersaults, shinning up that tree in the yard and perching there like a monkey above the patrol, the men who never thought to look up. So quick she was, once she'd got the idea, quick as ... the flick of a wing. She could do the whole alphabet now, could spit on her finger and trace words on the breakfast table ... and read. More words every day: Charlie, parrot, bread. Liberty. To Liberty prove true. Em could print that now. It was like watching something surface or rise like bread. Don't forget to put the 'a' in; bread, not bred ...

That'll be Rosie. She'll have bred by now. What has she, four back in Nottingham? Knows what she's doing, she'll manage. She'll have to: Molly heaves a sigh. Much as she hates to admit it, Joan is right. Mary's nearly done. Been here for years, longer than any of us. Part of the furniture. Let her out and she drinks herself stupid till they take her back in again. Poor old soul: suppose she's hoping she'll just drop one day. Just drop and not have to worry about anything anymore. Like me.

She leant back against the wall. The slit of air was barely visible now. Sing something. Yes: that was something she could do. That might help. Bridget was in the next cell; she should be able to hear. Though the walls were thick as ... not bricks. Stones. Stones.

Sing what?

Something rousing, something rebellious: *Lilliburlero bullen a la ...* Nah. Not in the mood. No point being rebellious when you're locked up. Four not so pretty maids all in a row: Molly, Bridget, Maggie, Betty. What state were the other two in? Probably dead to the world. Something to be said for drink. That Marsden with his list: he's had it in for Maggie ever since she farted in church that time. Which made Bridget laugh; 'so long as you can laugh', that's it, according to Bridget. But no laughing now. Not in that collar.

Sing for Bridget. The walls can't be that thick ...

Oh ye'll take the high road, and I'll take the low road ...

***

The old woman hovered over the bed. The cloths she was holding flapped like broken wings. 'Push! Push!'

'What d'you think I'm bloody doing?' Rosie grunted.

The contraction eased. Rosie took a deep breath and relaxed her grip on the wooden sides of the birthing stool. How long now? She looked up at the clock on the shelf. Three hours ... nearly there, surely to God ... with a groan, she grabbed the stool again. Mary kept hovering, now and then jabbing a cloth at the glistening forehead. 'There now, dearie, there now; it's coming, won't be long now ...'

Throwing back her head, Rosie hissed: 'How long's long?' She squeezed her eyes tight ... *coming, yes, oh hell, hell's bells, yes* ... 'Now! Now, ready, now!'

Mary squatted, wobbled, and fell over backwards.

'Christ! The cloths, give me the damn cloths ...'

Sobbing, Mary shoved the cloths into the labouring woman's outstretched hand and pushed herself back up. Rosie snatched them, face scarlet, the veins of her throat corded. For one choked moment the whole world was an agonised blur ... then release. Sudden, blessed release. The baby was out: out and bawling.

Groping for the child, skin slick with sweat, fingers fumbling clumsily round the slippery small body, all she could think was *fishy, fishy, fucky little fishy ... swim if you can ...* before heaving herself up and lurching towards the bed with the mucky little thing squirming in her arms. Gingerly, she lowered herself. The baby kept squalling ... *shut up, shut up or I'll smash you ... no, no, don't, what's wrong with you*? Rosie clamped the tiny body hard to her breast, let the blind gums search, find and latch on. The letdown, the lovely, lovely letdown: she looked at her baby and sighed. She closed her eyes. If only she didn't have to open them again, if only she could just keep lying there, just keep feeding and being fed, just sleep the soreness away, not have to do anything ever again ...

Some hope of that. From under half closed lids, Rosie watched Mary hobbling about the room, filling the bucket, soaking the mop, squeezing out washcloths that dripped and dribbled redly into the sink. And all the time there was this drumming, this thudding rhythm, like some band marching past, some procession; except there wasn't. The drum was inside; the drum was her heart.

Mary leant over, dabbing at the baby with a freshly wrung cloth. 'See? See? They always come ...'

So they do, thought Rosie. So they do. One born every minute. 'Well done, well done, didn't you do well, didn't you just? The baby, now, we need to cut the cord ...' Mary pulled scissors from her apron pocket. Rosie jerked forward.

'Give those to me ... give, give! I know what I'm doing, give them here! Christ: never thought I'd be doing this again ... here, hold still ...'

Mary handed over the scissors and steadied the baby, breath held, intent on the snip, the tie. The baby started squalling again. Rosie handed over the scissors, lifted her child and returned her nipple to the searching gums. In the sudden stillness, Mary crossed herself. Rosie glanced up. 'Hail Mary, is it? Mary full of gin?'

'I am no such thing! Nobody ever saw the sign of liquor on me except down the town. Ticket of leave. What was I supposed to do?'

'You had your ticket of leave?'

Mary nodded. 'Twice.'

'So why on earth are you're still here?'

Mary tapped the side of her nose knowingly. 'Yes. Done my time, I have. Couple of times over. Last one a year ago. They took me back. Drunk and disorderly, you see. Had to. Can't seem to stop myself. Something about being outside that gate, turns me into a proper public nuisance. Matron Raine, she just goes, back again, Mary! Well, don't need to worry about a midwife then, do I? You'll do the job again, won't you? And I go yes, Matron, yes. I'll do the job. Always do the job.'

Rosie wrapped the cloths tighter around the baby and wedged the tiny being carefully between bolsters. She held a handout to Mary, who staggered but managed to hold on as Rosie pulled herself up. One step at a time, they made their way across to the sink. Mary went back and hovered over the baby while Rosie cleaned herself and pulled on another shift. When she came back and lowered herself, groaning, on to the bed, the old woman patted her arm. 'A girl. And a bonny one too.'

Rosie picked her baby up. 'A girl. God help her.'

Gently, the old woman touched her fingers to the baby's downy head. 'A bonny one, isn't she just? Give her here. It's all right, I know how to hold a baby.' Rosie hesitated, then shrugged and handed the baby over. What did it matter? Dropped now or dropped later? She hadn't the strength ... Mary bent her head, making kissing noises. She hobbled over to the sink.

'Hoi!' Rosie sprang upright, swinging her feet over the side of the bed. 'Come back! Give me my baby, you silly old biddy! What the hell do you think you're doing?'

Mary had emptied another saucepan of clean water into the sink, talking the whole time. 'Warm enough, yes, yes. Let's get rid of that nasty sticky stuff, eh? There now, atta girl: bonny little bonny. Here you go, here you go ... *Hush, little baby, don't you cry ...*'

Humming, she lowered the baby into the water.

Rosie steadied herself against the wall. To her amazement, the baby didn't cry, just stretched and turned her little face blindly from side to side. Rosie wrapped her arms around herself and sat hunched, aching, poised to be there in a second. But Mary was holding the little body firmly, surely; how many babies had she washed in that sink? Where were they now, all those babies? She smiled as Mary swaddled the child and handed her over. 'Couldn't have done better myself. Thank you.'

Mary beamed. 'There you are, then. Never been known to throw the baby out with the bath water, not me!'

Rosie lay full length on the bed, baby at her breast. 'Never would have thought I'd be doing this again. Thought it was all over, red rover.'

'How many have you had?'

'Four. In Nottingham. Two boys and two girls. Her brothers and sisters. That she'll never see. That I'll never see again.'

'What about your man? Who's looking after them?'

'He'll be long gone.'

'Gone where?'

'Dead.'

Mary clicked her tongue. 'Ah. Sorry, dear.'

'It's all right. We knew it was coming. We knew before I was nicked it was only a matter of weeks. The sooner the better, he said. The sooner the better, once you're gone, Rosie. He had the cancer, you see. So it would have been goodbye anyway.'

'But the children?'

'They're with my sister. He'd not been able to work for months, so it was all down to me. Rearing them, feeding them. Not his fault, mind. Shocking, the pain he was in; you wouldn't wish it on anybody. Only then I went and got nicked. Over a year now.'

Mary sat on the edge of the bed and sighed. Silence, except for occasional little baby noises. The old woman frowned. 'So where did this little one come from?'

'What does it matter? He's not going to be any use to her. Or me. He's a lag as well ... what are you doing?'

Mary had gone to a cupboard. She pulled out a blanket and spread it over mother and child before fetching a mug of water. Gratefully, Rosie drank before falling back again. She put the baby on the other breast and watched, smiling, till the nipple popped out of the small mouth and the baby's eyes closed.

Mary nodded approvingly. 'That's the way, that's the way. Turn and turnabout, don't want to get lob sided, do we? I should have some wool fat left ...' She hesitated, then patted Rosie's hand. 'You won't say nothing, will you? About my little trip? See, normally I have girls helping, but on account of the riot, on account of youse all being out there in the yard, I didn't know where anybody was. And I didn't want to go looking on account of I didn't want to leave you and they could have ducked off or been hiding somewhere ... anything. It could happen to anybody, couldn't it? I mean, losing your balance, easy done ... but you saw what a good job I did of the bathing and cleaning up, didn't you? I've been delivering babies for nigh on twenty years now; more than that if you count Liverpool. That's where I grew up, Liverpool; delivered my first there. My sister's little boy. He'd be a middle-aged man now. They started me in here pretty much soon as I come out ... no different, really. Except you don't have to go round to people's houses, and you don't have to worry about the cold. One little mite, I'll never forget, froze to death. Left out in his perambulator. Don't have to worry about that here. But no different, really. The babies still come.' She patted the small bundle on Rosie's chest. 'The babies still come. What are you going to call her?'

Rosie studied the old woman, frowning. 'Don't know. I thought maybe after one of my own; but that don't seem right somehow. Nothing wrong with Mary, I suppose.'

'No, no, not Mary. Far too many Marys. Bonnie. That's what I'd call her. Like she is.' Rosie looked down at the sleeping baby. 'All right. That'll do. Bonnie.' And closed her eyes.

CHAPTER THIRTEEN

At Home

Hands clamped around the large wooden box, Robert Gordon shouldered the bedroom door open, staggered in and dumped it at the end of the bed: how many damn boxes did the woman have? 'That's it. That will do. I'll shift the rest in the morning.'

Ann looked up from stuffing a pillow into its pillowcase. 'But there only are two more.'

'Don't care. I've been carting stuff up and down those bloody stairs for an hour. What's the big hurry?'

Ann punched the pillow and tossed it on to the bed. 'It would all have been done by now if you'd been back earlier, like you said. But oh no: always have to play the big fellow, don't you? Always have to be the life and soul of the party!' She turned to face him, hands on hips.

'Well, what's wrong with that, my dear?' Robert waved his arms expansively. 'Got to find out who's who, haven't we? Got to make ourselves known, meet the right people, haven't we? And what party? All I did was take Lockyer for a drink at the Barracks; least I could do. The man's taken the trouble to introduce me to that Storekeeper fellow, Tuckwell, and a few of the officers; people you'll need to work with as well, my dear, so wipe that frown off your face. Played a few hands of cards, just to be social. How was I to know you wanted every last thing unpacked tonight?'

'Seeing as how the boxes are blocking the hall so we can hardly get in or out, seeing as how we've got the children tripping over them now too, you might have worked it out. For goodness' sake, Rob: we need to get this house in order. There'll be no time tomorrow, I'll be at the Factory all day. You'll have to mind the children till we find somebody.'

'The children will be fine. Make time, take time! Why does everything always have to be done immediately if not sooner? What's the hurry? You've only just started, for God's sake. Nobody expects you to be on top of everything immediately.'

Ann picked up a second pillow. 'I do. I expect it. You just make up your mind, you start as you mean to go on: organised. That's all there is to it. First impressions, Rob: you're the one always telling me how important they are.'

Her husband cocked his head to one side and smiled. He sat on the bed, reached for her hand and pulled her down beside him. 'Relax! Being crabby and bad tempered before you've even started doesn't make a good impression.'

'I am not crabby and bad tempered!'

He raised his eyebrows; she had to smile.

'Look at that frown line.' He ran his finger down it. 'I'll swear it's got deeper.'

'Has not!'

'Let's see ...' He pulled her closer and brushed his lips over it. 'Definitely deeper. They come quickly enough, the wrinkles; no point encouraging them. Didn't you say you were in this for the long haul? So what's the big rush?'

'Oh give over, you! I did, and I am. All right, so I'm crabby. Is it any wonder? This has to work out, Robert, you know that as well as I do. I'm just so tired.' She clicked her fingers. 'I could drop off like that. I keep waking up in the wee small hours. And then I can't get back to sleep, so many damn lists in my head. And that man Marsden at the meeting today. That sticks in my craw, it truly does.'

'You mean about the rabbits?' Robert laughed. 'Never pick it, would you? Sheep, yes; but bunny rabbits?'

'It's not funny, Rob. And it's not the rabbits. It's not even just him, it's that damn two-faced wife of his. I was there, Rob, I saw the state she was in. She'd never have managed without that girl. And then she goes and tells him it the girl's fault! How unfair, how completely unjust is that?' Ann shook her head vehemently. 'And there I was, feeling sorry for the stupid woman, trying to make things easier for her! The man's obviously a bully, and she's scared of him, but that's no excuse for getting the girl dismissed, is it? I wish I'd shown him the scratches on that girl's arms. But who'd have thought? Who'd have thought?'

'Nobody.' Robert patted her knee. 'You're quite right. Completely unfair, of course it is. But beating yourself up about it isn't going to help. And there is a funny side, you know. Reverend Marsden and his bunnies. You've never seen an Angora rabbit, have you?' Ann shook her head; he chuckled and patted her knee again. 'Just you take a good look at Marsden next time he's around. It was the first thing came in to my head when you told me. Big flat face, red eyes, pokey little mouth; you've only got to add ears ...'

Reluctantly, Ann smiled. She leant against her husband. 'Yes, yes, that's all very well. But what about that poor girl? Sally: I don't know her other name.'

He put his arm around her. 'That's better. You take everything too much to heart, that's your trouble. I mean, it's pathetic, really. The ever so Reverend Marsden, laying down the law to all and sundry, and there's his own wife, running rings round him!' He chuckled again.

Ann's smile shrank. She shrugged off her husband's arm and stood up. Crossing to the window, she looked out. 'All very well for you men.' Robert got up and joined her, reaching his arms around her again. A few women were carrying bundles across the yard below; he craned forward. 'Sally, you said? There'd be a few Sallies.'

'I know. Don't worry, I'll make sure I get her other name when I see him next.'

'Look at it this way. She's well out of there, isn't she? Now you're Matron, you can find her a new position, a better position. Somewhere she doesn't have to wrestle with red eyed bunny rabbits.' His eyes were on the women below. 'Youngish, didn't you say? Plenty of people looking for a healthy young domestic. Ourselves included. Why don't you assign her to us? You're going to need a maid, aren't you? Well, there you are. Start with Sally.'

Ann glanced sideways; he was smiling slightly, his eyes on the young women below: about Sally's age. She pursed her lips: yes. She would find Sally another situation. But it wouldn't be in her house. Not with her husband. 'No, no, that would never do. What would I tell the Reverend, that I took her on because he unfairly dismissed her? Don't worry, I'll think of something.' The women disappeared round a corner. He came back and nuzzled her neck. 'What about dinner? I'm starving.'

'In the oven.' She smiled up at him. 'It'll be on the table by the time you get those last two boxes up here.'

* * *

In the Barracks, the older officers had settled into their armchairs, smoking and talking. Lockyer glanced up at the clock on the mantelpiece, leant forward and stubbed out his cigar. Time to go: he'd promised Mabel he wouldn't be late. The younger men were mostly gone already, out gallivanting God knows where. Some of the older men had been talking about that very thing, and he could see the problem. There were none of the established clubs, hunt balls, family visits to keep the young men occupied. So they drank. Gambled. Fraternised with jumped up jonnies like that architect fellow, Greenway.

Lockyer had mostly listened and nodded. He had met Greenway and found him good company, with a few useful suggestions for Lockyersleigh. He had half a mind to take the fellow out to have a look at the place. In his view, any young fellow worth his salt should be able to make a go of things, clubs or no clubs. Would they really have been so different at home? You're only young once, after all. No harm kicking up your heels once in a while.

The two playing cards down the other end of the table, for example, that was harmless enough, surely? They would be rostered on to the extra patrols, twenty minutes away yet. They were just filling in time, that was all. Lockyer glanced at the clock again and rose to take his leave.

He paused as he passed the card table. 'Hello, lads. Andrew, isn't it? One of our newer boys, aren't you? Settling in all right?'

'Very well, thank you Sir. I'm settling in very well. George here has been showing me the ropes.'

'That's the way. More than just a hand of cards, then?'

'Oh yes, sir, lots more! George has shown me heaps ...'

'That's not poker you're playing, is it?'

'It is, Sir,' George looked up with a smile and a shrug. 'We're on patrol duty, Sir. Just filling in time, that's all. Mr Gordon and the other officers had to go, but we've still got a few minutes before we're on duty. Good player, Mr Gordon. Hope to give him a better run for his money next time.'

'Money? I hope there was no money changing hands. I don't condone gambling.'

'Of course not, Sir. I only meant that I'd like to play better. It's a game of skill, you know.'

'Is that so? I thought it was a matter of luck; whether you got dealt a good hand or not.'

'Oh no, there's a lot more to it than luck, isn't there Andy? You've got to have a good head for numbers for a start.'

'Well, well, I'll take your word for it. It's a harmless enough amusement as long as there's not money involved. Who's winning?'

George flashed a grin and threw down his cards. 'Four of a kind, Andy! Can you beat that?' Andy looked at his hand, shook his head and tossed it in, looking up at Lockyer with a rueful shrug. 'Last one. He wins.' He pushed his chair back. 'Well done, man. Time to go.'

'Duty calls, eh? Good lads: you have a good evening now!'

'Goodnight, sir!'

They watched Lockyer walk out the door, chin thrust forward, hands clasped behind his back. George grinned at Andy. 'For chrissake, what's the point of poker if there's not money involved? Takes everything too damn seriously, does the Major. Never mind: win some, lose some.' He waggled his fingers. Andy pulled a wad of notes out of his shirt pocket and peeled off two. George pocketed them with a grin. 'Ta. That makes us even. Best of three, hey? Go again tomorrow night?'

'You're on. Right then: like the man said, duty calls.'

'Cock a doodle doo! Pity, I was on a bit of a roll, wasn't I? Just our luck to be rostered on first. Stupid bloody women. What on earth were they thinking? No, don't tell me: they weren't. What I'd like to know, is what good the Major thinks these extra patrols will do. Absolute bloody waste of time. Bet you what you like the stupid cows we're meant to be watching will all be tucked up in their quarters. It was only ever one or two that were ever likely to cause any grief, and they're in the cells. So it's a complete waste of time.'

'Only one or two, you think? Well, I hope you're right.' Andy shook his head. 'Seeing them outside the Factory, you know, marching arm in arm like that, it's a bit of a worry. There's a lot of them; I mean, if they ever did get any ideas ...'

'Ideas? They wouldn't know an idea if they fell over it in the street. And they've done plenty of falling over, believe me, in the street. Straight on to their backs. Puts me in mind of this poem my old schoolteacher used to read to the class. He fancied himself as a bit of an actor, you know, used to stand up and read to us aloud.' George clapped one hand to his forehead and waved the other theatrically. 'Water, water everywhere, and not a drop to drink ...' he grinned and nudged Andy ... 'or not a drop you'd want to drink! And yet they keep right on sending them, whole cargos of them. What for? Most of them you wouldn't touch with a barge pole, let alone your own!'

'That's not what you were saying the other night.'

'Yes it is. What I said was, pick your time and place, boy. You've got to pick your time and place.'

'So you really think Harry's is all right?'

'Oh yes. For definite. I'm working on it, don't you worry, I'm working on it. Come on, time we were out there.'

***

'Here she comes, here comes Kitty cat!'

'Can I catch her?

'Yes!' Lockyer swooped his small daughter up and looked over the mop of fair curls to the doorway where his wife stood smiling, his baby son in her arms.

'Hello, little Kitty cat! Mabel, my dear!' He set a protesting Kitty down and kissed his wife. 'You look exhausted; everything all right?'

'Yes, yes; been a long day, that's all. Never mind, you're home now.' Mabel held out their youngest son and Lockyer took him from her. 'Time for bed, eh, Freddy? Take him up now, shall I?'

In the big dining room, eight children of assorted ages sat around the table. They stood with their heads bowed while their father said grace. From the head of the long dinner table. Lockyer spoke to them one after the other, youngest to eldest. Mabel passed the plates, smiling at the eager faces; he was so good with them. A maid in a frilled mobcap put her head round the door. 'Will that be all, Sir? Ma'am?'

'Yes, thank you, Elsie. You may go.'

Lockyer glanced at his wife. 'Where's Janet?'

'Not well.' Mabel sighed. 'And I mean really; not a bit well, Edmund. This is the third time in the last month. Complains of a pain in her belly. We'll have to have her looked at. I've been run off my feet in the kitchen. Elsie has no idea.'

'Right. I'll see to it. Remind me later. Kitty, don't poke your nose. Billy, how are the chickens?'

In between hearing how the chickens had escaped and who could name most places in the globe of the world that sat on the sideboard, Lockyer's gaze flicked back to his wife. How pale she was, how worn looking. Everybody got tired, of course, especially with a household this size. Not like Mabel to admit it though. What ever happened, he suddenly thought, to the blue-eyed girl with flowers in her blond curls that he'd met in Ceylon? Nine children later, the blue eyes were faded, the grey threaded curls strained back into a bun. *Ma Belle*, who had followed him halfway across the world, no questions asked, had wilted. He expected he had too: slower, greyer, more creased. How would Dorothea have looked, he wondered; then, surprised at himself, wondered again.

He hadn't thought about her in years. It occurred to him that he had been married to Mabel considerably longer than Dorothea: 11 years to Dorothea's 7. One child from her: nine from Mabel. Delicate, Dorothea, always the nervous type. Neurasthenic, that was the doctor's word. Not like Mabel; good childbearing hips, his Mabel. Mabel was never sick, not unless you counted pregnancies.

He watched as she dabbed a napkin over Kitty's chin; he was a lucky man and he knew it. His people – and Dorothea's – had raised their eyebrows and talked among themselves when he'd married his second only months after losing his first. He'd gone ahead anyway, knowing that he was to be posted to Australia. And never a second's regret. Yes, he was a lucky man. However often work took him away, he still looked forward to coming home, to sitting down for a quiet chat after the children were in bed. Even on leave, showing her his latest painting and waiting for the purse of her lips, the nod and the comment. Even, sometimes, the suggestion; several that he'd had framed were the better for that suggestion.

He glanced around the room. Home was still a drafty old box with narrow stairs and a kitchen nowhere near the dining room. It was cold in winter and hot in summer. Mabel never complained. She was used to it, she said. Still: time and tide, time and tide. She was wilted and he was creased. The sooner the new house was finished the better.

Lockyersleigh: good name, if he said so himself. They'd have more room there, a lot more room. That was the thing about this country. So much room, so much open space, such wide horizons. So much still to see. Next year, definitely next year. Finish his term as magistrate, move out to where he could stand at his own front door and see for miles and miles and miles. He'd been thinking about it earlier, riding out after the Factory women. How odd and out of place they had looked, scattered about the banks of the river and further up under the trees, their drab skirts and jackets like blots on some ancient parchment. Outside: in the open, outside the factory, outside the walls of the town: how strange it must have been for them too. Wouldn't have known which way to look, would they? Especially not the ones straight off the ship, bundled into a coach or shipped straight up the river to Parramatta; it must have seemed to them that they had fallen right off the edge of the world. By road or by river, they could have had no idea what those pale huddled plants poking out of the water were, or those long legged, bald necked birds, running instead of flying. Pale trees with long strips of bark hanging down like panting tongues, strange pear-shaped creatures bouncing instead of running, saucer eyed faces peering down from the branches over your head ...

They could never have known anything like it. City born and city bred, most of them: creatures of closes and alleys and lanes, of narrow, confined spaces. The spaces in the Factory were pretty narrow and confined, it wouldn't have been so very different. But the country itself, east to west ... you could ride all day and never see another soul; narrow your eyes and squint into distance upon distance. Some of that distance was his now, claimed and named. Lockyersleigh. He could raise sheep, farm ... and paint. Paint his own landscape. That was his plan for retirement. He would go over his old water colours, make a proper record of his travels. Some he would retouch, some he would add to; his time would be his own. Yes.

Later, when the children were in bed, Mabel led him through to the front room and pointed at a brown paper package lying on the table. 'It came this morning. Go on; have a look!'

'Is it what I think it is?'

She nodded. 'Frederick Town. I'm sorry, I couldn't resist looking. I didn't think you'd mind. I think it's one of your best.'

He carried the framed water colour to the window and studied it.

'Yes, not bad. Not bad at all, is it? I've got the water right; you can see the depth. It'll be a major port, no doubt about that; the first in Western Australia. And British, too: see where I've planted the Union Jack?' He pointed to the swirl of flag on the cliff above the bay.

'Yes. Well done, dear!' Mabel patted his shoulder.

He smiled, reliving the time, the place; then his smile faded. 'Over here, see the inlet here? That's where I caught those two ruffians.'

'The sealers? Ugh, don't talk to me about that. Horrible, just horrible. Those poor women. I don't care if they were natives.'

'Indeed. You wouldn't treat your dog like that. I can well understand why a few sealers might get a spear in the back.'

Mabel shuddered. 'Ugh. Thank God you're done with all that.'

'Yes. Lockyersleigh awaits.'

'But perhaps one day ... you know, when we've got the children settled and there's just the two of us ... you might like to go back. To Western Australia, I mean. By sea, we could sail around the coast. I haven't been on board a ship since we left Ceylon. We could sail right into Frederick Town.'

'Now there's a thought.' He smiled at her. 'A very good thought. Yes. Not just yet, of course, but in a couple of years ... yes indeed. Once we're settled in Lockyersleigh.'

'Of course, dear, of course. Now ... where do you want to hang it? Here, above the mantelpiece? For guests to see?'

'No. No, I think its place is in my study.'

'But nobody will see it there.'

'I will. Come on, let's take it there now.'

Mabel followed him through to the small room at the back of the house. On one wall was a map of the world; on another a watercolour of an English port: Plymouth. Lockyer held the new painting up beside it.

'See? They're a pair. Then and now.'

***

Em opened her eyes; it was still too dark to make out more than mounds of sleeping bodies, not dark enough to fancy them gone, fancy herself back with Charlie in their own little attic. She turned onto her side. 'Scotty! You awake?

'Yes. What?'

'I can't stop thinking about Molly.'

'I know. And Bridget. Is it true they've put a collar on her? Like a horse?'

'Yes, it's true. Joan were on her way back from the Matron's office and seen them putting it on. It's horrible, a horrible thing. All metal with spikes sticking out so you can't lie down or anything.'

'That's wrong.' Sarah shook her head. 'Just wrong. She's not an animal. No human being deserves that. I don't care what they've done.'

'No. That's why tomorrow. At the gate.' Em punched her fists in the air, one after the other. Sarah shifted restlessly; Em propped herself up on one elbow.

'What's wrong? You're not going to chicken out?'

'No! No, I know we've got to do it. And the sooner the better: like Joan said; before they're ready, while they don't expect it. We might not get another chance. They've put extra patrols on. I just hope everybody turns up. It won't work if they don't.'

'Why wouldn't they? I mean, after yesterday ...'

'That's it. Yesterday. The women next to me in the carding room, I heard them going on about not making things worse for ourselves, and maybe not doing the ones in the cells any good either.'

'But we have to, we have to stick together, like Joan said. For Molly and Bridget.'

'I know, you don't have to tell me! We go for it, of course we do. It's just not everybody might turn up ... and it's not going to work if there aren't enough of us.'

'They'll turn up. They know we've got to stick together.'

'Yes. Well. I just hope you're right. The other thing they said was that Bridget might be let out, you know, in her collar. Like a warning. Scare people off.'

'Bastards! Joan said Bridget punched the guard because Betty pissed herself and he laughed. That's why they put the collar on. Must have really clocked him one. Wish I'd seen it! Joan thinks his nose is broke. That must have felt good!'

'For about ten seconds!'

'I know that! I'm not stupid, I've not forgot what Molly said. Don't lose your temper, Em, or that's not all you'll lose. But at least he got a taste of his own medicine. No harm you and me feeling good about that, is there?'

'God, no. None at all.' In the close breathing dark, they smiled. Em flopped back down and Sarah reached for her hand. For a while they lay quietly, fingers entwined, each in a world of her own. Then Em squeezed Sarah's hand. 'You know what it is, Scotty? What it is, is everybody's lost without Molly. Like, Bridget would never have hit him if she'd listened to Molly.'

'But Molly was there!'

'Not so she could talk to her or warn her, but. Not so she could stop her.'

'No, more's the pity. Funny, them being mates. I mean, Bridget: well, maybe it's just the eye, but sometimes I think she's not all there. And Molly's so smart.'

'Molly told me she got to know her when she done time in Thirds. Says they looked out for each other. Plus they're both Irish, I suppose. And both big.'

'Yes: I thought Molly was big, but Bridget's bigger. Wider.'

'And younger. And tougher: Molly told me. She done time at Moreton, only her and some other woman she got sent out with had this feud going. The real thing, blood feud. The guards were getting fed up having to break up fights all the time, so in the end they decided it was easier to split them and send Bridget back down here. Must have been women Bridget knew from Yorkshire. She milked cows on some big estate, did Bridget. Something about enclosures, Molly said; land being taken over. This woman set fire to a barn, that's why they were fighting. Sort of like Lizzie Adams and me, that's why Molly told me about it. To warn me off.'

'Well, she's right, isn't she? Just as well your Lizzie don't sleep in here.'

'She's not my Lizzie! No way ... wish they'd send her to Moreton Bay.'

'Sounds like Bridget's a lot better off here.'

'Yes. Though you still don't want to get on her wrong side. Molly says even her right side is tricky; you've got to watch every little thing you tell her to do, because she'll go straight off and do it. Like when she got stuck into the gate with that sledgehammer. Seen her do it; she were swinging the big hammer back and she looked straight at me. Or not straight: that cast of hers, it's so ... like, you don't know whether she means you or not. Whether she sees you or not. Do you think she could talk to two different people in two different places and see them both at the same time?'

Sarah yawned. 'Dunno. Don't care. We should go to sleep.'

'But whatever Molly says goes as far as Bridget's concerned. That's like me too: don't know where I'd be without Molly.' Em nudged Sarah. 'Funny, innit? We need Molly to work out how to get Molly out.'

'Not much funny about it.'

'No. No, there's not. Them cells!' Em shivered. 'Can't stop thinking about her, locked up in there. So big, you know, there'd be even less room. Seven days: one was bad enough. She's been that good to me, Molly. Never mind Bridget. Can't stop thinking ...'

'Wish you could stop talking. Go to sleep, for God's sake. Count sheep, or breaths or something. But in to yourself.' Sarah withdrew her hand and turned her back.

Em sighed and closed her eyes. She breathed in to a count of ten, out to a count of ten, like Molly had told her. No use. She stared into the dark. Sarah turned over and reached out her hand again. 'Em?'

'Thought you wanted to go to sleep.'

'I can't. I nearly was, nearly gone. But I'm all woken up now. Everything keeps buzzing round and round.'

'Like mosquitoes, innit? Only then they go quiet. That's when they bite you.'

'It's the relief, that's what it is. Just the relief.'

'What relief?'

'My bleeds.'

Silence: Em pushed herself back up on her elbow and hissed. 'You mean you thought you were pregnant?' She felt rather than saw the nod. 'But how could you be, when you were in Newgate all that time? Oh, Scotty: one of them sailors raped you, didn't he? Shit. That's it, innit?'

'No! No, nobody raped me.'

'But ... how then?'

'What's it matter?' Sarah folded her hands across her chest. Em flopped down on to her back. The two of them lay staring up at the dark. Em whispered first.

'No need to be shamed. I know what they're like.'

'Em, nobody raped me.'

'But ... how then?'

'How do you think?'

'You mean there's some other fella?'

Silence. Em felt Sarah shrug. 'On the ship. Second mate, he was. You know what it's like, down in the hold, all smelly and dark. Especially those last weeks, you've been there so long, it's that hot and smelly and smothery, you'd do anything for a breath of air ... well, I did. It wasn't just me either. You took any chance you could to get out of that hold, get up on deck, at least breathe fresh air for a bit. Some of the girls were at it from the minute we sailed out of Portsmouth. All the pretty ones, like you. Bet they were after you on your ship.'

In the dark, Em grimaced. 'Yep. You had to watch it. Never let yourself get caught on your own. Did he ...'

'I told you, it wasn't like that. I mean, he never forced me. He didn't have to. And I didn't have to either, and I didn't, not for ages. Not till we'd crossed the line. You mind crossing the line? So hot: everything all slippery with sweat ...'

'You mean you just let him? After Harry?'

'But that was it, Em, exactly it. After Harry. I'm never going to see Harry again, am I? Never ever. He'll be with somebody else by now, bound to be. Always did have the girls running after him. That's why I could hardly believe it, you know, me with my face. Because he liked me in spite of it. Just him touching it made it not even matter.'

'Only it does. He'll always remember you, Scotty. I mean, your mark: it's sort of like my tattoo ...'

Sarah squeezed Em's hand. 'Anyhow. I thought to myself, I thought, you've had that. Which is more than a lot of girls have. Nobody can take that away. You're out here and you've got a life to live. Not much of a life, maybe, but you don't have to make it harder than it already is. What difference is it going to make?' She shrugged. 'Didn't seem like that much to do, really, for a breath of air. Because it wasn't as if I didn't like him. He was a decent man. More than decent, really: he looked out for me. I was sad when we said goodbye. Know what he said? Have a good life, he said.' Sarah laughed. 'I must have looked at him funny, because he stuck his hand in his pocket and pulled out a penny. He set it on his thumb and went, Heads or Tails? I went, Heads. And it was, and he laughed and said, see? You're in luck.' She paused.

'He had this scar down one side of his face that puckered up half his eye; he'd been knifed in a fight as a young lad, running round the back streets of Glasgow. So he had a botched face too. He said my voice put him in mind of home, and I suppose it was the same for me. He was still broad Scots, even though he'd been a sailor all his life, pretty much. He'd sailed all over the world. He was quite old, that was the other thing. Sometimes we didn't even do it, we just lay and looked up at the stars and he told me about all different places he'd been. He told me about black men and yellow men, and elephants in fancy dress that people rode on and birds with wings that beat so fast it sounded like humming; and mountains of sand that changed shape depending which way the wind was blowing, and this sea of weeds, like a big rug in somebody's best room ... Sargasso, that was it. He said he'd never married because women took one look and walked the other way. I said I knew what he meant. He said he'd seen some of the roughest women on the ship pointing at him and sniggering behind their hands. I suppose he thought I wouldn't be so fussy. Well: he was right. I wasn't. I suppose I should have been more careful. It was just that he was old and a bit sad and I never even thought about falling pregnant. S'pose on account of him being old. That sounds stupid, and it was. Only then we landed and I didn't bleed and didn't bleed.'

Em reached across and pressed a shoulder. 'That's nothing. Half time mine don't come either. See, you're skinny, like me.'

Sarah covered the hand with her own. 'That's only since being nicked.

I suppose you're right. It's just that I've always been able to tell, right to the day. So I just naturally thought ... though I did wonder, because I haven't wanted to throw up or anything, like Ma did.' She paused, frowning. 'That Matron Gordon probably thinks I'm a real hard case. Remember, I told you I went back to where she told us to stay? There she was, giving off to me, and there was me, grinning all over my face. I'm sure she wondered.'

Em shook her head. 'I don't know, Scotty. I mean, it's hard to credit, you know? Do you even know his name?'

'Of course: what do you think I am? Daniel. Daniel Nicholson.'

'I didn't mean it like that. It's just ... I get it, you know. I truly do. I just know I couldn't.'

Sarah pulled her hand away. 'Nobody's asking you to, are they? I'm talking about me.' She turned her back.

Seconds later, Em whispered, 'I didn't mean it that way, Scotty. Sorry.' Sarah didn't nudge, she elbowed. Sharp and hard. 'What other way is there?' Em said nothing.

Sarah sighed and rolled back over. 'You know how they say men are all the same, only after one thing? Well, I'm not so sure anymore. Daniel was nothing like Harry, nothing at all. And I was nothing like me, or not the me that went with Harry. You know what it was with Daniel? He reminded me of my Dad. Before he got poorly. The way he talked. Dad used to talk like that, except with him it was all planning what he was going to plant, you know, what colour roses in what beds, what to put in so you had a bit of colour all the year round, even in winter. He was never outside Scotland in his entire life, my Dad, not even to see his own sister in London. If he had, he'd never have sent me; and if he hadn't sent me I wouldn't be here. But I wouldn't have met Harry either. Or Daniel. So that's just the way of it. Never know, do you?' Sarah sighed. 'Em?'

Em was asleep.

CHAPTER FOURTEEN

Face to Face

With a smile, Robert Gordon held out his hand. 'Thank you, Mr Tuckwell, thank you. My wife and I are fortunate; she has had Matron Raine to show her around the Factory and I have had your good self to show me around the Storerooms. We are both looking forward to working with you.'

Bill Tuckwell grunted and shook the proffered hand. 'Happy to be of assistance, Mr Gordon. Be prepared, that's what I say. Always be prepared. You will soon get to know our various suppliers and routines. I look forward to working closely with your good lady wife; the Reverend is much relieved finally to have found a new Matron, though Matron Raine will be missed of course. I expect the Reverend will make some special mention during the service.

'Service?'

'Church service, Mr Gordon. Mr and Mrs Raine are pillars of the church. No doubt I will see you and Mrs Gordon there on Sunday.'

'Ah! Yes, of course. My wife and I are very much looking forward to becoming part of such a Christian community. However: today is not our day of rest, is it? I know you are a busy man, so I shall detain you no longer.'

'Yes, there is always something on the go. Good day to you, Sir.' Tuckwell retreated into his office. Robert bowed and set off across the yard. Busy busy, busy: blah blah blah. All work and no play makes Bill a dull boy: dull as ditch water. Head full of lists and dockets.

He paused, sniffed and looked around. That was baking he could smell. Kitchens must be somewhere close. He could do with some breakfast. Why on earth did the man have to meet at such an ungodly hour? The Stores weren't going anywhere, were they? He sniffed again. No point going home, Ann would be gone by now. He sniffed again: good smell. Fresh bread. He followed his nose.

A woman came hurrying round the corner, dodging to avoid him. Blue jacket: Second Class. 'Not so fast, not so fast!'

The woman pulled herself up short, a flicker of annoyance crossing her face ... her young, rather pretty face.

'Where do you think you're going ... what's your name?'

'Lizzie Adams per Harmony, Sir.' She bobbed a curtsey and stood with her eyes lowered, waiting.

'Per Harmony, eh? Bumping into folk isn't what I would call harmonious. I'm sure you should not be running.'

Lizzie clasped her hands behind her back and looked up. 'Sorry, Sir, very sorry. I don't know, all the rules yet, Sir. I haven't been here very long, Sir. Per Harmony, last ship in, Sir. I'm still finding my way about. Sorry, Sir.'

She bobbed another curtsey. Not a bad little piece.

'Well, never mind. Make yourself useful and tell me which way to the kitchens.'

'Oh, I can tell you that, Sir, I'm just coming from there. This way.' She dimpled up at him and pointed behind her 'Straight down there, Sir. Bread's just out of the oven.' She hesitated for a second. 'Smells good, don't it Sir?'

'Indeed it does. And what were you doing there? Baking?'

'No, Sir. Returning some dishes from the lying-in rooms, Sir.' She clasped her hands under her chin and took a big breath. 'We've just had a new baby, Sir.' Raising his eyebrows, Robert looked her up and down. 'Indeed? You have certainly recovered well.'

'Oh! I didn't mean me, Sir ... Sir! You know I didn't mean me.'

'Yes, yes.' He reached out and chucked her under the chin. 'I should hope not.'

She lowered her eyes; fine eyelashes, he thought, and knows it.

'No, indeed, Sir. Better watch what I say, Sir, hadn't I? I wouldn't want you to get the wrong idea.'

'No. Indeed not. You can't be too careful.'

'No, sir. That's what Matron Raine said at my inspection, Sir.'

'Did she indeed? Well: I hope you met with her approval?'

'Yes Sir. It were just before the ... well, the disturbance, Sir. I were the first, on account of being an Adams. I don't think she ever got to the rest of us Harmony girls. But she said that she'd had a request for a maid of all work, you see, wanted immediately. Somebody young and strong, they wanted. And she could see I'd been in domestic service back home; so she said I might fit the bill.' She bobbed another curtsey. 'So I said, Sir, I said, just give me the chance, Ma'am.' She looked up at Robert and dimpled again. 'Lucky, wasn't I, Sir!'

'You were. Though you have a new Matron now.'

'Yes sir. So we've been told, Sir. P'raps you know her, Sir? Do you think it will make any difference, Sir?'

'Couldn't say. These things, you know, can't be too careful. There may be some small delay. Due to recent events. You must show the new Matron you are obedient and hard working.' He wagged his forefinger. 'Just you make sure you are!'

'Oh yes, Sir. I will, I certainly will, Sir. Just give me that chance, Sir.' She curtsied again.

'Can I please go now, Sir?'

'Yes, yes. The kitchens are along here, you say?'

'Yes, sir. Thank you, sir. Goodbye, sir.'

He watched the bob of her backside as she trotted off: cheeky enough little piece.

Don't even think about it, man. Not before breakfast. He headed for the kitchen.

***

The women were at it again. Like a buzzing hive, thought Lockyer, remembering the newspaper report. At least they were inside the gate this time. It was a restless, angry buzz. A few thumped on the newly repaired gate, but most huddled in groups, nudging and fidgeting. After a few minutes, word must have gone out from the ringleaders; the women linked arms like they had when they were filing back in the previous day. They started chanting, softly at first then louder. 'Bread or blood.'

Bread or blood: a familiar phrase. Food riot days, that was it: Liverpool, Manchester, London, the words echoing through streets haunted by gaunt men and haggard women. For all he knew, some of these women might even have been there, he might have ridden past some of them ... strange, thought Lockyer, strange the way one thing leads to another, one world to another world ...

He tried to do a rough head count. Not so many as yesterday: that was good. But still too many. Loitering with intent, thought Lockyer, definitely loitering with intent. He glanced round the yard. His men were posted at intervals, waiting for orders. From corners and doorways, small knots of women could be glimpsed, hesitant and whispering. The group at the gate weren't whispering, though, all of them were chanting now, making very sure they were heard. Lockyer moved closer to Ann Gordon's right side, just as Marsden, purse lipped and heavy lidded, moved in on her left.

'A monstrous regiment, Major.' The Reverend's voice broke across the rhythmic chanting. 'Remember your history? Mary Queen of Scots? As the Reverend Knox' put it: a monstrous regiment of women. Scotland or New South Wales, no difference. Who do they think they are?'

Lockyer nodded absently; his eyes were on Ann. Her hands were clasped at her waist, in what he already thought of as her typical stance. Her square jaw was set, her eyes narrowed, studying the swarming women. 'What would you like me to do, Matron? Shall I tell my men to go ahead and round them up?'

'No. No, Major. Wait.'

He waited. As did his men and the Reverend. As did the women. The chanting became quieter, gradually petering out. They stood silent, arm in arm.

Ann stepped forward, raising her right hand. Marsden moved to follow, but Lockyer laid a restraining hand on his shoulder.

'Good Lord, Major, what does the woman think she's doing? Reckless, quite reckless; come on, we must stop this nonsense. Give the order. Give the order!'

'Patience, Reverend, patience. Give her time.'

'Time, Major? There is no time!'

Ann glanced over her shoulder. 'Thank you, Major. Force of arms does not seem to have worked, does it? Let us see what force of reason can do.'

'Reason!' spluttered Marsden. 'What's reason got to do with it? They must be crushed immediately. We have given you authority, Madam, use it!'

'I intend to, Reverend. In my own way.'

Again, Lockyer restrained Marsden. 'Let her go, Reverend. Let us see what she can do. They might just be prepared to listen. It would certainly be easier if they did.'

'Thank you, Major.' Ann took a deep breath, clasped her hands tighter round her keys and walked into the middle of the yard. She stopped directly in front of the cluster of women.

'Ladies!'

No response. Again. Louder. 'Ladies!'

The women shifted uneasily. Neighbours nudged neighbours, elbows dug into ribs, heads tipped towards this small woman in her plain dark dress and sober bonnet, standing out in front of them on her own. Their eyes flicked from her to the men posted around the yard, back to her, then to what Molly had once called the long and the short of it: Lockyer and Marsden.

Right. Here we go. 'Ladies! I am your new Matron. Matron Gordon.' *Wait; get them all listening.* 'I had not expected our first meeting to take place in such regrettable circumstances. It is most disappointing, most.

Particularly given the events of the last few days. However, so be it. Since you have gathered here of your own accord, I shall make the most of my opportunity.'

The women glanced at each other, baffled.

'You are clearly aware that Matron Raine is no longer in charge. I repeat, I am your new Matron, Matron Gordon. Each and every one of you, for the duration of your sentence, will be answerable to me. For everything.' Ann paused again, scanning the women's faces.

'You will answer to me for your day to day activities: work, meals, rest. You will receive your assignments from me, your tickets of leave, and, as necessary, your discipline. Let me stress that word: discipline. I will reward obedience and hard work; I will punish disobedience and laziness.

'Over the next week, I will be visiting your workrooms. I will be making sure that each and every one of you has suitable employment. For instance, those women from the Harmony who have not yet been inspected and allocated work will be dealt with tomorrow.' Ann looked around; a few women fidgeted and exchanged glances. 'You know who you are. The delay is due to yesterday's regrettable and quite pointless disruption. You will be advised of any further changes which may be necessary. At present, whatever your regular work might be, you should be at it right now.' She paused again: *let it sink in.*

'After such disruption, I would have expected you to know better. I would have expected you to make up for lost time, not waste it. What for? That is the question. What can you possibly hope to gain? After such outrageous behaviour, the last thing you need to do is bring down more trouble on your heads. Can any single one of you step forward and explain to me what exactly you think to gain, what exactly is the point of this ... circus?' Ann paused, looking round. 'Anyone? Or two of you perhaps? You may appoint two spokeswomen. Clearly, I cannot speak to all of you at once. You have my word that your spokeswomen will not be penalised in any way.'

Silence, followed by a flurry of whispering and nudging: several women went into a huddle, waving their arms and shaking their heads. Eventually, a stocky dark-haired woman linked arms with a lean angular one. They looked at each other and stepped forward.

At a respectful distance in front of Ann, they curtsied.

'Joan Campbell per Morley.'

'Agnes Rowley per Janus.'

Ann inclined her head and gestured for them to continue. They looked at each other; looked at each other again. The taller nudged the shorter and she stepped forward. 'Permission to speak, Ma'am.'

'Permission granted, Joan Campbell.' *Finally, someone I don't have to look up to ...*

Taking a deep breath, Joan gestured towards the gate behind her. 'Thank you, Ma'am, thank you. Well, now. See yon gate? For all you've fixed it, it's still just a gate. We got through it once, we can get through it again. Not that we're planning on doing that, not at all. The only reason we did it once was to make you listen. To show you that there's only so far we can be driven. We're already paying for whatever we done, we don't need more taken out of our hides. That's the first thing. You can only drive human beings so far. Isn't that right?' She turned to Agnes, who opened her mouth, shut it and ducked her head.

Scottish. That's it, hen, take your time! Joan scowled and nudged her companion; Agnes shook her head. Joan took a deep breath and seemed to make up her mind. 'In for a penny, Ma'am, in for a pound. It was the whole lot of us, you see. No just three or four, the whole lot of us. Though that's the next thing. Punishing us all on account of what one or two at the laundry did, that's no fair. That's no just. Never mind we're on short enough commons as it is. I mean, have a look at us: how many rosy cheeks do you see? How many round bellies? The thing is, Ma'am, we all of us made up our minds to do what we done. Because you're the Law, and the Law's meant to be carried out fair and just, and it wasn't. It wasn't. That's why we did what we did.' Joan cleared her throat and glanced back at the other women. There were nods, even a spatter of applause.

'As for today, well it's the same only different. It's the same because it's about what's fair and just: it's different on account of having only just happened, where the other, it was coming for weeks. What today's about is them four women in the cells. Because it was all of us, not just them. So putting them in the cells, that's no fair or just either. Molly and Bridget, Maggie and Betty, they were no worse than the rest of us.' She paused, glancing back at the other women, acknowledging their nods of encouragement. 'Ringleaders, you talk about ringleaders. The thing about rings is they go round and round, so there's no single one that's the leader at any one time. It's all of us. It's all of us in this together. So if you're going to lock them four up, by rights you should be locking us all up. Whatever punishment you give them, you should give us. You're still docking our bread and sugar, you're still starving us, aren't you? Is that not enough? How are we expected to work if you dinnae feed us? That's what we're here for, isn't it, to work? That's the reason it's called a Factory. Well, you're not getting any work out of them in the cells; and you won't get any work out of us either, not if you keep them in there. So that's it, that's what we decided. You can lock us up, you can stand over us at the wheels and the looms, but you cannae make us spin, you cannae make us weave. We'll just sit and do nothing till you listen.'

Joan's throaty voice reverberated across the yard; when she finished, nodding and folding her arms under her bosom, the women cheered. Ann didn't have to look over her shoulder to know how red Marsden's face would be or how straight the line of Lockyer's lips. *Steady now, steady ...*

The cheering died away. Ann clutched her keyring tighter. *You could cut the air with a knife ... wait. Make them wait.*

Agnes Rowley stood with her eyes on the ground, one hand tugging at the knuckles of the other. Ann winced at the sound of them cracking. Joan Campbell stared straight ahead, lips compressed.

'I hope you mean what you say and that is not a threat, Joan Campbell. Agnes Rowley, I hope you are not making matters worse for yourselves.' With a panicky glance at Joan, Agnes shook her head rapidly. Joan lifted her chin and met the Matron's eyes.

'The thing is, Matron Gordon, we dinnae think they can get worse.'

Dark eyes locked into dark eyes. *Don't look down. Do not look down.* Joan dropped her gaze and Ann allowed herself a tight little smile. 'Let me make one thing very clear.' She raised both hand and voice, her gaze sweeping around the yard. 'It is not for you to decide when you will work or how. That is my job, with the authority vested in me by Her Majesty the Queen. You are all convicted felons, don't forget. You must pay your debt to society, use your time in here to make amends to the society whose laws you have willfully broken. I will decide whether you spin or weave, wash clothes or mend slops ... or pick oakum; I will decide whether you are fit to be let out on assignment.'

Take your time. Let it sink in. 'And I will decide which punishments fit which crime. Is that clear?' She looked straight at Joan. 'Until this recent disturbance, I knew nothing about any of you. Names, occupations, nothing. I was prepared to wipe the slate clean, make a fresh start. However, I must now think again. It remains to be seen whether you are any the wiser for this 'standing up' as you call it.'

That's it. Slow and steady, slow and steady. 'Very well. If one is punished, all should be punished. I grant you that. So. You all deserve to be punished. All of you, including the four in the cells, have brought this upon yourselves. You have threatened, robbed, and damaged property. Yet you have the nerve to complain of unfair treatment. What would the good citizens of Parramatta, whose shops and properties you made free with, have to say? No doubt some of them feel unfairly treated too. No doubt some of them would call it unfair, not to be paid for their goods. Is that not so?'

Crack, went Agnes' knuckles. Up went Joan's bosom and chin.

'One of you will come with me now: Joan Campbell, you. I will make a note of your 'things', as you call them. And I will consider how soon those in the cells might be released. You cannot expect better than that. As your new Matron, you may rest assured that when you come to me, if you have a fair case, you will be given a fair hearing. Good behaviour – that is, hard work and obedience – will be rewarded with good treatment. You are here to serve time, not waste it.'

Silence. Ann clapped her hands.

'For now, every woman in this yard is to go back to her place of work immediately. Major Lockyer, please see that they do so.'

Lockyer saluted. Ann pointed at the two women. 'Agnes Rowley, you may go. Joan Campbell, wait there.' She raised her hand. 'All of you, listen, and listen carefully! You are dismissed. Joan Campbell will be your spokeswoman. I will hear your case; I will consider when those in the cells might be released. Go straight to your workrooms. You will be told in due course what decision has been reached. For now, take yourselves off and make up for the time you have wasted.' She clapped her hands once more. 'Off you go! Quick smart! Major, can you get your men to tidy that rubbish up as well?' She waved her arm at a pile of discarded planks beside the gate. 'The sooner we put this all behind us, the better. Follow me, Joan Campbell.'

Lockyer called his men and moved toward the gate.

The women scurried off.

Marsden fell in beside Ann. She set off, then glanced over her shoulder. Joan Campbell was not following. She beckoned, but the woman shook her head, staring pointedly at Marsden's back. Ann sighed, turned and laid her hand on his black sleeve. 'Reverend, I really must apologise. This silly business has taken up far too much of your valuable time already. I know what a busy man you are. I can deal with the Campbell woman and report to you afterwards. No need to hold you up any longer.' She leant confidentially towards him and pointed in the direction of the workrooms. 'What I would really appreciate would be if you could look in on the workrooms. Just on your way past: a glance from you would soon settle them. You know the ones we need to keep an eye on better than me.'

Lips pursed and frowning, Marsden looked after the disappearing women. Finally, he nodded. 'Yes. Yes, well. I do have a number of fairly urgent matters to attend to, as you say. The Lord's work is never done. And you actually seem to have restored order, for the time being at any rate. A promising start, Matron!'

She patted his sleeve and smiled.

'A firm hand, that is the important thing. The velvet glove, believe you me, is not much use without the iron fist. Give them an inch and they will take a mile. And you will not always have the advantage of novelty.' He rubbed his hands together briskly. 'Very well, then: I leave the woman in your capable hands. I do have a number of appointments in town, but I will be sure to cast a shadow on the workshops as I pass.' He nodded and made off after the last of the women. Ann turned and beckoned Joan. 'Follow me, Joan Campbell. Quick smart.'

With Joan a few steps behind, she set off briskly for her office.

CHAPTER FIFTEEN

Solitary

Out of the corner of her eye, she caught movement. There ... there, on the floor, right in the middle of the cell, a scuttling black bead ...

Molly swung her feet up on to the bed and hugged her knees. The cockroach paused, its feelers probing the air. *Don't be silly. Stamp on it, go on! Squash it, grind your foot on it, round and round, grind it flat!* Eyes trained on the spot, she lowered the tips of her boots to the floor. But they knew when you were going to go for them, those feelers just knew; it would be out of there, under the bed where she couldn't see it. Hunt the cockroach.

It still wasn't moving. Why not? What were those feelers telling it? A long, frozen moment ... then the cockroach scuttled towards the cell door. *Hah! Making a run for it, giving them the slip: lone cockroach bid for freedom!* The insect disappeared through the slit between door and floor.

Molly felt a ridiculous urge to cheer.

Instead, her stomach rumbled. What sort of an excuse for applause was that? She clapped her hands.

Well. That passed a few minutes. Thank you, Mr Cockroach. What next?

Bridget. She kept coming back to Bridget. Those white-ringed eyes as they clamped the collar round her neck, those frantic fingers clutching at metal ... the thought had woken her once, twice, three times in the night. Maggie and Betty? They'd have been flat on their backs, dead to the world, snoring the night away. But Bridget ... how had Bridget got through the hours of darkness?

She had sung last night, sung her heart out. Ballads, choruses, songs the two of them had swung the sledge in time to, songs she'd heard Bridget singing when she was helping old Jake dig the vegetable patch. Digging dirt: better than splitting stone. For a few seconds last night, after waking the first time, she'd fancied she'd heard Bridget moving around. She'd sat up, pressed her ear to the wall, called; but no. Nothing but her own wishful listening, nothing but the wishful hope she'd helped ...

It was Bridget who had kept her sane, those first days in Thirds. Not that the other Third Class women had baited her much; she was too big for the usual stand over treatment. Plus she was Bridget's mate. They hadn't know what to make of her, from the day she'd taken the sledgehammer from the guard, walked over to Bridget, set it down, and shaken her hand. Then picked it up: one, two three: swing up, swing down. Up, down, up, down till the stones split and scattered. That was what they did in Thirds, day after day after day: split stones. Broke their backs and hammered their heads till the walls blurred and dust dizzied the air.

She had set herself to count how many stones were in the wall. To keep her mind working. That was how she'd found the marks. Not accidental scrapes and scratches, these were deliberately scraped and gouged. There were crosses, triangles, crude initials. There was the row of neatly scored lines, as if somebody was keeping count ... of what? The score of some game, the number of bets they'd won? How many? Seven lines: did that equal seven years? Had he served his sentence, got his ticket of leave, was he outside somewhere now? Or had he just given up? Then there were the letters ... an L, a T, and an awkward C: harder to do curves. The marks must have been made by the builders, the men who had set stone on top of stone and mortared them all together. Stone equals wall equals prison equals prisoners equals men. Men who each had a name, a mark different from every other mark. Men who took the trouble to make a mark that was his and nobody else's. The graffiti of unknown builders, all that was left to show they'd existed. L: Larry or Les, or maybe Leo, Leo the lion? T for Tommy, C had to be Charlie: the more Molly peered, the more marks she found ... creeping along the bottom, perching at head height, lurking in corners.

Molly found Bridget a mark that could be a B; your head's cut, said Bridget. But she leant in close and ran her fingers over the rough surface, smiling as she recognised the grooves in the sandstone. She couldn't read, but she did know her initial. It was like the brands on her cows, she said, you didn't need them yourself, but other people did. A herd of black and white Herefords, for example. At first, you'd think there'd be no way you could tell them apart. But it didn't take long. 13 she had, 13 that were hers to milk. A Bridget's Dozen, said Molly. Bridget chuckled over that for days. What were the cows' names? Think, think: Bridget had told her often enough. The first two were easy, already named when she started: Daisy and Buttercup. Moo and moo, said Molly, but Bridget said no, each cow was different, each one had a different name. Flower names: all flower names. Right, so 11 more.

Think. Think.

She counted them off on her fingers. Pansy, Primrose, Rosebud, Snowdrop. Carnation, Poppy, Daffodil, Marigold, Bluebell, Dandelion ... but that's a weed, Molly said. Yes, said Bridget, kicked like a bloody mule. What was the last one? Not a flower, she'd run out of flowers, but she was Bridget's favourite: Topsy. Yes, Topsy with the crooked horn. Molly nodded, pleased with herself.

Bridget didn't have a lot to say ... until you got her started on her cows and her horses. The two heavy horses which pulled the plough were called Samson and Goliath. Bridget slept in the barn loft above their stable; she kissed their long, gentle eyed faces every night on her way up to bed. When the ploughman got sick, she fed them; she plaited their manes and tails for the show, she brushed them till they shone.

When the barn caught fire, she untied them from their stalls and got them to the doors so they could escape, so they could thunder off into the night. The next Sunday, the minister thanked the Lord for sparing the dumb beasts. Bridget could have told him that the Lord had nothing to do with it. Should have told him, said Molly. Bridget shrugged. 'Nah. They'd just have wanted to know what I was doing out and how come I wasn't up in the loft asleep. Just as bloody well I wasn't, eh?'

Molly shook her head. Bridget had evidently been involved in the land riots, but she never had worked out how come she wasn't asleep in the loft. The big woman just tapped her nose. When Molly asked if there had been any fighting, she nodded fiercely. 'And were you hurt?'

Bridget looked at Molly and out the window. She tapped the side of her nose again and sang:

They hang the man, and flog the woman,
That steals the goose from off the common;
But let the greater villain loose,
That steals the common from the goose ...

'Do you like that one, Moll?'

'I do, Bridget. I do.'

Enclosures: Molly looked round her cell. Couldn't get much more enclosed than this. Far above her, daylight crept in through the strip of window. But when she checked the spy hole in the door, it was dark. She frowned, then realised she was looking at the back of a guard; he was leaning against the cell door. She leaned in close.

'What d'you reckon then?' he said. Liverpool, she thought: scouse accent. Like Mary.

'Better tell him, I suppose.' London?

'I reckon. In case she does herself a mischief. Or more of a mischief, by the sounds. Better let him know.'

'Swear to God, she was on all fours when I went in there, pawing at the floor. Jumped up when she saw me, let out this wild sort of whinny. That's when I twigged; woman thinks she's a bloody horse! Reared up against the wall, rolling these crazy eyes. Made me think of this mare I had once. Cost me a packet, she did: top sire, and already won a couple of big races: great turn of foot. And jump? Jump anything you put her at. But one vicious bitch: I've still got the mark where she bit me. Ended up shooting her. Laid her ears back once too often.'

Molly moved away and stood staring at the wall she'd sung to last night. Bridget: It had to be Bridget. Crazy eyes: she could see them, white ringed, staring in different directions. Her big hands, trying to lift that collar. Demented. Unless ... any chance it was some kind of act? Stop them parading her around, collared? No: wouldn't even occur to her. It was real. She was gone. Molly dropped to the bed and sobbed.

Sometime later ... what time? She had lost all track of time ... the food hatch scraped open. She took the tin tray. 'Thank you. What's the time? Have you been told when to let us out yet?'

'Midday. Two prisoners due out this afternoon. Not you. No chance.'

Not me. That'd be Marsden. Pray for, prey for. 'What about Bridget?'

The guard grunted and dropped the hatch.

The tray shook in her hands. Bread and water. Water and bread. She lowered herself down onto the bed. Sit. Eat. Keep your strength up. For how long?

Her and her immoral soul. Maggie and Betty, they'd be the two let out. Be glad for them.

Bridget must be in a shocking state, God help her. If she was no threat, though, maybe they would let her out. But then what? Some asylum, some madhouse? Was there one? The guard probably didn't know any more than she did.

Parade her around in that collar: the wages of sin. Or courage.

Take it off. Leave her alone. Molly looked up at the strip of sky. You wish. You so bloody wish. She closed her eyes; she couldn't get Bridget's out of her head ...

Bridget's laugh: the way it used to ring out across that yard. That *hahaha hohoho* laugh, that shake-your-whole-body laugh. But some sledges were just too heavy ... Bridget was broken. Just ... broken.

What would they do with her? Would they keep her in Thirds, or was she too much of a liability? Would she even get to see her again, and would Bridget know her if she did? What would Thirds be like without Bridget?

Sit. Eat. Keep your strength up.

Why? For when you get out of course.

Why? What the hell for?

Stop it. What the hell for? Em, think of Em. Think of teaching her, looking out for her. Em would be waiting for her, would run up and give her a hug. And what about the others? Joan: they hadn't put her in the cells either. Lucky Joan. Maybe that man of hers will come and get her. Wonder if she's told the new Matron yet? That was her on the far side of the yard when they were holding Bridget down, so she'd know, she'd have told the rest of them ...

Eat. Try to go to sleep.

But then I won't sleep tonight.

How much did you sleep last night?

Count fleas.

CHAPTER SIXTEEN

One on One

'Joan Campbell. Wait for me here.'

Closing her office door firmly behind her, Ann crossed to her desk, leant forward on her hands, and closed her eyes. A moment, she needed a moment.

Done. Done. So far so good. She shook her head and looked at her clock. Still only nine o'clock, the day barely begun: *how time flies when you're dispersing a mob*! Wryly, she smiled: *like something Robert would say. Funny, but also not.*

She picked up the clock and peered at the wheels and sprockets inside the glass case, the same way she had peered when she was a child back in Portsmouth. Strange, how such little wheels and sprockets could transform carefree girls whose plaits kept coming undone into middle-aged matrons with not a hair out of place. She turned the clock in her hands, studying each side. She had always liked that about it, the way you could see the mechanism through the glass, could see what was, quite literally, making it tick. Time: not flying, not dragging, just turning little wheels round and round, all through today and into tomorrow ... tomorrow and tomorrow, like the man said. Whatever side of the world you were on, and whether you'd remembered to wind your carriage clock or not.

It had belonged to her mother. Not that her mother had a carriage, she had simply seen it in a Portsmouth shop and liked it. It was small and elegant; the polished brass looked well on the drawing room mantelpiece. First thing every morning, her mother would wind the clocks: the one in in the bedroom, then the one in the kitchen, then the carriage clock in the drawing room. Smiling down at her daughter, she would open its glass back and show how the little brass key fitted on to its pin, how to wind it till it was tight but not too tight. Working parts, she called them: *always look after your working parts, dear.*

When her mother's working parts began to need looking after, it became Ann's job to wind the clocks. When she married Robert, her mother gave her the clock as a wedding present. It had accompanied her to Limerick, it was with her here in New South Wales; she could still look at it and see her long dead mother, clicking her tongue, drumming her fingers on her armchair. *I thought you had more sense.* With a sigh, Ann set it down. *I have now, Mother*

Enough: think. What are you going to say to this woman?

She found her list of names and ran her finger down it. Joan, Joan, Joan: how many Joans would have been through this place? Here we are: Joan Campbell. Glasgow: yes, well. Only has to open her mouth. Widow, twice married, domestic service. Receiving stolen goods. Thirty-eight. Not much older than me. Doesn't look it: dark eyes, good features: attractive enough yet; hasn't let herself go like most of them. Wonder if there's still a husband in Glasgow? Doesn't matter. Call her in. Get this over and done with. Ann got up and opened the door. 'Joan Campbell? You may come in now. Stand there, in front of the desk.'

Hastily, Joan pushed herself off the wall, bobbed a curtsey and did as she was told. *Don't be so bold, do as you're told*, if she had a penny for every time she'd heard that ... Last time she'd been in here, she'd been given a sermon on swearing. Raine, Raine, go away ... creeping around the place like that, what did she expect, her charges to be reciting nursery rhymes? As she'd said to Molly afterwards, didn't have to listen, did she? But anyhow, no more Raine. She looked at the bent head before her: would this one be any different? What was she doing now, scribbling away in her book? Joan looked around the panelled walls, pausing at the picture of Queen Victoria above the door; wouldn't want to get on the wrong side of that one, would you? She tried to picture the heavy jowls lifting in a smile, gave it up as a bad job. At the other end of the room were the armchairs, the fireplace, and the sheepskin rug. Not for the likes of her. Bare boards, bailed up in front a desk, that was the place for the likes of her.

How long was the woman going to take? *Just trying to wear you down: stand your ground, girl.* Joan stared at the wall behind the new Matron; something was missing. What? Something she remembered from last time: the Virgin, that was it. You could see the outline where the picture had been taken down. The Virgin with the pudgy baby that Molly said looked like Marsden might have done while he still had a mother to love him. Joan had laughed: that man? A baby? Spare me, she said. The whole time Matron Raine was sermonizing, she'd kept her eyes on that image, pictured herself putting baby Marsden over her knee and smacking his backside. See how he liked it. She wondered if Rainey had taken it with her, or if the new Matron was the one who had taken it down.

Ann dotted a full stop and looked up. Under the date was printed, in capital letters, 'Joan Campbell (per Morley)'.

'So. Joan Campbell. What do you have to say for yourself?' She held up a warning hand. 'Before you start, understand that any argument about the release of the women in the cells is strictly off limits. You have made your point; it is now a matter for the authorities.' She paused. 'Any further insubordination will do nothing to bring about their release. Quite the reverse, in fact. The authorities may conclude that a longer time in isolation is required, precisely to teach you and your fellows a lesson. Each case will be judged separately. Meanwhile, the governors and I expect the Factory will resume normal operations without delay. However, I undertook to hear these "grievances" of yours. So. What are they, these so-called grievances?'

Joan hesitated. 'Well. Matron Gordon, Ma'am. It's a bit hard to know where to start, really. Except that we're none of us fellows.'

'Being smart is not a good way to begin, Joan Campbell. You know very well what I mean. You are here to tell me what so called grievances can have led you women to so forget who you are and why you are here. Do so. Ringleaders, for example. You would have me believe that you all held hands in a big circle and made up your minds together. That is, of course, nonsense. Clearly, a few of you decided to stir up trouble and persuaded the others to go along. Since you have been chosen as spokeswoman, I presume you are very grateful not to be in the cells yourself.' *There: let's see what you say to that, Joan Campbell?*

The woman pressed her lips tightly together; Ann could almost read her mind: *in for a penny, in for a pound.*

'Begging your pardon, Ma'am, the reason they chose me was because they reckon I've got the gift of the gab. And you said I wasn't to be penalised. And you might say it's nonsense, but just ask any of us. We did all agree to do what we did. We never sat round holding hands or anything, when would we get the chance to do that? But we did agree. Time goes slow in the Factory; we've been making up our minds for days and weeks and months. All the little things, over the days and weeks and months they pile up, see. The bread and sugar just tipped the pile over, so to speak. I put it to you, Ma'am, was it a fair thing to dock everybody's rations on account of a few laundry girls kicked up their heels? Even Thirds said it wasn't fair, and they don't even get sugar in their tea to begin with. But they still stood up with us; so much the worse for Bridget Murphy. Ma'am, half of us never even knew we'd done anything wrong till we sat down for our meal. Most of us weren't on laundry duty, weren't anywhere near the river. The thing is, you see, the thing is, not only is it not fair, there's no sense to it. If you want decent work out of a body, you've got to put something decent in, stands to reason. You've got to feed her. It's not a big ask, Matron, enough bread to line your stomach and sugar in your tea. Not a big ask.'

Ann wrote the letters ABC underneath Joan's name and looked up. 'I should warn you that I'll be noting down all you say.'

Joan's eyes dropped to the page, flicked up again. She raised her eyebrows. 'Well, Ma'am, I s'pose that would be your job. But what's the alphabet got to do with it?'

So. She can read. All right ...

'That's for me to know and you not to ask. I am waiting for you to mention some grievance I haven't heard of before I take notes under these headings. I suggest you get on with it.'

'Well then, Ma'am: grievances. I hope I can take you at your word, that you meant it when you said you wouldn't penalise me for speaking my mind.'

'You can. You have my word.'

'Because what I'm saying is what's on everybody's mind, not just mine. Just like all of us felt the draught after some mongrel broke the window in our sleeping quarters. Chucked a stone, middle of the night. I won't repeat what he yelled, Ma'am. There was broken glass all over the floor.'

'You have reported this, I presume?'

Joan shook her head. 'Who to, Ma'am? They'd just say we done it ourselves.'

'That sort of behaviour is certainly not to be condoned. I will look into it. And see to the repairs. Did any of you see anybody? It would have been dark, of course.'

Joan sniffed. 'Don't need to see, Ma'am. It's not the first time. Young troopers from the Barracks, Ma'am, coming back late and the worse for wear. Shortcut across the yard, they do. Shouldn't be allowed.'

Ann made a note. 'Very well. I will make enquiries.'

'Will you Ma'am? Mean to say, I know we're the crims, or we wouldn't be here, but it still don't make it right for them to be throwing stones. Whatever we done, we're paying for it, aren't we? Shouldn't need to pay twice, should we? That there window, that's government property, isn't it? And besides, it gets back to the same grievance, don't it? Being punished when we never done nothing. And even the ones that did do something, the laundry girls, it's not like they hadn't done their work, not like they were playing hookey or drunk and disorderly, nothing like that. They'd done their work, the laundry was in the baskets ready for carrying back up. It was only a few minutes playing up. Just letting off steam, having a bit of a laugh.' Joan held out her upturned palms. 'I mean to say, what happened then was like what's happening now, only back to front.'

'What? What on earth do you mean?'

'Because then we were all being punished for what only a few done, and now you're looking to punish a few for what we all of us done. If you take my meaning. Ma'am. Of them in the cells, Molly's the only one was even at the laundry. Like I said, it's not like they were drunk and disorderly or wrecking stuff. It was a sunny day, Ma'am, that's about the height of it. Even a convict can't be miserable all the time. So they kicked up their heels a bit. Who were they bothering? Apart from Matron Raine and her man?'

Stop, stop it right there.

'That's enough! I am not here to listen to excuses. Kicking up their heels: what do you think this is, some kind of music hall? Who do you think you are, Joan Campbell?'

Joan opened her mouth, shut it again. She shuffled, clearly wondering if she'd gone too far. Then she shook her head defiantly. 'Nobody, Matron. Same as all of us. We're all of us Nobodies now. We stopped being Somebodies the day we boarded one of those hulks.' She pointed at Ann's book. 'Didn't think I could read, did you, Ma'am? We're not all of us ignoramuses. I mightn't know what all the big words are, but I can read enough to know what's going on. Like in court when they asked me if I understood the case against me.'

'And did you?'

'Certainly I did. I done it. No two ways about it. How else was I going to keep a roof over my head? Never hurt nobody; just shifted a bit of stuff about. From them as would never miss it to them as were happy to pay for it.'

Receiving, receiving, rhymes with, deceiving. How many times would judges have heard this kind of yarn? Poor, hard done by ...

'So you say, so you all say. How would you know what would or wouldn't be missed? If you're a Nobody, you have nobody to blame but yourself. You've run amok, you've rampaged through the town and frightened decent law-abiding folk out of their wits, all for a bit of bread and sugar. Did you really think you would get away with it?'

Joan put one hand to her back, the other to her forehead, and swayed.

'What's the matter with you? Are you ill?' Ann stood, frowning.

'Yes. I mean, no. I mean, I've been better. I was going to come and tell Matron Raine. I was, swear to God I was, only then there was yesterday and everything went out the window. I am pregnant, Matron. With child. I've been on my feet all day. Could I have permission to sit down a minute?'

Receiving, deceiving ... no, look at her, maybe not ...

'Normally, no. But in this case ... you do not look well. Yes, you may sit down.'

Ann rose from her desk and crossed to the window, turning as Joan leant back with a sigh in Marsden's chair.

'That's better. All the excitement, see, and not enough to eat ...'

Don't miss a chance, do you? 'How far gone are you?'

'Three month or so.'

'And who is the father?'

'Nobody that'd be known to you, Matron.'

'But who is known to you, I trust.'

'Oh yes, Matron, oh yes! Known to me all right.' Joan smiled, her hand stroking her stomach.

'And is there any prospect of him making an honest woman of you?'

With an earnest nod, Joan looked up. 'Well, Ma'am, I do believe there is. If I can take his word for it, which I do believe I can. He swore he would, or I never would have ... you know, Ma'am. I'm just waiting on word from him, that's all.' She hesitated. Ann, who gestured for her to go on. 'It was like this, you see. I'd been assigned me to him and his wife: domestic duties. On account of his missus being sick and taken to her bed and couldn't look after the house or his two wee boys. At death's door, she said she was ...'

'Are you telling me you committed adultery with a dying woman's husband?'

'No, Ma'am! Well, yes; only it was nothing like that, honest! See, she'd taken to her bed, only she'd taken to it a couple of years ago, and there was no sign of her mending ... or ending, if you take my meaning. She said she started feeling poorly straight after the boys were born: twins they were. The old woman next door used to come in and do for them, only she died.

Worn out, prob'ly. That's where I came in. He did his best, Tom did, but what with the inn to look after, and customers to serve, and two wee boys running wild ... well. Run ragged he was, run ragged. And there's her lying on her back with the curtains drawn, not even fit to cook him his dinner.'

Ann opened her mouth, closed it again. Joan kept talking. 'So. So anyhow, there's me, doing my level best to look after them all. Swear to God, I worked like a black. I was sorry for her, you know, at first. Really, I was: that scrawny and pinched looking she was, shuffling about like an old granny. So I did do my best, I did, spit and polish and cleaning up after them two boys. Right little brats they were, nobody to look next nor near them. And I'd give him a hand in the bar now and again too. I done bar work back in Glasgow ... anyhow. The long and short of it is, I tried but it was never good enough. She was always whingeing about some damn thing or other. It wasn't just me either, she'd be on at Tom as well, have you not done this, have you not done that? What man's going to put up with that? A man needs a wife, not somebody making his life a misery one minute and telling him he'll be sorry when she's gone the next. And then what's he supposed to do when she has gone? Anyhow, the long and the short of it is, he kept on and on at me and I did, Matron, in the end I did give in to him.'

Joan lowered her eyes and stroked her stomach again. 'So God forgive me, here I am. And maybe it was a sin, but I think there's worse. He was that desperate, Matron, I couldn't say no, just could not say no to him one more time. Only then didn't some nosey old biddy think it was her duty to tell his Missus, and all Hell broke loose. That was it; I got sent back. That's how come I'm here, Ma'am.' Joan heaved a deep sigh.

So what do I believe out of all that? Apart from the 'could not say no' bit ...

'I see. Is that all you have to say?'

Joan held out her palms again, like she was making an offering. 'Just this; just this. Most of us, Ma'am, most of us has learned our lesson. Most of us just want to serve our time and be done with it. You can check, Ma'am, you can check. It'll be in those books of yours somewhere. Tom Kennedy, that's his name. Innkeeper. The Traveller's Rest. On the Sydney road.'

'Does he know you're pregnant?'

'Yes. I told him when I left.'

'When was that?'

'Six weeks ago.'

'And you knew then? That you were pregnant?'

'Oh yes, Ma'am, you can always tell, you know, once you've had a couple ... not the sickness, though there's that; more the general feel, if you take my meaning.' She ran a hand over her breasts. 'Glasgow or New South Wales, don't matter, same sort of feel, tenderish and full up, same sort of queasiness ... I'm from a big family, Ma'am. I got a lot of experience; never mind a couple of my own that'll be running round their aunt's place back in Glasgow right now; at least, I hope and pray that's where they are ... but that's it, too, the other thing, that's what else I had to say. By your leave, Ma'am, by your leave, of course. Not just on my own account, I'm a few months off yet, but there's others, there's Rosie, now, she's just had hers ...'

Ann started: of course, the one they led out of the yard. Damn: she should have gone and checked.

'... a little girl. And they're both doing fine, but that's because Rosie's had four and knows what she's doing, it's no thanks to Mary that's in charge of the lying in. She might have been good once, I'm sure she was; but she's well past it now, Ma'am. Old dear doesn't know if she's coming or going halftime. Whereas me, me, Ma'am: I brought every one of my sister's bairns into the world, every last one, never mind a couple of my own, and all as hale and hearty as could be. Or they were. Last time I saw them. Three year ago now ...'

Joan's hands paused in their circling, then resumed.

'So, anyhow, that's what I'm saying. Old Mary's past it. Ask anybody, they'll tell you. Just an accident waiting to happen. Now, if you're looking for somebody with plenty of experience, somebody who's done the rounds, knows what's what ...'

'Enough! That's quite enough. This is not about midwifery, here or anywhere else. Stick to your grievances, Joan Campbell. Yesterday, as well as that nonsense at the gate: there are proper procedures, you know. You should have spoken to the proper authorities. But instead you ran riot.

Instead you took it upon yourselves to break through the Factory gate, to do willful damage to public property, to loot and intimidate: in short, to behave like criminals. Grievances? I think we are the ones with the grievances.'

Joan sat up straighter. 'Begging your pardon, Ma'am, not so much criminal as desperate. Report it? Who are they, these proper authorities? When have any of them listened to any of us? What way have we of getting them to listen to the likes of us? Who, the gentlemen on the committee? They'd run a mile before they'd speak to any of us. Reverend Marsden, he can't speak for preaching. The troopers, the police, all they do is round us up like so many sheep. But we're not sheep; nor goats neither, whatever the Reverend says.' Joan threw up despairful hands. 'Ah, what's the use? Molly's the one you should be talking to, not me. She said you'd have to penalise us, penalise, that was her very word. Consequences, she said. On account of we did damage property and we did nick bread ... though some of the bakers handed loaves out to us, did you know that? And scraps and leftovers? So there's bad consequences and good consequences, and what we were looking for were some good consequences for a change.'

Ann frowned and made a quick note. 'You mean Molly Malone, who's in the cells?'

'I do. And just so you know, she was the one that told us to come back into the Factory and get back to work. So that makes it all the more unfair, don't it? I mean, penalise away, but be fair about it. It might not sound a lot to you, extra bread or a bit of sugar for your tea. But it's a lot for us.'

'Tea's not tea without sugar, is it?' Elizabeth Raine ...

Joan slumped back in her chair, fingers splayed over her stomach. Ann tapped her pen on the desk.

Lying in rooms: I'll go straight there. Poor old thing, she probably is past it. Not so sure about Madam Joan here though. No hurry, no hurry.

'We will talk about your situation later. And as for Mary's: well, you've had the necessary experience, but so have plenty of others. You're not actually a midwife, are you?'

Joan sat forward earnestly. 'Might as well be. I could do the job,

Ma'am. Honest. My cousin was a midwife and I used to go with her all the time when she was called out ... she was training me up to take over from her. Only then I got nicked ...'

The door swung open. Both women started. Robert Gordon stepped in. 'My dear ... oh.' He raised his eyebrows, looking from Ann to Joan, who pushed herself to her feet and stood gripping the back of the chair. He raised his eyebrows at Ann. 'Sorry to interrupt. I gather there has been a further incident. I came to check that everything was all right.'

Ann went back to her desk. *Knock: she must tell him to knock.*

'Thank you, Mr Gordon. There's been a minor disturbance, yes, but it's all over now, all sorted. I have almost finished here. You might like to wait down there.' She gestured towards the far end of the room. Robert hesitated, then mock saluted and strolled down to the sofa. Ann sat down at her desk and made some more notes before looking up into Joan's ... what? Curious? Cynical? Anxious gaze?

'I have heard your grievances, Joan Campbell. They will be dealt with. You will be told if you are to come and see me again. For now, you are to go around the workrooms and inform the other women that their grievances have been duly noted. Tell them that normal rations will be restored along with normal behaviour. The sooner the better, as far as I am concerned. As for the women in the cells, I will see them this afternoon. Meanwhile, the sooner you get back to work the better.'

'So will you let them out, Ma'am?' Joan clasped her hands.

'I said nothing of the sort. I said I would see them this afternoon. You are dismissed.'

Joan hesitated still, hands on her belly. 'And you will consider ...'

'You are dismissed, Joan Campbell. You will be told if I need to see you again. Now go.'

Ann pointed to the door. Joan curtsied and left.

Ann closed her book sharply and turned to look at her husband. Robert patted the space beside him on the sofa. 'Attagirl. That's the way. Come and sit down.'

'I can't.' Ann closed her book. 'I have to go to the lying-in rooms. One of the women has just had a baby. The Harmony inspections don't start till 11: I just about have time.'

Robert had stretched out in an armchair, penknife out, idly cleaning his fingernails. She stood over him and held up a key. 'Well, Mr Storekeeper. Have you worked out what all your keys are for yet? This is a spare to my office: do not lose it. And don't forget to lock up after you.'

She flipped him the key and was gone.

CHAPTER SEVENTEEN

Bygones

Sarah stood in the middle of the yard under the solid grey tree trunk, looked up and shook her head: just the notion of a woman climbing a tree, who would even think of it? Em had explained to her the how: the run, the leap, the low, steeply angled branch that you swing up onto. Climb high enough, she said, and you could see over the wall, down to the river and the laundry clearing and the wilderness beyond. 'Goes on forever, Scotty, true!'

Now, Sarah put her hands to the trunk and craned upward. 'Em! Em!'

She jumped back as Em dropped to the ground beside her. 'Scotty! What time is it?'

'What time is it? Where the hell have you been? I've been looking everywhere! You've missed the whole bloody thing, Em, you that was so full of it, you that was telling everybody to be there or be dammed! You chew my ear half the night ... then you don't even show up!'

Em gaped. 'You mean ... ? Shit: Shitshitshit! I'd no idea, I lost track, just totally lost track of time. Was it alright? Did they all turn up ... apart from me?'

'Yes; pretty much.'

'Sorry; so sorry! What happened. Tell me! What's happening about Molly?'

'Don't know yet. But you know that new Matron? She came out all on her own, no Marsden, no Major, and she talked to us. And she said she'd hear our grievances and she took Joan off with her to be our spokeswoman.' Sarah paused, frowning. 'What do you mean, lost track? How could you lose track?'

Em clapped her hands to her head and groaned.

'You look awful. What's up?'

'Lizzie Adams, that's what's up.'

'Oh no. Don't tell me you've been fighting again?'

'What, and go back in the cells? Not that stupid. Neither's she. More's the pity. That was the first thing she said, how she never wanted to see the inside of a cell again. Let bygones be bygones, she goes, we're all in the same boat now.'

'Well, what's wrong with that? She's right, isn't she? And we'll be in a boatful of trouble when they come checking the workrooms and we're not there! Come on!'

Em rubbed her eyes. 'Yes. Right. Coming.'

They hurried across the yard, Em chewing at her fist. When Sarah smacked her arm, she grimaced and shoved it under an armpit. 'You know, for a couple of minutes I even thought she might mean it, that same boat stuff. 'Cause it weren't me seen her, it were her that called out and come across to me. I just kept going like Molly said, only she caught me up. So I pulled up and said, going to the meeting? She shook her head and I give her a filthy look, like, why the hell not? She jumped straight into how she couldn't on account of having just been assigned and told to report to Tuckwell. That she would if she could, but if she didn't turn up they'd change their minds and not let her go, I could see that, couldn't I? And I said nothing, on account of I actually could ... I mean, if it'd been me ...

'Anyhow, I just sort of shrugged. But then she goes, want to know where? Meaning, where she'd been assigned to ... I just shrugged. Made no difference to me. But then she bats her eyelashes like she does and says, Sydney town. Tuckwell's told her to be ready to go tomorrow. Rainey must've done it last thing: I mean, none of the rest of you Harmony lot have even been inspected yet, have you?' Sarah shook her head. 'Adams, see. Top of the list.'

'Half her luck. You should be pleased. Won't have to look at her anymore.'

'But don't you see, Scotty, that's where Charlie is! Think she don't know that? Then she smirks and tells me she's seen him. Seen Charlie.'

'Your Charlie?'

'Geez, what other one is there? Says she seen him on the docks at Sydney when they were being unloaded off the ship; and that he seen her. Then she sniggers like she does, and says she were going to tell me only I was too busy beating her head in. Swear to God it were all I could do not to beat it in again and bloody strangle her while I were at it! But I didn't. I didn't. Not even when she shows me how she puckered up and blew him a kiss.'

'Did he blow one back?'

'She says he did. But she would say that, wouldn't she, no matter he did or he didn't, just to stir me up. Lying cow. Always was.'

'But Em, that don't mean nothing. Or what it means is you know he's all right and you know to start looking round the Docks. So what if he blew her a kiss? You'd do that to anybody you used to know if you saw them out here, wouldn't you? Don't have to mean anything. Maybe he meant the kiss for you.'

'How in hell do you make that out?'

'Cause he'd have known she was on her way to the Factory, and he knows you're here. Doesn't he?'

'He might. But he might not. I don't know what he knows. He knew I'd be convicted, but how would he know where I was sent? Or when? Last time I seen him they were leading him away. He heard me, I know he heard me, because I saw him turn his head and I were shouting at the top of my voice that I'd find him, that I was on my way. Plus Smithy sent word that he'd got a mate of his who worked on the Docks to tell Charlie about my sentence, that I was on my way to Sydney and to look out for me. But I've no way of knowing if that message ever got through.'

'You've no way of knowing it didn't either. I mean, he might've been on the lookout for you.'

‘But why didn’t I see him when we docked then? I was looking.’

‘Any number of reasons. It’d be dead easy to miss someone; wrong time, wrong place, wrong boat …’

‘But I don’t know, Scotty. I don’t know, do I? What if he didn’t? For all he knows, I could be dead.’

‘Come on, Em, they weren’t going to hang you for breaking and entering!’

‘No, but I could’ve got sick or died on the way out or something. Because he knows I don’t change my mind, he knows it’s him or nobody. He knows that pretty much the only thing that would stop me would be if I were dead. We didn’t get tattooed for nothing.’

‘Solemn vow and tatt, eh?’

‘Yep!’ Em patted her shoulder. ‘You’ve got a few tales to tell, haven’t you, puss?’

‘Bur how does Lizzie Adams fit in?’

‘Because she’s after him, of course! Always has been. It was only meant to be me she dobbed in. She thought he was off on this other job, only Smithy changed the plan at the last minute ‘cause he found a better one that needed the pair of us. She never meant for Charlie to be nicked. But he doesn’t know any of this, doesn’t even know he’s got her to thank for being here. He’ll just think she must’ve got nicked too.’ Em shook her head. ‘Some big house in Sydney, she said. Near the harbour. The docks. The docks where she seen him!’

‘Yes, but Em, it’s not like she’s going to be let out to wander round the docks now, is it?’

‘She’ll work it out, don’t you worry; she’s smart enough. She’ll ask around, she’ll find him. And she’ll tell him I’m dead. Act all sad, if there’s anything she can do, anything at all, bat her eyelashes. Damn her, damn her to hell! Scotty, what am I going to do?’

They stopped in front of the carding room door. Em’s fist was in her mouth again. Gently, Sarah pulled it down. ‘Well: you could try the new Matron, Em. Why don’t you do that? Tell her you got a good report last time, and that you heard they were looking for domestics in Sydney?’

'Scotty, there's just been a riot, remember? You think she's going to be handing out assignments? No chance. No, I've got to think of something else. That's why I climbed the tree, just to get up where I could think. There's got to be some way.'

'But what about you at least try? I mean, what else have you come up with?'

'Sweet FA. Can't think. I wish Molly was here.'

'Molly? God knows what state she's going to be in when they let her out. You can't go pestering Molly.'

'Not pester, just talk! Did they say how much longer they were going to keep her?'

'No, but it might not be that much longer. Depends on what Matron Gordon thinks of what Joan has to say.'

'You think Joan will get into trouble?'

'Well, Matron Gordon gave her word. In front of everybody. That Joan wouldn't be penalised. In front of everybody. Reverend Marsden and that Major Lockyer and Matron Gordon, they were all there. The Major had his men posted all round; we were just waiting for him to give the word and for us all to be rounded up and clapped in irons. But he didn't. And then she walked out on her own, right out into the middle of the yard, and started talking. Ladies, she said, like she did before ...' Sarah grinned. 'It was funny, you know. Everybody looking round, like, who, me? And then she started on with the usual stuff about knowing our place and debts to society. Anyhow, the long and the short of it is that Joan and Agnes were chosen to be speak for us and tell her what our grievances were. Don't know why they chose that scaredy cat Agnes, she never said a word. It was all Joan. Joan was great: lock one up, lock the lot of us up, she said. Let Molly and the others out. Or get someone else to do your spinning and weaving.'

'She said that? Joan?'

'Well, not exactly that, but that's what it came down to. I was waiting for Marsden or Lockyer to butt in, but they didn't. It was all her, out on her own, talking. And not the repenting or wages of sin stuff, about what was actually going on. She couldn't say when they'd get out of the cells, but she was going to get the Factory back to normal as soon as possible. For everybody. Then she dismissed us and I came looking for you. Quick, she's not looking ...'

The supervisor's back was towards them; Sarah pushed the door a little further and they slipped in.

***

After Ann had gone, Robert sat stubbornly on: did he know what his keys were for: indeed! Keeping people in and keeping people out, that's what keys were for. The right people and the wrong people. You just had to know which one was which. That was the trouble with Ann: if she spent more time on who was who and less worrying about what was what, she'd make things a lot easier for herself. He pulled out his wallet and added her office key to his collection. It was considerably smaller than the key to the Storekeeper's office, he noted with some satisfaction. They fitted neatly into his waistcoat pocket.

A knock at the door: he strode across the room and opened with a flourish.

'Mr Gordon! What a surprise; I was looking for your wife.'

'Major Lockyer! I'm afraid you've missed her, she is just this minute gone. I almost missed her myself; called in on my way to the Store, you see, just to check that she was all right. Those wretched women!'

'Yes, indeed. Nothing like as bad as yesterday, though. They are all back to work now, thanks to your wife. Most impressive she was, most impressive. Just took charge, cool as a cucumber, no nonsense. You must be very proud of her.'

Yes: got the nonsense out of her system a long, long time ago.

'I certainly am, Major, I certainly am. Salt of the earth, my Ann. Determined, you know? Once she sets her mind on something, there's no turning her.'

'Yes. I wanted to see how she got on with Joan Campbell. She didn't say anything, did she?'

'That would be the woman here when I came in: bold looking baggage, but not bad looking? Ann had obviously dealt with her, she sent her packing as soon as I arrived.'

'So there didn't seem to be any difficulty?'

'No.' Robert waved a dismissive hand. 'Ann would have given her short shrift. All over by the time I arrived. Don't have any details, I'm afraid, she had to rush straight off. But she was fine.'

'That's good. No doubt she'll tell us the upshot of it when we meet later on. And there was one other matter ...'

'Nothing urgent, I hope.'

'No, no: need a new domestic, that's all. Our old cook has been taken ill and my wife needs someone to take her place. I thought your wife could find us a Factory lass. Sooner the better, really.'

'I'll be sure to mention it. Where are you headed? I was about to go and make a start on those police requisitions. If you're going past the Store, we might walk together.'

Lockyer nodded. 'Certainly ... you ready?'

The Major waited while Robert locked the door, then they headed down the stairs. 'Police requisitions, eh? Yes: you will be a busy man, Gordon. The stores are like the ships; they just keep coming.'

'So it seems. Though Mr Tuckwell does have everything shipshape; I met with him this morning.'

'Shipshape, ha! Good way of putting it. Very capable fellow, Tuckwell.'

'It certainly seems so. Very businesslike. After you ...' They set off across the yard. Robert cleared his throat. 'You're a family man then, Major?'

'I am. My wife's name is Mabel.'

'Any children?'

'We certainly do: ten, all together.'

Robert chuckled. 'Good Lord! I thought I was doing well with four, but you've really been a busy boy, haven't you? Especially since, from what I hear, you are much away; quite the explorer. Absence makes the heart grow fonder, eh?' He gave Lockyer a nudge. 'Never mind the old fella!'

Lockyer raised an eyebrow. 'We have been fortunate. I have been married twice, Mr Gordon. Mabel is my second wife; my first died in Ceylon. I met Mabel there before being posted here.'

'Ceylon, eh? A true servant of empire, then!'

Lockyer shrugged. 'Usual army career. We arrived here April 1825. Complete change, as you would know. It takes some time to adjust, does it not? We had hardly settled into our house when they sent me off to Brisbane. Army wives, Gordon: they are a pretty long-suffering lot!'

'Indeed, I think you'd find Ann in agreement with you there.'

The two men strode on. Lockyer broke the silence.

'At the time, as I said, it was the last thing I needed. But that trip up the Brisbane River: I would not have missed it. Marvelous. Nothing like it: sailing up a river that's barely even been mapped. Miles and miles of open country, and the colours, Gordon, the colours! So different! The birds, the flowers ... I do a bit of painting in my spare time, you see. Landscapes. I've had a couple of the best ones framed. Give people a better idea of the potential of this place. You and Mrs Gordon must come and see them some time.'

'We would very much enjoy that, thank you. We shall hold you to it. You are a man of many talents, it appears. I would never have picked you for an artist.'

'Oh, I do not claim to be one; not the kind they hang in galleries at any rate. It is my hobby, my relaxation. New landscape like this, it's a gift. So much that has never been seen before, you know; never mind painted. For the record, apart from anything else. Natural history, you know, that sort of thing.'

'Good for you, sir! I have to confess, drawing a straight line is challenge enough for me! I do take your point. Keeping a record: absolutely essential.'

'Just so. A sort of logbook, you know? I've never been much for writing up logbooks, far too tedious. But give me a pencil or a brush and I'll make you a likeness. Never had enough time to work on it, though, develop a proper technique. It's something I've promised myself in my retirement. I'm handing in my commission. As I believe you have already done.'

'Yes indeed, I'm a step ahead of you there. The regiment was being posted to India, and I have to say, Lockyer, I did not fancy it: not at all. Cows wandering round the streets, malaria, mad rascals running about, heat blazing or rain teeming. But of course, I am forgetting, you would know ... though perhaps Ceylon is different. All very well when you're a young blood, but once you've got a family and children, all of that, you start looking for something a bit more settled, don't you agree? So when Ann got offered the position of Matron and I got the Commissariat job, we jumped at it. Thank you, by the way, for putting me in touch with Bill Tuckwell. Most useful.'

'Not at all, not at all, anything I can do ... yes, you are right about the family. We old married men, eh? You and your wife came out here together?'

'Yes. Let's see: 1812, that's when we were married. My God: that's fifteen years. Fifteen years! Hardly credit it, would you? I met Ann in Portsmouth when the regiment was stationed there. We had a year in Ireland – Limerick – before coming out here. Sailed in 1817. Been up in Newcastle for most of the last ten years.'

'Clearly you've taken to colonial life.'

'Yes. Yes, I have to say that it has suited us well. We even had our eyes on buying some property, but unfortunately it fell through.'

'Shame. There's land for the taking, and plenty of it. I've bought a property myself: Lockyersleigh, we've called it.'

'Is that so? Whereabouts, if I might ask?'

'Outside Sydney, a bit further north. But we won't be ready to move for a couple of years yet.'

'Not ready to leave civilization, eh? I'll admit, sir, I'm no explorer. All those empty spaces, no society, nothing to occupy oneself; give me city life any day.'

'O, you'd be surprised. Depends on your interests, of course. I thought I'd seen some strange things in India and Ceylon, but nothing to equal what I've seen here. Just the wildlife: emus, goannas, kangaroos, native bears. You would think the good Lord might run out of ideas, but no! Big ones, little ones, square faces, pointed faces, thin tails, tails like paddles; they hop, they crawl, they run, they waddle. And then there are the natives. You know, at first glance all you see is brown skin and fuzzy hair. Bur sit down and draw them, and they're as different as you and me.'

'You've had a bit of contact with them, by the sounds of it. No trouble?'

Lockyer shook his head. 'Mainly as guides. Couldn't do without them. In my experience, Gordon, you leave them alone, they'll do the same for you. You just have to keep a weather eye open, that's all. I've done a few sketches to show Mabel. Makes it easier, you know. Instead of trying to answer all the questions – what do you mean, scars? What kind of fur? – I can just pull out a drawing.'

Robert nodded and stopped; they had reached the Storekeeper's office. They shook hands and Lockyer walked on, head forward, hands clasped behind his back. Robert watched till he turned a corner; he did go on a bit, the old Lockyer. Meant well of course; the man knew his stuff, that was obvious. Took everything so goddam seriously; though he supposed you would have to, taking off for months on your own like that. Bound to catch up with you after a while, all that trekking about in the heat. Lockyersleigh, for God's sake. Just a fancy name for Lockyer's place. And ten children! No wonder his poor wife needed help. Four was plenty, Ann and he had long since agreed on that.

CHAPTER EIGHTEEN

Time Please

Midday. Her carriage clock ticked, her pen scuffled along, pages turned: peace and quiet. Not for much longer, though. Ann sighed, looking at her list for the afternoon: talk, talk, talk. So many words: a man of words but not of deeds is like a garden full of weeds ... where did she remember that from? Her old nursery rhyme book ... what about a garden full of rabbits? She sighed and dipped her pen in the inkwell.

Outside, at the top of the stairs, Elizabeth Raine paused in front of the brass plaque on the door: 'Matron'. It had been one of the first things she'd ordered after her appointment. And kept polished: it could do with a polish now. Never mind, she told herself; not your worry anymore. She's probably run off her feet, just as you were at the beginning. First things first. You can't stay long, remember; you can always call another day if there are things she wants to ask. Just get her to sign off on those papers. Mary Jane Lewis, orphan, four years old, hereby released into the care of ... She should have seen to it herself, of course, but what with one thing and another, it had entirely slipped her mind.

She tapped on the door. How was she managing, plain little Mrs G? Such an appalling start: you wouldn't wish it on anyone. As Edwin said, she was well out of it. Taking the child was a good deed, particularly fitting for a past Matron, as the Reverend had remarked over tea. Save the child from her mother's fate, wretched woman: dragged in off the streets, died in childbirth. Father? Anybody's guess. Edwin was perfectly agreeable, bless him; suffer the little children, he said.

She would train the girl up; she would need extra help once she set up her school, once she advertised and the enrolments started coming in. She would limit numbers of course; top drawer only. Accomplishments extra; she would have to find a music teacher. Taste and tradition, that was her mission: to bring taste and tradition to this cultural wilderness. She knocked again, more loudly, drawing herself up to her full height at the sound of footsteps.

* * *

In the yard at the back of the lying-in rooms, Mary Jane was dragging a stick backwards and forwards along the paling fence: clip clop clip clop, like a horsey. Mary leaned back in her seat, vaguely watching the child, more intent on what was going on inside. Rosie had a visitor.

That Joan with her questions, with her eyes prying into every corner: had Rosie told her about the fall? Always ready to help, was Joan, Mary knew that didn't she? Far too bloody ready, ready to take over, that's what Joan was. She'd heard her talking to Agnes Rowley: 'soon as she falls off the perch.' Soon as she was pushed, more like.

A loud wail startled Mary to her feet: too late. The child had tripped and banged her head against the fence. She sat bawling in the dirt. Mary hobbled across and opened her arms.

Inside, Rosie waved Joan goodbye. She looked down at the sleeping Bonnie and stroked her downy head thoughtfully. Joan wasn't the only one with experience of babies and childbirth. When Mary came in towing a wriggling, sobbing child, she got up and pulled out a chair.

* * *

Joan walked slowly, in no hurry to pick up her needle and start stitching again. So Rosie had had no problems: well and good, of course. Pity, though, that she'd nothing to add to her list for Matron. She had asked, but according to Rosie it was all straightforward. And of course, she'd nothing against Mary; God help her, she needed a rest. Worn out, that was all. Like she'd said, an accident waiting to happen. She'd be far better off sitting out in the sunshine with the other old biddies. They didn't eat much, did they? Weren't doing anybody any harm ...

Not how she meant to end her days, though, not in this place. Not for Joan Campbell, thank you very much. She laid a hand on her belly: Tom, Tom, what is keeping you? Over a fortnight since that woman finally snuffed it, and still no word. Though he'll have had the funeral and the relatives to get sorted, never mind the pub. Still. Bloody men! She looked across the yard to where three troopers were walking toward the gate, one with a bandage on his face. Must be the one Bridget punched. God help her, she wouldn't be throwing any more punches. One of the troopers glanced in her direction; she quickened her pace. They would not be in a good mood, they would want to know what she was doing out, why she wasn't at work, quick, duck around the corner ...

***

Andy patted his wounded comrade's shoulder and shook his head in sympathy. Hard to credit any woman could pack a punch like that. Downright unnatural. The gentle sex? Some joke that was: you'd never think they were even the same species as his Emily.

'Well, there's thoroughbreds and there's mules,' grinned George. 'Never mind, mate, we'll stand you an extra round on Andy's stag night.'

His mate rolled his eyes and gingerly touched his bandage. 'Don't know if I'll be up to it.'

'Up to it? It's your nose, mate, not your pecker! 'Course you will! Come on, I thought we were getting a bite to eat.' George and Andy took him by the elbows and led him on.

***

Time for lunch. Robert locked the door behind him. All done: forms filled in, signed, ready to go. He had a pretty flash signature, if he said so himself; added a bit of style to those dry old requisitions. He looked around the yard; there they were, the poker playing lads. He called out and hurried after. Young fellow with the bandage: that mad Irishwoman. They should lock some of those women up and throw away the key. He joined them, feeling in his breast pocket; yes, cards there ready. 'How goes it, lads?'

***

Elizabeth Marsden laid her knife and fork side by side and picked up a brass bell cast in the form of an Elizabethan lady. Under the bell of the brass skirt, two slender legs on hooks tinkled when she shook them. Her name was Bess and she was a present from Elizabeth's mother. Once, in another world, Bess had rung for Elizabeth's practice time; she had tinkled continuously after a particularly good performance. Even yet, Elizabeth sometimes rang her continuously when she'd finished. Nobody else knew she was Bess. Years of polishing had rubbed away her features; but her tinkle still felt like applause.

Marsden wiped his mouth with his napkin, nodded, and Bess rang sharply. Sally came in to clear the table. Marsden sat back comfortably: he did enjoy a well-done lamb chop. 'Very good, dear, that was just right. I shall have to take lunch at home more often!'

Elizabeth dabbed at her mouth, twitched a smile. Sally cleared the plates and left the room. Setting them down rather hard in the kitchen, the maid looked out the window at the rabbit hutches, and muttered 'at least I'll be shot of him. And them.'

In the dining room, Marsden announced that he he'd sort things with Matron Gordon and everything was under control. They would have a new maid very soon. 'Oh dear; I am sure there are many people in more need than we are! I feel so much better now, I am sure I can manage quite well with Sally.'

'Don't be silly, Elizabeth. The wheels are in motion. I told you, everything is under control.' He stood up. 'I will be off. You need not wait up: I have a number of meetings. There has been some incident in the cells. Hopeless, hopeless. However … these little things are sent to try us! You are still quite pale, my dear. You should go to bed early.' He pressed his mouth against her forehead and left the room. She waited till she heard the front door close, then tinkled Bess again.

'Sally? Sally!'

* * *

Bridget looked up at Lockyer with one eye and snorted. Defiance? Hardly. You had to meet a man's gaze to defy him. Lockyer's habitual frown deepened. The woman was in a truly pitiable state. The flesh around her newly exposed neck was red and raw; she stood backed up against the wall. The collar had been returned to its hook in the station; the Sergeant had returned and was waiting for orders. Lockyer rubbed a baffled hand across his forehead: what were they to be? What on earth could you do with the woman? What would Marsden do? For once in his life, even Marsden, he suspected, would be at a loss.

She seemed harmless enough now. He leant forward, holding his hand out to her. She cringed, squeezing even deeper into the corner; if she actually were a horse, he thought, her ears would be laid flat back against her skull. One white ringed eye fixed his, the other fixed the floor. What to do, what to do?

Disconcertingly, the image of his newly framed painting flashed up in his mind, but not the deep water or the flag: the image he didn't paint. The two brown bodies sprawled on the sand, their bruised faces and closed eyes: his own Mabel's face, wincing as he told her the story.

The Sergeant coughed, shifting from foot to foot. The Major didn't seem to hear. He coughed again. Bridget shook her head.

'The infirmary. She will have to go to the infirmary.' Lockyer turned toward the door.

'Right then.' The Sergeant moved forward. Bridget bared her teeth and pawed at the mattress, one eye on him, one on the floor.

'Sir, I might need a couple of the boys.'

Lockyer paused and nodded. 'Yes. Yes, you do that. The infirmary, Sergeant. Get her out of harm's way. A room with a lock: not a cell, though. Somewhere safe. With a mattress, somewhere to lie down. And blankets. Is that clear? Right. Lock up now, but be straight back, understood?'

The Sergeant saluted and stood aside to let Lockyer leave the cell. He dived after him, tugged the heavy door closed and turned the key. Lockyer didn't look back, he was already halfway across the yard. No, he wouldn't mention it to Mabel. No point upsetting her. Or himself.

'Major! Major Lockyer!'

Tuckwell. With a sigh, Lockyer stopped and waited for the newly appointed clerk to come puffing up. Tuckwell took a minute to catch his breath, then started. He had just this minute been talking to Reverend Marsden, and the arrangements for Market Day were all in place. The guards had been rostered on, had they?

Lockyer looked at him blankly. Tuckwell clicked his tongue and shook his head: had the Reverend forgotten to tell him about the market? Such a lot on his mind ... Not before time, was it? The Factory was way too full ...

Lockyer pulled out his notebook and scribbled himself a reminder. Yes, he would see to it. Was there much interest? Tuckwell nodded; the Reverend was expecting quite a few takers. Chance to clear the decks, and not before time. Lockyer simply nodded. Matron Gordon was in her office, was she? She was: Tuckwell had run the latest assignment by her only that morning: one of the new arrivals. Adams, Lizzie. Per Harmony. A domestic. The very thing he wanted to see her about, said Lockyer and strode on, past the carding room, along the corridor, up the stairs.

* * *

In the carding room, Em and Sarah sat side by side among the other carders, their hands rhythmically moving the toothed wooden paddles forward and back, forward and back until the rough became smooth, until the matted wool fibres fell soft and spinnable. Not that either girl's mind was on her hands. Em was casing the Factory, room by room, yard by yard, wall by wall. Sarah was strolling round the gardens at Holyrood, looking at the herbs she and her Dad had planted – lavender, rosemary, rue – then the flowers – geraniums, lilac, verbena, and roses, lots of roses: pinks and reds and a single white climber. Suddenly, her hands stopped moving.

'Em,' she hissed. 'Em!'

'What?'

'We were supposed to go to Matron's office. We never did.'

***

Lockyer passed Elizabeth Raine going down the stairs as he went up; he bowed but did not stop. What on earth did she want? Never mind: he knocked on Ann's door, went in at her call. Ann rose to greet him, glancing at her clock. He was early. Quick word before the meeting, he said. Their cook was sick. Mabel, his wife, had organised for a doctor to take a look at her. That was all done; what they needed now was a new domestic. Sooner the better, really. A Factory lass, one of the younger ones, somebody Mabel could take in hand and teach. Fit, healthy; the sooner the better.

Ann's eyes lit up; she believed she knew just the one. She sat down and pulled her day book towards her. A frown flickered across her face.

'While it's just you, Major ... what's this I hear about Bridget Murphy?

***

In her cell, Molly looked up at her window and tried to guess what time it was.

CHAPTER NINETEEN

Once Upon a Time

'Didn't expect a visit from Joan. Didn't think she'd manage it. She's a smart one.'

'She's a smart one all right. Where there's a will there's a way, and there's a will, believe you me.'

Rosie glanced sharply at the old woman in her chair by the door. 'You know she's pregnant, don't you?'

Mary didn't look up. She hugged the sobbing child in her lap closer. 'No. I did not.'

Rosie moved back to the bed. 'Well, she is. She's just told the new Matron.'

'There, there.' Mary jiggled the child in her lap; the sobs were easing. So: pregnant. She pinched her lips in tightly; didn't make any difference. She'd go for the job anyway, say it was meant for her, settle right in, bairn and all. Mary eyed the brown spots on the back of her hand; when did there get to be so many?

'Wanted to know about the birth, of course.' Rosie lowered herself on to the bed. 'Had a cuddle.'

Mary pushed the child off her knee and sniffed irritably. 'Off you go, that's a girl, off you go and play. Wanted to know about the birth, did she? I just bet she did. Told her I fell over, did you?'

'No. Why would I? Made no difference, did it? Like you said, it could have happened to anyone.'

Mary Jane was still clinging; the old woman pushed her away again. 'Here's your stick. Go on, shoo! Off you go!' She turned back to Rosie. 'Didn't, but, did it? Happened to me. Doddery old biddy me.'

'So it did.' Rosie eyed the thinning hair, the wizened throat and rheumy eyes. Not much of her, she thought. Joan's not wrong. 'Bears thinking about, don't it?'

Mary Jane trotted back and laid the stick across the old woman's knees. Mary snatched it up. 'Off you go, I said! Away on out of here before I tan your hide!' She threw the stick out the door. 'There! Outside, now, outside!'

Mary Jane ran out. The old woman sat back, her lips pinching in and out.

There was a heavy silence. Finally, Rosie got up and pulled another chair close to the old woman. She sat down and took hold of her hand. 'Mary, it's me. I'm not trying to get rid of you, I'm trying to help you. What are you going to do? You know yourself you're not going to be able to manage much longer.'

'I've a few years in me yet! She'd have me out on my ear tomorrow!'

'No, she wouldn't. She's just thinking ahead. And I was thinking too. I was thinking that Joan's not the only one to have had a few bairns and know what she's doing.'

The old hand quivered: skin and bone, thought Rosie, skin and bone. 'I'm talking about me, Mary. We could do it together, you know. The two of us. I could go and see the Matron. I mean, you know every inch of the place, you could show me. She'd see the sense of that, anybody would. Save her any bother. You could help me and I could help you.'

Mary stared at their two hands. 'What, you mean take turns?'

'Something like that.' Rosie smiled. 'None of us getting any younger.'

Mary shook her head and closed her eyes. Rosie let go her hand and checked on the baby. Sound asleep. When she turned round, Mary was leaning forward, clutching the edge of her chair. 'They'd never allow it. Would they?'

'Don't see why not.' With a little grunt, Rosie swung her feet up on to the bed and lay back.

'Worth a try.'

Mary rocked to and fro, nodding. Abruptly, she pushed herself to her feet and went to the wall cupboard. Opening it, she pulled out a small cloth bag, kissed it and turned toward Rosie. 'Catch!' She tossed the bag and Rosie caught it. She turned it slowly in her hand, feeling the silk of the faded ribbon, crumbling the grains inside.

'A lavender bag?' She held it to her nose.

Mary nodded. 'No scent, lost its scent years ago. Damn near as old as I am. Came out with me on the ship. Used to bury my nose in it. Long time ago.'

'What did they do you for?'

'Murder.'

'What?' Rosie gaped at the old woman.

Mary chuckled. 'That shook you, didn't it? Never think it, to look at me now. Murderess. That's what she called me, that's what she mouthed at me the whole way through the trial. But in the end the only charge they could make stick was manslaughter. Anderson. That was the name. I was their nursemaid after Gino died.'

She paused. Rosie opened her mouth, then thought better of it. She waited.

'Gino was my husband. Half Itie, you see. Mother was Italian. Sailor. Until his ship went down and all on board were lost.' Mary pointed at the lavender bag. 'He gave it me. I wasn't bad looking myself, believe it or not.' She shook her head.' Ancient history. Ancient history.'

Rosie wriggled up straighter on the bed. 'Well? Go on ...'

'It's not a very nice story. For somebody that's just had a baby.'

'Don't be silly. Take my mind off my aching arse.' Rosie patted the bed. 'Come on, this is softer than hard wood. You could do with a rest.'

'Yes. Yes, I could that.' Mary settled herself at the opposite end of the bed.

'Well. Well ... Liverpool is a big port, you know, ships from all over.

Blond men, black men, slant eyes. Like I said, Gino was half Itie. Beautiful he was, if that's a word you can use for a man. The longest eyelashes ... and knew it. Oh, didn't he just! Like they all do. I used to get these nightmares after the news of the drowning and.it was them eyelashes I'd see, round this big black hole, with fish swimming in and out ... crabs, scuttling and nipping ... used to be when he was away I'd shut my eyes and picture those eyes of his, but I stopped that once he died. Cause then I'd start thinking about what the crabs were doing to them.' She held out her hand and Rosie tossed her the little bag. 'See this? Last thing he give me before he sailed. No scent left, no good any more. Like me. Lived too long, that's my trouble, far too bloody long. Anyhow: Gino and me got married and they were the best two years of my life. But then the Toscana went down and all were lost and they were the worst.

My sister took me in. I got work as a cleaner. I started doing for Mrs Allsop; proper sweetheart she was, God rest her soul. Probably about as old then as I am now. Anyhow, she got sick. Bedrid for months, she was. I looked after her till she died. Her son in London came up then, and he shook my hand and thanked me. And he give me a recommendation to the people in the big house just down the road. Mr and Mrs Anderson. Money coming out their ears, they had. I thought to myself, you've fallen on your feet here, girl, you surely have. Little did I know.

Rosie patted Mary's hand.

'Anyhow, I was nursemaid to their son Teddy. Seven year old he was, and a spoilt brat. Not a patch on my Tony.'

'You had a child?'

Mary nodded. 'Still have, somewhere. I hope. Tony: short for Antonio. The spitting image of my Gino. But I doubt he remembers his old mam.'

'Go on.'

'Well, the Andersons were at some big garden party and it was a sunny day so I took Teddy out for a walk. I went by my sister's place, which was close handy, and I picked up Tony. I did that every so often, you see; otherwise I hardly ever got to see him, my own son. In the daytime, when he was awake. And Teddy was an only child, so he liked having another to show off to because Tony was only four and couldn't do stuff like Teddy could. Anyhow, Tony was in the pram and we were walking along the towpath by the river ...'

Mary blinked hard and swallowed. 'Sorry. Stupid, after all these years, stupid. But there it is. Anyway, the long and short of it is, we stopped for a rest and Teddy started skimming stones in the river. I'd lifted Tony out and he tried to copy him, but of course he couldn't do it, he just toddled toddled about. Teddy started yelling "Fetch! Go fetch!" Then Teddy grabbed him ... he was a big lad, stout ... grabbed him round the middle and bounced him up and down. "Yap yap," he went. I can hear it yet: "Yappity yap yap!" Then he dropped him. Where the bank was steepest. Tony rolled, that fast he rolled, and he fell into the water. Straight under he went, then up again, his little face all streaming and gasping and I jumped in. I just managed to get hold of him and drag him back to the bank. It was that slippery, and he was bawling and thrashing about ... then the next thing, Teddy's gone. He's run up on to the bridge, the bridge Tony would have been swept under if I hadn't jumped in. He's jumping up and down and yelling 'come on, come on' and shaking the rail.' Mary sighed and shook her head. 'Well. The rail broke. Teddy fell in.'

Mary's eyes were brimming. 'What was I supposed to do? Tony was bawling his head off, I couldn't leave him. I ran with him in my arms, ran screaming for help. This man saw me and dashed over, but by the time he'd jumped in Teddy had gone under again.' She swiped a hand across her eyes. 'So there you are. I'm a murderess.'

Rosie sat up and moved to the end of the bed. 'That's awful. Just awful. But not murder, Mary. Just ... just nothing you could have done.'

'But there might have been, if I hadn't been holding on to Tony. It might never have happened if Tony hadn't been there. Dereliction of duty, they called it.' Mary sniffed. 'Anyhow. That's why I'm here. And why I'm in here, if you see what I mean.' She looked around the room. 'Making up for it. Been making up for it ever since.'

'How long?'

'Fifteen year.'

A squeak: Rosie lifted the baby, brought her back to the bed and guided the blindly seeking mouth to her nipple. 'Must have delivered a hell of a lot of babies.'

'Yes.' Mary reached out and stroked the small head. 'Lost count. Bonny wee Bonnie, eh?'

'I don't know. Mary might be better.'

'Oh no. Bonnie. Keep it Bonnie. Too many Marys.'

'Like Rosie. Too many Rosies.'

'Nottingham, you said?'

'That's right. Near Sherwood Forest. Robin Hood, you know?' Rosie grinned wryly. 'Outlaws. Like us. Nothing much special about me, though; no murders. I just stole stuff. After Edward died. Framework knitter, he was. I made lace. Fancy work. Not much fancy work here.'

'What sort of stuff did you steal?'

'Bit of this, bit of that: cutlery ... clothes ... what I got done for was a greatcoat. They followed me home from the pawn shop.'

'What about your children? Four, you said.'

'That's right. Young Edward, and William, and Annie and Kitty. My friend next door took them in, God bless her. I got word once, after I'd been here a year. Off this woman I knew who got sent here as well. It was a note and it said 'dear mother we are all rite. Yours E.' That's Edward, the eldest. And then 4 thumbprints, each with their initial. It's stitched into my skirt. He's a good boy, he'll look after the others. Like his father.' Rosie looked down at her baby. 'What would they think of you, I wonder?'

'This one's father's a convict, ain't he?'

Rosie nodded. 'Martin, his name was ... is, I suppose. Carpenter by trade: he was building stables for the people at the place I was assigned to, him and that other bastard. I used to have to take them out their dinner.' She shrugged. 'Martin was nothing like Ed, but Ed was gone and I wasn't. You can't spend your life weeping ... and that was the thing. He made me laugh. Real strange it felt, to be laughing again ... and with a man. Only that put his workmate's nose out of joint. He didn't see why Martin should be getting it and him not, so he shoved me up against the stable wall and

… oh!'

Rosie covered her mouth. Mary heaved herself from the bed and curtsied stiffly. 'Matron Gordon!' Mary glanced at Rosie, on her feet and standing over her baby. 'We were just having a rest. We'd only just got the new little one to sleep, you see.'

'I see. I was told we had a new arrival. That is why I am here. You are the mother? Rose Watson?'

Rosie nodded.

'And you are well? The babe is well?' Ann looked from Rosie to Mary. Both nodded.

'Boy or girl? Have you got a name?'

'Girl, Ma'am. Bonnie. Her name's Bonnie.'

'That's a pretty name; and she looks a pretty enough child … what I can see of her. What about the father? Do we have a second name?'

Rosie and Mary exchanged glances. 'Watson,' said Rosie.

'You mean you don't know the father's name.'

Rosie shrugged. 'Martin Brown. There'd be a few Browns about, Matron.'

You're not wrong there … and when would she ever see him anyway?

'You never know,' Mary patted Rosie's arm. 'You never do know, Rosie. Maybe he'll come looking for you. One Market Day …'

Market Day again; to market, to market, to buy a fat … Tuckwell. Good name. Still, the man seems to know what he's doing …

'Yes, Mr Tuckwell has already spoken to me about Market Day.' Ann eyed Rosie. 'Too soon for you, I think. You will hardly be there.'

'No, Ma'am.'

But maybe another time. It is a way out, I suppose. Though who's going to take her on with a baby? Ann bent down and stroked the downy little head.

***

Another baby: and another on the way: Joan Campbell's. Unless that man of hers comes good. More mouths to feed. Back in her office, Ann sat down at her desk and sighed. A knock at the door.

'Come in … Major Lockyer!' She stood and waved him to a seat, but he shook his head.

'What can I do for you?'

'I have brought Molly Malone for her interview as you requested, Matron.'

What? That time already?

'Thank you, Major. Bring her in.'

Lockyer held the door open. The big woman strode to the front of the desk, one of Lockyer's men hurrying after. She stood with her hands clasped behind her, feet planted wide, eyes fixed on the wall. In spite of herself, Ann flinched. The woman was so pale, so gaunt, like a ghost. *She has been in solitary, remember. What do you expect?* Ann lowered herself into her seat and looked up at Lockyer. He turned towards his charge; he was not much taller.

'Right, Molly.' He nodded. 'You know to behave yourself.'

Molly glanced at him indifferently. Her heavy-lidded eyes flicked from Lockyer to the woman on the other side of the desk, then to the wall behind. Ann sat up straighter in her chair. She waved a dismissive hand.

'Thank you, Major. The Constable can wait outside.'

Lockyer raised his eyebrows. 'In view of this woman's record, Matron …'

And your man barely comes up to her shoulders …

'I said, your man can wait outside the door. I shall call when I am done.'

'The usual procedure …'

'This is my procedure, Major. Should there be any need, I will call.'

'Very well.' The Major bowed and stepped back. 'As you please. You heard, Jones. Wait outside the door. The least thing, Matron, insolence, lack of respect, you call. Don't stand for any nonsense.'

'Don't worry, Major. I do not expect to.'

Lockyer followed his man out. Ann looked down at her day book, then up into those deep set, dark circled eyes. What now, said those eyes, as clearly as if their owner had spoken.

What now indeed? Ann pushed her chair back and crossed to the window overlooking the yard. *Bit of distance, that's what I need* ... She turned around.

The woman had turned as well; they stood facing each other. Ann wrapped her hands around the keyring at her waist and took a deep breath.

'You are a long way from Ireland, Molly Malone.'

Molly tipped her head to one side and grimaced. 'True. By time and by tide at any rate.'

What's that supposed to mean?

'You have been here five years, I believe? What age are you now?'

'I am in my forty fifth year.'

'Not married, evidently. No other family?'

'I am not married. My family is in Ireland. My brother's and my daughter's.'

'You have a daughter? Illegitimate, I suppose?'

'Her father was killed before we could marry. Our Maeve is wed, though, with bairns of her own. That'll be half grown by now.'

Father killed ... Like Letitia's.

'I see. And the father of your child, he did not provide for you? He made no provision for his daughter?'

'He made no provision for being killed. He never knew he had a daughter, more's the pity. He'd have been as good a father as my own.'

Take your time. Take your time.

'Also, presumably, dead.'

'Oh yes. Long gone.' Molly looked around the room. 'Knew nothing about any of this, thanks be. Neither him nor Charlie.'

'Charlie? Is that your daughter's father?'

'Yes. Though like I said, Maeve never knew him. More's the pity. All she's got is his fiddle. He was a great fiddler; he could earn more from one night playing at some hooley than a week pushing a weaver's shuttle.'

'Hooley?'

'Celebration. Dance. Get together.'

I see what Marsden means: literate. Educated, even. 'According to your records, you are guilty of assault. Of causing grievous bodily harm.'

'I am. I did. Guilty as charged.'

'A violent crime. A brutal attack.'

'Yes.'

'You show no remorse.'

'Remorse? That's a hard word. Yes and no.'

What am I supposed to make of that? She doesn't sound remorseful; but there again, what does remorseful sound like? Fierce enough looking: those dark circles under the eyes, those scars on her head ... but she doesn't sound fierce. She was the singer at the laundry, according to the notes ...

Molly shifted, clasping her hands in front instead of behind. *What's she doing, should I call? No, why would she? She's just settling herself. Hasn't spoken to anybody for days, remember. Right then; come on, Molly Malone, what else have you got to say for yourself?*

'Yes and no. And what exactly is that supposed to mean?'

The pale face softened, the lips twisting.

'Matron Gordon, so. And you never said. You've some nerve; I'll say that for you.'

'You'll say no such thing! Insolent is a hard word too. You mind your tongue, Molly Malone.'

'The other day, Ma'am, that's what I mean. Standing there cool as you please, telling us you were just visiting. Just visiting!' Molly chuckled.

Ann drew herself up as she had when the crowd of women had come milling round her and Robert. 'At that time, just visiting is exactly what we were doing. My husband and I. We were certainly not expecting to be set upon by such a mob. Led by you. My difficulty is not your guilt. All of you are guilty, after all, or you would not be here. My difficulty is that you confess quite readily to violent crime, but appear quite unrepentant. If it has done nothing else, the time you have served here should have at least caused you to reflect upon the error of your ways. But you seem to be quite indifferent.'

'Confess, is it? I have never been to Confession in my life and I have no notion of starting now. I'll leave that to Matron Raine.'

'You are insolent ... again!'

'No, Ma'am. I'm Presbyterian.'

Ann looked down at her hands to hide the involuntary twitch of her lips. She flexed her fingers. 'You admit, then, to inciting riot? You admit that you are a troublemaker?'

Molly lifted her chin and replied, slowly and deliberately. 'What your difficulty is, Ma'am, is entirely up to you. But begging your pardon, why would I go to the bother of making trouble when it's out there readymade and waiting? Why would I pick a fight when I've already lost the biggest fight of my life? As for inciting to violence, where was the violence? Yes, there was damage to the gate, but that's property. Where was the damage to flesh and blood? Did any of your smart young soldier laddies get so much as a scratch?'

'A broken nose is a lot more than a scratch.'

'That was after we broke out, not before. That had nothing to do with the break out. Begging your pardon again, Ma'am, but there's only so much even a lag should have to take. The man had it coming.'

'Enough! No wonder your head has been shaved. Not that it seems to have taught you anything.'

Was that a sneer? And a shrug. Take your time, take your time. 'I see from your records that you have been sent back from assignment twice.'

'Records? And who did the recording, were they there? Did they record that the only reason I got sent back from Lloyds was because they were returning to England? That I was there for a year and more and it wasn't just me got sent back, it was the cook and the groom as well? Did they record that Mrs Lloyd gave me a tin whistle?' Molly sniffed. 'I doubt it. But it's the truth, for all it's the word of a violent offender.'

There was a pause. *What else? Keep her talking ...*

Molly nodded towards Ann's desk. 'For all I know, that whistle's still at the bottom of one of those drawers. Decent folk, the Lloyds. Sydney town, that was.'

'Indeed. You feel qualified to pass judgement, do you? You are not backward in coming forward, are you?'

'No, Ma'am. Should I be?'

Ignore that ... keep going ...

'What do you say to your second return? I suppose I am to believe that there was no assault there either?'

'Depends who's doing the assaulting. That was Sydney as well. Big house, upstairs downstairs, you spent your life running up and down stairs. The long and the short of that one, Ma'am, is that my lord and master wouldn't take no for an answer. So when I shoved him off for the umpteenth time, wasn't it just his bad luck that he'd chosen the top of the stairs to grab me? Bumpety bumpety bump, down he went, all the way down, effing and blinding all the way. The air was black and blue, I'm telling you! Anyway. He broke his ankle. Look before you lech, I said, look before you bloody well lech ...'

Look before you lech; save that one for Rob ...

'Hard to believe now, of course.' Molly rolled her eyes. 'But I wasn't bad looking once. When I'd a head of hair instead of a scabby scalp.'

This was not the interview she'd intended to have. Ann returned to her desk, sat down and picked up her pen. Careful: don't let her see ... She wagged the pen to and fro. *Dangerous, remember? Could be telling you a pack of lies, leading you up the garden path ... What was it Marsden said? Malice afore thought, that was it. Plausible, I'd say plausible was a better word. The best liars are always plausible. Might trip herself up yet.*

'You are from the North of Ireland, I see. Per the Resolution.'

'That's right. County Antrim. A little place called Templepatrick. We moved there from Belfast after my father retired from the printing business; he was a typesetter. Not that he really retired; carted his letterpress out with him and turned the shed in the backyard into a another print shop for the Northern Star.'

Ann started, unable to hide her surprise. *The Northern Star: the United Irishmen's paper! Wolfe Tone, the '98 rebellion, all that mayhem, all that bloody madness. Fifteen years later, Robert's regiment posted there because they still weren't over it, still needed an army to keep them ... under. Keep them under ... Her father a typesetter: who was this woman?*

'I see you know it, Ma'am.'

'I recognise the name.' Ann set her pen down. 'Not that I have ever read it, of course. However, my husband's regiment was stationed in Limerick before we came here. The uprising had long since been quelled, but unfortunately there were still disturbances. Unrest. The regiment was stationed there to restore law and order.'

'Serving King and Country, then. Well: King anyway.'

'King and Country. Exactly.'

1798: the Year of Liberty. Wolfe Tone and his United Irishmen. Some liberty; the whole of Ireland up in flames ... Talk about scabby scalps, there were plenty of them, plenty of cut and bleeding ones too. The whole country was bleeding, north to south, Belfast to Dublin. Even on our posting, so many years later, you'd still see them, the walking wounded ... or the not walking, the crippled and the maimed, begging on street corners. That song, that fiddler at the market: 'you haven't an arm and you haven't a leg, haroo, haroo!' She probably knows it. She could probably sing it ...

'Does that explain it, Ma'am?'

'Explain what?'

'Violent times, Ma'am. Violent crimes.'

Don't give an inch ... Ann drew herself up. 'I fail to see how it could. There can never be any excuse for criminal behaviour.'

'I was 16 in '98. There was a war on. North to south, crime and violence, violence and crime. It's what I grew up with.'

'As did many others. Who did not become violent criminals. Who did not abuse their liberty. Who had more respect for the law, who understood the consequences.'

'Consequences? Since when have consequences stopped anybody? I'm not making excuses either. What I'm saying is that sometimes you have only one answer in you.'

Molly's gaze returned to the wall, her eyes wide and unfocussed. Ann went to speak, then changed her mind and waited. Silence. After a long moment, she glanced at her clock and tapped her pen. 'It would be your father, I presume, who taught you to read and write.'

A vague nod. 'You presume right, God rest his soul.'

Molly blinked, then shook her head and looked Ann in the eye again. 'You'd also presume that he was a rebel, wouldn't you? And you'd be right. My father was a United Irishman. A violent criminal, according to the likes of you and your husband. Like father, like daughter, so. But here's where your accordinglies go wrong. He was for a United Ireland, he was for liberty, head and heart, heart and head. But he never drew blood for it. He never struck a single blow, my father. It was your English troopers that struck the blows, your bully boys that broke into his shop and wrecked the place: papers, inks, moulds, rags, whatever ... stacked them round that big wooden brute of a press and set fire to it ... went up like a rocket ... they're your violent criminals! Arson, that's the word, arson!' Molly's eyes were white-ringed, wild.

Ann bit her lip. *What to say?*

'It was a war. Dreadful things happen in wars.' The words rang hollow, even to herself.

Molly didn't seem to have heard her. 'The bloody heathen that stood over my father, the bastard who flung methylated spirits in his face and then set him alight, he's your violent criminal. Blinded him. 1797, that was, before it had even started. Hard to fight when you're blind.'

Stay still, don't move. Don't say a word. She's been in isolation, remember, all this in her head ...

'Fifteen. I was fifteen. Ma used to send me over with his lunch. I'd only just handed him the basket when we heard the clatter of hooves, the thumping and hammering at the door. He was the only one there because it was a Sunday, but they were behind with the next issue, so he'd gone in specially ... anyhow. He shoved me inside a cupboard and stood in front of it. If you're for wrecking, he said to them when they came charging in, the press is through there. He didn't move, just stood there while they barged past and started wrecking the place.

'When they'd done, the Captain came back and grabbed my father by the collar. He shoved him against the cupboard door. I was crouched down inside, peering through the lattice work. He still never moved, not even when that bastard flung the meths. Not even when he pulled out his tinderbox.' Molly closed her eyes. 'Even after he'd poured the stinking stuff, even after he'd tossed away the empty can, I don't think my father believed he was going to do it. I don't think he believed anybody could do that. But I saw that bastard's face leaning in, I saw it lit up in the flare when the sparks flew off the flint. I saw his fat pink lips. I saw him laughing before they turned and bolted.'

Molly swayed. Around her, the room seemed to shift, the air itself to be reeling. 'And I'm out of the cupboard and he's screaming and I'm dragging him outside to the tap and turning it on full bore and shoving his head under ...'

So many years, going over it and over it ... alone in that cell ...

Molly had taken hold of the desk to steady herself. Ann started towards her but was waved away. The tick of the clock on the desk between them seemed the only movement, ticking world to world. Molly leant there, shoulders shaking. Finally, she shook her head, straightened up and folded her arms under her chest.

'Better call, hadn't you? Better call. Woman must be demented. Probably is. Probably am. Was for sure when I saw that bastard again. Twenty years later. Twenty years and my father long dead. But not forgotten, not that day, not that smell of burnt flesh, not that sound of my father screaming. Twenty years later, that same Captain and his men came clattering into my brother's forge. His horse had cast a shoe.

'I knew him the second I set eyes on him. Older and fatter, busting out of his uniform, but him, him! The same fat pink lips, the same ugly wee spits of eyes.' Molly's laugh was a whiplash. She thrust her two hands out in front of her, fisting them. 'So being the violent criminal I am, Matron, well, grabbed the tongs, didn't I? Pulled the horse shoe out of the fire, didn't I? White hot it was, so bright, so blazing ... and I rammed it into his fat cheek. And no, I didn't blind the bastard, but by Christ I branded him!'

The carriage clock ticked. And ticked.

Molly dropped her hands to her sides and shrugged. 'So. There you have it. Guilty as charged. Transported for Life. Or something like it.' She grimaced. 'You're quite right. Never did learn to mind my tongue. You've got to want to learn, you see. You've got to want to learn.'

CHAPTER TWENTY

Love and Marriage

Ann sat at her escritoire with her head in her hands. She didn't move, not even when Robert came up behind her, put his hands on her shoulders and kneaded gently. 'Thank you, thank you. That's nice ...'

'Long day, eh?'

'I have not stopped ... and just as I'm about to lock the door, Bill Tuckwell turns up and hands me this.' She picked up the list on her desk and fanned it at him.

'What's that?'

'The list for Market Day. Tomorrow.'

'Market Day?'

'Marriage market. Marrying them off. The women. Marsden's idea, apparently. Men come to the Factory and pick a wife. Too many men, you see, not enough women. Parramatta, Sydney, whole damn colony. The farmer wants a wife – except here it's the convict. *Hey ho, my deario, the convict wants a wife*! So. Seems they line the women up for the men to inspect. Sometimes they will have one picked out already, seen her when she was on assignment or on her way from the boat. Some have made enquiries, some are just there to have a look. Anyway, they take their pick and check with us. Then we let the woman know. She can say no, she is allowed to say no, Tuckwell made a big point of that. She might be due her ticket of leave, for example, or just been assigned and decided that was a better bet.'

Ann pulled a face. 'Devil you know and the devil you don't. Anyway, if she says yes, off they trot to Reverend Marsden to be joined in holy matrimony. Hurray! They're off our hands. No longer our problem. On their own heads be ... whatever comes next.' She set the list down. 'But at least no is a possibility.'

'What, no to a chance to get out of the Factory? Not much of a possibility.'

'Apparently some do say no, and not just because of what I just said. Bill Tuckwell told me he remembers one "customer"... they're all "customers" to him ... anyhow, this pert looking customer about a year ago turned round to the man who'd picked her and asked what sort of pin money he was offering. Then told him she'd changed her mind, it wasn't enough!'

Robert laughed. 'Pin money! That's rich ... not! Got to admire the hide of her, though. Think she was marrying for love.'

Ann looked up at him, eyebrow raised. 'What, like us you mean?'

He kissed the top of her head. 'Yes, dear. Like us. Exactly right.'

'The children ...'

'That's all right, they can stay with me. You'll have to be at this market, won't you? To market to market ... to see how they jig ... The children will be fine. They can run about the Store.'

'Seriously, can you take them? I haven't got anybody yet ... you're not too busy?'

'Not yet. I'll say this for Bill Tuckwell, he runs a tight ship. Yes, that's fine.'

'He likes his i's dotted and his t's crossed, doesn't he? Marsden has him well trained. That's excellent, dear, thank you. One less thing to worry about. It'll get better once I get into a routine, I know it will. It's just that they keep springing things on me and forget that nobody's told me. There's so much to remember. Don't think I've talked so much in years, hear how scratchy my voice is? And I don't rattle on anything like Elizabeth Raine. Oh, keep doing that, please. I'll sleep tonight, and that's for sure.'

Robert smiled and kept on kneading. In a few moments, he bent to nuzzle the top of her head. 'Pretty cosy set up, eh? Matron and Storekeeper? All expenses paid, or about to be.' She leant her head back against him and smiled. He cupped her breasts. For a few seconds, she let herself drift; then set her hands firmly on top of his and lifted them off.

'Not now, dear, not now. I've got to finish this. Make sure I've got it all memorised ... and dinner. Haven't even thought about dinner yet ...' She frowned, shaking her head.

He took her chin between finger and thumb. 'Know what? I was in the kitchens earlier. I could pop over again and have a quick chat to the cook. See if she'll put something together for us.'

'That's a good idea; that's a very good idea. Would you?' Ann picked up her list.

Moments later, she looked out the window and saw her husband disappearing in the direction of the kitchens. Easy come, easy go, that was Robert. Hard to stay angry with. Drove her demented half the time, but he had his moments. The army really should have done more for him. He should have been able to get something solid out of the years he'd served instead of having to come up with a hare-brained scheme like Burragorang. What did he know about buying a property or running a farm, back at home, never mind out here? One day, perhaps. Storekeeping, that'd keep him occupied.

You could have done an awful lot worse, Matron Gordon. Wouldn't even be here if it wasn't for him, would you?

She scanned the list of hopeful husbands; none of the names meant anything to her. Never mind: they might after tomorrow. And then there were the Harmony women that she still hadn't got to because she'd spent too long with Molly. And those two scamps of girls that she'd sent for ... and Joan. Joan knew what she wanted, all right. Which was fair enough: she liked that about her. What to do about old Mary, though?

And what to do about Molly. Molly Malone. She stared out the window.

* * *

Marry for love: Robert chuckled. That wasn't what made a marriage, Ann knew that as well as he did. No, you married somebody you could get on with out of the bedroom as well as in, somebody with a good head on her shoulders, somebody who made life easier. He'd got Ann out of her little stumble ... stumble, tumble ... all those years ago and he'd never regretted it. They'd done well: she'd taken on New South Wales and made the best of it. Took things as they came, didn't look back. Kept a weather eye on the books, turned a blind eye if she had to ... not that she had, lately. He'd be losing his touch. Right now, he was happy enough being Mr Matron. Mr Storekeeper Matron. Worth her weight in gold, the old Ann.

She'd have that list memorised by the time he got back: like the keys. This morning, as he'd left to meet Tuckwell, she'd been sitting on the edge of the bed studying that damn key ring again, key by key. Memorizing them, shutting her eyes and testing herself. He shook his head: woman had lists on the brain.

A few years and they should have enough to buy a decent block of land. No more sucking up to banks or senior officers. Gentleman farmer, that was the ticket. He smiled to himself. That was the ticket of leave for him.

***

'This Market Day duty we've got, what does that involve?'

George tilted his chair back against the mess hall wall and grinned. 'Ah! Not really a market, Andy, more of a circus. They line the lovely ladies up, you know, our factory belles, such as they are ... then single men can come and take their pick. They come from round here, from Sydney, or they might be passing through and just taking a look. Then they pick a ride; I mean, bride.' With a grin, he nudged Andy. 'As the Bible says, mate. Multiply and replenish the earth. We won't have to do much. Good for a laugh, usually. The women are all on their best behaviour, chests out, batting their eyelashes, you know, chewing their lips to make them redder.'

Andy smiled. 'What about the men?'

'The men are a bit of a mixture. Anybody and everybody, really. Settlers from some god forsaken property after somebody ... anybody ... to do the needful for them, and yes, that does mean everything you're thinking. You get dockworkers, tradesmen, shop keepers: mostly ex-convicts, ticket of leave men. Checking out the goods. Matron Raine and Bill Tuckwell run the show. I expect Bill will be in charge this time; give the new Matron a chance to learn the ropes.'

'So we're pretty much just in case?'

'That's right. Just in case any of them step out of line. Last time there was a scrag fight. You could see it coming a mile off; tart knows this man, see: ex-convict, ticket of leave, dock worker. She's simpering and making googly eyes at him and waiting for him to stretch out his hand and whisk her away from all this ... but then he walks straight past her! Seen a better-looking piece further along! Her face, mate: priceless! Anyhow, they call the second one's name and she's walking past the first when number one trips her up. Then they're at each other screeching like those bloody cockatoos last night, biting and punching till the second boots the first fair in the guts and we manage to pull them apart. Fistfuls of hair, ripped clothes: took four of us!'

'What did he do then? The man, I mean?'

'Him? He just stood there grinning. There we were, dragging them off by the hind legs and what's he doing? Wandering on down the line to see if there's a tastier one!'

'And did he take her? The second one, I mean?'

'He did. And she trotted along like nothing had happened.' George shrugged. 'You'd cry if you didn't laugh, I swear, cry if you didn't laugh! Anyhow, that's tomorrow. Hardly the kind of marrying that's on your mind, is it?' He leant across confidentially. 'I've got it all organised. Harry's, I mean. We've got the night off, we can sign out early. Got the other lads all lined up.'

'I been thinking, though, George; what if we're seen? What if Emily's father finds out? The chief surgeon? What's he going to think?'

'He's going to think you're a red-blooded boy who'll make his daughter a good husband, that's what he's going to think. Don't you worry: bet you what you like he did the same when he was a young bloke.'

'Doubt it. I mean, seriously. He's a church elder. They watch over Emily like a hawk, him and his wife.'

'Yes, I've heard the Missus is a bit of a dragon. Must run in the family; didn't you say Emily couldn't stand the one in London?'

'You don't think Emily could turn out like that?'

'Not if you show her who's boss from the word go. Stag night: what it's all about. Done thing. She'll expect it. Then she can say she's reformed you.'

'Reform? What do you mean?'

'Well, every daddy's girl needs a sinful young man to reform, doesn't she? Before she promises to love, honour and obey. Obey: remember that! Anyhow, Harry's is all settled, so there's no pulling out now. Now. You ready for that return game of poker?'

'Right. Right. And I'll damn well beat you this time.'

'Now, now, don't be in too big a hurry! You know what they say ... lucky in cards, unlucky in love ...'

* * *

Molly sat staring up through the thick dark; she couldn't even make out the window slit. It seemed darker because she'd been out, she supposed: she'd had to hold her arm over her eyes as Lockyer and his man steered her across the yard, up the stairs to the Matron's office. She winced. What had got into her? A right exhibition she'd made of herself, raving on like that in front of that woman! Matron, jailer, whatever. She put her head in her hands and squeezed her eyes until the dark shuddered.

Stop it: look up. The Gordon woman hadn't called the guard in, had she? Like she'd said, the woman had some nerve. Very different kettle of fish from Rainey, that was for sure. So that was good. She'd just sat there and listened. Until she'd mentioned the Star: the face of her!

Limerick, she'd said. That would be right, they'd put troops all over. But it was what she said later, did she mean it, that was the thing. About somebody to copy out lists, and did she think she could do that sort of work. Of course, of course she did! Molly held up her fingers and flexed them. Sooner rather than later, Matron Gordon had said, sooner rather than later. A couple of hours each day, getting those lists done. Why would she say that if she didn't mean it? It was good, wasn't it? Keep flexing those fingers ...

Dark, dark, dark. Like it had been for her father. Three whole years of opening his eyes to darkness: this was nothing to that. *We just have to learn to thole, my dear; just put up with whatever life gives us to put up with.* Right or wrong, fair or not fair, be patient. Take your time, don't let time take you. Good word, thole. Pity she hadn't tholed in the smithy that day ...

There's a time and a place, a place and a time, my dear. Father dear: if you could see me now ... this time, this place?

Stop. Think high, think sky; think yourself out of it. Think yourself back to the garden at Templepatrick, sitting beside him to read the newspaper. The Northern Star, the Belfast Newsletter: talk to him, cheer him up, keep talking. Talk him through the bitter fighting and the bloody fallen at Donegore, at Antrim, at Ballynahinch. And when the talking was done, put your arm around him and hold on.

Wolfe Tone, Henry Joy McCracken, her own Charlie: just names now. Irishmen united in death: so many deaths. Though Father never knew about that last one. For her Father, Charlie was always the one that got away, the one who was coming back from America to marry his daughter as soon as it was safe ...

Our big chance, Molly, thrown away, tossed out the window! She could hear his voice, hear him going over old speeches and letters to neighbours, or just to himself, the light he couldn't see glinting off the web of scars round his eyes. Irish poetry, he recited, screeds and screeds of it, stored away in his brain like honey: she'd be up feeding Maeve in the next room, and she'd hear his voice, the words plucked out of the air like notes from a harp.

He had talked once about getting her harp lessons. Her twelfth birthday, that was, he'd taken her to the Belfast Harp festival. The loveliest sound in the world, did she not think? She did, oh she did: at the time. But then she forgot. Such a civilised, elegant instrument: far too elegant, far too civilised for her. Give her a fiddle any day. And then it was too late for lessons. Then the Star disappeared, along with the picture of the harp on its masthead.

Feeding Maeve, early and late, listening to him, thinking of the hours he must be lying awake, thinking through the dark. Like her, now. Strange, that the light should wake him; but it seemed to. Up with her baby, the hum of his voice came with the light sliding under the drapes. She'd take the baby through and read to him until they heard Sam opening the big doors to the forge and his hammer on the anvil. And her Father would say, your brother's up and about, you'd better get yourself out there and give him a hand. *You can leave the bairn here, I'll mind her ...*

Picking him posies of this and that from the garden: what's this one, Father? Watching him smile, trace petal and leaf, guess, teach himself, memorise. Taking his veiny, ink stained hand and resting it on her belly: and where do you say he is now, this Charlie of yours? America? Well, what are you doing here, then? He'll come back once it's safe, Dad. Well, you can't wait forever ... This year, next year ...

She never told him about the chase through the docks. Nor about the shrill flares exploding along the harbour wall; he never knew about the shots and the shouts in the night, the scream, the splash, the silence.

She said nothing about sometime, never.

He sat and rocked the baby while she did the bookkeeping that paid the bills. He chose her daughter's name: Maeve was a great princess, he told her, a Queen. In the old days, in the days of Finn and the Fianna. The book was in his bedroom, she could see it still ... it was Maeve's book now. And then he touched his hand to his brow, as if there was something he'd forgotten to say. *But are you sure now?*

Are you sure that man of yours likes it? The child's name, I mean? Maeve? Have you written again? What does he say?

He says you couldn't have chosen better. He used to call me his princess, you know. Up on Cave Hill. Two years. You'll be off to America now. That's right, she said, pressing his hand.

As he turned his face to the wall and left them.

As she too had left them. Maeve and her Frank, little Molly and whatever other bairns had come since. Sam and Abby, tearing away in the forge, her own nieces and nephews running about: not a day went by that she didn't think about them, didn't wonder what they were doing now ... and now, and now. And there, and there, and there: *Templepatrick, Castle Upton, Mallusk, Umgall, Donegore, Ballynure, Ballyclare, the Sixmilewater: all the fields, all the roads, and the path down to the river ...*

Did Maeve still stand up for her, the headcase of a mother that had them all dragged through the courts, that had her poor brother's life savings wiped out paying for the flash lawyer that got her sentence reduced to transportation? The lawyer who told them that she was off her head, that she hadn't known what she was doing when it was the one thing in the world that she had known, the one answer she'd had to give ...

Dark, dark, dark. Did they still talk about her? What did Maeve tell her own little daughter about her namesake? Did she still play the fiddle, did she tell the little girl stories about her grandfather Charlie, how he played that very fiddle in his green cockade, how he lived and died? To Liberty proved true?

How he hid with Henry Joy McCracken and the rest up on Cave Hill, how her grandmother, the girl that was once herself, climbed up to meet him, to lie with him in among the yellow gorse and look down at Belfast Lough and talk about America as if it were as far as you could go ...

And Sam, her good brother, he and his Abby, up at the crack of dawn, bellows going, the fire lighting up the dim old forge, the clang of the hammer and the stars sparking off bright curves of metal; the hiss of water as he plunged the horseshoe or the ploughshare or the door hinge into the rusty metal bath to cool. The sweat glinting on his forehead, the swing of his big arm ... her Father used to wonder how on earth he'd ever bred two such strapping big children: *must be your mother's side, I was always a skinny wee runt ...*

Her good kind brother and his kind, good Abby: they were well matched. Telling her not to worry, Maeve and Frank were just down the road, they'd keep an eye on them ... Busy road, Antrim through Templepatrick to Ballyclare and Ballynure: plenty of coming and going, good spot for a blacksmith's shop. Her big brother that she used to think was so slow, that she used to tease till he lifted his fist to her: so damn sharp, aren't you, so damn sharp? Want to watch you don't cut yourself! He lifted his fist, but he never brought it down on her, for all she deserved it.

You want to watch you don't cut yourself; exactly what she had done. Don't cut off your nose to spite your face: again, exactly what she had done. She was sorry now, for all she'd sworn to the judge that sorry was the one thing she'd never be. Yes, the bastard had got no more than he deserved, he was branded for life ... but what had she got? What had her family got? Far, far more than they deserved. For herself, she'd got rid of the rest of her life. Years of it, thrown away in a few minutes, a few mad, murderous minutes. A violent criminal: yes, that was her. How do you plead? Intent to kill, yes. Grievous bodily harm, yes.

At least her Father never knew.

Funny thing, Em's lad being called Charlie too. Brought it all back. So long ago now, 1797, 1798: another century. He was just a blur now, a pale floater in her mind's eye. Which was not how he was at all: nothing far away or floating about Charlie. Even after they killed him he was everywhere, she could not get away ... *the haunt of him, the lungeing, lurching nightmare, teetering along the harbour wall, his hand splayed bloody on his chest ...* She would wake with her mouth stretched to scream, but no sound coming out ... so.

So. She'd set herself, then, to remember him the way he was, not faint or floaty but fine boned, square jawed, hazel eyed. She would kneel by her bed, cross her fingers, and re-make him, inch by inch, limb by limb: his walk, his talk, the tilt of his head ...

So. So the years passed, passed like she could never have imagined they would. Book keeping, keeping books, helping Sam and Abby. Keeping her Father, keeping Maeve. Watching the child grow, teaching her, seeing his curls on her head, the set of his chin; thinking, but he'd be ten years older now. Would he be grey? Bald? A year. That was all they'd had together, barely that: and half of it snatched and secret, on the run, hiding out on Cave Hill ...

By the rising of the moon, by the rising of the moon;
The pikes must be together by the rising of the moon ...

Could she still do it? She closed her eyes: not like she used to, not so she could nearly put out her hand and touch him. Not for years. Unless she thought of him bent to his fiddle, playing that tune, that long lick of hair falling over one eye, the crookedy mouth, the foot keeping the beat ... nodding for her to join in ... *by the passing of the years, by the passing of the years ...*

She hoped Maeve still played. Something left, at least. To show he existed. To re-member him.

Enough. Enough. Think about the living. Em, Ginger Em. The girl had a temper on her, same as she'd had herself. Only sixteen: same age as she'd been when Maeve was born. Strange, she hadn't thought of that before. Sixteen good years they'd been, with the kindest mother and the best father in the world: whereas Em, what had Em ever had, living like an alley cat, like that tattoo of hers, in and out back doors, up and down drainpipes, God knows what. She'd go looking for her as soon as ever she got out.

The Matron had said that should be tomorrow, after the committee meeting. Should be: Unless Marsden objected; which he would. He surely would. But the Matron had said she would see to it. They couldn't keep her locked in here forever, after all. She shivered. Yes, they could. What was to stop them?

Sleep, dammit, go to sleep!

There was the song she used to sing after they brought her back his fiddle, the fiddle Maeve still had, the fiddle that would be handed on to little Molly. She sang it because it was something to do; she sang it because there was nothing else to do. She sang it because he'd taught her, and he'd taught her to show her that words didn't have to make sense because at that time she still thought they did.

Shule, shule, shule-a-roo,
Shule-a-rak-shak,
Shule-a-ba-ba-coo ...
Here I sit on Buttermilk Hill;
Who could blame me, cry my fill;
Every tear would turn a mill ...
Johnny's gone for a soldier!
Oh my baby, oh my love;
Gone the rainbow, gone the dove;
Your father was my only love;
Johnny's gone for a soldier!

CHAPTER TWENTY-ONE

Time Out

The new Matron wasn't doing too badly, mused Marsden as he walked home. All things considered. No shrinking violet, though, certainly not. A tad too sure of herself, in fact. Lockyer seemed to like her. Time would tell. Time: every day he hoped committee meetings would not last quite so long. Every day, they seemed to last longer. Meeting after meeting: it went on and on. He was ready for that steak and kidney pie. He was very fond of steak and kidney pie.

'Excuse me, Sir! Excuse me!'

The man hailing him looked vaguely familiar. 'God bless you, Mr ...? I don't think we've met ...'

'Sorry, Sir, I'll just catch my breath. Glad to catch you, Sir: Tom Kennedy. If you remember, Sir. Traveller's Rest.'

'Ah, yes: Kennedy: you're the publican. That was right, after church a fortnight ago. You were asking about that woman: Joan Campbell, if I'm not mistaken.' Marsden congratulated himself. 'What can I do for you?'

'Well, Sir, I was just wondering, given all the disturbances lately, if Market Day was still on? If you remember, I was interested in that same Joan Campbell.'

'Indeed, I do. And are you still?'

'Certainly am, Sir. Certainly am.'

Marsden congratulated himself. The man might have changed his mind if he'd heard the Campbell woman was in the cells. He held out his hand. 'The Travellers' Rest: One of our more respectable houses, if I'm not mistaken.'

'Yes, Sir. Thank you, Sir. I like to think I keep a decent place. I do my best, Sir, but as I explained to you last time, since the wife's died, I am badly in need of help. I cannot run the pub and look after two boys and keep house all by myself. It was bad enough when my wife was still with us, her being what you might call an invalid, you see. That was why we got a domestic in the first place: the woman Joan Campbell. She was only with us a few months, but it made all the difference. Good worker, Reverend. Suited well. And the boys liked her, they're always asking about her.'

'Why did you return her then?'

'The wife died sudden, you see, very sudden. Big family, and they've all of them been down for the funeral, then there was a bit of property to sort out. Anyhow, they've gone back to Newcastle now. On top of that, my barman's taken off, God knows where. That's the thing, you see, Joan's done bar work, knows how to pull a beer. Which is a big advantage.'

'My condolences on the loss of your wife. The Lord giveth and the Lord taketh away. It must have been a shock.'

'Well, it was, and it wasn't, Reverend. She'd not been well for a long time, you see. But there again, to happen so sudden ... shocking. It was.'

'Well, her suffering is over; she is in a better place. The funeral has been conducted, I presume?'

'Yes, Sir. Her folks, you see, one of them is a minister, and he did the necessary. So I didn't need to disturb you, Sir.'

'Indeed, it is a duty with which I am all too familiar. However, we must look to the future, must we not? It seems I shall be marrying rather than burying. Tell me, Kennedy, is Joan Campbell aware of your intentions?'

'She is, Sir. There is something of an understanding between us. So can I take it Market Day is still as arranged?'

'You certainly can. I will be happy to tie the knot for you and see you make an honest woman out of Joan Campbell at the same time. Come along tomorrow, my man, I shall be on the look-out for you.'

'Thank you, Sir, thank you very much indeed. I will be there, I certainly will. Good night, now!'

'Good night.'

Marsden watched Tom Kennedy stride off; well and good, he thought. If only all his cases were that easy. Now: time for that steak and kidney pie. He turned in off the street.

Elizabeth was practising: good. Something he didn't recognise; also good. The same old hymns every Sunday did get a tad wearisome. He opened the door quietly and went through to the drawing room, where she was leaning forward over the piano, peering shortsightedly at the music. He raised his hands to clap, then sniffed. 'Elizabeth! Is that burning I smell?'

She swung round to face him, sniffed and sprang to her feet. 'Oh dear. Dear oh dear: the pie!' She gulped. 'Sally must have forgotten about the pie!' She fled to the kitchen.

Marsden frowned. Sally? Had Lockyer not collected her? That was what they'd finally agreed, that he would pick her up on his way home. He was very pressing; nothing would do but the girl start as soon as possible. Ah well: he had been warned. He should have been to pick her up by now; perhaps he had thought better of it and changed his mind. No, that wasn't like Lockyer. Puzzled, Marsden went through to the kitchen. Elizabeth was at the bench by the sink, scraping blackened pastry. No sign of Sally.

***

Despite her care, the door to the sleeping ward creaked: Em flattened herself against the outside wall. No moon: the world waited in darkness. She darted across the yard to the big tree, swung herself up to her branch and crouched, eyes on the corner around which Molly would come.

A denser shadow, then a moving shape: the big woman reached the tree. Em jumped down and hugged her. 'Thought you'd never get out! I been worried sick; Christ, you look awful.'

'Thank you, dear. Tell me something I don't know. It's all right, don't fret. Tough as old boots, me. They let me out yesterday. No warning, door open, straight back to the oakum. Thirds, but she got me out like she said. Matron Gordon, I mean. Said she would, and she did. Marsden wouldn't have been happy. And I heard about what she did at the gate. We might have hit it lucky at last.'

'So you know I wasn't there? But do you know why?' Molly flicked Em's plait and nodded. 'Sarah told me when she gave me your message. Lizzie Adams: honestly, Em. Thought you'd learned some sense.'

'But she's been assigned! To Sydney town!'

'So? You won't have to see her face anymore.'

'Did Sarah tell you she'd seen Charlie? Blown him a kiss?'

'So? What about it? You know what it's like, coming down that gangplank with no idea about anything ... see somebody you know, of course you're going to wave, or do something!'

'That's not it, you know it's not. She'll find him, tell him I'm dead or something.'

'And why would he believe a word Lizzie Adams says? Got him nicked, didn't she?'

'But he don't know! They dragged him off before he could even look sideways. It were me that seen her, pointing up the stairs ... and Smithy got me word as well. In Newgate.'

'See? If he got word to you, he'll have got word to Charlie.'

'How do you know, but? They keep a tighter watch on the men, divide them up more. He might just think she'd been nicked like him. Feel sorry for her. Then she'd start talking old times, bat her eyelashes and give him some sob story. I know what she's like and I'm not risking it, Moll, I'm just not. I'm out of here. Don't give me that look. I am. And no, I'm not mad, I've worked it all out. The whole time you've been in them cells, I been puzzling over it till my head's fit to burst. I've worked it out, every last bit. Only I need your help. No, don't shake your head, at least listen! You know the wall that runs from the main building to the workrooms? What's on the other side?'

'Fleet Street.'

'That's right. Get over that wall and you're out!'

'Em, that wall is a good twelve foot high.'

'I know how high it is. I been studying it. See them sandstone bricks, the way they're rough on top? They'd give you a toehold. If you had a rope and something to tie it to, you could do it. I been right round every single bit of wall, and there's this one place. You know just past where the workrooms are? There's a couple of metal bars drilled into the wall, one above the other. Must have been going to put in lights or pulleys or something, only they never got round to it. That's all I need.'

'What do you mean?'

Em hugged herself. 'It's like Charlie and me studying how to do jobs. Get a rope looped round them bars, climb up; they're big enough to balance on; bottom one, then the top, then you'd easy reach the top of the wall. But the first one's too high, I'd need a lift to be sure of getting the rope up and around. Then I thread it through, then I tie it so I can climb up ... that's you, Molly. I want you to piggy back me. Once I've got that rope there, I climb up on the first bar and from there I can reach the second ... and from there I'm on top of the wall. Take the rope, find somewhere to tie it, let myself down the other side. There'd be a bit of a drop, but it shouldn't be too bad.'

'Jesus Christ, Em, you're off your head! What on earth do you think you are?'

'Cat's Whiskers.'

'In your dreams!'

'I can do it, Moll. I know I can. You've never seen me, me and Charlie. You don't know. I never knew myself till we done what we did. I just need that lift to begin with. And a rope. I need a rope. You said you were back at the oakum?'

'Yes, I'm back at the oakum. In the meantime, she said. For a couple of weeks, she said. Then she'd see.' Molly closed her eyes and leant back against the tree.

Em crouched beside her. After a while, she reached out and stroked the bald head; Molly's eyes snapped open. 'You're mad, mad to even think about it. Though that's not it. We're all of us mad in here. But there's mad and there's mad. You that can't stand the cells: you've heard about Bridget, haven't you?' Em nodded. Molly shook her head. 'Damn them to hell ... anyway. Is that what you want? Because you'll be straight back in there the minute they catch you. You know that, don't you? With a collar too, likely as not.'

Em clenched her hands together and shook her head. 'They won't catch me. I'll jump first. I am never going back in them cells, never: no way in the world. But I'm not staying in here neither. That's all there is to it.'

'Em, use your head for god's sake! Look, why don't you go and ask to be assigned again? This place can't hold any more, they've got to get the numbers down. You're strong and healthy, you're not in any kind of trouble: or not yet. You wouldn't have to wait long, people are always looking for domestics, especially in Sydney town. If your Charlie's all you say he is, he'll be looking out for you. He knew you were going to be in court straight after him, didn't he?' Em nodded. 'Well? So he'd be watching the ships unloading, wouldn't he? That's probably what he was doing when he saw Lizzie Adams.'

'But then why didn't he see me?'

'How would I know? Too late? Too early? Couldn't get out? If she saw him, he must be working round the docks somewhere ... not locked up, at least. But his time's hardly his own, is it?'

'No, I s'pose it's not ... but still, he's got no way of knowing where the hell I am ... or if I'm even alive. And she'll find him. She'll lie ...'

'It's still worth waiting, I tell you! They'll be looking to assign as many as they can, and youngest and fittest will be first to go.'

'But they could send me anywhere. Miles and miles and miles away, middle of bloody nowhere! Charlie's here in Sydney, and so's she ...'

'Look. Even supposing you could get over that wall, which is a pretty damn impossible suppose ... what's going to happen then? They'll be straight after you. They'll catch you, and Charlie too. Then you're both worse off. I mean, do you even know that she really did see him? If she's that big a liar, couldn't she be telling lies just to get back at you?'

'I thought of that. But no, that look in her eyes: for once in her life,

Lizzie Adams were telling the truth.' Em grabbed Molly's hands. 'You don't know my Charlie, he's smart. Really smart. They won't catch us, we'll take off, we'll hide. Place like this, that's easy: we'll just disappear. Like needles in a bloody big haystack, or hay bush, or whatever they call it out here. Like we done before, when we were on the run. There's this big wreck of a house in the country outside London that Smithy uses.' She paused, looking across the dim yard. 'We'd just done this big job for him and he sent us there to lie low. Kind of a reward. We were there a whole week, doing whatever we liked, living off whatever we could find. Best week of my life, Molly, true. The best week ever.'

She let go Molly's hands and hugged herself. Molly looked at her and shook her head. No use talking. Off with the bloody fairies. 'No noise. That was the first thing. No noise, nothing; just waking up to the light all soft, and leaves fluttering where the window was broken ... and Charlie there beside me ... there were blackberries in the garden, we could just go out and pick them ...'

'Blackberries? Jesus, Em, think you're going to find blackberries out here? Nah, I'm not even going to talk about it. Come on, or we'll get sprung. Last thing I need. I'm going.' Molly heaved herself up and stretched her arms as high as she could reach.

Em stayed crouched under the tree, chewing her knuckles, glowering. Her voice floated thin and bodiless. 'I'm doing it. I'll get Bridget. That's it, I'll get Bridget. She's supposed to be under guard, but they're not bothering much. They've got her on a long rope ... see, there's the rope, just a matter of untying ...'

Molly grabbed Em by the shoulders and shook her. 'Don't you dare! Don't you even think about it, you little brat!'

'I will. I will think about it.' Em didn't struggle. She stared at the ground, chewing her knuckles. 'It's not selfish, it's not! Or if it is, it's still my life! My whole life!'

Molly let go. With a sigh, she took the limp, shivering body in her arms. So little of it. She leant back against the tree. 'So. I'll need a day or so to get the rope.'

Em jumped up, wiped her nose and flung her arms around her friend. Molly took the chewed hand and rubbed it. 'All right. Now. Explain to me again.'

CHAPTER TWENTY-TWO

In the Dark

Rock-a-bye baby, in the treetop
When the wind blows, the cradle will rock
When the bough breaks, the cradle will fall
And down will come baby, cradle and all ...

In the darkness, Rosie hummed the tune and thought the words and stroked the downy little head at her breast just like she had stroked four others, once upon another time and another place. A time with their father sitting next to her; reaching out his hand to stroke as well: *we were all like this once, Rosie. Every last one of us.* And then ... Kitty, it was ... shat herself, and he said *full of shit* and they had to laugh. He was already sick.

Every last one, once: every women inside these walls, every man hauling on ropes down the docks or hammering nails in the middle of nowhere, every good citizen lined up in the pews of a Sunday ... old Mary there, sleeping slack jawed in the next room. Martin Brown: would his child look like him? Would he see a child running about the streets some day and stop and look again? No chance ...

What did they do about christening here? Marsden, she supposed. Even ministers, even magistrates, they'd all been like this once. Once upon a time, long ago ... She stared into the dark. Until the bough breaks ... *down will come baby, cradle and all ...*

A faint wail. But not Bonnie: Rosie tensed. From the next room, a faint creaking. Then nothing. No, something: something moving. She held her baby tighter and pushed herself higher up the bed. The door was half open, as Mary had insisted. Now, it opened wider and a stooped shape shuffled through. It picked up a dish clout and started wiping the table, round and round and round and round.

Rosie set her baby carefully down in the middle of the bed, wedging the child between bolster and blanket. Intent on not making any sudden movements, she was easing herself off the bed when Mary tripped, throwing up her arms with a terrified wail. Rosie lunged and caught her just in time.

'Hold on, hold on ... I've got you! Mary! Mary, it's all right, it's all right!'

She half carried the old woman back to her bed. She craned, listening ... unbelievably, not a sound from Bonnie.

She pressed a hand to her pounding heart. The only other sound was the harsh wheeze of Mary's breathing. The old woman opened her eyes.

'Where? What?'

'You walked in your sleep. I think. Where do you think you are?'

'Too late, I'm too late ...'

'Yes, it's late, but you're all right, you're here with me, Rosie.'

'Am I? Is the baby's all right, that's the main thing, is the baby all right?'

'Yes. The baby's all right. Sound asleep.'

'Good, good, very good.' Mary reached out her hand. 'How are you feeling, my dear?'

Rosie took it. 'Well, apart from nearly having heart failure, I'm all right. Stiff and sore. Leaking all over the place. But it's you I'm worried about. Mary, who am I?'

A frown flickered across Mary's face; she raised a hand to her forehead. 'Must have been dreaming.' She smiled and nodded. 'That's it: dreaming. Rosie, you're Rosie. Sorry. Must have scared the living daylights out of you.'

'You certainly did. Not too much daylight, though. It's the middle of the bloody night. I thought you were a ghost at first.'

Mary sniggered. 'Not yet, dearie, not yet! But someone fell overboard, see. And nobody saw it but me and I kept shouting and telling them and they wouldn't listen. And then I had to unwind the rope for the lifeboat but it wouldn't come ...' She shook her head. 'Wouldn't come. But I'm all right now.'

'Are you sure? I thought you were going to walk right out the door.'

'Oh no, not without a lifeboat. That's Jesus, he's the one can walk on water. The rest of us just have to sink or swim.' Mary spread her arms wide. 'I'd like that, just go floating down the river.' She tried to sit but fell back down again.

'You'll do nothing of the sort. Not while I'm around.'

'No. Not while you're around, dearie.' Mary yawned. 'I'll go back to bed now. Sleep, I mean sleep. You should too. You need your sleep. Don't wake the baby.' The old woman turned on her side and curled up Rosie waited, yawning. She was just about to go when there was a voice.

'You won't say anything, will you? To that Joan? 'Cause you know what she'll say, don't you? Bats in her belfry, she'll say. I can hear her. But it was only a bad dream. Anybody can have a bad dream.'

'I won't say a word. Don't worry about Joan. Remember our plan. You and me.'

'Oh yes. You and me. That's right, I'm not gone yet. There's still you, you and baby Bonnie. Now you lie down and rest, dearie. You need your sleep. I'll find the wool fat in the morning. Ni' night.'

Rosie sat on, listening to Mary's breathing deepen and slow. Then she tiptoed back and lay down beside her baby: *down will come cradle, baby and all ...*

***

In the close breathing dark, Sarah tossed restlessly. From the far side of the room, Joan pushed herself up on an elbow and hissed: 'Give over, will you?'

'Sorry. Can't sleep.'

Joan pulled a pillow out from under her and tossed it. 'Here. Take this. I took it from the lying-in rooms.'

'But what about you?'

'It's all right, I took two. Nobody using them. Try it.'

Having a pillow helped, but not with getting to sleep. What was taking Em so long? Why couldn't she leave Molly in peace? What if they got caught, what would happen to Molly then? They kept a tighter watch on the Thirds. Why did Em have to drag Molly into it anyway, what could Molly do? Apart from talk some sense into her. Sarah sighed: she wished!

'You're not serious!'

'I am. I am. Dead serious.'

Mad. Mad: but wouldn't listen. The only one Em listened to was Molly, but Molly was in no state ... it wasn't fair. But then, nothing was. Mad: the way she went on about that Charlie of hers. She'd never been like that. Except ... yes, she had. Stealing that shawl, that was mad. But silly mad, not off your head mad.

Funny, Molly having a Charlie too. Common enough name, she supposed. Yet never married. Probably could have, you could see she'd have been good looking once. The time was out of joint, she said, whatever that meant.

Molly wasn't as one track minded as Em: when Sarah had told her about Daniel, all she'd said was 'atta girl. Half your luck.'

Cats whiskers, for God's sake. What did Em think Molly could do? About Lizzie Adams or anything else? Funny, really. Molly so big and Em so little. It had made all the difference, meeting the two of them. The way Em could turn cartwheels, the way Molly could talk ... it kept you going. Kept you thinking of ways.

She had been thinking of ways ever since talking to Jake. All the women talked to Jake as they went past the garden, even if it was only to say hello. He was an old man and he lived in the shed at the bottom of the garden and he was lonely. Talked to his potatoes and carrots, Joan said. Nothing wrong with that: she remembered her own father sweet talking his roses.

She'd told Jake about him and he'd asked about Holyrood and she'd only just got to carding in time. She'd told him how she used to help in the castle gardens and then at home as well: potatoes and carrots and silver beet and parsley and scallions for making broth. Jake smiled and nodded, nodded and smiled, told her how he missed his son. His son had been gone a year now. The old man sighed. Not as fit as he used to be, could do with a bit of help with the garden. Not really work for a woman, though. But if she was a gardener's daughter: if, like she said, she could tell the herbs from the weeds: well, maybe.

That was how they'd left it. He'd have a word with the new Matron, what would she say to that? Yes, she'd say, yes please! Later, in the carding room, she realised that the new Matron would recognise her. Sarah Scott per Harmony ... per bolter ... and they still hadn't reported ...

Joan said she and Em should both go in the Market Day line up tomorrow. She'd laughed; what would she do that for? Who was going to pick a wife with a face like hers? Why would she go looking to be rubbished? She'd long since settled for life on her own. Digging and weeding, planting and harvesting; but she'd have to say sorry to the Matron first. Crawl, grovel, whatever.

Molly said it was the Matron who'd got her out of the cells. She would, she'd go and see her, with or without Em. First thing. Sorry, sorry, sorry: so much to be sorry about ...

The door opened quietly; Sarah turned over. 'Em!' she hissed, 'Em!'

CHAPTER TWENTY-THREE

Husbandry

Ann checked her clock: half past nine. Time enough. The Market wasn't till midday. She opened her day book. Those two girls: she should follow up on those two girls. Emily Kelly and Sarah Scott; Scott was off the Harmony, so she could tick her off that list too. Not now though: she looked at the pile of letters on her desk, then raised her head sharply at the rap on the door. It swung open. 'Reverend Marsden! This is a surprise. Sit down, sit down ...' She gestured at the chair before her desk.

'Good morning, Matron, good morning.' Marsden rested his hands on the back of the chair and scanned her desk. 'Working hard, eh? Good to see, good to see!' He sat down, slapping his thighs and leaning forward. 'Getting ready for your first Market Day, I presume. Don't worry, Bill Tuckwell has it all under control. He'll show you the ropes. Good man, Bill. You'll be impressed, I guarantee. He has the Market running like clockwork. I was inspired by the good book itself, you know: the book of Ruth, to be precise. As I'm sure you remember, Matron, Ruth is a stranger in a strange land and Boaz picks her out from among the women working in his fields. Good husbandry, you see, in every sense of the word.' He smiled and nodded. 'Marriage: that's the thing. The best way to fight immorality. Only the other day I was approached by one of our prospective husbands, asking about the Market. You may recall, I advised not putting

Joan Campbell in the cells? How right I was, Mrs Gordon, how right I was! Joan Campbell is the very one he's after. According to him, they even have some sort of 'understanding', whatever that may be. She was on assignment to him until quite recently; and gave satisfaction. At any rate, the man is definitely keen. He will be attending today and I expect to be asked to do the necessary and join them in holy matrimony.'

He paused, clearing his throat. 'However, that is not my present errand. To business: you will remember our discussions about the convict Sally Lewis?'

'I most certainly do.'

'My wife Elizabeth, as I believe you observed yourself when you first met her, is of a nervous disposition. It has come to my attention that, in my spousal concern, I may have been rather too hasty in dismissing the Lewis woman. However ... what's done is done. Major Lockyer has already had her removed to his home, where it must be hoped that she will provide satisfaction. I meant to mention it the other day ... a domestic, a cook, that is what we need. Have a look through your lists, Matron ... somebody to start immediately. Elizabeth, as you know, is musical: she plays every Sunday and sings in the choir as well. Visitors to our church often remark on the standard of the music. She cannot be both at the piano and in the kitchen.'

'She is fortunate to have such a gift. I look forward to hearing her.' *Don't smile, don't smile.*

'Yes, gifted, that is a good word. I look forward to seeing you and your husband in the front pew, alongside Mr and Mrs Raine, next Sunday. Normally, of course, I would invite you for afternoon tea, but you will understand that, in the absence of domestic help I am reluctant to ask Elizabeth.'

Ann allowed herself to smile. 'I am sure your wife appreciates your efforts on her behalf, Reverend. As a matter of fact, I do have a woman in mind; newly arrived per Harmony. I know she has domestic experience. She had in fact already been assigned, to quite an eminent Sydney family, I believe: Luttrell?'

'Yes, yes, Luttrell the surgeon ...'

'Earlier this morning I received a note from Mrs Luttrell, advising that they no longer require her services. It seems they have acted on a neighbour's advice and employed some dependent relative instead.' Ann pulled her day book towards her. 'Matron Raine made the arrangement; Elizabeth Adams is the woman. Bill Tuckwell has been overseeing it all; would you like me to advise him to transfer Adams to you? On approval, of course?'

Marsden rubbed his hands together. 'Yes. Yes, you do that, Matron. Without delay; this is most satisfactory. Bill will have the relevant papers ready, he can get her to me straight after the market.' He frowned. 'But you are quite sure the Luttrells don't want her? I would not want to put them out ...'

'Quite sure. Mrs Luttrell's note is perfectly clear. She apologises for any inconvenience.'

'Fine woman: fine family. Well, in that case, problem solved. I will speak to Bill myself on my way down and have her sent out. Save you the trouble.' Marsden glanced at Ann's clock and scraped his chair back. 'Good Lord, is that the time? I must be on my way. Good day, Mrs Gordon, we will meet again at the Market.'

The door closed behind him and Ann sat back in her chair, chuckling. Fortunate indeed! Her smile deepened as she made a note. 'Call from Rev. Marsden. Cook/domestic. Elizabeth Adams per Harmony. Tuckwell to organise.' She wondered how Marsden had found out what had really happened; he obviously knew. That silly woman: just as well she plays better than she fibs. Though you would have to think she's actually done Sally Lewis a good turn ...

She had started on yet another list when the second knock came. She clicked her tongue in annoyance. What now?

'Come in!'

Two faces, damp and shiny, appeared at the door; it must be raining. She glanced at her window. It was: not good for the Market ... maybe it would ease.

'Well well. Sarah Scott, I believe. And Emily Kelly. Finally.' Hovering just inside the door, they curtsied, glanced at each other and spoke as one.

'Yes, Ma'am. We have come to say sorry, Ma'am. For everything, Ma'am. Especially, we are very sorry we didn't wait when you told us to.'

'Stand in front of the desk.'

Ann scanned her desk. Harmony and ... Janus, that was it. She pulled the papers towards her. Such a pity about that mark on the girl's face. Born with a brand, so unfair: so different from that Captain of Molly Malone's. Strange to think of: him with his branded face riding through the Irish countryside on one side of the world and the woman at the other end of the branding iron pacing a cell on the other ...

'Well? Sarah Scott? Emily Kelly? What do you have to say?'

The two exchanged glances. Again, they spoke as one. As obviously practised ...

'Just that we're very sorry, Ma'am. About bumping into you like that. And not waiting to be dismissed. We never meant to be disobedient, we just didn't know any better. We're very very sorry and it won't happen again.'

'And how many times did you practise that little speech?'

Yes, yes, check with each other. Having a little mate always helps. Especially at that age.

Em lifted her chin. 'All the way over here, Ma'am.'

Sarah elbowed her. 'But we really are sorry, Ma'am. Really and truly.'

Sorry you got caught, you mean ...

'Let's start with you, Emily Kelly. You having been here longer and therefore, one would like to think, more aware of how to behave. Per Janus, correct?' Em nodded.

'Do you know who Janus was?'

The girls looked at her blankly.

'He was the god of entrances and exits. In pictures, he is shown with his face looking both ways. Ins and outs. Comings and goings. Looking before and after. Whoever named your ship would have known that. Pretty suitable, don't you think?'

What on earth made me say that? Whoever named the ship needn't have known it at all, they'd have had lists, pulled names out of a hat. Shiploads of lists.

'Wipe that smile off your face, Emily Kelly. What's so funny?'

'Nothing, Ma'am. Nothing. It is funny, that's all. The looking both ways, I mean. Ins and outs. Like having eyes in the back of your head.'

'What workshop are you in?'

'Carding, Ma'am. We're both in carding.'

'Indeed. You would do well to keep your eyes on your wool.'

'Yes, Ma'am.' Another elbow from Sarah: Em glanced sideways but tossed her head and went on. 'Sorry, Ma'am. It's just ...'

'Just what?'

'Just that it puts me in mind of London, Ma'am. That's all. 'Cause that's what you did, coming and going, going and coming. And you had to be looking both ways the whole time.'

'And what was it you did in London?'

An even harder elbow.

'Ah ... tumbling. That's it. I'm a tumbler, Ma'am. Was a tumbler. Back in London.'

'A tumbler. What does that even mean, a tumbler? I think that's nonsense, Emily Kelly. It's certainly not what's in my notes. Breaking and entering, that's what is in my notes.' Em glanced at Sarah's wide eyes and bit back the 'why'd you ask then?' She looked around the room and shrugged. What did it matter, now?

'I could show you, Ma'am. I used to show folk sometimes. I mean, with your permission, Ma'am.'

A horrified little gasp from Sarah. Em shrugged. Tight lipped, Ann tapped her pen on her desk. Keep them under, don't forget. But there again ... lists, lists, lists. Where's the harm? She was curious ...

'Go on then.'

Em started. 'Ma'am?'

'I said, go on. You call yourself a tumbler. Prove it.'

Em flashed an incredulous grin and darted to the middle of the long room, halfway between Ann's desk and the armchairs at the far end. Ann stood up sharply: what now? Em stretched her arms up high. A deep breath, a spring, and ginger plaits flew. Head over heels: a cartwheel. Tumbling.

Silence. Sarah's hands were clenched, her eyes fixed on the floor. Em went up on tiptoe again ... spring, flip, tumble ... and repeated herself. She stood where she had landed, perfectly still for a moment. Then she flourished a bow. 'See, Ma'am? See how you have to look both ways?'

It must have been her at the river that day ... circus, fairs, yes; but that's not what brought her here ... breaking and entering, that's what brought her here. Burglary.

Ann permitted herself a grim smile. 'I do see. And I did ask. Tumbling indeed. You have misused your talents, Emily Kelly. Which is a great pity. There is a time and a place for everything.'

Em pressed her fist against her mouth.

'A time and a place, Emily Kelly. The sooner you learn that lesson, the better off you will be.'

'Yes, Ma'am.'

'What about you, Sarah Scott? Have you any such surprises to show me?'

'Oh no, Ma'am. I can't do nothing like that.'

'Just as well. As I said, this is neither the time nor the place.'

Ann glanced at her clock. 'However, you have come of your own accord to apologise, albeit belatedly. That, at least, is a hopeful sign. Emily Kelly, your call of nature story was clearly nonsense; however, given your youth, perhaps you can learn your lesson. For now, I intend to take no further action. But be warned. I will be keeping a close eye on you both. You will need to prove yourself deserving of my clemency. Emily Kelly, you will go to the Carding Rooms directly and make up for lost time. Understood?'

'Yes, Ma'am.'

'Be warned; one more step out of line and I will not be so lenient.'

So light she was, light as a feather ...

'Work hard and do as you're told.' She glanced at Tuckwell's list. 'I see you are not in attendance at the Market?'

She's pretty enough ...

Em shook her head. 'Not me, Ma'am, not me. Not up for marrying, Ma'am.' Ann raised an eyebrow. 'Is that so? Well: there is no hurry. Learn to behave yourself first.'

'Yes, Ma'am.'

Enough. You haven't time for this. 'Very well. Dismissed. Straight to the carding room, Emily Kelly. And I will check. Sarah Scott, you stay. You are from the Harmony, are you not?'

'Yes, Ma'am.'

A squeeze of Sarah's arm, and Em left. *Haven't seen the last of her. Something to do with red hair? Though you'd think she'd take her chance at the Market ...*

Sarah kept her eyes on the floor.

'Well, Sarah Scott. What about you?'

'What about me, Ma'am?'

'Will you be lining up?'

'What would I do that for, Ma'am. Who'd want me?'

Shouldn't have asked. Poor girl. Ann pulled the Harmony manifest towards her. Sarah coughed. 'So begging your pardon, Ma'am, seeing as how you let Em do her tumbling, can I ask you something? I mean, may I be permitted?'

Damn: give an inch ... 'You may.'

'Well. There'd be no point me lining up, you understand that, Ma'am. But there's something I could do where it wouldn't matter about my face. What I wanted to ask, Ma'am, was if you could see your way to assigning me to work in the garden with old Jake. See, I was talking to him and he said he needed a helper. And I said I'd done gardening but he said it wasn't women's work, but then I told him about my father. He was the gardener at Holyrood castle and I used to do all sorts for him. I know about planting and mulching and pruning. Vegetables, too, because I had to do the garden at home as well as up the castle when he got sick.' Sarah stopped, catching her breath. 'So anyway, Jake thought about it and he changed his mind and he was going to ask you. I mean, if I could work there. In the garden.'

'You mean Jake Barnes? I hope you've not been making a nuisance of yourself. Holding the poor man up ...'

'No, Ma'am, I haven't, Honest. It's just ... he's getting on, and his back plays up and he can't do the digging like he used to. It was all right when his son was here, but his son's been gone near a year now and Jake's worried he's never coming back. I could do it. I'm strong, Ma'am, see that arm?' Sarah flexed her right arm. 'I mean, you got plenty of girls doing carding. I'd be a lot more use out in the garden. To the Factory, that is. If you saw fit, Ma.am.' She paused. 'There. That's what I had to ask. Thank you, Ma'am.'

Ann drummed her fingers on the desk. Mary, and now Jake: all the mouths to feed ...

***

Andy and George stood in the lee of the wall with their collars turned up.

'Never rains but it pours,' grumbled Andy.

'It's easing, though. Sun's out. They're getting started; look, there's Tuckwell.' George pointed across the yard to where Tuckwell, Marsden and Ann Gordon were standing round a table over which a tarpaulin had been roughly draped. Several men clustered nearby, a motley crew of sou'westers, capes and a single umbrella. The women from the Factory huddled under an archway. Ann Gordon walked out into the middle of the yard and beckoned. They straggled forward; she lined them up.

'Right. Better get out there.' George moved forward, Andy beside him. 'Pretty miserable looking lot. But then, what d'you expect? Here, this is where we usually stand. Near enough and far enough.'

They stood to one side of the line of women and watched the Matron bustle up and down the line of women, checking names, gesturing at an untidy jacket here, a loose strand of hair there.

'What's your pick, Andy?' said George. 'Don't see my little redhead, dammit. Not much among the younger ones. There's that one that stood out and spoke at the gate, see, the dark busty one. Joan something. Bit overripe, but not bad.'

'I thought you said to keep away from the older ones.'

'Did I? So I did: see? Told you I've got your best interests at heart!' George scanned the women again. 'She's not that old. Plenty up front still.

Not like the one beside her, flat as a board. She was at the gate as well: back-up, I suppose. Never opened her trap. Look, Tuckwell's calling the punters now.'

***

Agnes nudged Joan. 'See him yet? Your Tom?'

Joan shook her head, her eyes on the main gate. 'They're only just arriving. He's got a fair way to come. He'd have to get somebody to mind the boys, lock up, all of that.'

'What do you think of the rest?' Joan scanned the men and shrugged. 'Much of a muchness. See that skinny wee runt talking to Marsden now? That's Eileen's man. So she'll be off. Good luck to her. Not much else: except for the tall one with the umbrella: must be a good six foot.'

'Him with the moustache and the side whiskers? Fierce looking bugger, ain't he? Wouldn't want to argue with him. Must have a few bob though, with the umbrella and all.'

'Ssh, here they come.'

Marsden had waved the men forward. George and Andy stood to attention, watching them stroll across the yard. The short skinny man went straight to the even shorter and skinnier Eileen and took her hand. She beamed and trotted meekly after him to the table. The other men strolled up and down the line, stopping here and there as their fancy took them. Several stopped by Joan, but she kept her eyes on the ground. George grinned and nudged Andy. Tuckwell sent the skinny couple on to the table where Ann sat with a ledger in front of her. Two of the men came back to the Reverend, pointing and asking questions. He nodded and stroked his chin and said a few words. They went down the line again, beckoned and returned with two women in tow. Those remaining stood perfectly still, staring straight ahead. The tall man stopped in front of Joan. She didn't look up.

'You. Look up.'

She did. He beckoned. She took a step forward, lowering her eyes again. He walked around her slowly, then reached out and lifted her chin.

She shook her head. He raised his eyebrows, shrugged and moved on.

'He likes you!' hissed Agnes.

Joan tossed her head and bit her lip.

'Still no sign of that Tom.'

'Shut up.'

Where was he, where the hell was he? Bloody men ... *Tom, Tom the piper's son ... stole a pig and away he run ...* Don't be stupid, Joan Campbell. If Tom Kennedy was a wrong one, then she gave up on the lot of them. She shifted from foot to foot, her eyes fixed on the gate.

Agnes hissed again. 'Look, Joan, look! Him with the whiskers, he's talking to Marsden. Joan, he's pointing at you, he is, him with the whiskers!'

Joan folded her hands over her belly; starting to show, like Molly said. She closed her eyes. God dammit, Tom, where are you? Where are you?

Reverend Marsden looked up at the tall man. 'Nothing serious, Sir. Petty crim; receiving, that sort of thing. Like so many of them, bad company. Easily led, no proper guidance. I know for a fact she has done bar work. And domestic of course. As a matter of fact, I'm surprised she's not gone already. I had another fellow asking about her just the other day. He's a publican too: I'm surprised he's not here. He said something about an understanding, so I should warn you. She might say no. We do need them to say yes, I'm afraid.'

'Understanding, Reverend? First come, first served, that's my understanding.'

The man turned and strolled along the line again, pausing occasionally. In front of Joan, he stopped once more and beckoned. She shook her head. He raised his eyebrows and pulled a handkerchief from his pocket. He held it up and shook it out. It was fine and white, with a dainty lace border. Joan looked from the handkerchief to the pale blue eyes, to the gate, to the eyes. Thin lips curved; he reached for her hand and turned it over. He draped the handkerchief across her open palm and folded her fingers around it. Joan opened her mouth, shut it again. He closed his hand on hers and led her to the table.

Half an hour later, the unchosen women were filing back to their workshops and the sun was drying out the puddles. George and Andy made their way back to the Barracks. 'So what did you think of it all, Andypandy? Told you the dark busty one would go. Which was your pick, you never did say?'

'Yes I did. The one down my end, the fair haired one with the freckles.'

'I see. Like freckles do you? Emily got freckles?'

'Certainly not. Her complexion is perfect. English Rose.'

'Ah! Perfect English Rose is it? A rose without a thorn ... except now she's got you, you lucky prick!'

At the table, Ann stood listening to Marsden and Tuckwell congratulating each other. One of the best they'd had in a while: six more beds, six fewer mouths to feed. She was about to leave them to it when a man came rushing up, red faced and sweaty, his boots caked with mud. He tipped his hat.

'Matron Gordon, you must be Matron Gordon? Reverend Marsden ... Mr Tuckwell ... I'm late, I know: swear to God, I thought I was never going to get here. Sydney Road's shocking; I got bogged.' He looked around. 'Where are they? Where's Joan?'

Marsden shook his head. 'Tom Kennedy! Too late, man, too late: your bird has flown. Your bird has flown.'

CHAPTER TWENTY-FOUR

Moonlighting

The night was clouded. Anaemic and indifferent, a full moon slid from cover, ghosting the empty yard. The two figures flitting across it dived for wall shadow, crouching where the overhang of the main building offered deepest shade, where a single dash could take them to the end wall.

'Christ, that wall is big. Are you still sure, Em? Take a good look, now, go on, just take a good look! It's not too late to think again, not too late; for there'll be no thinking again once you're up there, no going back then. You are absolutely sure and certain?'

'Absolutely. I am.' The smaller figure lifted her skirt and began to roll it up. 'What do you think you're doing?'

'Tying my skirt up. So it don't get in my way.'

'I see. Well, no, I don't, but never mind. You know what you're doing. You'd bloody better.'

Em barely nodded, intent on her skirt. 'Full moon. Never mind. Light my way.'

Molly looked up into the night sky: *By the rising of the moon, by the rising of the moon ... the pikes must be together by the rising of the moon ...*

Em's hand on her shoulder made her jump. 'Give me a hand tearing this. Like this, see?'

She had wriggled out of her petticoat. Her excuse for a petticoat, Molly thought, it was that threadbare. Easy ripped: but what for? Say nothing. She tore the petticoat into strips as she had been told.

Em lifted the strips and bandaged her knees. Molly watched, admiring the quickness of the girl, the deftness ... 'Not forgotten how, have you?'

Em flashed a smile. She looped the rope carefully over one shoulder, tucked the end in at her waist. With a shiver, she stood up. 'Right. Ready.'

Molly stood beside her, both flattening themselves against the wall. Molly gave Em's plait a gentle tug. 'Right. So we run across. I get myself ready and braced next the wall. You jump yourself up on to my shoulders. I stand straight and steady and step back. You get your balance and throw. Throw like we practised ...'

Em nodded. 'Throw the rope. Get it over the bar. You step forward again, I feed it through and grab the other end. Tie the knot. Use the rope to pull myself up on your shoulders, jump, climb.

'Get a hold on that bar, pull onto it then push myself up. Untie the rope, throw again ... top bar. Once I'm on that top bar, I can reach the top of the wall. Untie the rope, pull myself up. Yay! I'm there, laying along the top. Oh Molly: I'll wave!'

'You'll do no such thing, you'll look for somewhere else to tie that bloody rope so you can let yourself down the other side without breaking your neck!'

'All right, all right!'

They stared at each other, locked in their vision. Em flung her arms round Molly and they held each other tight.

Molly loosened her grip first. 'That's it. Don't you dare wave. Just get yourself the hell out of my sight and anybody else's. Here we go!' She ran to the wall, stretched out her arms and braced. Seconds later, she felt Em's hands, knees, feet on her back. *Liberty ... to liberty prove true ...*

***

Crouched in the shadow of the wall, Molly strained to see. *Where are you, Em? And what the bloody hell am I going to do if you fall?*

Top bar: dear God, she's done it, she's going to do it ... standing, yes ... spring ... yes! She's up there, look, a silver leg, an arm ... by the rising of the moon ... atta girl, go! What are you looking round for, get on with it!

What shall we do with the drunken sailor?
What shall we do with the drunken sailor?
What shall we do with the drunken sailor ...
Early in the morning!

Molly swung around: there, over there! Troopers, bloody troopers. Yes, but not on duty. Half a dozen of them, lurching about, raucous and reeling, must have been out for a night on the town. Jackets unbuttoned, shirt tails hanging out. Short-cutting through the Factory to the Barracks ...

She looked up. There was Em, clear as anything, crouched like a cat in the moonlight, looking round, what the hell is she looking for? Somewhere to tie her rope, dammit, it's too long a drop otherwise ... Now what? Bloody hell, waving, silly little ass, waving!

Molly moved out from the wall, punched her fist in the air, shook her head and pointed at the troopers: go! Go! Em seemed to understand and squatted ... but she was still visible, still moonlit ... creeping towards the corner, the drainpipe, yes, of course, but slow, so slow ... the moon lighting her way, but lighting her as well, silvering her ...

Turn them; keep them looking the other way. Quick, before one of them looks up. Molly flattened herself against the wall again: where, but where? The tree, Em's tree, that was it.

She stood clear of the wall, opened her mouth and sang.

Put him in the hold where the rats can't get him,
Put him in the hold where the rats can't get him ...

Not like them, caterwaulers: never mind that now, make them hear, make them see! She ran across the yard, then paused, chest heaving: they were in a huddle, they were all over the bloody place, they hadn't heard ...

She sucked her breath in hard and waved her arms. Louder!

Stick them in the hold so the rats can get him,
Stick them in the hold so the rats can get him,
Stick them in the hold so the rats can get him ...
Early in the morning!

'Hoy!'

'What the hell is that?'

'It's one of them fuckin' women!'

'What's she doing out? Grab her!'

'God dammit, it's the big bald bitch!'

Hounds, she thought, hounds baying ... she flung her arms around the tree. Em's tree ... where was that bloody branch, the one you swung up on ... there! Molly flung herself upward and heaved, kicking her legs ... missing.

'Now where the fuck is she?'

'There, look, over there!'

No Em to give her a boost ... Molly leapt again. *Can do, can do ...*

One leg was hooked over when rough hands grabbed the other one. She gasped, struggling to keep her hold, but they had her by the knee, two hands, four, six, clutching, yanking, dragging her down. Rough bark scoured her hands; with a sob, she let go. She landed at their feet with a thump. 'Told you, the big bald bitch. Legs spread and all!'

She scrabbled to get up, but the kick gutted her.

'She's the one they warned us about, isn't she? The one they said was dangerous?'

'That's her. Not too fucking dangerous now, is she?'

The gob of spit dribbled down her cheek. Grabbing hold of her arms, they heaved her to her feet. A stab of pain from her ankle: she staggered into a shoulder. The shoulder swore and shoved her away. Her ankle gave and she fell.

Kick. Kick. Kick.

'Get up, you stupid cunt!'

'Dammit, how're we supposed to get her back? I'm not carrying that!'

'Drag her, I suppose. You reckon she was trying to do a runner?'

'Where the hell to? There's no way out. Meeting somebody, more like.'

'Bloody hell, who'd want to meet her? Even on a dark night? Never mind fuck her?'

By the rising of the moon, by the rising of the moon ... Molly lunged for the last speaker's legs; with a startled curse, he fell. She drew back her fists and pummeled his balls; his yells split her ear drums.

'George! God dammit, get her off, boys, get her off him!'

Lurching to her feet, she hobbled away. The bullet ripped through her back and lodged square in the middle of her chest.

CHAPTER TWENTY-FIVE

Out to Dry

Parramatta
December 1837
My dear Letitia

Thank you for your letter, as always, so welcome. From what you say, your boys are turning into fine young fellows; you must be very proud! I do hope my Christmas package arrives in good time, and that they will like the bird pictures. The birds here are so colourful; is it the same in New Zealand? Though there are not many songsters; you really can't count the kookaburrah, or laughing jackass, which seems to me a far better name for him! There is one black and white bird which they call a magpie, though it's quite different from the one at home. Nasty, swooping thing: but it does have a lovely song. I hope you like the pressed flowers; like the birds, the native flowers are very colourful, but quite scentless. How I should like to smell primroses again!

You keep saying that my dismissal was really a blessing in disguise. Thank you, my dear, I know that you mean well. You have always been a loyal daughter, despite the miles; you know what a special place you have in my heart. Friends here have said similar kind things and I am touched, I truly am.

It is the unfairness of it that really sticks in my craw; that through no fault of my own I have lost a position to which I have given nine years of my life. And I don't think I flatter myself when I say that the Female Factory would not be what it is today without me. You only have to read the newspapers. They routinely refer to it not as the Factory, but as Gordonsville or Gordon's Aviary or some such term, even in their court reports. I do believe I have been a good and faithful servant. I believe I have succeeded where others would have failed. I believe I have done a good job.

Nine years, my dear, nine years! So many women, children too; it has got to the point where I may actually bump into them down the street. The better ones, of course, the ones who did not give up, the ones who stayed the course. They come up to me and ask if I remember them. It is really quite gratifying; I do like to hear how they are getting on.

So. It is hard. To have built up so much, then be dismissed so casually! So unfairly! Robert is, of course, full of apologies. He swears that he went nowhere near the lady concerned; I have lost count of the number of times he has told me he did not touch some woman or other! As far as that goes, to be perfectly honest, my dear, I really could not care less. I have long since given up caring about his propensities in that direction. Ours has never been a conventional marriage; I cannot forget that I ... indeed, we ... have benefited from that very indulgent nature of his, given the circumstances of your own birth. That, I hastily add, is not intended to cause you pain; as I have told you many times, your father was a soldier and a gallant gentleman, my dear. Had he returned from the war, our lives might have been very different. But it was not to be. I have no doubt he died bravely, fighting for his country. Robert has never cast my indiscretion up at me; I have long since decided to turn a blind eye when he strays. You need not worry about me on that account, my dear. I have much less patience with his loose tongue than his loose behaviour,

I did think he had finally gained some common sense. Private indiscretion is one thing; public indiscretion quite another. Gossip: that was how word got around, simply gossip. Simply his inability to keep his mouth shut, to not give those who have long been jealous of my success their opportunity. As for Caroline, well, even as a child she was foolish; not disobedient so much as just plain silly. Easily led. No doubt I should have kept a closer eye on her, certainly on the company she was keeping; but what time did I have to do that? And after all, I was not able to keep an eye on you, my dear, was I? And look how well you have turned out! No, Caroline has made her bed; she may lie on it.

So, here we are. Robert holds forth with his usual verve on what he calls the 'puritanicality' of society here. I have to remind him that the days of the 'sans culottes' are long gone, if indeed they ever did have much influence beyond the infamous excesses in France. He puts his usual jolly face on it, but being a publican is certainly not all that he might have hoped. It is certainly a come-down from his position as Storekeeper. This year has been difficult for both of us.

I have written again to Governor Bourke; I have quoted from his own original letter of dismissal. It is here, right here in front of me; 'no blame was attached to her', he writes. In view of that acknowledgement, in his own hand, I am hopeful that my application to be reappointed will receive favourable consideration. We await his decision.

Ann put down her pen and opened a small drawer. She took out Bourke's letter and read yet again what he had written. No blame: surely, now that Robert had his publican's license, his establishment could be seen as completely separate from the Factory. He would have no need to even enter the premises, nor Caroline either, come to that.

She replaced the letter and sat flexing her fingers; she hoped they were not becoming arthritic. Crossing to the window, she drew the curtain and looked out along Fleet Street towards the tall sandstone building, golden now in the late afternoon light. It was her favourite time of day.

And the women: Gordon's birds. The Factory itself: Gordon's Own, Gordon's Temperance Society ... plain Gordonsville, that was the best. Because it was a little city of women, wasn't it? Surely it was some sort of acknowledgement, that her name and the Factory's had become one? There was nobody else with her experience, nobody who understood the assignment system as well as she did, nobody who knew how many beds there were, how many children could be looked after at any one time, what stores to order weekly, monthly, yearly. Nobody else knew the best systems for monitresses and portresses, which women could be depended upon, which could not. Surely to God the Governor must see that.

Nine years. Nine years' worth of women. All shapes, all sizes: young, old, middle-aged; good girls and bad girls ... remember that silly song they used to sing?

> *Good girls sit like this,*
> *Bad girls sit like that ...*
> *But girls that won't obey ...,*
> *Girls that say their say ...*
> *Have this and this to pay!*

With actions, they did it with actions. Remember the four of them who used to sing it down by the river, what were their names? Did it matter? Elizabeth, Elsie, Betsy and Bess ... setting their laundry baskets to one side, standing up in a row ...

Good girls sit like this ... legs together, *bad girls sit like that ...* legs apart*: but girls that won't obey, girls that say their say ...* knees up hard, then *have this and this to pay ...* gut kick, face kick, fall down dead ...

Remember standing just outside the gate above the path and listening to the voices floating up ...

Voices. That was what stayed with her, the voices. Women talking, women just talking and talking. To each other, to themselves ... to her. All that talking, all that spoken air, all gone ...

Can't be miserable all the time, can you? Nottingham or Liverpool or Newcastle or Sydney, don't matter, feels the same ... look before you lech ... she'd shouted that at Robert only the other night when he'd come home several sheets to the wind ... again.

You've some nerve, I'll say that for you ... Molly Malone. *Life: or something like it.* Molly again. *'She died of a fever, and no one could save her' ...* because it wasn't a fever. It was a gunshot.

What happened to them all? Where did they go, all the Joans, all the Sarahs, Sallies, Rosies? Somewhere out there, they must be somewhere out there. Or else mad, like Bridget Murphy. Or dead. Like Molly Malone. *'Now her ghost wheels her barrow' ...*

There had been nothing she could do. Not a thing. There was just a body; just a dead, dumped weight. Dirty because it had been dragged; it was black and brown and torn and tattered. When they straightened her skirt in the dead house, leaves fell out. A dark rosette of clotted blood bloomed where the bullet still lodged.

There had been nothing to do but turn away, nothing but sit and listen to Marsden praying for the Lord to have mercy on this lost sheep ... sheep! She'd wanted to laugh; laugh like Molly Malone would have laughed.

Emily Kelly, the tumbler. Whatever happened to Emily Kelly? She disappeared around the same time. She hadn't thought about her for years. Doing cartwheels in her office that time, those first frantic weeks, her long red plaits whizzing as she turned head over heels. How did she end up, the tumbler? Ginger Em they called her. In all the panic and fuss about Molly, they hadn't even found out she was gone until the following night. Gone. Simply nowhere to be found. Vanished into thin air. What ever happened to Ginger Em, they used to ask. She shook her head, went back to her desk and picked up her pen again.

If the answer is yes, obviously we will stay where we are. If no, we will move. Try somewhere new. Robert's public house should not be hard to sell. Parramatta as plain Mrs Gordon would be simply too difficult.

In the meantime, my dear, I send you every good wish at Christmas. I suppose you will have the turkey all ready. I never look forward to cooking a turkey in the heat. I confess that even after all these years, I still cannot quite believe in Christmas here.

To think it is twenty years since we parted! Twenty whole years! Yet however land and sea have separated us, you are still my beloved daughter. I have never forgotten you; this very moment, my hand is around the locket with your curl of hair inside. If only we, like the birds, could fly across the seas so that I might see you and your dear little boys!

Your affectionate mother Ann Gordon.

She was copying out her daughter's address when Robert came in. He touched her shoulder and dropped an envelope on to her desk.

She kept writing.

Robert coughed. 'Come on, Ann. This'll be it. See the stamp? Better open it.'

She stabbed a full stop and set down her pen. She licked the envelope, sealed it and set it carefully in the tray for posting. She picked up her paper knife, then the official envelope. She slit it and paused, closing her eyes.

Robert grunted impatiently and crossed to the window. Below, people bustled up and down the street, stopping to chat, pulling children along, going into shops, coming out of shops. Up and down, to and fro. Busy busy. Parramatta was a busy town now; a hive of activity, as the older residents said; you wouldn't know the place. But he knew the place, he knew the people in Parramatta; people in Parramatta knew him. It had become their home.

He frowned and swung to look at the woman at the desk. No, escritoire. She insisted. Her and her damn escritoire. With that noisy bloody carriage clock ticking away on top. 'For God's sake, Ann: tell me you've got it. Can you not just tell me you've got it?'

She refolded the paper, returned it to its envelope and set it down, blank side up. She looked up at him and clasped her hands together.

'The Governor begs to inform me that my application, regretfully, has been unsuccessful.'

'What? What the hell? That's outrageous! How can you not have got it? Who else in this damn place ...'

He trailed off before Ann's unblinking stare. 'No, dear. You're the one that's outrageous, remember? You and Caroline. Hardly surprising, I suppose. You always did say she took after you.' She held out the letter. 'Here. Read. It won't take you long.'

He snatched, skimmed. Took a step forward, took a step back, read it again. Then he crumpled it up and fired it at the floor.

'Begs,' he snorted, 'begs! What rubbish: his lordship wouldn't know how! When has he ever begged?'

Ann got up and picked the crumpled twist of paper from the floor. She smoothed it and returned it to its envelope. 'Your successful wife has not been successful, dear. Not this time. This time, she has not been able to put things right. We shall have to sell up. We shall have to move.'

He looked down at the deep-set eyes, the high cheekbones, the compressed lips: the face he relied upon. 'Ann, my dear; I am so sorry.'

'Yes.' She sighed and rubbed her hands together. 'Well. So you should be. Never mind. I should have preferred to go in my own time, but nine years is nine years. I at least have nothing to be ashamed of.' She opened her correspondence drawer, set the letter on top of the other one and closed it. She pushed back her chair. 'I think I shall go for a walk.'

She looked at her clock: five o'clock. Yes. An evening stroll. Some fresh air. At the door, she paused, turned and smiled. 'Never mind, dear. Your second chance.'

He looked his question.

'To be a gentleman farmer. Your ticket of leave, remember?'

* * *

Down in Fleet Street, it was a warm evening. Ann walked towards the Factory, stopping, as she had so many times over the last year, opposite the entrance. Such a handsome building. She wondered about Mr Greenway; you never heard of him these days. Did he stop here too, and look back? This was a good place to stand; did he feel proud of his handiwork? Surely he would. It must be satisfying to know your name would last as long as the building did. Who knew? If he'd stayed in England, nobody might even have heard of him. Like her.

What about her? Would they remember her too? Not so much, she supposed: no Government House, no streets and carriages, no flags, no sheep. But her name was there, in the books. In the court reports. On factory women's lips.

The sky was streaked pink; in the sunset glow, the factory looked almost cosy. Hah! Tell that to the Mollies of this world ... Ann sighed. So many times she had walked in and out that entrance, in and out, never stopping to think what it meant. For the women inside: for the men outside. It seemed wrong, somehow, that you never knew which in or out was going to be your last.

Honey: it was the colour of honey. With the women inside it like so many bees, buzzing away, building their honeycombs ... worker bees. That might be something she could do: keep bees. She stood motionless, hands clasped around invisible keys.

'Mrs Gordon!'

Her hand flew to her chest.

'Mrs Gordon: I'm so sorry, I didn't meant to startle you!'

Ann recovered herself and smiled. 'Sarah! Sarah Scott! Sorry: Sarah Barnes, I should say. How are you, my dear? Oh my: haven't they grown!'

She smiled at the two little boys peering out from Sarah's skirts.

'Oh yes. Into everything, they are. I'm well, thank you, and I hope you are too, Ma'am. I didn't mean to startle you so ... were you going in?' She nodded toward the Factory. Ann shook her head. 'No. I have no place there now. They have a different Matron.'

'So I heard. Couldn't hardly believe it, Ma'am: I mean, don't seem right, do it? There'd be nobody like you, Ma'am.'

'Thank you, Sarah, thank you. No, I'm saying my goodbyes, I'm afraid. We will be moving shortly.'

'Oh really? Not for good, I hope; may I ask where?'

'You may, but I can't tell you. It's not yet decided. It will be for good, though. For better or for worse, as they say. It's certainly been for better as far as you're concerned, hasn't it?'

'Oh yes, Ma'am. I've never looked back, Ma'am, never since you gave me my start in the garden. Such a stroke of luck seeing you, too; I was on my way into the Factory to ask for you. I didn't know how else to get in touch and I thought you'd want to know.' Tears welled in her eyes. Funny, thought Ann, that strawberry mark doesn't look so dark now. Maybe they fade with age. Or you just forget about them. She looked down at the little boys. No, no sign of a mark on either. The next generation, to whom the old world was just a name ... she wondered how much of their mother's accent they had. When she looked up again; the girl ... she still thought of her as a girl ... was wiping her eyes.

'Sarah, what is it?'

'I wanted to let you know that old Jake is dead. It's all right, Ma'am, he just went off in his sleep. He was always the first up in the house, so when he wasn't in the kitchen Matt went into his room and found him. Just lying there dead.' She sniffed. 'Well. He was done, he told me so himself. So I suppose it was time.'

Ann clicked her tongue: what to say? Sarah wiped a hand across her face.

'Poor Matt. They were pretty close, you know, him and his Pa. He's that grieved.'

'Well, of course he is. My dear, I am truly sorry. When was this?'

'Yesterday. Only yesterday. I'm seeing to it now. The funeral, I mean.'

'What on earth age would he have been? He was an old man nine years ago!'

'Eighty. He was eighty years old. His back gave up on him, you see, and then his legs. He reckoned he was useless. But he wasn't. Matt rigged up the wheelbarrow so he could sit in it and reach up and prune stuff.'

'Good for him. When is the funeral? I would like to pay my respects.'

'Would you really? That would be lovely, Ma'am. Matt would be that pleased. If it hadn't been for you, Ma'am, giving me leave to help Jake ...'

'Yes, yes. You did well.' Ann looked down at the two little boys. 'What are their names?'

'Matthew ... after his Dad. And Jacob, after his Gramps. We're going to meet the minister, I'll have to keep going.'

'Yes, on you go. Please pass on my sincere sympathies to your husband. When did you say the funeral was?'

'I didn't. This Friday, Ma'am. Eleven o'clock in St John's.'

'Good. I will see you again there.'

'Thank you, Ma'am.' Sarah glanced across at the Factory. 'Some memories, eh Ma'am?'

'Yes; yes indeed. Some memories. Do you remember Molly Malone, Sarah?'

'Oh yes, Ma'am, how could you not remember Molly? And Em, Ginger

Em, and me only just off the boat ... I'll never forget them. Either of them.'

'Did anybody ever find out what happened to her? Ginger Em? Did you ever hear anything?'

Sarah glanced at Ann Gordon sharply. So many years of silence, so many years of remembering that night so long ago when she'd lain awake, picturing the two of them sneaking out, crossing the yard, over to the wall, the lift, the climb ... the shot.

Hearing the shot.

'Nobody ever found her, Ma'am, did they? For all their searching?'

'No. Nobody ever did. There one day, gone the next. Like she'd vanished into thin air.'

'Well.' Sarah looked up at the Factory. 'Don't suppose it makes any difference now.' She hesitated. 'No, don't suppose it does. Thin air's sort of right, Ma'am. She went over the wall, Ma'am. See that end bit of wall?' She pointed. 'Molly helped her. They worked it all out between them.' She shook her head. 'Mad, they were. Mad.'

'She climbed that wall?'

'They've built it up since, another couple of feet, but it was still big. Maybe that's why they made it bigger. Maybe somebody found out, or maybe somebody suspected. But who, Ma'am? Who?' She shook her head. 'Mad, they were, mad. She explained it all to me, how Molly would give her a boost, the rope, them metal bars ... she was done for breaking and entering, remember? She could do cartwheels, balance on a sixpence ... Remember that time she done a cartwheel, right in your office?'

'I certainly do! Well, well! I never ...'

'No, me neither. And I've thought and thought and what I reckon must have happened was them troopers showed up before Em was over: the wall, that is. And Molly got them to go after her instead. I can see Molly doing that, can't you, Ma'am?'

Ann nodded. She could. She certainly could.

'Cause they shot her in the back, didn't they? Like she was running away. Wicked, Ma'am. Don't care what anybody says: that was wicked.'

Ann stared at the sandstone walls and said nothing. There was nothing to say. 'Listen, Ma'am: I'm going to have to run or I'll miss the minister. But thank you, Ma'am, I'll hope to see you at the funeral, at St John's, then? I can tell you anything else I think of then if you like.' She took her little boys' hands. 'I think about her too, you know. I wonder if she ever found that Charlie she was so mad about.' She shrugged. 'Never know, will we? Just never know.'

Ann stood watching the now distinctly matronly figure bustle off down the street and disappear around the corner. She looked back at the Factory, at the end wall: yes, she could see it like Sarah told it: over the wall. Over and out, into thin air. Thin air. She turned and walked back along Fleet Street.

* * *

On the far side of the Factory wall, down beside the clearing, the river whispered quietly to itself, sluicing stones, swirling stray insects and fallen branches along and along, lapping against the flat rocks where Factory women still came with their baskets and their dirty laundry.

Now, the clearing was quiet and still: no laundry baskets, no piles of clothes, no buzz of voices.

From the trees, barefoot and soundless, walked a slender figure. At the edge of the clearing she hesitated, crouching and looking carefully around before darting across to the rocks and kneeling beside the river. She scooped water into cupped hands and drank. Once, twice: the third time she splashed the water over her head and shoulders, shivering as the cool trickled over her skin.

She sprang to her feet and perched, bird like, her dark head tipped, listening. Nothing. She stretched up her arms and turned a cartwheel.

www.ingramcontent.com/pod-product-compliance
Ingram Content Group Australia Pty Ltd
76 Discovery Rd, Dandenong South VIC 3175, AU
AUHW020137130726
429791AU00003B/85

9 781922 454102